P9-CFU-150

Breathtaking Praise for
CHRISTINA DODD

"Christina Dodd's talents continue to grow
and readers are guaranteed pleasure
and true enjoyment."
—*Romantic Times*

"Christina Dodd just keeps getting
better and better."
—Debbie Macomber

"Memorable characters, witty dialogue,
steaming sensuality—the perfect
combination for sheer enjoyment."
—Jill Marie Landis

"A beautiful, sensual love story filled with
mystery, intrigue and adventure....
A book to curl up and enjoy."
—June Lund Shiplett
on *Treasure of the Sun*

"A very special romance—heartbreaking and
heartwarming, original, beautiful, compassionate,
and well written. It is a story you'll never
forget.... Ensures Christina Dodd
a place in readers' hearts."
—*Romantic Times*
on *Candle in the Window*

BOOKS BY CHRISTINA DODD

Candle in the Window
Treasure of the Sun
Priceless
Castles in the Air
Outrageous
The Greatest Lover in All England
Move Heaven and Earth
Once a Knight
A Knight to Remember

BY CATHERINE ANDERSON, CHRISTINA DODD,
AND SUSAN SIZEMORE

Tall, Dark, and Dangerous

Published by HarperPaperbacks

ATTENTION: ORGANIZATIONS AND CORPORATIONS

Most HarperPaperbacks are available at special quantity discounts
for bulk purchases for sales promotions, premiums, or fund-raising.
For information, please call or write:
Special Markets Department, HarperCollins Publishers,
10 East 53rd Street, New York, NY 10022-5299
Telephone: (212) 207-7528 Fax: (212) 207-7222

CASTLES
IN THE AIR

CHRISTINA DODD

HarperPaperbacks
A Division of HarperCollins*Publishers*

HarperPaperbacks
A Division of HarperCollins*Publishers*
10 East 53rd Street, New York, NY 10022-5299

If you purchased this book without a cover, you should be aware that this book is stolen property. It was reported as "unsold and destroyed" to the publisher and neither the author nor the publisher has received any payment for this "stripped book."

This is a work of fiction. The characters, incidents, and dialogues are products of the author's imagination and are not to be construed as real. Any resemblance to actual events or persons, living or dead, is entirely coincidental.

Copyright © 1993 by Christina Dodd
All rights reserved. No part of this book may be used or reproduced in any manner whatsoever without written permission of the publisher, except in the case of brief quotations embodied in critical articles and reviews. For information address HarperCollins Publishers, 10 East 53rd Street, New York, NY 10022-5299.

ISBN 0-06-108565-0

HarperCollins®, ®, and HarperPaperbacks™ are trademarks of HarperCollins Publishers, Inc.

First HarperPaperbacks printing: July 1993
Special edition printing: September 1998

Printed in the United States of America

Visit HarperPaperbacks on the World Wide Web at
http://www.harpercollins.com

❖ 10 9 8 7 6 5 4 3

To Arwen
My Pragmatic Daughter

Who knows the value of a dollar.
Who frequently and pointedly reminds me that the
only time anyone notices our housekeeping
is if we don't do it.
Who knows that her mama needs lots of love and
who gives it so generously.

ACKNOWLEDGMENTS

My grateful thanks to my editor, Carolyn Marino, for taking the time and energy to teach me the skills of a professional writer.

To my critique group: Pam Zollman, Anna Phegley, Paula Schmidt, Barbara Putt, and Thomasina Robinson; thank you all for your continued enthusiasm and support through so many pages and so many seasons.

"I learned this, at least, by experiment; that if one advances confidently in the direction of his dreams, and endeavors to live the life which he has imagined, he will meet with a success unexpected in common hours. . . .

If you have built castles in the air, your work need not be lost; that is where they should be. Now put the foundation under them."

—Henry David Thoreau

1

England, 1166

She had all her teeth.

Raymond heaved a sigh of relief. She was wrapped in too many layers of clothing to see aught else, and she fought him with all the strength in her slight body, but her teeth glimmered behind her blue lips and they made a sturdy clinking as they chattered together. That meant she was young enough to bear children, in reasonable health, capable of warming his bed.

He tried to lift her onto his horse, but she twisted in his arms, flinging herself down onto the woodland path and scrambling away with a desperation he respected. Respected, but ignored. Too much was at stake for him to pay attention to a woman's apprehensions.

She floundered in the snow that misted the ground. Catching her, he wrapped her in his cloak, bundling her so tightly that her hands and feet flailed uselessly. With a heave, he tossed her face down in front of the saddle and mounted before she regained her breath. "Steady, Lady Juliana, steady," he soothed, patting her back as he urged the horse forward.

She battled against his solace, kicking her heels and trying to slide away. He didn't understand her persistent opposition in the face of such odds, nor did he understand the impulse that drove him to try and comfort her as if she were some wild bird he could charm to his hand.

Perhaps her refusal to scream appealed to his sympathies. She'd made no sound since he'd stepped out from the trees, only fought him with determination and silence.

Then again, perhaps she couldn't say anything. Bundled as she was, with her head bobbing beside the horse's belly, he couldn't see her face, and he began to wonder if she could breathe properly. Leaning down, he groped for her face, and those same strong teeth he had admired bit deep into his fingertips. He jerked his hand back with a grunt and an oath, shocked by her violence yet not truly surprised.

Hadn't he compared her to a wild creature? His own carelessness was responsible for his pain, and he sucked the drop of blood from his skin and then tucked his hand into his armpit to warm it.

Her breath froze as she panted harshly, the sound rending the still air. Scratched from the sky by bare, ice-tipped branches, the snow sifted down relentlessly, filling the spaces between the dried leaves with a thin layer of white. Damn, it was cold, and getting colder by the moment. "We'll be there soon," he said aloud, and held her firmly as his promise brought renewed strife.

He topped the hill, and the blast of frigid air snatched his breath away. Here the threatening blizzard threatened no more. It was reality, and the world disintegrated into a narrow, white passage that opened as they moved through and closed behind them. The woodcutter's hut stood not far ahead, yet he worried about the lady, now rigid where she lay over the horse. He leaned over her to give her all his body warmth and peered ahead.

Dug into the hill, the hut had proved a godsend for him, providing a stock of fuel for warmth and a store of dried foods. Traveller's provender, he'd guessed, provided by Lady Juliana of Lofts and used by him for her abduction.

"Just a few more steps, my lady." His breath froze on the muffler before his mouth, but he thought it fair to warn her since she seemed so averse to his touch. Sliding out of the saddle, he pulled her down. She tried to stand; her legs collapsed, whether from cold or fear he didn't know. Like a bear with a haunch of venison, he dragged her along and swung wide the door. "We're here," he said unnecessarily. "I'll stable my horse close by the door. The fire's just beyond. If you'll sit on the straw until I can carry you in there . . ."

Her wide eyes glistened in the dim light as he dropped the bar, then she bolted into the little room beyond. Through the slats of the feeding pen, he watched as she frantically paced the length of the tiny room.

A fire burned in a pit in the middle of the wood-cutter's shed. The smoke rose to a small hole in the thatch, melting the flakes as they drifted in. Drawn by the flames, she held her hands out and looked around, dazed. All the cracks in the walls had been stuffed with cloth, the window had been covered with a blanket. A rough bed laden with furs stood in one corner and his gear lay in another. But the only door lay behind him, and she couldn't reach that.

To give Juliana time to adjust to her surroundings, he took his time feeding and grooming the hardy gelding that had served him so well, but at last he could delay no more. "We'll be cozy enough, my lady, to weather the storm here."

She blinked away the snowflakes melting on her lashes and stared at him, and he wondered what she saw that made repugnance curl her lip so expressively. He was only a man, albeit a tall one. "You need to remove your damp clothes," he said.

He expected her to try and run again, but she seemed hypnotized by him, treating him with the attention one might give to a ravenous bear. She flinched when he removed his cloak from around her, then her cloak, heavy with snow. Working the gloves off her hands, his gaze remained fixed on her face, wondering what lay beneath the overhanging hood and the drooping muffler.

This woman he would spend the rest of his life with, and he was torn. Since the day King Henry gave her to him, Raymond had wondered what she looked like. Now he would see her, but what would a few more moments matter?

Her shivering calmed his brief cowardice. As he untied the hood and unwrapped the muffler, he realized she was more than just young and healthy.

Not a pruny widow at all. Not an invalid, not a whining witch. This Lady Juliana was smooth-skinned, tall, and fair. Not beautiful, although as low as his expectations had been, he might have thought so. Wisps of burnished copper hair escaped her hat and waved around her forehead. Her lips were too full for her thin face, sculptured as it was by high cheekbones and square jaw. Her vividly blue eyes slanted up at the corners, but they never blinked. She didn't want him undressing her or rubbing her hands to bring the circulation back. She projected an explicit message; this hut was a prison and he the lowest of gaolers.

Unwillingly, his pity stirred. Raymond of Avraché knew the sense of imprisonment too well.

"Your face is very white," he said. A round, purple scar marred one cheek, also, but he didn't mention that. "Are you frozen?"

She only stared, wary as a wolverine at bay.

"Your freckles float like tidbits of cinnamon on the clearest wine." He lifted his hand to touch the fascinating specks, but she jerked her head aside. Prodded by her silence and her distaste, he queried, "You don't want me touching you?" He reached out again. "Then tell me."

She stumbled backward. "Nay!"

"Ah." He relaxed. "You can speak. I wondered if we would ride out this blizzard in silence. Would you like me to build up the blaze?" Carrying wood to the fire pit, he stacked it in a pile beside him and knelt. "It's going to be a bad storm, did you realize? Nay, of course not, you couldn't have realized, or you wouldn't have come out in such weather." He glanced at her, pleased to see her creeping close. When his gaze touched her, she leaped back almost guiltily, and he turned back and fed the flames. "Surely a lady as exalted as you could send someone to the village to do your duties. You are Lady Juliana of Lofts, are you not?" She didn't answer, and he swivelled toward her. "Are you not?"

She stood off to the side, closer to his woodpile but not so far he couldn't touch her. He reached out his arm toward her, and she admitted, "Aye."

His eyes narrowed against the smoke; he studied her tense figure and wondered what she planned. Her hands opened and closed on nothing; she stood braced for action. The brave girl looked like a squire before first battle, all nerves and anticipation. Slowly, he turned back to the flames. Listening to her every move, he chatted, "In sooth, 'tis good. You can say only 'aye' and 'nay.'"

Behind him, a chunk of wood shifted, lifted.

"If a man must be trapped with a woman, what more could he desire than to be trapped with a silent one?" He waited, the hair on the back of his neck raising. He heard the faintest of indrawn breath. He twirled around, saw the log descending toward his head, and dove into her. The log smacked his shoulder so hard his arm went numb, then flew out of her grasp. Together they stumbled backward and sprawled onto the hard-packed ground. It knocked the breath out of her, but she'd almost knocked the brains out of him.

Although he understood desperation, he couldn't help shouting, "What in the name of Saint Sebastian do you think you're doing?"

His shout echoed in her ears. She shut her eyes and cringed away from the blow that would follow.

Nothing happened.

He lay on her, a motionless weight. He sighed and asked, "Are you hurt?"

She shook her head and opened her eyes a slit. A muffler left only his eyes and mouth exposed. He was watching her intently, trying to see more than she wished to disclose. A woolen cap covered his head, black hair hanging ragged beneath it, but she knew she didn't recognize those shoulders. He was a stranger, a man, one of the creatures she dreaded most. A shudder racked her. Sympathy deepened in his gaze, and somehow that brought a measure of courage back to her cowardly soul. She didn't want his sympathy, and she rejected it even as another shudder shook her. "Get off."

The corners of his eyes crinkled, and she knew he grinned at her. "Not only can you speak, you can give orders."

"But can you obey?" she snapped.

He sobered, weighting his words with more significance than they deserved. "Indeed. I'm a well-trained monkey, didn't you know?"

His bitterness confused her. He stood and shook his arm. He lifted it, twisted it, and when he was satisfied it would work, he said, "You've a fine swing, my lady."

She stared up at him, trying to discern his features and his mood. Her gaze travelled down to his scuffed leather boots, up to the fine material of his cape, aging now, and she wondered at him. Her back against the wall, she scooted up until she had her feet under her. "What's a monkey?"

His amusement returned. He extended his hand, demanding she take it, and said, "Come close to the fire where I can watch you, and I'll explain."

"Nay."

Her lips had scarcely formed the word when in one giant step he stood next to her. She realized anew how tall he was, yet she had nowhere to move. Sensation was returning to her feet, and with it the prickles of frostbite. Her teeth created a tapping noise that embarrassed her, but she couldn't seem to stop.

"'Tis foolish to spite yourself. Come to the fire."

Her teeth chattered even more, but she came, making a large circle around the proffered hand, afraid he would touch her if she didn't obey.

As he intended. It irritated her that he knew so well how to manipulate her, like some conniving puppeteer with his doll. It irritated her more that he did it for her own protection, leaving her no room for rational objection.

"I'm betrothed to a man who'll show you the color of your gullet for this." The words burbled to her lips without thought, but she was glad when he looked alarmed.

"Betrothed? To whom?"

"To Geoffroi Jean Louis Raymond, Count of Avraché."

"Ah." He relaxed, and knelt to unwrap the frozen wool around her ankles. "Have you been betrothed for long?"

"Aye, over a year."

"A reluctant suitor, then?"

"Nay! That is—we were betrothed by proxy in the king's own court."

"Yet you're not wed?"

She shifted uncomfortably. "I was ill."

He peered at her. "You don't appear to be ill."

"I was ill, then my children were ill." He still looked politely incredulous. "Then it was winter, and 'tisn't safe to cross the channel in the face of such gales. Then it was summer, and I couldn't travel before the crops were in . . ."

She realized how ineffectual she sounded when he chuckled. "Ah, a reluctant bride. I trow the court found your hesitance most amusing."

"Nay!" she protested in horror.

"And Henry, too, must have roared with laughter at the insult to Lord Avraché."

"That would be most unfortunate. No insult was intended"—she said it in hopes of convincing him as well as herself—"for he's a fierce warrior. A Crusader."

"Crusaders are not necessarily fierce warriors, my lady. Some are snivelling cowards." He busied himself with her shoes, lifting her feet to peel them off one by one.

She toppled and almost fell rather than grab him. At the last moment her dignity overcame her good sense, and she gripped his shoulder. Many layers of clothing lay between her fingers and his skin. Not even his body heat could penetrate the damp and cold which still enveloped him. Yet this was the first time she'd voluntarily touched a man in over three years.

This man couldn't know that, but he'd coerced her by holding her off balance. If only he would look up, but he never removed his gaze from the toes he was unwrapping. Humble as a serf, she thought bitterly. As if this man could ever be humble. Every gesture, every tactic was planned and executed with forethought and intelligence. Aye, he'd known how much she feared his touch, and had forced her to touch him first.

Perhaps he wished to prove he was only flesh and blood, but she understood the danger of flesh-and-blood men. Oh, aye, she understood. Stroking the circular scar on her cheekbone, she protested, "My betrothed is not a snivelling coward. The Saracens captured him, and he escaped by stealing one of their own merchant ships and sailing it to Normandy."

His hands were warm; her feet were cold. His hands were strong, yet he massaged each muscle as skillfully as a healer and brought the blood rushing back.

"You shouldn't believe everything you hear, my lady."

"It's true!" She should have been alarmed at his easy dismissal, but his amusement robbed the words of their menace, and she found herself offended instead.

"Indeed?"

"Aye, indeed." She hopped a little, intent on convincing him. "King Henry sent me a letter informing me of my betrothal. In it, he described my betrothed and his history."

Unimpressed, he asked only, "How did he describe your betrothed?"

Disdainfully, she repeated the lyrical phrases. "As handsome as the night, as strong as the north wind."

"You don't believe it?"

Melting snow dripped off the tip of her nose. She dabbed it with her sleeve. "Am I a fool? If he were lame and half mad, still would Henry weave a web of poetry around him. The king wishes to forestall my objections until the marriage is performed."

"Then most likely his heroism is an exaggeration, also."

Biting her lip, she felt it crack beneath her teeth and tasted the salt of blood on her tongue. She had betrayed herself with logic, but she repeated the suspicion she both clutched as security and rejected in fear. "I don't think so. When they can, the Welsh come to plunder the land I hold for the king. He wouldn't give the protection of that land to a weakling. Lord Avraché is a man to be feared."

He squeezed her toes. "Fear him not. He's just a man."

It struck her then. The man who knelt at her feet spoke French, as she did, as did all the nobles in England, but his accent sounded like none she'd ever heard before. He came from the court, but what had brought him here? "You know him?"

He laid one gloved hand flat against his chest. "I? The count moves in the highest circles, but his lineage, character, and reputation have been blared about by various untrustworthy sources."

"Nay," she answered thoughtfully. "Not everyone who's been to court has spoken with the king, I suppose."

"Nay, indeed. I'm in no position to judge the truth of your Avraché's character." He chuckled and shook his head. "Nay, indeed."

"But do you know . . . ?"

"What?" he urged.

"Is he related to the king?"

"So they say." His broad shoulders lifted in a shrug. "But who isn't? Henry's related to most of noble Europe, and whoever he's not related to, Eleanor is. The queen, I mean. Queen Eleanor."

"You should show her more respect," she rebuked. "So Avraché is the king's cousin. Is he very rich?"

"The king?"

The impudent fellow's eyes shone big with innocence above his muffler, but she didn't believe it. "Avraché. Is he going to gobble up my lands as if they were whey?"

He looked down at her bare feet. "I have hose you can wear to keep you warm." He reached for his bags and fumbled inside. She didn't think he would answer, but at last he admitted, "Avraché is the only son of a wealthy family."

Rancor welled in her. "Then Lofts and Bartonhale will account for nothing to him."

"Not at all, my lady." He kept his head down and smoothed the dry but ragged hose over her feet. "His parents are less than generous. To keep him on a short leash, they've kept him without funds."

"But he's Count of Avraché."

"At birth, they granted him one of his father's many titles, but although they promised, they have never given him the income from the lands."

"How old is he now?"

"Five and thirty."

A groan eased from her. "He's getting old."

He laughed as if he were startled. "I've heard he's . . . well preserved. At least, you won't have to worry about your lands. He'll care for them as if they were his own."

The protest burst from her, propelled by her possessiveness. "The lands aren't his. They're mine. I'm my father's only heir, God rest him. When I was a child and he loved me, he insisted I walk every rood of Lofts, meet all the people, for if I did not, he said, I would be cheated out of what is rightfully mine. Now I am heir to my husband's estate, God rest him also, and I have found that to be a hard truth. Men would take from me by stealth or treachery."

"You are sole heir to your father's lands and your husband's lands?"

His words struck her with the force of a spring flood down the river. How had he lulled her so she admitted to such wealth? No doubt he knew the extent of her holdings—such adventurers always did—but she'd confirmed it in a betrayal as unpremeditated as it was unexpected. Who was this scoundrel?

She reached for his face; he jerked back as if she would strike him. Sulky, she said, "Your scarf." This time, he remained still as she stripped the material away.

She dropped it as if it burned her hand.

His green eyes, his absurdly long, black lashes should have warned her of trouble.

The man was handsome. More than handsome: alluring, intriguing, with a calm, still demeanor that warned of deep waters, and which offered rewards for exploring them. His ebony hair swept his shoulders and invited a woman's touch. Clean-shaven, his cleft chin was broad and proud. The smooth hollow of his cheeks caught her eye and dismayed her soul. She pushed his hat off, and his hair tumbled wildly. Black as a raven's wing, with an unruly curl, it grew longer than she liked, yet her gaze lingered on the shining mass and on the barbaric gold earring that glittered in one ear.

He was, she realized, kneeling at her feet patiently waiting for her appraisal to end. Obviously, he was used to having women—hordes of women—stare at him. It made her angry, to class herself with a legion. It made her angry, too, to be so affected by his appearance.

Rude as her own ten-year-old daughter, she sneered, "You have big ears."

Startled, he blinked. A smile crept up on him, curving his sensual mouth as if he couldn't resist it.

Oh, God, his smile added to his beauty. The corners of his eyes tilted up and crinkled—he wasn't as young as she'd first supposed. Dimples creased his cheeks. His lips, chapped with the cold, begged to be soothed. She found her hand clutching the cloth over her middle to appease the churning of her stomach. She'd never thought that someday, somewhere, a man would affect her this way.

How was it possible? If all the men in the world were marching toward a cliff like lemmings into the sea, she'd throw tidbits before them to tempt them along. Her father had ranted that she was too sensitive, too easily offended when a man treated her like meat, to be sold, bartered, consumed at a lord's leisure and for his pleasure. So why could she see the comeliness of this man, this villain who had so cruelly abducted her?

He rose to his feet, and her words tumbled over each other. "My betrothed is here at this very moment."

Considering her, he asked, "Here? Where?"

"On my lands." A variety of expressions raced across his face, and none could she define. Flushed with her falsehood, she wiped her face and dislodged her hat. It fell to the hard dirt floor. She didn't like the way he stared at her, so she dove for the hat.

He restrained her with his hand, and instinctively she kicked at him. "My lady, I thought we were beyond that."

Bracing herself against her panic, she satisfied herself with a glare.

He picked her braid up in his hand, weighed it, pursed his lips. "Let us hope your betrothed is as well protected from this storm as we are."

Did he notice how short her hair was? Did he realize that, if unbraided, it would reach only to her shoulders? And what did he surmise from that? What conclusions did he draw?

His gaze slid down her body, stuffed like a sausage

into her winter dress. "How many layers of clothes do you have on?"

Embarrassed that she'd looked at him and even more embarrassed that he'd seen her, she flared, "That's my business and none of yours."

When she'd tried to hit him with the log, his shouting had made her cringe. Now she wished he'd shout again. His face lost all expression, like that of a man whose fortune would be foretold with one roll of the knucklebones. His eyes chilled to green icicles, his quiet voice lowered until she had to strain to hear it.

"If the lady of Lofts should freeze to death while in my care, it would soon become my business. When your men would hang me up by the neck, it would be my business. When they would tie me to four horses, one limb to each, and would whip them and tear me—"

She covered her face, too tired and cold to deal with the images he evoked, and his indignation faded.

"So. We are agreed. It is my business what you have on because you must remain alive for me to retain that blessed state. Shall we remove the outermost layer at least?" He held his hands back, palms out. "With the purest intentions."

She doubted that, but pure intentions or no, it had to be done. Already the wet of snow seeped through the first cotte to the other clothes she wore. Cautiously, she backed up and tugged at the laces closing the long gown of rough homespun she wore for outdoor winter work. Resentful of his scrutiny, she snapped, "Are you not cold?"

"Of course." He shrugged off his mantle, tossed it over the top of the cloaks. "But when a man's been to hell, a blast of winter revives him."

She stared at her fingers, inalterably tangled in the laces. "Have you been?"

"To hell? Certainly. And back."

It was one thing to suspect she was in the hands of the devil, quite another to have it confirmed. Her teeth began that dreadful clattering again, and he observed her through narrowed eyes. "My lady, how many years do you carry?"

"Eight and twenty."

He clicked his tongue. "Still so impressionable. You're not a child."

"I know. Forgive me, but I'm cold and I'm tired."

"And hungry, in sooth. I have only oatcakes, but—"

"I'm not hungry." Instinctively, she denied the animal in her belly, the one who demanded sustenance regardless of her fears. Well did she understand the significance of breaking bread with the enemy.

"You're not hungry?"

His amazement seemed forced to her, and she wondered crazily if this man knew her mind. She didn't want the devil's cakes, no matter how tempting. Without a doubt, she knew that if she ate them, she would never return to her world again. Her fingers were still caught, her brain still muddled, but she insisted, "I have said so."

"Sit at the table." His hand was gentle on her arm. He led her to the bench and pushed her down. "I left wine warming." He touched his finger to her nose. "And don't tell me you won't partake of that."

Her refusal withered on her lips. When he ordered, she obeyed. Not because she doubted herself, but because he displayed a natural assurance that withered defiance before it could flower. Very well, she would take the wine and simply hold it, not drink it, just to appease him. Petulant about even that concession, she asked, "Who are you? Why have you taken me?"

Moving back to the fire, he lifted the lid of a pot. The scent of red wine rose through the air, and while he ladled it into a cup, he said, "You had no chance of reaching your home. Didn't you realize that?"

He sounded inexplicably concerned, indefatigably honest, and she searched his face, seeking the truth there, knowing she'd not recognize it if she found it. She sighed, jerked her hands free of the lacing, and found her palms wrapped around a cup of mulled wine. The heat seeped through to her fingers, cramped with cold, and a painful recovery began.

"Drink." He urged the cup toward her face.

She closed her eyes to better savor the aroma, and found the seduction greater than she had imagined. Native herbs and a savor quite unlike any other ascended on the steam. Opening her eyes, she found him before her, his face level with hers, his gaze compelling. "Drink," he said again, and, mesmerized, she swallowed the steaming brew.

No matter how good the wine tasted, no matter how it warmed her, she had to know her fate. "Why—?"

"Drink it all."

One look at his expression, and she gulped the wine to the dregs and thumped the cup on the plank table. The way he spoke irritated her. Slowly, as if he considered every word before it crossed his lips. Raspingly, as if the words whispered up from deep inside him, from where his thoughts resided. And that place was deeper than a wind-directed whirlpool.

It lured her, tried to suck her down, used her

weariness against her. That deep place in him tried to communicate with her. It used the strength of his large body. Rest on me, it whispered, I will protect you. It used his eyes, green like the sea during a lightning storm. Trust me, it whispered, I won't hurt you. More than the wine or the food, *he* beguiled her. Her eyes pricked with tears, and her sigh wavered most awkwardly. Three years, and some stranger imagined she could trust him.

Before she could question him again, he asked, "Are your men-at-arms so unruly they won't escort you?"

"What? Where?" She spread the laces wide and fought her shoulders out of her brown homespun cotte, revealing another gown beneath it.

He grasped the rough wool at each of her wrists, tugging until her arms were loose. "To the village. That is where you'd been, was it not?"

"To see my old nurse. She's not expected to live through the winter, you see, and she was asking for me." Angry for justifying herself, she stood, pushing the cotte over her waist, and found his hands over hers. She jerked her hands away, glaring up at him. In his face, she could see nothing but impatience and a good measure of anger.

"Where were your men-at-arms?"

"Sir Joseph escorted me himself. He is my chief man, a crony of my father's."

"Where is he *now*?" Raymond enunciated the words clearly, wanting the explanation faster than she wanted to give it.

This man, with all his sensibility, would think her a dolt for her terror, just as Sir Joseph did, just as her father had. But they were her terrors, emotions she couldn't control, and defiantly she said, "He refused to come back with me, saying the storm was too intense and we would freeze ere we returned to the castle."

Raymond seemed to be thinking. "Did you doubt him?"

"Nay."

"Is there a reason you had to return? A sick child, perhaps, or a dying mother?"

"My children are well. My mother is dead."

He slid down the cloth, his hands too firm on her hips for her comfort, but he didn't linger and she didn't dare complain. "But regardless of his warning, you determined to go home?"

"Aye." She waited for the explosion, the rain of contempt from the logical man. Instead she heard his incredulity.

"And this Sir Joseph refused to accompany you? He let you go, knowing you would perhaps die as you made your way home? Knowing you might wander away from the path under the influence of wind and snow? Knowing he could lose his mistress?"

"Well." She opened the lacing on her next cotte. "You must understand, he's an old man."

"He's a man who has outlived his usefulness."

He pronounced judgment as if he had the right. Filling her cup again, he noticed her trepidation. Unsmiling, he said, "Don't fret. I'll tend to it."

"Tend to what?" He only handed her the cup, and in her distress, the liquid sloshed dangerously close to the edge. "Oh, please don't say anything to Sir Joseph about this. He would say I'd been complaining about him, and—" The way he watched her gave her pause.

"Pray continue."

"—and Sir Joseph can be very unpleasant," she mumbled. Not for the first time, she wished Sir Joseph roasted in hell. But that was a wicked, ungrateful thought. Once more, she touched the scar on her cheek, then her hand slid around into her hair behind her ear. Another scar puckered the skin there, long and jagged.

"Climb into bed and finish your wine."

"You jest."

He lifted the covers and held them in silent command.

"I will not." He'd never told her who he was or even why he'd brought her here. His concern for her safety masked a greater goal, and she'd be a fool to forget it.

He looked impatient, but she had wine courage running in her veins. "I will not lie down for you or with you. Kidnapping an heiress is a time-honored way to win a bride and a fortune, but others have tried to force me to marry them and I refused. Just as I refuse you, you scurrilous maggot."

He suddenly loomed over her, a tall, strong, furious man, and she flung her arms up to protect her head.

But no blow struck her.

"Sit," he said in a tone that belied the fury in his eyes.

Lowering her arms slowly, suspecting a trick, she eyed him. He still looked tall and strong, but disgust had replaced anger. Her cowardice sickened him, and she shrivelled inside. Obedient now, she sat atop the musty straw pad.

A profound silence settled over them as he tucked the furs around her ankles and tight around her waist, and placed a cloth over the smooth log that served as pillow.

She didn't know what drove her, even out of the depths of her terror, to defy him still. Perhaps it was her fear of the man. Perhaps it was her fear of herself, of the care he pretended to take for her, of this strange attraction she felt for him. Perhaps she'd just been forced to the brink of endurance. But she stared into his cold eyes and whispered, "I will not bed you. Better to fling myself on the flames or chain myself to the life of a serf."

The frost in his gaze dissolved into emerald fire. With his hands on her shoulders, he pushed her back. "Never say such a thing again. Never think it, never wish it on yourself. The chains of a serf are not for you, my lady."

"Nay, but they would fit well around the neck of the scum who dreams of bettering his station with my title."

He released her as if she had burned him. "If ever I have the good fortune to meet Geoffroi Jean Louis Raymond, Count of Avraché, I would advise him to shackle you to the marriage bed until you learn a better use for your tongue than speech."

2

Geoffroi Jean Louis Raymond, Count of Avraché, reflected gloomily on the debacle he'd made of one simple abduction.

Juliana was an heiress, with two attractive castles and accompanying rich demesnes. She had been given to him by King Henry, had refused, for the most specious of reasons, to come to wed, had made Raymond of Avraché a laughingstock of the court.

Why, then, had his fury abated when faced with the panic of this one disobedient woman? He'd wanted vengeance on Lady Juliana for her reluctance to be wed, yet when he saw her, so frightened, so brave, he was unable to wreak retribution. And she was only a weak woman—even if she did pack a ferocious wallop with a log.

But after he knocked her down and subdued her, he became aware of her delicacy. Although her clothes wrapped her in a disguise of pudginess, the body beneath was fine boned. He found himself awaiting the removal of every garment with the anticipation of a pasha previewing his latest concubine. The innermost cotte had been just as ugly as the outermost, but it couldn't completely conceal the slender waist, the curves at bust and hip. Her face lacked the narrow beauty popular at court, yet her sweet mouth, her shadowed eyes, tempted him to hold, to caress, to comfort until her resistance melted into passion.

Rummaging through his bags, he found the stamp bearing his family seal, and with his fingertip he caressed the crude representation of the bear etched therein. With slathering jaw and upraised paws, it threatened death and dismemberment to every enemy of his clan. A mere woman had no chance against the might of the bear—so why hadn't he taken the lady who slept in such exhaustion?

Angrily he tossed his seal back into the bags. He wasn't like the legendary founder of his clan: fierce, strong, maddened in battle. He was more like a mother bear reproving a cub with a blow of one big, soft paw.

Rolling his wet hose down his legs, he hung them by the flames to dry. Would God he had another pair, but Juliana wore his extras, and he was too soft-hearted . . .

So some other man had tried to pressure her into marriage.

And she had refused? Refused what kind of offer? Had some suitor put that purple scar on her cheekbone with a blow of one ringed hand?

He knelt beside the fire, feeding it wood to see them through the night, and the glowing red of the coals matched the fire in his breast.

From now on Lady Juliana would go nowhere without a guard. His blood boiled when he considered how easily any man could pluck her from her lands and force marriage on her. Any knave could have beaten her into submission, used her ill, taken her.

Raymond had not used her ill, not beaten her, nor even taken her.

'Strewth, what kind of knight was he? Gone were the days when he slashed his way through life, sword and mace his constant companions. There had been a time when jousting, fighting, killing had brought him honor and enough wealth to maintain himself. The prizes of war had slipped into his purse, and he'd never considered the grief, the ruin that followed in his footsteps. He'd been to hell, he'd told Juliana. So he had, and he'd risen from the flames with his old self burned away.

True, he had been a knight on the Crusades. He had been captured, and he had indeed stolen a ship to return to Normandy.

But Juliana didn't know about the years he'd lived with the Saracens.

Or did she? Was that the reason she'd refused to come on the king's command and wed him? Did all of Christendom know of Raymond of Avraché's frailty of will? Was she disgusted by the tales of his cowardice?

Was that why she called him scum?

He warmed his hands until steam wafted from his damp sleeves and stared at the sleeping lady, stared until his eyes burned. She would be passionate, wouldn't she? She would be giving and kind, and welcome him to her hearth and into her body. Take her, he urged himself. It wasn't too late. Impregnate her. Climb into the bed with her, be between her legs before she woke properly. Then he would have the lady in marriage without falling back on Henry's strength, on Henry's orders.

He leaned across the fire pit and draped a wool wrap over her, so if the furs shifted, she would still be protected. Then, lured by her warmth, he slid one chilly hand beneath the covers, touched the flesh he coveted. The firelight blessed her fine skin with a glow. He wanted her, and this gentle lady . . .

He sniffed. The odor of scorched cloth irritated his nose. Wool? He glanced at his hose, but they still hung out of reach of the flames. Then what? . . . Struck by an ugly suspicion, he leaped up. His drawers were smoldering, and he slapped at himself to muffle the impending—and appropriate—blaze.

Juliana sat straight up. In the dark room, the fire smoldered red. The storm moaned as it died a slow death, and the cold it brought pressed in, unfazed by the weak attempt of the embers to hold it back.

On the bench across the circle of stones, the stranger slept. His head rested on his arm, he'd pulled his knees close to his chest, a single ragged blanket covered him. Across the hut, the horse, too, wore a blanket, and a better one than his master.

Even in repose, the man seemed taut, vigilant, with none of the rumpled softness of slumber, yet he hadn't taken advantage of her weakness the night before. With her weariness abated, her basest suppositions disproved, she wondered if she'd misjudged him. Now she'd had a full night's sleep, now she had her wits about her, and she realized a few things about the man.

He spoke like a learned knight. Would such a man brave a blizzard to kidnap her? True, his scuffed leather boots and formerly fine cape indicated a need that could drive a man to desperate measures. They could also be a disguise to fool the brigands who so freely patrolled the roads.

So if he was not a knave, why was he here, on her

land, in her hut? Was he an errant knight, or a free man seeking work? Had bad fortune taken everything from him, and he was too embarrassed to speak of it? With a skillful application of feminine handling—surely she remembered how to handle a man—she could discover his misfortune without hurting his pride.

Today she could draw him out, question him about his background, and at the same time establish a relationship untainted by their genders. It was possible. Until three years ago, she'd known men she called her friends. Had welcomed them to her home, joked with them, confided in them. Now she shunned such contact, but for the sake of her safety, she could do it again. She would do it again, for the most important thing was this; he hadn't raped her.

They'd spent the night together, and he hadn't forced himself on her with cruel hands and grinning mouth and vicious intentions. For she knew that if the man had been determined, he could have plundered her defenses. This was no puny knight, ablaze with a dream of riches, but a man who knew what he wanted. He looked to be eighteen hands high, and she had reason to know his hard muscles covered hard bone. His restraint alone absolved him of almost every guilt, and if she couldn't completely acquit him, she hoped her suspicions would prove to be for naught.

Ablaze with resolve, she sat up, dislodging the furs around her, and, as if to test her courage, his eyes opened. Like a warrior ready for battle, he assessed her, and there leaped to his face a ravenous hunger.

The terror returned, making her cower when she had resolved to be strong.

"Are you thirsty?" he asked.

She nodded, and marvelled at him. How strange

he was. Unlike any other man she'd ever met, he seemed to have his desires under control.

"I'll heat more wine." Sitting up, he rubbed his eyes.

His gloves had no fingers. His dexterity was greater, but the gloves had not been knitted in that manner. He'd cut them, and the gloves had suffered in the wearing. Perversely, that made her cast her fear aside. "No more wine," she said with parched tongue. "Water, I beg you."

He rose. "I'll collect the snow that has blown in around the door."

While he mounded his cooking pot full, she asked, "Is it morn?"

He pawed the ashes away from the still-glowing embers, arranged kindling and logs, and blew until the wood lit. "Perhaps. The snow piles so deep around the hut we are—" He hesitated.

"Buried?"

"Snowed in," he said.

She pointed at the ceiling where the smoke whirled before escaping. "Not completely buried, but I think I detect a warmth that comes with a snow-bank's protection."

"Warmth?" He grinned, a wry twist of his lips. "Warmth is an exaggeration, I believe."

As he turned and handed her a cup of chilly water, she remembered that the covers which had kept her warm last night had been denied to him. His kindness nagged at her; she didn't wish to be indebted to him. She drank the cup dry, then, brisk as a mother hen, she said, "Here." Swinging her legs down, she plucked the wool blanket from atop the bed and swung it around his shoulders.

He huddled into the blanket, and, as she stood close, she could see the blue tinge to his skin. She said, "Sit there, and I'll cook us a warm meal. What food have you?"

"I've a loaf of bread I bought in the village."

"I'll toast it."

"And some cheese, some oats, some onions, some dried meat, some dried peas, some dried fruit, some ale—"

She held up her hand. "Toasted bread should be enough." He looked up at her with big, wounded eyes, and she yielded. "But I'm hungry enough to eat a stag. Perhaps some oats with stewed fruit, also."

"Is that all?" He sighed.

His shoulders drooped in the exaggerated imitation of a child, and that pretense sat so ill on his massive frame that she laughed. The bubble of amusement startled her. How long had it been since she'd smiled? Too long, for it felt too odd and a little like a surrender. Turning to his gear on the table, she picked up his bags. "Is the food here, or—"

He plucked the bags out of her hand before she could open them, and pushed her toward the shelves against the wall. "There are my own supplies and the supplies left for those too weary to wander farther."

"Shall we be snowed in indefinitely? I mean, should we be cautious about our supplies?"

"I fancy the wind lessens. If it ceases, I'll try to force the door."

"Would you?" She clasped her hands prayerfully. "I would give anything to be safe behind my walls."

"Safe? From what do you seek to be safe?"

From someone like you, she wanted to say, but she hadn't the courage. Her gaze slipped away from his;

she found herself staring at the row of neatly arranged jars and bags.

His sardonic voice drawled, "With a snowdrift as your castle and a man such as I as your champion, you're as safe as is possible."

"Of course. I didn't mean . . . " She stole a glance at him. Most definitely, this was a man who had faced misfortune. He was beautiful, aye, but not in the first bloom of his youth. The stubble of his beard grew black and thick on his chin, and his tanned skin showed signs of a relentless sun. Responsibility had marked him with tiny wrinkles around his eyes, and as he watched the flames, his mouth drooped.

She could handle this man, if only she'd take herself in hand and stop blundering about. Keep the conversation impersonal, talk about things men like to talk about, subtly probe into his background. She blurted, "Where was King Henry's court when you left it?" Oh, that was subtle, she chastised herself.

But he answered readily enough. "Moving about his domains on the continent with the speed of a youth, which he is not anymore, although no one has the crust to tell him. His retainers complain, but I've come to think it's the way he keeps his kingdom under control. No one ever knows where, or when, he'll arrive."

While sorting the bits of chaff and small stones from the oats, she muttered, "You learned much from him."

"I didn't hear you."

"I asked what kind of fruit you want." She peered into the leather sacks that protected dried foods from rodents.

"Apples. Since my return, I can't get enough of good English apples."

"Don't apples grow over the channel?"

"Not with the tang of these."

His smile spoke to her soft heart, and she tossed a goodly handful of apples into the bubbling stew. The scent made her stomach growl, and she remembered her trepidations of the previous night. She dismissed them as fantasy, brought only by hunger and distress, and told him, "I've heard Queen Eleanor returned to England."

"She did," he acknowledged.

"I've heard she's distressed with the king."

"That kind of gossip spreads like the floods of spring." He reached for the spoon and stirred the pot. She thought he would say aught else, but he gripped the handle until his knuckles turned white. "Henry is a fool."

Startled, she protested, "You're bold with criticism of your betters."

"Henry's my king, and he holds my allegiance. That doesn't mean I have no opinion of his good sense, or lack of it." His mouth was grim. "You never reproached your father? Or your husband?"

"Neither my father nor my husband was king of England and lord of half of France," she answered roundly. Picking up the bread, she glanced around. "Where's the knife?"

He rose from his place by the fire and took the loaf from her. "*I'll* use the knife."

The way he spoke reminded her of her attempt to smash his head. Abashed, she gathered bowls as he hewed a chunk of bread and skewered it with a stick.

Extending it over the flames, he said, "Neither your father nor your husband had the potential to build what Henry has, nor the potential to destroy it. He's within a breath of uniting his lands into one kingdom, firmly in control of the lands of his father, of his mother, *and* his wife. And what does he do? He flaunts a mistress in front of his queen. His proud queen. The queen who divorced the King of France for him."

"Love . . . changes. Grows greater or lesser with time and circumstances." She was an expert at this. To avoid looking at him, she stirred the pot so vigorously the oats could never scorch.

"Love? I don't know if there was ever love between them. But there was infatuation, at least on Eleanor's part. She'd been married to Louis, and he was so holy he dispensed marital favors only sparingly. When she saw Henry, young and virile as a bull—"

"She's older than Henry?"

"Aye, and that makes his defection particularly galling."

"Any woman could understand that," she acknowledged.

"Any *man* could understand that," he snapped.

The flames illuminated his handsome features, and she was stricken anew by a sense of his power. This man carried his arrogance easily, without effort or thought. She knew that whoever he was, whatever he did, he was master. Her prolonged scrutiny brought his gaze to hers, and he lifted his brows in query. Hastily she said, "The porridge is ready." She spooned it into the bowls, accepted a piece of crusty bread, and seated herself on the bed. Testing his knowledge, she said, "But the king is known to have liaisons outside of his marriage. There's never been any talk of his fidelity."

"*Henry's* fidelity? Ha!"

She savored the flavor of cereal and fruit with closed eyes, and when she opened them she found his gaze fixed on her face. A half-smile decorated his mouth, but whether because of her pleasure or Henry's doubtful fidelity, she didn't know. Briefly, her doubts of the night before returned. Was this the king of hell? Had she damned herself to stay with him eternally by the eating of his food? As she watched, he tucked his hair behind his ears to keep it out of the way, and she saw the earring again.

A barbaric earring of hammered gold, so large it expanded the pierced lobe. The pain must have been extraordinary, and she couldn't imagine what had made him allow such a license. He glanced up to see the cause of her sudden silence, and she launched into speech. "I've heard the nobles keep their wives and daughters away from the king."

"Unless they want a favor," he acknowledged. "But this girl, this Rosamund, is different. Henry flaunts her, keeps her in the royal residences."

As she ate, she debated the wisdom of telling him all the gossip the minstrel had passed on. But he knew so much, was so intimate with the players, she couldn't resist. "During her autumn travels, Eleanor found Rosamund living at Woodstock."

He put down his spoon. "At that most beloved royal residence?"

"So I was told."

"Does Henry believe Eleanor will submit tamely to his disrespect? Before she was Queen of France or of England, she was Countess of Poitou and Aquitaine. Her lands are almost half of Henry's empire."

She scraped the last bits of apple from her bowl. "What kind of woman is she?"

"A marvelous woman." His smile spoke volumes of his fondness. "No queenly figurehead is she.

She understands the politics between France and England, and understands the politics *within* France and England. Without her help, Henry could never have come so far, so quickly." He took her bowl and gave her another helping of the oat and apple mixture.

"Surely you believe she's one of the lesser sex."

He sidestepped her challenge. "But greater than most men. She's borne Henry seven children—three healthy, living sons, and perhaps a fourth at Christmastide."

Juliana's heart contracted with sympathy for the beleaguered queen. "She carries a child?"

"Which Henry sent her away to bear on English soil, so he said."

"Perhaps the king doesn't realize how he offends her with his exhibit of this Rosamund."

"He does, never doubt it, but rather than placate the queen, he'll display his power over her subjects. He'll spend Christmas at Poitiers, at Eleanor's own home, to introduce his son Henry to the Poitevin lords. The second son, Richard, is Eleanor's designated heir to Poitou and Aquitaine, but the king will introduce Henry the younger as their future sovereign." He set his bowl aside with a sigh of satiation or aggravation. "Our liege is a splendid tactician."

The way he said it made her look at him. "Don't Poitevins recognize the young Henry as their overlord?"

"Poitevins are a flighty people, with a tendency to break into rebellion every time Henry turns his attention elsewhere. If the queen should go to them and request their assistance—"

"They'll gladly rebel," she finished. "And mayhap rebellion would spread. Glad I am that I've plans to make improvements to my castle."

His attention homed in on her. "Improvements?"

Should she tell him? Would it impress him that she had the foresight to strengthen her defenses, or would he see a weakness he could exploit? "Additions to the curtain wall," she said, watching him as closely as he watched her.

He leaned forward, his hands on his knees, his eyes sparking with zest. "Your outer bulwark needs reform?"

"Aye. I've been told of the progress made on the design of castles manned by the Crusaders, and I resolved to take advantage of those designs."

Obviously pleased, he told her, "I can help. I know a bit about castle design."

Did he indeed?

Leaping up, he went to the door and gathered snow in his arms. Close to the outside wall of the hut, he piled the snow on the packed dirt floor and formed a mound. "There's the outcrop your castle is situated on." He drew a wavy line around three sides of the mound in the packed dirt floor. "There's the river that protects you. The keep sits here, on the highest point, and in it you have your great hall, your storage cellars, perhaps a well, since you're so close to the river." He stabbed his twig into the summit, and around it like a fence he laid kindling.

"My kitchen is in the undercroft, also," she said, challenging him.

"In the undercroft?" He looked as astonished as every man looked when told. "Why would you want it in the undercroft?"

"'Tis easier for the servants to bring dinner up the stairs. 'Tis easier to boil water when the well is close at hand. 'Tis just easier."

"Than having a kitchen hut in the bailey?" He shrugged. "Such things are a woman's concern, and although I've never heard of such a madness, 'tis not for me to complain."

She stared at him, open-mouthed. None of the men she knew—not Sir Joseph, not Hugh, not Felix, not even her father before his affections had changed— none of them would have dismissed the location of the kitchen with such a bow to her knowledge.

"Have you had trouble with the fire below?" he asked, looking interested.

"Nay." Eager to explain her innovation to someone who appreciated creativity, she said, "We built a fire pit into the bare earth, well away from the columns that hold up the flooring of the great hall. We put a flue high above to siphon the smoke."

"So the flue is not a hole in your defenses."

"Aye." She rubbed her palms on her skirt, and she shared the greatest triumph of all. "And the food comes to the table warm."

"Leave it to a woman to improve the living conditions, I always say, and leave it to the men to improve the defenses." He pointed his thumb toward his chest. "That's me. Now here is the wall you have now. The bailey is this open area surrounding the keep. In it, you have a garden, a stable, perhaps—"

She wasn't listening anymore. She simply stared at the mound he'd made. He knew the layout of her castle. Not that it was an unusual castle. Except for the kitchen inside the keep, it was typical of the first stone castles built after William the Bastard had conquered England. But this showed he'd studied her home, as if he were a stone mason or a carpenter seeking work—or a warrior intent on conquest.

He said something impatiently, and her mouth went dry as she looked at him. This man was no simple carpenter.

"You want to add another curtain wall?" He spoke as if he would repeat the sentence into infinity, or at least until she answered him.

"Nay." She cleared her throat. Keep him talking. He couldn't learn anything she didn't choose to tell him, and if she could just keep him talking, she might discover his purpose. "I want to strengthen the present curtain wall—not that it's not strong enough," she added hastily.

"What changes will you make?"

She realized reluctantly she would have to tell him, minimizing the deficiencies while sounding airy and positive. "There's little protection atop the wall for the archers. I want to add stone merlons for them to hide behind and arrow slits for them to shoot out of. I want to add a tower and gatehouse"—she glared—"stop shaking your head at me!"

He smiled at her irritation. "You need an outer curtain wall."

"What good would another wall do?" Picking her words with care, she said, "I already have a wall, strong beyond imagining."

"A castle needs circles of defense to be effective, one inside the other, each stronger than the last."

"There's a moat around the wall." Waving her finger at his creation, she ordered, "Dig a moat on that toy castle you built."

He did as he was told, saying, "Also built, no doubt, when the first William conquered England."

Irked by his patronizing air, she nodded.

"That was one hundred years ago! The new

designs are built with many circles, so the attackers must scale many walls, dodge many missiles, face many arrows." In a fever of enthusiasm, he erased the newly dug moat with a sweep of his hand. He laid kindling along the side of the hill not facing the river and excavated a new moat right beside it. "See, with your site, you have a mighty advantage. With the addition of an outer wall from one bank of the river to the other, you'll have an impregnable castle. We could build a tower here and here"—he placed tall sticks into the corners of his outer wall, overlooking the river—"and the men-at-arms you placed there would have a view of the surrounding countryside for miles in any direction."

"Towers on the inner wall would produce the same results," she answered primly.

"We'll build towers on the inner walls, too," he agreed. "But first, this curtain wall. We'll construct a gatehouse, an impassable stronghold." He rubbed his hands in anticipation and sorted through his kindling for just the right gatehouse.

As he placed his stubby, rounded piece of wood in the middle of his outer wall, she wondered when the construction of her castle had moved beyond her control, why this wanderer waxed so enthusiastic about bolstering her fortifications, and why he spoke as if he would supervise the construction. "Of what use is a gatehouse?"

"Your gate is the weakest place in your defense. It's a hole in your wall."

"A necessary hole."

"Of course, a necessary hole. I didn't tell you to close it, did I?" He looked impatient with her dithering. "Within a properly constructed gatehouse, the enemy is funnelled through a small space where stones and boiling tar can be dropped on their heads, and a portcullis can trap them. A properly constructed gatehouse can be the key to an enemy's defeat."

She stopped debating. Why was she playing devil's advocate? She'd conducted this argument with Sir Joseph, only he defended the old ways and she argued for the new. She'd yielded to Sir Joseph, but the man before her spoke knowledgeably about the things she'd hungered to know. Only a master castle-builder could know more.

The thought lingered, and she turned it in her mind. Only a master castle-builder would know more. A master. A master of men, of many crafts. She had thought this man a master, with a master's authority and a master's control. She'd been so frightened by him, she hadn't been thinking straight, but . . . She studied him and his creation. Could it be? Was it possible? Choosing her words carefully, she said, "You have studied castles extensively."

He held his hands out, fingers spread wide, with all the dirt and splinters and melting bits of snow visible for her to see. "If I did not study castle design and construction, I would not be free today."

A free man. Not bound to any lord, he was a free man. To earn the privilege of freedom, he had had to perform services so valuable to his lord he had been released to make his way in the world. Buoyed by the hunch she now knew to be the truth, she accused, "You're the master castle-builder I sent for!"

3

In places, the snow drifted up to Raymond's waist, but he plowed through, breaking the way for his new liege. He could hardly believe he'd made Lady Juliana believe he was a master castle-builder.

A master castle-builder, in charge of design and masonry, carpentry and smithery. Of all those trades, he understood only design, for a knight must sum up a castle's defenses to conduct a successful siege. He brightened. But really, how hard could it be to build a curtain wall?

From behind him, Juliana said querulously, "Master Raymond, I hope you know how disappointed I am in you."

He stopped and drew in great breaths of the frigid air. "My lady, I am moving as quickly as I can."

"I wasn't talking about our progress," she snapped. "I sent for you last spring as soon as King Henry granted me permission to expand the castle's battlements. He also included a royal recommendation to hire his finest castle-builder, and a promise to send him ere the summer waned. It is now only more than a month until Christmastide. Where have you been?"

He looked around at the primal forest: trees draped in shades of white and blue, hills rolling with snow. He looked at the sky, still pregnant with clouds. He looked behind at Juliana, who led his horse and glared. "My lady, I don't believe this is the time or the place—"

"Master Raymond, I'll decide the time and place," she interrupted. "You spent the summer lolling in Henry's court, no doubt, accepting the tributes of his nobles for your construction of his castle on the Dordogne."

Her repetition of his name and his newly assumed title irritated him. It was her way of reminding him of his station, of telling him not to presume on the events of the previous night and this morning. Tucking his hands into his armpits to warm them, he protested, "My lady, your imagination—"

"My imagination needs no prompting. You come to me when the winter is hard upon us, expecting to live at my expense until spring." She stepped closer to him. "Well, think again, Master Raymond. Aye, you will remain at the castle—if I allowed you to leave, only the angels know when you would return—but there are duties I will assign you."

"Any duty you assign will be an honor, but as master castle-builder"—the title tasted strange on his tongue, so he repeated it—"as master castle-builder, there are other duties I must perform to prepare for construction in the spring. That is why I came when I did."

"What duties are those, Master Raymond?" she demanded.

"Digging and . . . " She wanted him to forget her panic of yesterday, but she had become a nagging fishwife. He wasn't used to such treatment, and he resented it even as he groped for inspiration. ". . . and tool making," he finished triumphantly.

"The ground's frozen."

Her tone put his teeth on edge. "I'll make pickaxes."

"Hmm." She pushed at him. "Move on. It's cold."

Doing as he was told, he couldn't resist saying, "I did advise against trying to reach Lofts Castle today."

She ignored him. Ignored him as royally as she had done everything since his "identity" had been revealed. But she was selfconscious about her arrogance, for her voice quickened and she seemed more indignant than her suspicions would call for. "Why didn't you tell me who you were?"

He bowed his head in what he hoped was subservience. "I was, as you said, late. I hoped to smooth your temper before revealing my identity."

"And to observe the layout of my castle," she guessed. "Are all castle builders as arrogant as you?"

"Have you never had a castle builder work for you before?" He cursed the hope that colored his tone, and floundered on a patch of ice hidden beneath a drift.

She caught him before he fell, and looked pleased, perhaps at her own daring, or perhaps at his clumsiness. Brushing the flakes from his cloak while he wiped his face, she answered with a courtesy absent from her previous conversation. "Nay. My father never chanced it, for during Stephen's rule no one dared lower their defenses long enough to perform any but the necessary repairs. Henry came to the throne, and we waited and hoped. When the king tossed the Flemish mercenaries into the ocean and brought the bandit-barons to heel, our hopes were fulfilled."

" 'Tis easier to keep order with the threat of king's justice," he said.

She agreed readily enough. "If not for that, I would have been battered to the ground when my father died two winters ago."

"Without the firm hand of a lord, men do all they dare to do and still not break the law." She flinched, and he asked, "What enemies have you?"

"Enemies?" The bitter smile rested ill on her piquant face. "No enemies, only the men I once called my friends."

"I see." For the most part, he did. Friends turn greedy when confronted with a chance to enrich themselves, and her friends had proved fickle. "Your husband?"

"Millard was a sickly youth, and my father's ward. He died ten years ago while I was in childbed with my younger daughter."

No regret shadowed her face, no recollection of love nor faded sweetness. That union, he surmised, had been a political one, arranged by her father to add to the family's wealth. An unimportant part of her life, and not the reason for her back-stepping caution.

"That was also the time Richard was born to the queen and designated as the queen's special heir to Poitou and Aquitaine. My elder daughter carries eleven years, born the month Henry ascended to the throne." Her mouth smiled, but her eyes dimmed with sadness. "My father said my fertility prophesied the events of a nation." Flushing as if she'd said too much, she demanded, "Why do you stand there? We'll never get home before dark if you don't move."

"As you say, my lady." Turning back to his exhausting job, he wondered if this half-formed plan of his was worth carrying out, if Juliana would see through his ruse, and what she would do if she did.

One flake of falling trouble interrupted his musing, and he looked skyward. Another flake, and another, floated on the still air. "Saint Sebastian's arrows," he swore. "Now we're in for it."

"Should we go back?" she asked.

"We should never have left," he answered savagely.

She sounded abashed when she said, "Cavilling at our dilemma will accomplish nothing."

"It will make me feel better." But he already felt better, for someone had had to make the judgment to leave the hut. Juliana had taken the responsibility without flinching, and if he didn't agree with her decision—well, at one time, he'd made some painfully stupid decisions, too.

"I thought it best to try to reach Lofts Castle during the first break in the weather. The squirrels' coats grew abundantly this year, and the caterpillars were thick on the ground, so I know it's going to be a hard winter. We could have been trapped through the new moon."

He blinked against the snow, now hurtling along on the freshening breeze. "The wind's at our back. We will arrive on the wings of the storm."

His conjecture proved ridiculous. By the time they crossed the drawbridge, the wind howled and snow blinded them. He had his arm around Juliana, carrying her, and his gelding plodded behind them with many a reproachful nudge. The bailey was empty. No one patrolled the wall walks. The keep had no door on the lower level, a primitive defense and very effective, but it meant Lady Juliana would have to wait until a ladder was lowered to enter her own home.

Raymond shouted and kicked at the stable door for too long before the stable boy came running. The boy's eyes widened. He backed from the two frozen figures who resembled nothing so much as walking snowmen.

"Care for the horse," Raymond snapped. "I'll take care of the lady."

The boy responded to the anonymous voice of a lord, and in moments, the horse was being groomed and fed. As Raymond peeled the icy scarf from Juliana's face, another man stepped out of the shadows. "M'lady?" His voice rose. "M'lady Juliana? Saint Wilfrid's needle! What be ye doin' out in a storm such as this?"

"Coming home," she croaked.

"Oh, m'lady, we hoped ye holed up somewhere, but we were afraid ye'd do this." He clicked his tongue and eyed Raymond with more curiosity and less respect than necessary. "Well, blessed be th' moment o' yer return. I'll go tell 'em at once."

He raced outside, but two more stable hands ran forward, and their jubilant cries gladdened Raymond's heart. So they liked their lady, did they? He watched as they piled their own blankets on Juliana, and listened as the almost frozen woman thanked them in their own English tongue. So she'd troubled to learn the language of her servants, had she?

They, too, watched him with such intense curiosity he found himself wondering what reception they gave their guests when unaccompanied by the chatelaine. Raymond would have been happy to remain in the stables, but because of the hay, no fire was allowed, and only the animals' warmth kept it above freezing. "We must get to a fire, my lady," he warned.

"Is your steed settled to your satisfaction?" She hardly waited to hear his reply. "Then let us go."

Without hesitation, she plunged out the door, and as Raymond followed her, he discovered why. Two forms struggled down the ladder from the open upper door of the keep. Shrieking wildly, they flew lightly toward Juliana. Juliana threw out her hands, and raced toward them.

Her daughters.

They met in a mighty clash, falling in the drifts, wrestling, kissing. Halting at a respectful distance, Raymond couldn't see their faces, but implicit in the gestures was a frantic concern. Love shone around their little group like the rays of a star.

Amazed, he stared, his eyes smarting, his feet hurting from the cold. He'd heard stories of affection between mother and child, but he'd discounted it as a romantic tale, or a reality only for peasants. As Juliana and her daughters stood and walked, clasped in each other's arms, toward the ladder, he made a resolution. He resolved he would be part of that magic circle one day. One day, Juliana and her daughters would run to him when he returned to them.

First the girls, then Juliana hitched up their skirts and crawled up the ladder. Raymond followed close behind, to guard against a slip, he told himself. In sooth, he wanted to examine this bond between mother and daughters, and see if there were rivals for the affection he coveted.

A young man-at-arms stood in the entrance, shouting, "M'lady? M'lady, 'tis glad I am t' see ye, but how came ye here in this weather?" His exultation died when his gaze met Raymond's. The same curiosity that waylaid the stable hands seemed intensified in this youth, with the added fillip of hostility.

Juliana and her children went into the dark passage, and Raymond elbowed the soldier aside to follow them. But the soldier closed in behind, following on Raymond's heels as they climbed a short stair. Raymond noted and approved the narrow turns that gave all advantage to a defender, but he didn't linger. Ahead of him, the door burst open and light streamed out.

Inquisitiveness and a bump from behind drove him into the great hall, and he squinted against the smoke generated by the roaring fire. After his isolation of the past weeks, the room seemed to be overflowing with humanity. Squeals of maidservants mingled with the deeper shouts of men as they all milled in excited circles around their mistress.

Through breaks in the crowd, he could see two caped figures clinging to Juliana, one a child's size, one almost the size of her mother. That gave him pause, for although she'd said her elder was eleven, he hadn't realized that daughter would be a woman. Juliana had an arm around each one, not releasing them as the maids fluttered around her. Her cape, her hat, her gloves were pulled from her while she kept hold of her children.

"Are you both well? Have you kept warm?" With a smile, Juliana turned to the younger child. "Are you wearing shoes, Ella?"

With a pout, Ella stuck out her shod foot.

"Good girl," Juliana praised.

"And you, Margery? Did you—"

"Mama, I hurt myself," Ella interrupted.

Juliana didn't seem truly concerned, but she asked, "How did you hurt yourself?"

"I hurt my finger." Ella held out the injured digit. Raymond noted the child hadn't replied to the question, but Juliana leaned to kiss it anyway.

"She tried to stir the fire when no one was looking and burned herself on the stick," Margery said.

Ella made a rude noise. Margery made one right back.

"Girls." Juliana reproved them automatically, and reached out to stroke Margery's cheek. "Are you well?"

Margery smiled and nodded, but Raymond could see her chin trembled. Margery was fast approaching the difficult time of her life. Childhood would soon be left behind, for in the form of her body she gave notice of a coming beauty.

Juliana gave her cloak to Margery, her gloves to Ella. "Put those away, please." Margery clung a moment longer, and patting her shoulder, Juliana promised, "We'll talk later."

"Mama, who is that man?"

Ella's voice was audible throughout the hall, and dozens of eyes fixed on Raymond. "He's not important," Juliana said firmly. "Please obey me, girls."

Not important? To be so dismissed in the hall where one day he would rule . . . His surge of fury took Raymond by surprise. He *was* important. He was cousin to the king, heir to great tracts of Norman lands, heir to an ancient title. Never again would he dance for his supper, scamper to avoid the lash, work like a peasant. And if the Lady Juliana thought he could be so easily dismissed, her mind would have to be altered.

He was glaring at her, he realized, for although he stood in the shadows some of his hostility had projected itself across the hall. The color which had returned to her cheeks eroded. She pushed her children toward the great bed in the corner and faced him with squared shoulders and quivering chin. Raymond almost laughed at her heroics, so irrelevant in a room filled with her men, and wondered why her fear seemed genuine. He stepped forward, intent on stating his true name and true intentions, and be damned to her feelings, when the young man-at-arms stepped between him and his mistress.

"What are ye here fer?" the soldier asked, resting his hand on the scabbard that held his knife.

Well-muscled shoulders and a variety of scars proclaimed battle hardening, and the thread of steel in his demand returned good sense to Raymond in a rush. In a low, controlled voice, he said, "I am the master castle-builder, sent by King Henry to raise a wall on his majesty's property."

The young man's eyes narrowed. "I'm Layamon, chief man-at-arms in Sir Joseph's absence. What's that golden bobble ye're wearin'?"

Used to the amazement his barbaric decoration engendered, Raymond caressed it and smiled without humor. "'Tis the mark of an ordeal I once endured. I wear it to remind myself of the pain."

"Guess fashions are different where ye're from." Layamon extended a hand, but not in courtesy. Palm up, it demanded an accounting of this stranger. "Ye have, o' course, proof o' his majesty's command?"

Damn! This Layamon wasn't quite as trusting as Lady Juliana, who had never thought to ask for evidence. Raymond reached for his purse and selected a letter. Layamon took it cautiously and turned it toward the fire. Afixed in red wax was Henry's seal, and Layamon's face lit with recognition. "'Tis indeed from th' king," he pronounced, and unfolded the document.

Raymond said, "As you can see from the first lines, our liege thinks highly of my abilities." Of his abilities to seduce Lady Juliana, but he didn't repeat the lines

Henry had penned. Instead he watched the young man's eyes as they moved in a random pattern over the page, and relaxed as he realized Layamon could not read. As he had hoped. But Juliana could read, or so she said. Would she want to peruse the document herself? Or would she not want to embarrass her man-at-arms by indicating doubt in his wisdom? Sipping mulled wine, she watched Layamon wistfully, and Raymond nudged the young man. "I believe your lady wishes to speak to you."

Layamon's head jerked up in obvious guilt, and he stammered, "Aye. She probably wants t' know about th' drawbridge." Raymond slipped the king's letter from Layamon's limp hand and back into his purse.

She called, "Layamon, about the drawbridge. What were you thinking, leaving it down?"

The young man said earnestly, "M'lady, it seemed t' me we should leave it open anticipatin' yer return."

"Anticipating the arrival of every army in England and Wales, you mean."

"Nay, m'lady." Layamon tugged his forelock as he contradicted her. "Not in this weather. No army marches in this weather."

"Why, there weren't even men patrolling the wall walks." She paced in a circle, her mouth a tight line. Glancing toward her daughters, she lowered her voice. "What do you imagine would have happened if I had returned to find my children kidnapped?"

"Ye'd have had me strung up," Layamon answered. "But I did keep men on th' wall walks until th' first one came in wi' a few toes frozen. I knew ye'd not want t' waste yer soldiers in such a way. Ye've told me, many a time, that if I'll take care o' th' men, ye an' Sir Joseph'll take care o' th' defenses."

His simple, honest reply seemed to melt her indignation, and she looked down at her own painful toes.

Layamon was right, Raymond knew. No army could march in this weather. Even if an enemy arrived, by himself or in a small group, he'd be hard pressed to do more than seek the comfort of the fire. Would the lady see the logic of it, and would she admit it if she did?

She proved her mettle when she said, "You did well. But let's close the drawbridge now, shall we?"

"I've got men out there right now sweepin' away th' snow. They'll pull th' supports an' swing it up." Layamon's bow was eager and brief. "I'll go check on them."

She spoke before he escaped. "Order cook to prepare an extra rasher of bacon for each man tonight, with my thanks. And take this"—she removed a horn cup, decorated with filigreed silver, from its place at the head table—"for yourself, in gratitude for your good judgment."

The cup was too fine to give to a man-at-arms, regardless of his status, but before Raymond could protest, Layamon himself said, "Nay, m'lady, 'tis too grand fer me."

He tried to thrust it back at her, but she refused. "The gift is given. May you find happiness in every brew you drink from it."

The young man still held it out, but she turned back to her children, now poised in the doorway, and Layamon's gaze caressed the cup. Recalling his duty, he would have tried again to return it, but she waved him aside. "The drawbridge," she reminded him sharply.

Stumbling over his own feet, Layamon disappeared into the stairwell. Ella's treble voice broke the silence. "That was Grandfather's cup."

"Aye." Juliana's own voice rose to fill the room. "'Tis a fitting gift for the man who will soon take command of my garrison."

Almost as one, the people of the great hall gasped.

"Sir Joseph?" asked Margery.

"Sir Joseph has earned his rest. The duties of chief man-at-arms have become too great for his aging shoulders. 'Tis time another man took his place." Juliana made her pronouncement calmly, but her gaze sliced to Raymond almost as if she sought his approval. Before he could give it, she remembered the hospitality due a guest. "This man is Master Raymond, our castle builder, come to us at last. Give him drink, dry clothes, and a place by the fire. Tomorrow he'll pick his men from among my serfs and put them to work."

The servants looked at him with the curiosity and wariness of people unused to strangers. He held their gazes, his strong, steady, and reliable. They relaxed, and he pushed his hood and hat off. From every woman with eyes to see rose a gasp, and three buxom maids eagerly started toward him. He couldn't resist glancing at Juliana to see how the attention affected her, but her almost-pained gaze startled him.

She commanded, "Fayette, you help disrobe him, also."

Juliana's own maid stepped away from her mistress, seemingly puzzled at the instructions, but Juliana gestured, and the girl bobbed an obedient curtsey. Fayette's knowing smile as she advanced on him told the tale; she knew how to pleasure a man. Juliana had given him the choice of one of these four women, or all of these four women, but he didn't want them. He wanted Juliana, and he would use any method to possess her. He waved the women back. "I care for myself, but if you could prepare warm food for your lady and me, you would have my sincerest gratitude."

"He's probably fat," he heard one mutter, none too quietly, and with a smile he removed his cloak.

Fayette looked him over with frank appreciation and took the discarded wrappings. Pressing herself against him, she asked, "Are ye sure?"

"Quite sure." His gaze wandered to Juliana, now ensconced in the master's chair by the central fire, a daughter on each knee.

Fayette must have seen, for she hugged his waist and said, "Ah, nay, ye'll not have luck in that direction. She don't trust any man, an' after all these years. Better take me, I'll give ye a good buckin'."

"Thank you for your counsel," he replied in a manner that imparted the opposite, and she stepped back in an offended flurry.

He advanced on the fire and warmed his hands. Through the flickering red glow of the flames, he watched the little family and said, "My lady, I must send for my construction crew. With your permission, I will do so at once."

He had pierced her motherly haze. Had she been interested in his reaction to such a bounty of womanly pulchritude? Had she hoped he would choose a mate from among her maids, or had she hoped he would not? Her frown gave nothing away, and she said, "A construction crew? Strangers? Here in my castle?"

"Without a doubt," he said reassuringly. "My master mason, my blacksmith—"

"I have a mason," she offered. "I have a blacksmith."

"And grateful I am for them. My own masters will have need of their skill. But to undertake a project of this magnitude, men with the proper training are necessary."

"How many men?"

He stroked the gold earring and made a pretense of thinking. "Ten men."

He suspected she would protest any intrusion into her home, and she didn't disappoint him. "Ten men? For one wall? That's an invasion force."

Craftily, he offered, "If my men offend you perhaps I could make do with one man."

Her relief was palpable. "One . . . aye, you can bring one other man."

He veiled his triumph as he added, "And two women."

"Two women," she said slowly. "Why do you need two women?"

"Why does any man need a woman?" He stared into the fire, projecting his will with silent might. *Believe the women are for me,* he prayed. *Believe they will keep me busy in the night. Believe they will succeed where your servants failed.*

Her inner debate was extended and painful, and made it too clear the maid's words were truth. Juliana trusted no man. At last she said, "As you wish. Send for your crew. How soon can you be started?"

Struggling to keep his triumphant grin off his face, he assured her, "Three weeks."

"Build a castle wall?" Raymond's chief knight and companion paced across Lady Juliana's bailey. As the sun peeked above the curtain wall, it shone on his changeless expression. "We do not know how to build a castle wall."

Years of shared hardship had taught Raymond to read Keir even when he was most enigmatic, and now Keir clearly believed his friend had developed maggots in his brain. With the charm of a practiced courtier, Raymond asked, "What's the difficulty? The building can't be as arduous as the breaching."

Keir didn't respond to the charm. Sometimes Raymond wondered if Keir knew what charm was. "You do not know anything about the trades, any of them."

Raymond smiled guiltily as they stopped on the drawbridge. "I thought a wall built about halfway down the hill." He pointed. "See? I have Lady Juliana's men already busy with pick and shovel, digging the foundation."

Keir's tone was flat. "You are the least skilled man I have ever met."

"The snow has melted, but the ground is still half frozen, and the other half's mud. It's hard work for the men."

"You do not even understand the intricacies of a waterwheel."

"The local mason has increased his order of sandstone from the local quarry. The lead quarryman tried to put us off until spring, but I convinced him—"

"I was a blacksmith," Keir allowed.

Raymond dropped his courtly facade. "I had not forgotten. Nor had I forgotten you learned it the hard way—at end of a Saracen whip. I had hoped you would help me with this deception, but if you can't face the humiliation of such work again, I won't press you."

"I know you would not." Keir hooked his thumb in his belt and gazed at his hand. Only his thumb and forefinger remained, the others gone to some distant amputation. Projecting a fierce satisfaction, he said, "For that reason, I do as you desire. Besides, smithery is not without its dignity."

Resigned, Raymond waited for the insult, and Keir didn't disappoint him.

"More dignity, in fact, than mucking out a stable."

"A fact you delight in recalling," Raymond accused.

Keir smoothed his droopy gray mustache, which stood in stark contrast to his dark brown hair. "Not at all. I do not have to recall it. I seem never to forget it."

Not for the first time, Raymond wondered if all natives of the island called Ireland were so unemotional as to be almost unreadable. He thought not; he preferred to think his friend's constraint was rare.

"The Infidels had no use for a Christian knight's skills, and we were, after all, nothing but slaves." With hearty goodwill, Raymond slapped Keir on the back. As Keir regained his breath, Raymond added, "This proves even the Infidels dance to God's own plan. If my master had not forced us to learn the trades—smithing, carpentry, masonry—we would have never escaped. Now, we use those trades again to gain me a bride."

Clearly, Keir didn't understand the sense in such subterfuge. "I would like to remind you, however, that although I possess the skills of smithery, those skills will not build a castle. I cannot hide your ignorance beneath the cloak of my knowledge, for I have no such knowledge. Why not just tell her who you are and demand she wed you?"

"Because she'd refuse, and I abhor the thought of besieging my future bride."

"It is not because of your ordeal with the Saracens, then."

Keir's shrewd guess made Raymond remember to whom he spoke, and he lifted his big hands in a gesture that exposed, for Keir only, the depth of his embarrassment. "A true knight would not let so little a thing as a woman's emotions dictate the course of his destiny."

"A true knight would not allow others' opinions alter the course of his compassion." Keir clasped his hands behind his back in a characteristic gesture. "Still, I wonder why she would avoid this union. King Henry rewards you with two fine castles, but he rewards her, too, with a husband who'll not beat her nor steal from her, and some women, I have heard tell, call you comely." He inspected his friend without a smile. "Although I could never see it, myself. So what is wrong with the woman?"

"That I intend to discover."

"I have another question to ask," Keir said.

"I hide nothing." Raymond spread his fingers wide, opened his arms to embrace the inquisition.

"Why a master castle-builder? If you would come to the woman in disguise, I can think of a thousand masks more fitting to your skills and station."

Raymond raised his foot and planted it atop a knee-high pile of cut sandstone. Propping his elbow on his thigh, he watched the men scurrying below in the mud and the ice. In the secret place in his soul, he'd made his plans. He would give Juliana the respect, the romance, the adoration the troubadours sang about, and she would fall in love with the man she called Master Raymond. By springtime, he would be spending every night beneath the covers with the lady of Lofts. He'd learn every curve of her slender body, kiss every sweet place. Perhaps he'd put a child in her belly, and a lady as sweet as Juliana would easily forgive the father of her babe.

Yet he wouldn't tell Keir, for Keir didn't understand

romance or subtlety or any of the ways a man wooed a skittish woman. Instead he said, "A new curtain wall is more than just a castle improvement to the Lady Juliana. It is security. It is safety. It is all the things I will be to her one day soon, and I want her always to associate me with such guarantees."

"I see." A look of insight passed between the friends, and Keir asked, "Why do you suppose that man is coming up the hill at such a great rate?"

Raymond followed Keir's gaze to the elderly bald-headed ruffian who had stopped at the ditch to revile the workers. "I don't know, but he presumes much." The stranger started back up toward the gate, and when he reached the drawbridge, Raymond stepped forward. "May I assist you, old man?"

Raising fierce blue eyes, the stranger growled and swung his walking stick so sharply the wind whistled before Raymond's knees. Raymond jumped back and watched with disbelief as Keir stepped aside. "You let him go?" he asked incredulously.

"It is not the duty of a blacksmith to interfere with visitors to the castle," Keir answered without expression.

Nor was it the master castle-builder's duty, Raymond recalled as he watched the old man limp into the stables.

"No one stops him. No doubt he belongs here," Keir said. "All castles have their eccentrics."

"Aye, that they do." Raymond turned back to his friend. "Did you know I would ask your help in building a wall?"

"When I arrived to hear you greeted as master castle-builder, my suspicions were aroused," Keir acknowledged. "It's of no consequence. I live to serve you, you know that."

Grateful for this devotion, yet embarrassed by its excess, Raymond protested. "You honor me too much."

"I owe you more than my life. Yet I cannot help but wonder—how will this scheme advance your suit? Just because she's a woman is no reason to so dishonor her."

Raymond scuffed his toe in the dirt. "I mean no dishonor to her." And he didn't. If only she hadn't charmed him. If only she hadn't grown sweeter with every passing moment. He had lapped up her kindness like a starving cat lapped milk. "She is so scornful of Lord Avraché, of his connections and his marriage potential."

"She told you about yourself?" Keir asked, much struck.

"Aye, and I'm a pragmatic man. By hiding my identity I've been doing what I can to smooth her ire." He pushed his hair back from his face. "Besides, I put my faith in the women."

One corner of Keir's long mustache lifted in what passed for a smile. "Ah. The women."

Wickedly exuberant, Raymond chuckled. "Aye. The women."

4

"*My lady, are you ill?*"

A hand on her shoulder brought Juliana awake in a rush. "What? Is there a problem?"

"You were moaning in your sleep. Are you ill?"

Sculpted by morning's light, an aged woman's face swam before Juliana's bleary eyes. "Nay, I'm well." She pressed her hand to her chest. Was she well? Her heart beat so hard she could feel the thump. She panted as if she'd been running.

"You must have been having a nightmare."

Remembrance flared in Juliana, blotting out the old woman, the great hall, the early morning bustle with its intensity. It hadn't been a nightmare. Not at all. She clenched her teeth against the pain. It had been a dream as sweet as honey, as hot as burning pitch. A demon-driven imagining, filled with a man of midnight hair and emerald eyes.

All her previous dreams of men and lust had also been dreams of pain and abuse. And never, ever had the lust been on her part. What bewitchment had brought such madness to her mind?

She pressed the scar on her cheek as a remembrance.

No man cared for a woman's feelings. No man lusted after a woman without trying to force himself on her. No man . . . but Raymond. He was kind and respectful, and he wanted her. It shone in his eyes and announced itself in the unconscious gestures of a man toward a woman he desires. Why was he different?

Reality returned and seized her by the throat. Because any man with his face and body never had to force a woman.

Embarrassed by her own sensations, Juliana asked sharply, "Who are you?"

"My name is Valeska." The serving woman stood with the edge of the bed curtains clutched in her hand. Her voice was thick and guttural, and Juliana couldn't tear her gaze from the hypnotic brown eyes.

"I don't know you."

It was an accusation, but the crone's voice was soothing. "I came for the master."

"The master?"

"For Raymond."

"You're one of the women he sent for?" Juliana swung her feet over the edge of the bed and prepared to hunt him down.

"Will you be rising now, my lady?" This voice was different from the first. The lilting accent and deep, sweet voice reminded Juliana of a melody, and she blinked the sleep from her eyes.

"Who are *you*?" she demanded.

Fair-skinned, fair-haired, this old woman would have been tall but for a twisted back. "I'm Dagna."

"You came with the master . . . castle-builder, too?"

A frown puckered Dagna's forehead. "I came with Raymond." She cocked her head to one side and looked at Juliana from the top of her head to the tips of her toes. "She's a pretty thing, but timid."

Valeska plucked at the sleeve of Juliana's chainse with her yellowed fingers. "I hope these are only her sleep clothes. Unsightly, they are, and old."

In a rush of indignation, Juliana realized the brazen women were talking about her. About her, as if she were a child, or invisible.

"What about that shawl?" Dagna asked.

"From the ship?" Valeska sucked her lip into the gap between her teeth and eyed Juliana. "Perfect."

As she darted away, Juliana demanded, "Where's Fayette?"

"Fayette?"

Juliana lowered her head like a heifer about to charge. "My maid."

"Oh, Fayette." Dagna dismissed her with a shrug. "We told her we'd take care of you this morning."

Valeska returned with a speed that contradicted Juliana's impression of age. Valeska tossed one end of the richly patterned silk shawl to Dagna, and like acrobats trained to work together they wrapped Juliana in it before she could protest.

"You women are insolent," Juliana cried, jerking it from her shoulders.

"You don't like the shawl? It is my own." Valeska showed all three of her teeth in a smile as she caught the shawl. She smoothed the rich pattern with her yellow fingers. "Dagna and I live to serve you."

"She would like the sash better." Kneeling before a battered trunk that had been placed close beside Juliana's bed, Dagna peered around her twisted shoulder. "It is because of Raymond we make this vow to you."

"Vow?" Alarmed at such unwanted fidelity, Juliana shook her head. " 'Tis no vow. Speak no—"

"Such vow?" Dagna smiled at Juliana. Her teeth were many, but brown as aging ivory. "The vow is real, but we will not speak it if it distresses you."

"What is he to you? Is one of you his mother?" Even as Juliana asked, she knew it to be a ridiculous question.

The women guffawed with delight. "His mother?"

"You flatter us, my lady. Nay, we are no kin of Raymond's."

These women were common, wanderers from some foreign country who by some mad chance had arrived in her home. They reminded her of the minstrels and players who travelled from castle to castle, but they were more. Much more. Raymond had misrepresented them to her, and she was angry. "Then why do you speak of him so familiarly? Of what use are you to him?"

Valeska's brown eyes widened. "We travel with him, mending his clothes, cheering him."

Juliana asked, "Singing to him?"

"There you are, my lady," Dagna said approvingly. "I do sing to him. Would you like me to sing to you?"

"Nay."

Taking the rejection with equanimity, Dagna promised, "Later."

This devotion they displayed to Raymond amazed Juliana, and that they would extend that devotion to her . . . as if she were an extension of him. . . .

Valeska tried to tie the brilliant red sash around Juliana's waist. Juliana slapped at Valeska's hands, then cried, "Ouch!" as she inflicted a tiny cut on herself with Valeska's long claws. Staring accusingly at the muscular old woman, Juliana said, "Now look what you've done."

Valeska finished fastening the sash before taking

Juliana's hand. "My lady, you'll just hurt yourself if you struggle. Would you like me to read your life in your hand?"

"A mountebank's trick," Juliana said. "I have no desire to have my palm read."

Smoothing the flesh, Valeska crooned, "Such pretty skin. Easily hurt, fine and pale."

Bent old Dagna stepped close to Juliana's other side. Holding her hand next to Juliana's, she marvelled. "Look how fair Lady Juliana is. The sun has made my skin brown and wrinkled, with these ugly splotches, and see"—she traced the upstanding veins—"as many paths as a forest. I am not hurt so easily as you, my lady."

Her big blue eyes peered up into Juliana's. Made uncomfortable by the intimacy, Juliana glanced aside—right into Valeska's brown gaze.

"That's right, my lady. Men think women are delicate, but we women know better. A woman should be spirited, tough, prepared to weather the storms of life."

Dagna chimed in. "A woman should rise from the flames of adversity stronger, wiser."

"A woman should strike back at her enemies and cherish her friends."

Juliana glared at the two crones who pressed her so close. "Do you mean I should strike you?"

"Ooh." They pulled back.

Valeska sighed. "Ooh, my lady, you'll have to determine whether we're friends or enemies, won't you?"

Juliana pushed them aside. "I'll go ask your Raymond."

"Ah, a wise idea." Dagna winked at her, one wrinkled eyelid twitching. "A wise idea, indeed."

Exasperation exploded from Juliana in a muffled shriek, and she looked wildly about for Raymond. He wasn't in the smoky hall, and that surprised her. Every day since Master Raymond had descended on her household had been long and stressful, full of private, yet necessary conferences with him about his damned wall.

Her wall, she corrected herself, and wished she could find some way to correct him. He acted as if it were his wall, or perhaps their wall. Yet she didn't know how to contradict him without further intimate discussion.

Snatching her cloak, she sought Raymond in the bailey. This early week of December had brought a brief return of autumn. Warm days, sweet with the remembrance of summer past, were followed by cool nights, crisp with the promise of more winter. The snow had melted except for the small piles of slush hidden in the shady corners, and mud coated the grass. She grimaced as she tried to avoid the deeper puddles.

Raymond and a strange man stood on the drawbridge—the open drawbridge—and she stalked toward them. Her people bowed to her as she passed, but she returned their greetings with little cheer. When she spoke to Raymond, what would she demand? That he make two ancient women stop being helpful to her? That he throw them out to face the oncoming winter? Charity doomed this mission to failure. Her own foolishness made her miss her step, and as she wiped mud from her skirt she heard a familiar voice taunt, "Well, there's a pretty sight. A soiled lady in the pigsty where she belongs."

For one brief moment of weakness, she shut her eyes.

Sir Joseph had returned.

She'd tried to pretend it didn't matter when he came or what he said, but she'd been lying to herself. These past years, he hadn't been the biggest part of her misery, but he was the most constant. Taking firm hold of her courage, she faced him.

Trouble. Already Sir Joseph brewed trouble. He held Layamon by the ear, and that young man danced at the pain. "Let go of Layamon," she ordered loudly enough for the half-deaf warrior to hear.

"Let go of him? Let go of him? Let go of a thief, a sneaking thief? Bah!" Sir Joseph spit on the ground close by her foot. "Lady Juliana, you're not fit to command. I've told you that many a time, and here's the proof. Do you know what this thief has stolen?"

"My father's goblet. And he didn't steal it."

"He stole your father's silver goblet," Sir Joseph brayed. As her words sank through his bombastic armor, he dropped Layamon's ear and cupped his own. "What did you say?"

"He didn't steal my father's goblet. I gave it to him."

Greater folk than she had cowered beneath Sir Joseph's fury, and Juliana had been raised to treat him with respect. He had been her father's closest companion, his greatest confidant, and Sir Joseph had expected—demanded—she retain him as her chief knight.

The passing of the goblet from her hand to Layamon's signified something different. To Sir Joseph she had declared, quite without words, that he had been replaced. She had given a valuable gift, and one he coveted, to a mere man-at-arms.

There could be no greater insult.

A palpitation started at Sir Joseph's feet and increased as it travelled up to his head. He chewed on words he couldn't articulate. He flushed red, the veins in his cheeks burst, bled beneath the skin. His rage was the greater for being without sound. His fanatical blue eyes blazed at her. He raised his staff.

Her every muscle clenched. She hugged herself, and her fingers bruised the muscles of her upper arms. The need for air brought black stars exploding before her eyes. Oh, God, he was going to beat her.

Blackened eyes, loosened teeth, the feeling of helplessness at a man's hands. Unconsciousness. Unconsciousness that didn't bring relief, only endless pain and the wish for death.

Something leaped into the periphery of her vision. Leery as a rabbit, she jumped, looked, expecting assault from that side, also.

But it was Raymond. Raymond with the stranger following close on his heels. They stopped when she saw them. Raymond sought her gaze, waiting for instructions. In his very stance—shoulders back, hands on hips—he declared his support. Support for her.

Oddly, Raymond's declaration came back to her, clear as if he'd spoken it today. "Sir Joseph is a man who has outlived his usefulness." Under the impetus of those words, she'd given command to Layamon.

She drew a fortifying breath. She wasn't sorry, Sir Joseph couldn't make her sorry, and damned if she'd apologize or retract.

Sir Joseph had threatened to strike her many times, and although he'd never done it, she'd always crumpled, then despised herself afterward. This time she said, "Hit me, or don't hit me, only know this is the last time you'll threaten me." She looked with conviction full into his blazing eyes.

Sir Joseph hesitated. This wasn't the response he had expected or desired, and he wrestled with disbelief and choler. The staff quivered; he desperately wanted to strike her.

She saw the moment good sense won out. He dropped his gaze. Stabbing his staff into the wet ground as if it were her breast, he snarled, "What are you doing to my fortifications?"

She didn't collapse from relief, but she wanted to. For the first time since her father's death, the wretched old man had given way. Sir Joseph had capitulated.

He swung his staff at Layamon. "Go on! Get on and see if those lazy sots you call soldiers have the castle secure."

Layamon jumped away from the stick, but he asked, "M'lady? What are *yer* orders?"

Layamon would pay later. Oh, yes, he would pay, for Sir Joseph's evil glare guaranteed retribution. But Juliana appreciated Layamon's courage. After somber deliberation, she said, "You may go, Layamon. After you've assessed the damage from the leak in the armory, see to the patrols on the wall walk. As Sir Joseph suggested. I'll take Sir Joseph to see the improvements on my castle."

Obeying her eagerly, Layamon sprang away.

Sir Joseph watched after him, shaking with a palsy that in any other man would be a sign of old age. "This is how you repay me for my kindness? By putting me aside like an old horse? I taught you manners when you were a child. I told you how to raise your children. I encouraged you to resist when the king wanted you to marry this Count of Avraché."

"If you'll come this way . . ." She waved an inviting arm, but Sir Joseph stomped into a mud puddle so hard it splattered her bodice; then he charged toward the gate. She sighed. She'd won a major battle; why did she feel the war had scarcely begun?

"A defeated enemy is a bad chamberfellow," said Raymond's voice close against her ear.

Still nervous from her encounter, she started, but he didn't seem to notice. "What do you suggest I do with him?" she snapped, although she'd been thinking much the same thing.

"Send him to your other castle." Reaching for her arm, he led her through the muddy bailey as if she were delicate as glass.

"He'd think it was exile."

"So it is, but better a brief unpleasantness than that troublemaker skulking about."

Sir Joseph bellowed from just inside the gate, "What are you doing, dallying with that young knave? Can't keep your hands off the men, can you?"

Raymond's fingers tightened briefly on her, then he moved forward to stand directly in front of Sir Joseph. "I am Master Raymond, the master castle-builder sent by my lord, King Henry, with instructions to strengthen this castle. I will be sure to mention your name when I report to the king." His smile showed broad white teeth, and Sir Joseph craned his neck to look up at him.

Sir Joseph studied him, eyes half closed in contemplation. Slowly, as though he were thinking aloud, he said, "I would have said you were a lord."

Raymond's smile got bigger and broader and a shade more vicious. "I am a lord. Lord of the castle builders."

"Pah!" Sir Joseph shook off his apprehensions. "Like as not you're some bastard son that toadied up to King Henry and bought the appointment."

"Like as not," Raymond agreed.

"But 'tis no shame to be a bastard son," Juliana said.

Sir Joseph flushed crimson again. "Well, this stupid bastard doesn't keep the serfs working."

Juliana waved to the muddy workers as they huddled around the fire and quaffed mugs of ale supplied from her cellars. "They've got to eat."

Sir Joseph snorted. "You're always too soft. If it were up to me . . . that young fool Layamon could never take my place."

"No one could ever take your place," she began placatingly. Then an unexpected gust of resentment swept her. "Just as no one could ever take my father's."

"*Your* father? He didn't want someone like you for a daughter, not even on his deathbed." Sir Joseph jabbed her with one sharp elbow. "Remember whose hand he held when he died? I wonder what he'd think if he could see this day's business."

"Maybe he'd think he held the wrong hand," she retorted, sick and furious with his jeers.

"I warned him about you from the day you were born. I told him to curb you with a large stick, but he was soft. He was so soft, but I reminded him of his duty." He laughed, a nasty snicker. "You're a disgrace to your family and a humiliation to your father. You're nothing but a whore."

Not a sound disturbed the silence of the bailey. Everyone had heard Sir Joseph's accusation, projected in the manner of the half deaf and with all the venom of a scorpion. Juliana had heard Sir Joseph's accusation—indeed, had heard parts of it—before. But never before had he admitted to his role in her father's absolute, continuing, and final rejection of her. Never before had he called her a whore. And never, ever had he spoken in such a fashion before her people, her friends—and Master Raymond.

She couldn't look at them. She looked, instead, out over her lands. Her lands, spread out before her in patches of wood and plain and village. Her lands, rich and fertile, alive with her cattle, her serfs, her villeins. She'd been the shepherd for this land and its folk, tending it, encouraging it, protecting it. From this land she drew her strength.

With that strength she faced the people who stared, peering up from the trench and out from the bailey. She faced the triumph that sharpened the hawklike features of Sir Joseph, and she faced Master Raymond.

She couldn't know the way she looked to Raymond: proud chin raised, copper hair soft around pale cheeks, mouth quivering, blue eyes muddy with anger too long restrained. He wanted to step forward, to defend her, but some wisdom curbed him. This was her fight. She wouldn't thank him for his interference, nor would she gain the poise she needed so acutely. Let her resolve this to her satisfaction.

In a clear, calm voice, she said, "Sir Joseph, you presume above your station. Go to Bartonhale Castle, and live there until you die."

By slow degrees, the satisfaction in Sir Joseph faded. He stared at her, then at the people standing around. Every face wore an identical expression, set in revulsion and rejection. If one man had reached down and picked up a stone, Raymond thought, every man would have picked up a stone, and Sir Joseph would have been consigned to the fate reserved for whores. A fitting justice for one so vicious.

"You may go now." Juliana dismissed him and turned her back.

The staff quivered in Sir Joseph's hand as he stared at the wimple wrapping her head, and Raymond nodded at Keir. Keir stepped forward and caught the aging fiend's arm in a warning grip. "The lady of the castle no longer requires you," Keir said softly.

Sir Joseph tried to wrestle free, and when he couldn't, called, "Lady Juliana! Lady Juliana, I'm an old man. I've lived here most of my life. Won't you have pity on an old man and let me stay?"

Never by any sign did she indicate she heard him.

Keir began to hustle him away, but Sir Joseph cried, "Lady Juliana! At least give me time to pack. To say my farewell to the place that has been my home these many years! I beg you—"

Raymond jerked his head at Keir. Keir almost wrenched Sir Joseph off his feet, but too late. Juliana was not immune to a woman's pity. Without looking at Sir Joseph, she pronounced, "You may stay until after Twelfth Night. The day after Twelfth Night, you will leave, regardless of your health or the weather or any other excuse."

Keir tossed an apologetic glance at Raymond, but Raymond only shrugged. He couldn't condemn Juliana's good sense in sending her opponent away, nor could he condemn her kindness to her obsolete commander.

Smugly, he realized one goal of his masquerade had been achieved; he had identified the reason Juliana had avoided marriage. Perhaps she had wanted some unsuitable man. The unbending old man's contempt, excessive though it had been, had made it clear it was nothing more than a foolish love affair.

She stood on the drawbridge, so still, so upright, unaware of his cognitions and seemingly oblivious to the gazes of her people. He thought she might break from the weight of her humiliation, and without a hint of sympathy—his experience with women told him that would bring the tears—he said, "My lady, I was hoping you'd come to inspect the progress. Would you like to go down?"

She trembled—as he'd suspected, tears were close—but she controlled herself, and his admiration grew. "My thanks, Master Raymond. I would like to inspect the progress."

Stepping to her side, he said, "If you would take my arm, my lady, I'll help you. It's very slick."

She stared at the outstretched limb as if it were attached to a loathsome creature, but after her encounter with Sir Joseph, he didn't blame her for suspecting a man's kindness. Catching his elbow, she followed him toward the ditch forming below her curtain wall.

Whatever scandal tainted her past and haunted her nights would be Raymond's to deal with as he thought best. He'd give her sympathy, support, kindness, passion. Without vanity, Raymond knew he could wean her from her useless longing and cure her of her fear. He never doubted he could do it.

Slanting a proud glance at her, he wondered if she realized how much confidence she'd gained today. He felt like a father with a precocious child, or a man with a lover.

That thought startled him. When had Lady Juliana become more to him than merely a challenge? When had respect and affection colored his view of her?

That was dangerous. Her devotion deserved to be cultivated, but if the spark of love ignited him with longing, wouldn't he long to confess his own secrets? Wouldn't he want to bare his soul? And when she saw the things hidden within him, would he survive the inevitable rejection?

Such an ill-favored attachment did explain these twinges of jealousy that stirred in him when he thought of Juliana with another man. He didn't love her, he couldn't judge her, and after all, what misdeed had Juliana committed that could be greater than his?

A pinch on his arm broke his concentration. "Stop frowning. You're frightening the serfs," she ordered. "When will the wall be finished?"

When would the wall be finished? He hadn't any idea, but he said, "That depends on the weather." She accepted that, and he continued, "Even as it sits, just one long moat, it's a deterrent to invasion."

She nodded.

"We'll work on it unless we have another storm like the one . . ." He trailed off, but she understood of which storm he spoke. Color came back to her face in a rush, and satisfied, he raised his voice. "We'll work until we're done, won't we, men?"

One villager, obliterated by mud, stood and tugged a blackened forelock. "We're idle this time o'year, m'lady, an' ye know there's never much work fer me father an' me. Not fer what we do. We don't mind workin' until yer ditch is dug."

"Tosti, is that you?" she asked.

"Aye, m'lady." He grinned, his teeth a marked contrast to his face.

"What do he and his father do?" Raymond asked.

"They're trackers," Juliana replied. "The best I have. They can find and flush any game, and when . . . and when someone is lost, they'll find him."

Tosti clenched his fists above his head. "Aye, why shouldn't we be th' best? We belong t' th' bravest lady in England."

Taken aback, she sputtered, "Brave? What do you—"

The men nodded toward the drawbridge where her confrontation with Sir Joseph had taken place, and with winks and smiles indicated their support. Again she blushed, pleased this time.

Raymond beamed at his workers and determined to give them extra rations of ale and meat. Assisting her in her climb back up to the gate, he said, "May I compliment you on the scarlet sash, my lady? It draws the eye and livens your gown, and reminds me that Christmastide will soon be upon us."

Across her face paraded a variety of expressions. Horror, discomfort, and remembrance mixed in such a curious blend he wondered if he would ever understand her.

She snapped her fingers under his nose, as rude and abrupt as she'd ever been. "That is why I came out here to speak to you. Those two . . . women you forced on me."

"Valeska and Dagna?" So his dear ones were working their magic. He should have guessed they'd contributed the sash. "Don't you like them?"

"Like them? Like them?" She tasted the words and evidently found them sour. "How could I not like two aging crones who insist on treating me like a queen? Who offer to sing to me and give me gifts they got by fair means or foul?"

"Good! Good, I hoped you would like them." He bowed hurriedly and backed away, keeping Juliana in sight while trying to get out of earshot. "Here is the drawbridge, my lady, can you find your way back?"

"They speak strangely. They move like young women. Can't you find them work with the horses?" As he ducked into the smithy, leaned against the wall, and laughed, he heard her yell, "They'll teach insolence to my children."

5

Children. Raymond feared them as he feared no man or beast. What did he know about children? He'd never been one. How could he please one? He didn't know how to play or what they enjoyed. He could court a woman; how did he court a child?

Awkwardly, he'd tried to talk to Juliana's daughters. Searching his mind for subjects that would interest them, he'd cornered them to discuss sewing. Margery had suggested he take his sewing to the maids, for she was too busy for such trivial matters, and whisked away. Ella told him she never sewed, never, never. Such activity was for softlings, and she whisked away.

Another time he'd suggested dolls. Dolls? Margery told him she was too old for dolls, and whisked away. Ella told him she never played with dolls, never, never. They were for softlings, and she whisked away.

In the end, he supposed it didn't matter, for, after all, what did he know about sewing or dolls? Yet he wanted into that golden circle surrounding Juliana and her children, and he was clever enough to realize he couldn't buy his way in, or fight his way in, or sidle his way in.

Shifting on the bench, Raymond pressed his back to the cold stone wall in the great hall and observed Juliana's children. Each to her own nature, they helped or hindered the clearing of the noon meal. Margery took her responsibilities as heiress and elder daughter seriously, ordering and assisting the servants as needed. She had Juliana's coloring and copied her mother's ways, but her long thin face resembled none in the castle; she must look like her father.

Ella, the younger, watched the world through bright eyes, and her laughter rang over all the sounds of the castle. Her blond hair hung free around her face, and she asked questions without ceasing. Nothing was exempt from her curiosity, and her fertile mind found endless opportunities for mischief.

They would like him if they knew him, but they refused to know him. The children treated him as warily as they treated Sir Joseph, as if he could turn vicious. They treated him the way Juliana treated men, and how could he combat a model as powerful as their mother?

There had to be a way to prove his reliability, but how? To women, he gave gifts, praised their beauty and made false promises. Surely it would work with children. He had no other plan. Catching Ella's gaze, Raymond graced her with his most beguiling smile.

Ella ducked behind the bench where Valeska sat spinning the fine thread Juliana preferred to work with. Valeska, ever his champion, spoke to the child crouched beside her. The girl glared at him. Valeska spoke more vigorously, and the child shook her head until her hair flew in a golden cloud. Valeska struck the spinning wheel; Ella stuck out her tongue at him.

Overcome by frustration, Raymond returned the

gesture with a vengeance. Ella's eyes lit up. She stuck her fingers in the corners of her mouth and rolled her eyes wildly. Raymond was impressed and knew how to gain her respect.

Pushing back his hair, he wiggled his ears.

Ella's mouth dropped. As if he beckoned her, she took one step toward him. Pushing back her own hair, she frowned in concentration. She squinted her eyes, puckered her mouth in a fishlike motion, extended her jaw. She might have been making faces at him, but Raymond knew better. In his boyhood, he'd seen others try to imitate him, but none could, regardless of their sincere desire and unending practice.

He grinned at Ella nastily and mouthed "Ha, ha."

Without trepidation, she marched over to him and demanded, "Show me how."

He stood, stretched. "I have duties to perform, else Lady Juliana would have my head. I need to consult with Keir about the construction." Walking away, but slowly, he halted at the tug on his jerkin.

"Can I come?"

He considered Ella, still manipulating her face in a mad attempt to imitate him. Except for a short period in his youth, he'd never seen the value of his freakish talent, but now he thanked whatever saint had blessed his cradle. While dolls and sewing didn't fascinate Ella, clearly ear wiggling did. "I don't know. You're only a girl."

Hands on hips, she corrected him. "I'm not only a girl. I'm Ella of Lofts."

And proud of it. With the instincts of a warrior attacking a breach, he sighed. "It's muddy outside and it's getting colder. You'd rather stay inside, be clean and dainty, work with your mother on her knitting." He was hard pressed not to laugh at her horrified expression.

"I won't be in your way." She was insistent.

Cocking his head to one side, he considered her. "Perhaps, Ella of Lofts, it would be wise for you to learn about a castle's defenses." Testing his influence, he belched.

Immediately, Ella began gulping air. "I already know everything," she boasted.

Her answering burp surprised him with its intensity. He glanced guiltily at Juliana to see her glaring at him. Planning a strategic retreat, he flung his cloak around his shoulders and took a step toward the door. "If you know everything, you have no reason to come with me."

"I don't know quite everything," she admitted, his phony reluctance pulling her behind him like a chain.

"Then . . . you may come."

His permission impeded her rush to join him, and her expression disclosed a little girl's second thoughts at joining this stranger. Brightening, she turned and shouted, "Come on, Margery!"

Margery halted, her arms full of tablecloths. She'd been observing the comedy with no small curiosity, Raymond realized, for she didn't ask where they were going or with whom. Shifting from one foot to the other, she said, "I'm busy."

"The servants can do that," Ella retorted. "Can't they, Mama?"

Ella wasn't asking if the servants could do their jobs. She was asking if Raymond could be trusted, and Raymond waited anxiously for Juliana's answer. Juliana bent her head over the ball of cream-colored yarn she was winding. "Is the gate open, Master Raymond?"

He hooked his thumb into the leather belt ringed

with his tools. "Aye."

"Are the men-at-arms patrolling the walls?"

From his place by the fire, Sir Joseph said spitefully, "Only if that young jackanapes hasn't called them all in because they might get cold."

"The men-at-arms are patrolling the walls," Raymond said.

Glancing at Sir Joseph, Juliana said, "'Twould do you children good to get out before another storm forces us to remain within. Do run along, Margery."

Raymond promised, "I'll look out for them." Ella glared at him suspiciously, and Margery halted in mid stride, so he added, "If they fall in the trench we'll dig them out."

Juliana lifted her head and smiled at him. The enchantment, the pure physical beauty of it, struck him, singed him like a bolt of lightning. He froze and stared. Through the pounding of his heart, he heard her say, "I sometimes think, Master Raymond, you move like a warrior. Did you train for the knighthood, then lose your sponsor?"

Did she know? Was she taunting him? He shook his head to clear it. Nay, not Juliana. Other women would find such torment amusing, but not Juliana. "I . . ." He couldn't think what to say, but she took it as a confirmation, as if he'd said, "Aye."

" 'Tis a sad thing when a man isn't able to follow the path of his heart." Satisfied with the size of the ball, she put the yarn into her workbasket. Another smile winged his way. Another bolt of lightning struck, and he could almost smell his good intentions burning. "But I'll trust you to keep my children safe from both an excess of mud and any stray abductors."

He staggered under the influence of her friendly

mirth, for he'd never seen her friendship directed at him. He staggered under the load of his lust. "You'll trust me?" he repeated, stupid as a fat lapdog after dinner.

"You've never lied to me. Would that all men had your code of honor."

Leaning again to her weaving, the unscarred side of her profile glowed against the light of the torches. Her chin thrust out as she concentrated, and she tucked her tongue between her lips. A mixture of amazement, consternation, and pure masculine appreciation buffeted him. She trusted him? Because he'd never lied to her?

Only about his identity, the identity of his crew, his mission here . . .

It hit him like a blow in the chest. This woman was his, given to him by his sovereign, and because of his own misdirected empathy with her plight, he'd strewn the path to their mating with stones and thorns. He wanted her, and he would have her—but only when she discovered he'd been lying to her.

Weighed down by horror, he found himself leaving the keep, crossing the yard, entering the smithy. The two young girls looked at him inquiringly. Lit by the fire, protected by a leather apron, Keir heated iron until it glowed red, then brought it to the anvil and began pounding it into shape. Concentrating on the shovel taking shape beneath his hammer, he said, "Greetings, my ladies. You honor my humble workplace."

Something about Keir—his solid shape, the calm that radiated from him—invited trust, and the two girls were no more immune than the cats who made themselves at home in his smithy. The girls relaxed, and Raymond congratulated himself until Keir asked, "What is your desire, Raymond?"

"*Master* Raymond," Margery corrected.

Any other man would have smiled, but Keir ruminated on her reprimand. After due consideration, he said, "*Master* Raymond and I have created a relationship quite unlike the one between lord and serf or master craftsman and apprentice. While the respect in which I hold him is real, it is all the more profound for being unspoken."

"Really, Margery," Ella said impatiently, "it's not as if Master Raymond is an earl or a baron."

Raymond forestalled anything Keir might say with a brisk, "Indeed not. Lady Margery and Lady Ella hoped, Keir, you would show us the diggings and foundation preparation."

Keir gripped the tongs with a dexterity that spited his missing fingers. "The master castle-builder should guide the young mistresses through the intricacies of construction. I do not possess the necessary skills of . . . communication."

Smiling with determined courtesy, Raymond said, "Do come."

Keir gestured at the forged pieces and unformed iron strewn about. "I am too busy."

"I insist."

"Much as I regret it, I must demur."

In a tone of triumph, Margery said, "See, Ella? If Master Keir doesn't utilize the polite form of address, it causes dissention and proves disrespect."

Raymond and Keir looked at the two ingenuous young faces watching them with rapt interest, then at each other. Keir put down his tongs and wiped his hands on his apron. "Let us proceed, Raymond."

Stopping by the stables, Raymond spoke briefly and vigorously to Layamon about the safety of the children and the necessity of maintaining a close watch for stray brigands or wayward mercenaries. He joined the small expedition as they crossed the drawbridge and started down the muddy slope. All the natural vegetation had been worn away by the ceaseless tramping of workers. The shallow trench originated where the cliff dropped to the river and followed that elevation around the face of the hill to the other side where, again, the cliff dropped off. It established an arc that slashed the earth to form the perfect bulwark, and Raymond glowed as he imagined the mighty wall he would create to dispel warriors who sought to take his land.

Aye, his land. His land, spread out in patches of wood and plain and village. His land, rich and fecund, alive with cattle, serfs, villeins. He would be the warrior for this land, protecting it from those who ravaged and gobbled with no care for the simple folk living there.

Juliana would dispute him, of course. She would call this property hers, but in no manner could any woman love the land like a man. Land represented more than just status, money, position. It was a place to be from, a place to return to, a home. These fertile lands, granted to him by his cousin Henry, came with a wife and children, a family ready-made. He gazed with satisfaction at the girls. From this land he would draw his strength.

A bonfire burned, lending ceaseless warmth to the air above and around it and none where it was most needed. A Saxon Christmas tune, liberally peppered with curses about the mud and the cold, rose from the trench. Tosti appeared over the top, dragging a laden bucket to add to the piles of oozing muck which rimmed the moat on the upper side. When he spied them, the whites of his eyes bulged from his blackened face, and he called down to his mates, "Hey, mud brownies, 'tis th' lord an' th' two little ladies from th' keep."

Heads bobbed as the workers jumped up and down like Jack-O-Straws in the hands of a babe.

"They do not act like this when we arrive," Keir observed. "Perhaps the Lady Margery and the Lady Ella should visit more often."

Raymond nodded and turned to the girls. "Doesn't your mama make sure you greet—" He broke off. Margery had her arm around Ella, and she looked at the men with an expression of horror. Ella cuddled close against her sister, and her wary gaze examined each muddy worker suspiciously.

"Why are those men staring at us?" Ella asked.

"This area is unprotected," Margery pronounced.

Keir and Raymond exchanged glances. With as much reassurance as he could muster, Raymond explained, "They're staring at you, my ladies, for you are their future mistresses." As the girls digested that, he declared, "This area *is* well-protected. We have the men-at-arms who patrol the walls, but more important, the first line of defense is the winter. No army can march in winter, for an army cannot feed itself without foraging on the land."

"It's not just armies a woman must beware of." Margery's large eyes were serious. "Even a man whom a woman believes to be her friend can turn against her to gain control of her wealth." She examined him from boots to knit hat as if she could gain his measure by his appearance.

"That's true, but no one can know an enemy by sight, and so one must make judgments according to wisdom."

"Whose wisdom?" Margery asked shrewdly.

Raymond crouched down until his eyes were level with theirs. "The wisdom of your elders, to begin with." Before she could object, he added, "Even more important than that is your own wisdom. Observe the people around you—all the people, not just the men—and make your decisions using your head, not your heart. But mistakes occur." He straightened. "I can help prepare you for attack. Do you know what to do should an unarmed man attempt to carry you off?"

She shook her head.

"What does your mother do when she's frightened?"

Quietly she said, "She freezes like a rabbit beneath the shadow of a hawk."

Raymond was startled. How misinformed Margery was about her mother's character! And why did she think such a thing? He told her, "You're wrong. Your mother's the bravest woman I ever met."

"*My* mother?" Ella queried, clearly staggered.

Picking his words carefully, Raymond said, "Before she knew my identity, she tried to hit me with a log." He rubbed his head in rueful remembrance. "She came too close to success for my own comfort."

Margery was impressed. "My mother did that?"

"Aye, she did. Will you be less courageous than your mother?"

The girls shook their heads in unison.

"Nay, of course you won't." Raymond turned his back on Keir. "Let's pretend I'm a woman and Keir grabs me."

Keir said drily, "I find it hard to pretend you are a woman."

"Try." Raymond heard Ella stifle a giggle when he continued, "I'm standing alone and unprotected, but perhaps my men-at-arms or an honorable man, or even another female friend stands not far off. My attacker approaches me, flings his arms around me." He grunted when Keir grabbed him from behind and jerked him so hard he lost his breath. "Now what do I do?"

"Scream?" Ella asked timidly.

"Aye!" Raymond tried to turn back to the girls, but Keir wouldn't release his grip. With a jab of the elbow and a stomp of the foot, Raymond freed himself and glared at his companion. To the girls, he said, "All women can scream. Let's hear you."

Ella let fly with one ear-piercing shriek.

"Good!" Raymond said. He pointed at the men-at-arms who crowded the wall walk, arrows drawn, weapons at the ready. "Your rescuers have arrived."

While Raymond waved a reassuring hand at the men, Ella hopped on one foot to display her pleasure.

"Let's hear you, Margery," he coaxed.

Margery stared solemnly at the soldierly exhibit, then emitted a squeak.

"Louder," Keir said.

Licking her lips, Margery tried again, but with similar lack of success.

"Like when I took your pig's bladder and popped it," Ella instructed.

Margery put her arms to her side, closed her eyes, and tried. It lacked the rage and fear that made a scream compelling, but Raymond approved it. "That's fine. Your next effort will be even better."

She opened her eyes and viewed her instructors. With her flushed cheeks and shining eyes, she looked less like a dignified adolescent and more like an excited child. "Teach me more."

"More?" Raymond scratched his chin, wondering how much he should teach them and whether their mother would approve.

"Teach us how you made Keir let go of you a few moments ago." Ella pointed at the place where they'd stood.

"Aye, teach us that," Keir said with awesome calm.

His tone expressed his intention to best Raymond, but Raymond only grinned. "Of course. I'd be honored to show you how to defeat an attacker as scurrilous as Keir." Swinging his hip out in a pitiful imitation of feminine stance and pitching his voice higher, he said, "Here I am, a lovely lady alone in the forest."

As Keir stalked around him even Margery giggled.

"When a knave most hideous snatches me from behind," Raymond continued.

Keir leaped on his back, but Raymond didn't bend.

"I scream." His gentle screech was blocked by Keir's hand, but Keir snatched his hand away immediately and shook it. Raymond returned to his normal voice to say, "You see, girls, if the knave tries to interfere with your first line of defense—your scream—you bite him. Then you scream again, louder." He bellowed in full-bodied male fury, reached up and jerked Keir's hair. Keir's roar joined Raymond's, and he catapulted over Raymond's head and came up standing.

For a moment, the two men crouched, facing each other, fingers splayed and hands outstretched. Their teeth shone, a snarl distorted their faces. They no longer looked like blacksmith and castle builder. They looked like two warriors ready to join a battle that would end with blood and death.

Into the silence their violence generated, Ella's thin voice piped, "Are you and Keir cross at each other?"

In slow degrees, the men recovered. The fierceness was absorbed back into their bodies, no longer visible, but not forgotten.

"Nay." Raymond passed his hand over his forehead as if to wipe sweat away, but his face was cold and white. "Keir and I are friends. We fight for fun, but sometimes we forget—"

"—where we are and whom we fight with," Keir finished.

The men smiled at the girls, but Raymond's lips felt stiff. The expression the girls wore betrayed their sudden skepticism, and not a man who watched from the trench nor the wall seemed any less suspicious. Raymond's lightning change of agenda betrayed his years as a tactician. "So you see, even friends can hurt each other. Keir and I are evenly matched, but when a man attacks a woman, that woman is at a disadvantage of weight and strength. To balance the weights, a woman must attack a man's vulnerable places. So if you are ever in peril," Raymond finished, "You scream, then strike repeatedly at your attacker."

"What if you're not sure you're in peril?" Margery asked.

"Be safe. Protect yourself. You can apologize afterward, and not many men will admit a girl could hurt them." Raymond's rueful smile acknowledged the male ego, then he waved at the men-at-arms. "Go back to your game of knucklebones," he called. "We're in no danger."

The men grinned and waved back, drifting away from the crenellations.

"Would you like to observe the diggings?" Keir asked.

A chance to wallow in the mud revived Ella's subdued spirits, and she lifted her skirt and clambered toward the top of the mound. Margery followed sedately, as befitting her age and dignity. Raymond and Keir assisted when the girls slipped and skidded. At the top, they looked down into the trench, fully as deep as any man standing.

"Hey, m'lord, wot do ye think o' it?" Tosti gestured from one end to the other.

"An excellent job," Raymond said approvingly. "How much farther down to bedrock, do you think?"

"I'm a better tracker than digger, fer certain sure. But wot I think"—Tosti struck the ground with his spade—"wot I think is that th' rock lies far below here. Don't ye think this is deep enough?"

Gesturing up toward the wall now standing, Raymond asked, "Isn't that wall set on bedrock?"

"Don't know, m'lord. 'Twas built long ago."

"Why are you calling Master Raymond 'm'lord'?" Margery asked curiously. "He's not a lord."

Tosti rolled his eyes. "Oh, nay, o' course not. He's only a lowly castle-builder. He's not th' son o' some great man. He's not used t' livin' wi' wealth an' power." His sarcasm rang out, and the men working the trench sniggered.

"That's enough, Tosti," Raymond commanded, but now Margery looked at Raymond, measuring, assessing, and seeing him more clearly than ever her mother did.

Ella leaped up and down, chanting, "He's a lord, he's an earl, he's a baron."

Too close to the truth for comfort, Raymond thought, and shifted uncomfortably. This called for drastic action. To distract Ella, he picked her up by the waist and swung her out over the pit. "Watch what you say"—she shrieked, and he looked, saw her laughing and swung again—"or I'll drop you into—"

Pain exploded in his groin. Below him, Margery drew back her fists, prepared to strike again, but with Ella weighing him down he overbalanced, fell onto his seat with Ella clasped firmly in his arms, and slithered down the steep slope into the muddy trench. Above him, he heard a gasp, then Keir and Margery landed beside them. Driven by agony, Raymond shouted at Margery, "Why did you do that?"

"You were threatening her," Margery sputtered. "You said if I were in doubt, to attack—"

Dumbfounded, Raymond stared at the girl, so young and valiant and filthy. "I was playing with her."

"She screamed," Margery said, defending herself. "And you said—"

"Margery's right." Keir's shaking voice betrayed merriment. "According to your instructions, she reacted properly in the circumstances. But I am so glad you were her practice victim. God help the man she seriously tries to injure."

Driven by the smirk on Keir's face and the woebegone girls, Raymond chuckled. The girls smiled feebly, then giggled, and at last the bedraggled group dissolved in hilarity. Already saturated, they rolled in the muck, slapped one another on the back, indulged in comradely mirth quite unfitting to their condition and position.

The diggers gaped at them, and when Tosti said, "M'lord?" Raymond waved a dismissing hand.

"M'lord," Tosti insisted.

"We've not run mad," Raymond soothed. "We just—"

"M'lord, look!"

The urgency in his tone broke Raymond's amusement. With his gaze, he followed Tosti's pointing finger to the rim of the trench.

Sword points and glistening edges. Armor and shields bearing an unknown coat of arms. Above him stood a great line of fighting men with swords pointed down. Down toward him and Keir and toward the girls who were his responsibility.

6

"*Your daughters are* still out with that simpleton knave of a castle builder, aren't they?"

Sir Joseph smirked as Juliana glanced outside for the dozenth time in this interminable afternoon. She wondered if Raymond would ever bring her daughters in, but she wouldn't give the old man the satisfaction of speculating aloud, for she'd come to give the master castle-builder her complete trust.

Well, almost complete trust. He would keep her daughters safe, even beyond the protection of her sturdy walls. Although he was no belted knight, still she knew he would. Raymond was tall, strong, honorable. She'd realized that after their sojourn in the hut. After all, what other man would have left her in peace when he stood to gain so much from her—especially when, in the end, she would have embraced the enchantment he offered with open arms?

If only Sir Joseph were in exile rather than sitting beside the fire with a loathsome smirk on his face. As the serving maids set up the trestle tables and covered them with white cloths, he jabbed at them with his stick. It was the kind of cruel entertainment that cheered him. At the same time, he jabbed at Juliana with a wit as sharp as any sword and a cruelty as bludgeoning as any mace. "Of course, why should you care if your babes are stolen away from you and raped? You've no more motherly feeling than a slime-bellied asp."

Before Juliana could defend herself, Valeska said, "You worthless, louse-ridden vermin." Her tone was as smooth as Mabel's ale, but Sir Joseph superstitiously hunkered inside his cape. "Leave my lady alone to do her needlework and listen to Dagna's song. 'Tis a romantic ballad of a knight and his true love."

"You call that music?" Sir Joseph spat into the fire. "I've put a live puppy on the fire and heard better music."

Dagna stopped singing, but her smile broadened and she never ceased strumming her mandolin. Her cheerful tune changed, grew oppressive, foreign-sounding, and she sang a few words in a language filled with guttural tones and nerve-scraping notes. Sir Joseph quivered and whispered, "Witches."

As Juliana sat before her loom and worked desultorily at the blanket she was weaving, she wondered if the old women really were witches. They had performed miracles she didn't understand. Her character had been tempered in the kiln of harsh experience, and though she allowed no one to weaken her with kindness, their cosseting didn't seem to have that effect. If anything, it nurtured and strengthened, like a sweet spring brew after a long winter.

"Your daughters must be getting cold as the sun sinks." Sir Joseph ducked back into the wide neck of his cape as Valeska cast an evil eye his way. "If you weren't such a mewling coward, you would go and seek them."

Fingering the red sash she wore about her waist,

Juliana glanced out the arrow slit. It was growing dark and much colder, and her daughters . . .

Her daughters, too, had grown to trust Raymond. Why else would they have gone with him? The weeks of proximity had dissipated their fear.

If only Raymond would bring them in. She wouldn't go and see what kept them. She wouldn't betray her anxiety so obviously, because as the time of his dominance faded, an increasingly spiteful Sir Joseph verbally rended her in the manner of one who knew her vulnerabilities and delighted in her pain.

She wanted to scorn him, shame him, force him to realize she was not the terrified fool he'd been dealing with. She no longer believed he would strike her, and she no longer wondered what cruelty he would perpetrate on her household next. But she *was* terrified of the secrets he could tell. She was afraid he would tell Raymond about Hugh and Felix and her father and those events which had destroyed her so long ago.

Although why she should care what Raymond thought, she didn't know.

Margery took one look at the shiny swords and produced the scream Raymond had asked for. Loud, long, and piercing, it contained all the terror of a young girl whose worst nightmare had come true. Diving for Ella, she dragged her sister into her arms and the girls huddled together—two muddy, scared children.

"Here's dirty work at the crossroads." A tall, well-formed knight held them hostage with the point of his sword.

A bobbing, florid-faced little man in armor echoed, "Here's foul play."

Raymond and Keir arrayed themselves in a wedge, pushing the girls behind them, as Raymond demanded, "Explain your purpose here."

"You're bold for a muddy peasant," the little man said, waving his sword close to Raymond's nose.

"He's not a muddy peasant, Felix," the other knight observed. "Listen to him speak. No serf of mine has travelled so far he speaks French with an accent like that."

The sword threatening Raymond's Adam's apple withdrew. Felix tried to scratch his head, but the chain-mail hood he wore deflected his fingers. By the time he had displaced the heavy hood enough to reach his scalp, all the men were gaping at him. When he realized it, he grinned, revealing a gap between his two front teeth. "Got a dreadful case of lice. Hope Juliana's got the herbs to kill 'em."

Raymond's concern eased. "Juliana?" he asked cautiously.

He was nudged from behind by the sharp elbow of a child, and one little head peeked around the curve of his hip.

The long arm of the tall knight—in Raymond's assessment, the knight in charge—reached out again. "Lady Juliana of Lofts. The mother of those children you've abducted."

The word smacked Raymond's mind and rang it like a gong. "Abducted?" He couldn't contain his laugh, and as he caressed the top of Ella's head, the tall knight's eyes narrowed. "I have not abducted Lady Juliana's children."

Keir dug a warning elbow into his ribs and said, "There would seem to be a mistake."

"Aye." The tall knight leaned forward, and placed

the point of his sword on Raymond's chest. "And you've made it."

Ella said, clear and high, "Be careful, Uncle Hugh. The mud's awful slick."

"My lady?"

Juliana opened the eyes she'd squeezed shut and pressed a hand to her forehead.

Valeska handed her the horn mug, filled to the brim with foamy ale. "Drink this. 'Twill ease your fears."

"I'm not afraid," Juliana snapped reflexively, then grimaced when she realized what she'd revealed. She smacked the woven cloth hard with the batten. "That is, I was wondering how long Master Raymond has been a master castle-builder."

"What a question, my lady." Valeska polished Juliana's loom with a cloth.

"Aye, a good question, and one deserving of an answer." Because Raymond sometimes forgets the names of tools and how to use them, Juliana wanted to say but didn't. Even though Sir Joseph was hard of hearing, she feared to express her doubts in front of him. Instead, she said, "Master Raymond has such an air of unconscious authority about him. How long has he been a master castle-builder?"

Valeska squinted at her reproachfully. "My lady, my memory isn't what it used to be."

Juliana didn't believe it, and she summoned a lad who struggled to serve a pitcher of ale. "Your father is Cuthbert, my carpenter, is he not?"

The youth grinned. "Aye, m'lady, th' best in th' village an' far beyond."

"What thinks he of Master Raymond?"

His grin faded. His intelligent face grew blank. "M'lady?"

"I asked what your father thinks of Master Raymond's building skills."

The youth scratched his head. "M'father? Why, he says Master Raymond's a right good . . . That is, Master Raymond never . . ." He let out his breath audibly, then jumped as the drooping pitcher spilled ale on his shoes.

Dagna ended her song with a discordant twang. "Look what you've done! Now clean up before you serve dinner." As the lad scurried into the darkness of the stairwell, she showed Juliana all her amber teeth in a smile and said comfortingly, "He's a good boy. He just needs more training."

And really, Juliana thought morosely, why did she care how competent Raymond was? The play of light and shadow on his face reminded her of a picture, and she wanted to paint him. The movements of his body reminded her of a melody, and she wanted to dance with him. The ripple of his muscles reminded her of a horse, and she wanted to ride . . . She caught herself with a gasp. She was a widow, a mother, a noblewoman betrothed by the king himself to a powerful man. She had no right to lust after a mere castle builder. But Raymond had proved to everyone he was a man to be trusted.

A man.

To be trusted.

To her, those phrases were totally unrelated, and nothing could change her mind.

Except that Raymond made her remember a time when men had been nothing to fear. His handsome countenance preyed on her mind, afflicted her gestures, brought forth the coquette she thought had died a painful death. But some women would only appreciate his beauty. Some women would dream about the liquid silk of his dark hair in their hands. They would make fools of themselves for a smile, and titter about the dimples it brought forth. Some women would let themselves be seduced by the long body, long legs, long thighs.

Juliana was not so foolish. It was the compassion in him that attracted her. The way he courted her children, anxious to be included in their play. The way he dealt with the maids, firmly dismissing their passionate ploys, yet treating them with such appreciation they loved him still. The kindness he showed to those two odd women, feeding them, tending them, letting them tend him when he'd proved to Juliana he could fend for himself. He and his absurd friend Keir made Juliana smile, freed her to plan a Christmas that would be truly merry, rather than a travesty of Christmases past.

"I hear them coming, m'lady," Valeska murmured in her ear.

Juliana looked at the old lady without recognition, then half rose as the sound of shrieking came in on the draft from an open doorway. Hurriedly she seated herself, and took hold of the batten. She assumed a serene pose and fed a thread through the warp of the wool.

As she expected, Ella ran in first, yelling, "Mother, Mother!"

Margery followed close on Ella's heels, no less vocal.

Both girls were barely recognizable.

Juliana forgot her forced serenity, forgot everything as she stood. In a voice no less loud than Ella's, she shouted, "What happened to you?"

"We fell in the mud," they chorused, giggling until they were convulsed.

"You fell in the—" Her gaze fell on Raymond and

Keir, equally blackened and hovering behind the girls like two shamed hounds. She drew herself up to her full height. "Explain this, if you please."

Raymond relished the vitality her anger brought to her, and he swept her an elaborate and flourishing bow. "Your elder landed me such a blow, she knocked me into the mud, and before I realized it, a delightful brawl developed. Keir and I"—Keir swept an identical bow—"were defeated handily by your miniature warriors."

Margery and Ella postured as great warriors should, grinning with overweening self-congratulation.

"My daughters defeated you? How is that possible?"

"A hereditary fierceness and a natural bellicosity, combined with feminine mistrust." Raymond grimaced with remembered pain.

"I really did it, Mother." Margery doubled her fist and thrashed the air.

Jumping up and down in little jiggling movements, Ella bragged, "You should have seen her, Mother. She defeated Lord Raymond before he realized the battle was even joined."

"The best way to defeat Lord"—Juliana's eyes narrowed as she refashioned his title, and she stepped toward the grubby group—"Master Raymond would surely be before the battle is joined."

As straight-faced as if he'd never participated in the mud fight below, Keir warned, "Do not discount your daughters' fighting skills."

Anxious to turn her attention from her daughters' too accurate assumption, Raymond said, "We would even now be kneeling before these mighty fighters, begging for mercy, but for our timely rescue by Felix, earl of Moncestus, and Hugh, baron of Holley." With the flourish of one presenting a gift, Raymond stepped aside to reveal the well-armored visitors hidden behind him in the hall. He anticipated pleased exclamations, but Juliana froze in her tracks, then frantically pushed her children behind her.

With a shock, Raymond recognized her. This Juliana was the Juliana he'd first met and subdued. The woman who had struggled for her freedom with every savage impulse.

The knights ignored Raymond with all the disdain of lords for a man of the earth, and when Raymond looked back at Juliana, she had conquered her panic with an effort Raymond could only salute.

"Welcome, neighbors. You surprise and . . . please us with your presence, my lords." She was clearly uneasy and wanting to flee. "You are old friends, and my daughters are cold. I hope you'll avail yourself of our hospitality while—"

"What is this madness of yours that allows you to leave your daughters in the hands of such inadequate nursemaids?" Hugh cast a fulminating glance toward Raymond, then toward Keir, who restrained Raymond with an unbreakable grip on his arm.

"They're not nursemaids!" Ella shouted.

"They're warriors!" Margery said, squirming as Juliana tightened her grip on her daughters' shoulders.

Raymond cringed at the children's bold defense. "Damn," he muttered, subsiding in Keir's clench.

"They sound like your father. Shouting when they should be learning their manners and minding their needles." Hugh pointed at the bogus castle-builder and the blacksmith. "These warriors"—he mocked them—"are without the intelligence to keep your valued daughters inside the walls!"

"And they allowed your daughters outside the walls without protection," Felix complained.

Sir Joseph chuckled with rich malice. "Did I not warn you of your negligence, *Lady* Juliana?"

Raymond and Keir exchanged weighted glances, but before Raymond could speak, Layamon stepped forward. Twisting his hat in his hand, he said, " 'Twas not quite as bad as that, m'lady. Master Raymond instructed me most severely about me duty afore he took th' girls t' see th' construction, an' I watched most heedful-like from th' wall. When I saw th' troop aridin' up, bristlin' wi' swords an' such, I called me men an' we surrounded th' lords after they surrounded th' trench wherein Master Raymond an' yer little ones were, ah, workin'.' " He moved with shambling embarrassment and peered at the aggravated neighbors. "Naturally, I knew th' noblemen, but Master Raymond had given me m'orders."

"My thanks, Layamon." Juliana nodded to the young man. With a strained smile at Hugh, she said, "I'm not so irresponsible as you believe."

Hugh's indignation withered at the sight of her white face, and he bowed. "A thousand pardons, my lady. I thought that"—he darted a glance toward the place where Sir Joseph sat—"I thought unworthy thoughts."

"Make yourself welcome," Juliana repeated. "I must tend my children."

The girls now shivered miserably. With the clap of Juliana's hands, the maids came flying and dragged out the great wooden tub from the corner where it had rested unused all winter. Warm water, heated on the anticipatory orders of Valeska, arrived in buckets from the undercroft. Dagna placed the great folding screen before the master bed to separate it from the great hall, just as she did every night when Juliana retired. As the women disappeared from view, the men seemed released from a spell.

With a glower that spoke volumes, Hugh stepped close to the fire. Short in stature, swarthy, and plump, Felix followed. He combined a habit of peering up from beneath his beetle brow with one of nodding his head to an unheard rhythm, and Raymond never doubted who made the decisions in the odd pair.

"You!" Hugh pointed at Raymond. "You'll do. Remove my armor." He held out his gauntlet-clad hands, challenging Raymond with his command.

As all knights did, Raymond had trained in his youth as a squire. Well he remembered how to remove another's armor, and Hugh's intended insult went astray as Raymond relished the chance to confront the baron.

As Raymond approached, Felix complained, "He's dirty."

"An understatement of the grossest kind." Hugh's lip curled as Raymond came into the light and the warmth of the fire. "You stink, my man."

" 'Tis clean mud," Raymond answered, stepping up, toe to toe and eyeball to eyeball. "Unlike the horseshit knights delight in."

Keir groaned, and Hugh lifted a fist to cuff the man he'd claimed as squire. Raymond's steady gaze weighed Hugh, and Hugh stopped with his hand clenched in readiness. "Who are you?" he whispered.

Raymond longed to tell him, but he itched to know all of Juliana's secrets, and Hugh was a simple man. He could be manipulated. The bride Raymond had come to claim was more than a conquest now; she was a mystery to be solved.

"I'm the king's master castle-builder," he told Hugh.

Hugh lowered his fist, but his rancor obviously flamed higher. Raymond wondered at such youthful animosity in a man of Hugh's maturity. The man perceived a challenge in Raymond, and his hostility grew.

"Bring him warm water," Hugh said. When no one moved, he shouted, "Warm water!"

Valeska darted about, clucking like a hen whose master was honing his axe. "Warm water," she screeched. "Get warm water for Raymond."

Hugh's lip curled as he watched Valeska appropriate a bucket from the long line of open-mouthed youths who carried it from the kitchen below. "Your mother?" he said sneeringly.

"God did not so bless me." Raymond plunged his hands into the water and shuddered as the warmth crept into the cracks and scrapes of his skin. After scrubbing the dirt away, he accepted with a smile the rag Valeska offered him. "My mother is ugly."

Valeska flushed at the compliment and ignored Felix's snicker. Using her yellowed knuckles, she brushed the flaky mud from Raymond's cheeks and beard. "There's more water warming for you below. You might wish to shave this day."

"Why?" Raymond asked.

She glanced at the knight glowering at them and lowered her voice. "He's a comely man."

Raymond looked, too. "I will shave."

"Let me see your hands," Hugh demanded. Raymond complied, thrusting his fingers so close under Hugh's nose the man had to push them away to view them. "They'll do. There's dirt under your fingernails, but what could I expect from a castle builder?"

Grinning, Raymond removed Hugh's gauntlets and gloves and glanced pointedly at Hugh's fingernails.

Hugh jerked his hands back and snarled. "Remove my hauberk."

His chain-mail cap slid off easily, revealing a receding hairline. The scars of some early encounter with a sword shone in red and white glory, lending him a fierce appearance and giving Raymond a respect for Hugh's fighting skills.

"Dreadful of me to challenge you below," Hugh said in counterfeit apology. "But I've long felt a responsibility for Lady Juliana and her family."

"A responsibility?"

"We grew up together, you understand, and I care for the little coward."

Felix piped, "I grew up with you. I was her friend, too."

Raymond scarcely heard him, and it seemed Hugh didn't either, so intent were they on each other. Holding the strings that tied Hugh's hauberk close against his neck, Raymond questioned him. "Coward? You call her a coward?"

"What else would I call a woman who refuses to visit her other demesne?"

"Not a coward," Raymond objected, remembering how valiantly she'd faced him when he snatched her from the teeth of the snowstorm.

Hugh laughed with loathsome superiority. "A coward, I tell you. She depends on Sir Joseph to tend Bartonhale Castle, to check the accounts and make sure the steward isn't cheating her. I've told her it's not wise to trust even so ancient and valued a servant, but still she huddles here at Lofts."

"Then she doesn't listen to you," Raymond observed cordially.

"She has listened to me through the years."

The strands broke in Raymond's grip. Hugh only smiled at this destruction of his property.

"She listens to me, too," Felix said.

"'Strewth! So old a friend as you"—Raymond flung the strings aside—"must have known her husband."

With a wave of his muscled arm, Hugh dismissed the husband. "Millard? He was a youth, chosen only for his wealth and too sickly to live long. He gave her only girl-children. Not man enough to keep Juliana's passionate nature satisfied."

This was the man, Raymond decided. The one who'd put Juliana in the position to be humiliated by Sir Joseph. The one who had no thought to her reputation. Had he been her lover? If once, then no more, for Juliana was his. His to protect, to cherish, and this shiny-domed warrior would rue the day he'd hurt her.

"As we've grown older," Hugh said with ever-increasing confidence, "we've found our affection growing and changing."

Raymond wanted to rip the hauberk off, and in the process take Hugh's head, but the respect of a fighting man for armor—any armor—kept his hand steady as he lifted it off. To retaliate for his control, he retorted, "Affection is like an hourglass. As the brain empties, the heart fills."

"How intelligent you are for only a castle builder." Hugh watched as Raymond examined the hauberk for injury or wear. "One would almost believe you had personal experience with chain mail—your concern is tangible."

Raymond handed the hauberk to Keir. "Clean it. Oil it."

"Why would a castle builder have experience with

chain mail?" Hugh inspected Raymond. Each muscle and sinew of Raymond's body was being measured by an experienced warrior, and Hugh might espy what Raymond wanted concealed.

Raymond glanced at Valeska, and Valeska understood. Calling to Fayette, she ordered, "Assist this lord with his underpadding, and take the armor from this other one." She glared at Raymond and Keir quite without respect. "Get you below, both of you, where you can be properly washed. You are leaving crusts of mud with every footstep."

Scuffling the reeds, Raymond muttered, "Who can tell?"

"Tarry not," she answered, her tone sweet. "Even now, the maids are carrying the water from the tub to the garderobes to flush them clean, so the Lady Juliana is done washing her babes. We will serve the evening meal without heed for two oafs who track mud on my floor."

She aimed a disrespectful kick at Raymond's departing backside, but Raymond needed no more urgings.

Before Juliana's clean daughters made their reappearance to sup on milk and bread and bid the visitors a fair night, a damp, cleansed, and shaved Raymond stood in the midst of the great hall. The smoke from the torches joined the smoke from the fire, lending a resinous odor to the woody scent. The head table was set with a white cloth and spoons and a trencher to be shared by every two diners. Kettles of stew were dragged from the depths of the keep by puffing pages. Ale splashed freely into the cups at the lower tables. A wine-filled flagon was placed on the head table.

Before the center place, the place of honor, stood a

tall silver salt, and with the ease of a hospitable host, Raymond said, "Lord Felix, you are the greatest lord present. You will, of course, sit before the salt."

Accepting that as his due, Felix agreed, "Of course."

Raymond picked up the stool before Juliana's loom. "Such a great lord should sit above even those at the head table." With his knee, he pushed apart the benches that stood in a line before the trenchers. "You should sit here, higher than the rest."

Felix bobbed incessantly, pleased for a moment. Then the consequences occurred to him, and he sputtered, "But I should sit beside Lady Juliana and share her trencher."

Raymond gazed with simulated awe upon the twitching earl. "You wish to yield your place to Lady Juliana? You invite her to sit on the stool alone, to eat from her own trencher?" He placed the stool before the salt with a mighty thump. "My lord, you honor her with your regard, and yourself with your courtesy." With his hand over his heart, he bowed. "Confess, you live at Henry's court when not visiting your estates."

Felix beamed, but Hugh said sharply, "You take much upon yourself, master castle-builder."

The title sounded like an insult, but, while washing, Raymond had regained control of his rancor. He would discover the truth about Juliana and these men who so alarmed her, and he would protect her as a husband should. With courtly charm firmly in place, Raymond said, "I have had the honor of serving Lady Juliana this month, and know well the esteem in which she holds her neighbors." The blandishment slipped easily from his tongue. "It will gratify her you hold her in such regard."

From behind him, a sound—or was it an awareness?—made him turn. Juliana had heard every word, and her thanks were all the more poignant for being silent. Her copper hair had escaped the plait that had bound it and trickled like liquid flame across her shoulders. Her slim hands were outstretched, open and giving. Her eyes shone like amethysts, and her smile conquered all fear.

With a bow to the lady, Raymond indicated the stool. "Lord Felix begs you to do him the honor of letting him sit at your feet."

"At her feet?" Felix interposed, real repugnance in his voice. "At her feet? At the feet of a woman?"

Displaying a flash of contempt, Juliana made her way to the table and sat on the stool Raymond pulled out for her. " 'Tis an exaggeration of courtly manners, Felix. I do not expect an earl of the realm to sit at my feet, nor anywhere near me."

Felix lashed out so suddenly he caught Raymond unprepared. His open hand almost struck Juliana, but she jerked back and, petulant as a child, he cried, "You've never forgiven me, have you? It was nothing! Nothing happened, and you've never forgiven me."

Except for Sir Joseph's crow of delight, the great hall was still. Every serf, every page, every maidservant waited to hear their mistress's response.

As Raymond watched, Juliana slipped away. She dwelt somewhere in the past, lived some experience that pained her. He couldn't bear the distance, and he laid his palm flat on her back. She shuddered, lifted her head, and looked at him. Green gaze meshed with blue, questions and comfort flowed between them, although who comforted and who questioned, Raymond knew not. His hand vibrated with the sigh he felt rather than heard, and the strength of her spine was so vital he wondered how he would respond when he touched her bare back.

That startled him—how long had he wondered such a thing?—and that astonishment was reflected in her face.

She turned to Felix. Her fingers stroked the scar marring her cheek. "Perhaps forgiveness is beyond me, but I have forgotten. Content yourself with that."

A collective sigh swept the room. Felix grinned and bobbed his head up and down in a motion as constant and repetitive as the waves on a pond. The captive audience bustled in a mass toward the tables.

The assault of sound and smell and sight seemed frighteningly mundane to Raymond. Hugh plucked Raymond's trespassing hand from Juliana's back, and Raymond let him. Keir moved to the end of the table and called Raymond to do likewise, and Raymond nodded, trying to appear normal.

But all the time he thought, *Felix?* Felix was the man who'd betrayed Juliana? Raymond looked again at the florid little rooster and, in his inattention, barked his shins against the bench where he tried to sit. He rubbed the painful bruise and stared at her without ceasing and marvelled, *Felix?* Felix had been her lover?

Nay. His disbelief was too intense, and Felix had himself denied it. Nothing had happened, Felix had said. He hadn't been her lover. She hadn't had a lover. The event that stained her past and made her a pariah in her own eyes was more than a simple love affair. It had been something dark, frightening, and Raymond was embarrassed by his own easy dismissal of her sin.

For had it been a sin, or had it been a crime?

When the meal was finished and the eating knives

had been sheathed, Hugh said challengingly, "Lady Juliana, tell us why your master castle-builder is digging such an immense hole in the ground."

"*We*," Juliana said firmly, "are digging the foundation for a twelve-foot-wide curtain wall."

"Eight-foot," Raymond said, correcting her.

She stared down her nose at him and summoned Fayette with the basket for the poor. "Twelve-foot."

Raymond didn't bother to hide his grin. "It depends on whose feet we use to measure."

Shocked to the tips of his slick black hair, Felix said, "He is insolent."

She tossed her sauce-soaked bread into the basket. "But he's the king's master castle-builder, and I trust his judgment."

"*You* trust him?" Hugh's shock was all the more conspicuous for being sincere. "You trust a man? A man whom you've known only a little while, who digs muddy holes for a few pence a day?"

Taking the wet towel Fayette offered, Juliana cleaned her greasy hands. Each finger must have required special attention, for she kept her gaze on them while she answered, "Aye."

Hugh's shaking finger pointed at Raymond. "Because *he* taught you to trust again? Is he in your bed yet? For I would remind you, Lady Juliana, that after your last scandal, it would be too easy to destroy your reputation and perhaps remove from you the guardianship of your children and your lands."

She grasped the edge of the table with her hands. "Your suspicions blemish the purity of your soul."

"The castle builder's a liar!"

"He is not!"

Embarrassment struck at Raymond. What would

his lady do when she remembered this spirited
defense? How would she overcome the humiliation?
For she would be humiliated. No woman so proud
she disdained the fawnings of an earl could be less.

"He hides the truth," Hugh accused.

Juliana folded her arms across her bosom. "What
truth?"

"I know not, but he's more than a simple castle-
builder."

Beside Raymond, Keir whistled under his breath
and said, "Lord Hugh is too observant."

"I thought him a simple man."

"Simple, but not stupid," Keir said, "and very determined to protect Lady Juliana to the best of his ability."

Raymond ignored him. The time of his own
unveiling was months away. It would be springtime,
at least, and by then . . . ah, by then, what? What
were his plans? Without ever telling Juliana who he was,
he had impressed her. Without knowing his reputation as
a warrior, she'd trusted him with her precious daughters.
Without actually seeing his credentials, she had trusted
him with the building of her defenses. Without knowing
his relationship to the king, without knowing about his
family's wealth, she'd come to like him. Without knowing
his reputation as a lover, would she come to his bed?

"I don't like him, either," Felix pronounced.

Juliana turned on him, and asked sarcastically,
"Why not, my lord?"

Felix reddened under the collective fascinated
gaze of everyone in the room. "He's, ah, insolent.
And he . . . he's more than he appears to be."

Keir muttered, "And that lord is a mimicking moron."

Raymond nodded agreement, but he basked in her
sweet defense.

"Look at him!" Hugh leaped to his feet. "Look at him. He swoons like a moonstruck youth over the chance to lift your skirt, and if you believe any different, you're a fool."

She did look. She looked, and in the tender appreciation of her gaze, all Raymond's plans seemed nigh on to being fulfilled.

"Sweet Saint Sebastian!" Hugh said. "You should see yourself. You look as moonstruck as he, for less reason. Do you think he sees you as some dream of love? Nay, he sees you as lands, as security, as an appetizing body."

Still she looked at Raymond, half smiling, relaxed, and from the place where Sir Joseph sat, hunched and malevolent, came an accusation. "She'd never pass the test of Saint Wilfrid's needle."

Raymond and Keir exchanged a puzzled glance, and Keir asked, "What is Saint Wilfrid's needle?"

Juliana lifted her chin. "Only a chaste woman may pass through the narrow passage in Ripon cathedral called Saint Wilfrid's needle."

"And you've proved you're not a chaste woman," Sir Joseph sneered.

Goaded beyond sense, Hugh shouted, "You're behaving like a whore!"

The sweet spell was broken with the repetition of that word Sir Joseph had chosen as a label. Not Hugh's grimace of apology, not Juliana's disgusted exclamation could stop Raymond as he rose from his bench and stalked toward Hugh. "I'll feed you those words until you choke on them."

Hand on his dagger, Hugh stepped forward. "Only a knight could fight me and win," he said. "Are you a knight?"

"Do you doubt I could fight you?"

"I doubt you are a castle builder. I wonder where you learned this courage, developed those muscles, learned to move like"—Hugh cocked a brow—"a knight."

Juliana looked troubled. Keir cursed under his breath. Raymond gritted his teeth.

"Mayhap Lady Juliana gives her trust too easily," Hugh said, snarling.

"My trust is none of your get," Juliana retorted. "If you wish to fight, then fight someone who—"

Layamon interrupted from the doorway. "M'lady?" He held a wet, shivering man in a traveller's cloak beneath his hands. As Raymond watched, Layamon pushed the fellow forward. In English, he said, "Nary a word can I understand from this knave, but he keeps repeatin' yer name an' waving this letter." He placed the paper in Juliana's outstretched hand. "It has th' king's seal on it."

Juliana examined the seal and looked at the traveller who had been so roughly treated by her man-at-arms. "What language do you speak?" she asked in Norman French, and was rewarded by a babble of heavily accented, rapid Poitevin French.

"My lady." The traveller fell to his knees. "My lady." He kissed her hands. "I have been treated ill by that peasant." He tossed his hood back, and his jowls jiggled in Gallic indignation. "He said he didn't understand me, but he proves he can speak a civilized tongue to you." With a large, white cloth, he dabbed at his damp forehead and wiped his mustache dry. "'Tis nothing more than part of the travails of journeying through such a barbaric land. If the king had not insisted, I would not have come at all." He mopped his cheeks. "Or at least not until spring." Hindered by his kneeling position, he produced a half-bow. "But of course King Henry was most insistent, and when he told me of your beauty and charm, he did not exaggerate."

He tried to kiss Juliana's hands again, and she seized the chance to speak. "I don't understand. Why did King Henry send you to me?"

Surprised, he gestured. "You asked for me."

Raymond's heart sank.

"I asked King Henry for no one. No one except—" Her gaze swung to Raymond and back to the portly man at her feet. She leaned down, peered into his eyes, and asked, "Who are you?"

"I?" The excitable Poitevin touched his hand to his chest. "I? I am Papiol." He struck a pose and lifted a finger into the air. "I am the greatest master castle-builder in all of the kingdom!"

7

Juliana stared at the jowled, expressive face of the stranger who called himself the king's master castle-builder. She watched him gesture, she saw his lips move. She knew he was speaking, but she couldn't hear him. She could only hear Sir Joseph, cackling with evil amusement. Somewhere inside her, hurt throbbed like an untended tooth. Somewhere inside her, tears welled for the poor, silly woman who'd trusted a man and been betrayed yet again. But she didn't feel the hurt or cry the tears, for all she experienced was anger. She could taste it, feel it roil in her veins, smell the fire and brimstone it engendered. Absolute fury shook her. She formed the words carefully, like a drinker who'd over-indulged in potent wine. "Who did you say you were?"

The man kneeling before her stopped gesturing, stopped speaking, stared as if she'd run mad. "I am Papiol, the king's master castle-builder."

He spoke with the deliberation of one speaking to an idiot, but she wasn't offended.

"Which king?" she demanded.

"My lady?" Papiol mopped nervously at his neck with the well-plied cloth.

"For which king are you master castle-builder?"

The bulging brown eyes bulged even more. "Why, for our sovereign liege, King Henry." Still on his knees, Popiol inched away. "May his line prosper."

"If you are the king's master castle-builder, then who is that?" She pointed at Raymond.

"My lady, I am not acquainted with any of the courtiers who surround you." Papiol paled when she glared at him.

"Just tell me if you have ever seen his leering, lying, deceitful face before."

Moving as if she were a fierce animal whose attack would be triggered by haste, Papiol turned his back and looked. Cocking his head to one side, trying to keep one eye on her, he said, "Nay, my lady, I have never seen this man before."

Juliana's breath flamed, her skin crackled from the heat of her outrage. She wanted to look at Raymond, to accuse her betrayer, but she found her body responded sluggishly to the commands of her brain, for anger consumed her energy. Her knees creaked like the timbers of a burning house as she stood. She raised her hand to point, and was surprised her fingernails hadn't grown to talons. "Kill him," she commanded.

Sir Joseph stopped cackling. The room stopped humming. Papiol fainted. Hugh reprimanded, "My God, Juliana!"

"Kill him," she repeated.

Hugh tried again. "Juliana, you can't just kill—"

She turned on him with a snarl. "Watch me." She snatched her eating knife from the table. Short and sharp, it would gut a man if used properly. She stalked toward Raymond, and Raymond prudently backed up. Backed up until he rested against the far wall and they stood well away from the table. As she jabbed with the knife, he caught her wrist.

"Allow me to introduce myself, my lady," he said softly.

"I don't want you to introduce yourself." She twisted her arm free and plunged at him. "I just want to bury your nameless body in a grave outside the churchyard."

He caught her wrist again, and again spoke so only she could hear. "I am Geoffroi Jean Louis Raymond, Count of Avraché."

Her breath cooled, caught in her throat, clogged it like ice. "I didn't hear you."

"I am Geoffroi Jean Louis Raymond—"

She slammed the sharp edge of her free hand into his chest. "This is impossible."

She was pleased to note he had to suck in some air before he could reply. "My lady, I vow it is the truth."

His gaze, frankly regretful, infinitely kind, curdled her fury into some lesser thing. Mortification, perhaps, or shame.

For the first time, she was aware of the people who observed them. Some had only observed through the past hours. Some had observed through the past days and weeks. All had seen too much, and she was going to have to face them. She didn't want to crawl away. Not yet. But humiliation tapped at the edges of her perceptions and before long it would drill into her being. She knew it. She recognized it.

"Sweet Juliana, don't look so." Raymond's bass rumbled with worry. "I never meant to hurt you."

She jerked her hand out of his grasp. Her knife clattered to the floor. "Don't say that!" She heard the shriek in her voice. Steadying herself, she lowered her voice to say, "Men never want to hurt women, but they do it so well."

"What can I do to convince you—"

"—who you are?" She pounced like a cat on a mouse. "I want to see the letter."

"The letter?"

Perhaps he feigned puzzlement, but she didn't think so. He wasn't as good an actor as he would like to think he was. "The letter you showed to Layamon. The one with the king's seal on it."

"'Strewth!" His horror made her all the more determined. "That letter's not for you."

"I never thought it was, but I want to see it now."

He fumbled with the tools on his belt and mumbled excuses, but he kept the king's letter on him—in case of trouble, the king's seal would provide protection—and in the end he yielded.

Juliana didn't know whether he gave in due to her indignation or to his own guilt. Once she'd read the letter, she just didn't care. Henry's jests were directed against her temperament—"shrewish"—and her looks—"horrific." His advice to the solitary bridegroom ranged from the crude—"swive her till she can't stand"—to the absurd—"seduce her." It was a missive written by a king who had never had to mince his speech. She turned her back on Raymond. If she could, she would have mutilated the parchment, but the words burned themselves into her heart, and she couldn't forget them.

Worse, they proved Raymond was who he finally claimed to be.

The wall where she leaned was cold stone, and she wished her heart were as hard and cold as that stone. It was not. It wept blood, it ached with betrayal.

"Juliana." Hugh sounded hesitant as he approached,

and she braced herself to look him in the face. "Juliana, what do you wish me to do?"

Hugh would be the vanguard of greater, more loathsome spectators, and, like a child who's been disciplined by her parent yet seeks comfort from that same parent, Juliana glanced back at Raymond.

More insistent, Hugh said, "Juliana. I'll kill him if you want, but we should first discover who he is."

Her knees collapsed. Hugh stood before her, Raymond stood behind her, and she fell backward like some hedgerow harlot. Raymond's hands caught her. He massaged her elbow, rubbed the rigid muscles of her back. He gave her the warmth to slow her shivering, loaned her the strength to stay erect—and Juliana hated that. She mocked her own emotions when she pretended to despise him, but she suggested, "Shall we rack him, or thrash him until he confesses his sins?"

"I suspected he was a knight and not the castle builder he claimed to be. He stands too proudly. He has the body of a fighting man. He must be a scout for someone who wants your lands or your money," Hugh said.

Felix's querulous voice called, "Juliana, have you been trifling with men again?"

Sir Joseph's hideous cackle grated on her nerves, and she realized that not only her knees were collapsing. Her hope for recovery, her shy, maidenly fantasies had been shattered. Startled by Hugh's query, Raymond was examining her from head to toe, and the humiliation formerly held at bay gripped her by the throat. She knew what he thought. She knew what he saw—a pale, gangly woman dressed in shapeless brown homespun and flaunting a red sash. A sash that pleaded for attention, that dreamed of style.

How pathetic.

No wonder he hadn't told her his identity. He didn't want a woman who'd been scarred by another man. He didn't want a widow with two children. He couldn't even understand why Hugh believed a man could want her. Raymond of Avraché was a lord of the court and—she snuck a glance at him and groaned—still as beautiful as the sunset.

"My lady—Juliana—please."

Raymond was a nice man, too, Juliana noted, for her distress seemed to break his heart.

"I will do all I can to ease this awkwardness. Please." His breath brushed her cheek, then a sword reached between them.

"Get your hands off her, you cretin." The point pressed toward Raymond's throat, and Hugh smiled unpleasantly.

She should have been grateful to Hugh, but he only stirred the night soil in the bottom of this cesspool. Wrapping her hand around the hand that held the sword, she swung it away. "Don't be a fool, Hugh. He's not a master castle-builder, or even a spy. He's Raymond, Count of Avraché, come to claim his bride."

Sir Joseph's laughter was cut as if by a knife, and Hugh's face mottled with rage. His sword and his hand shook under hers, and he shouted, "Raymond of Avraché?"

If there were any in the hall who hadn't heard his name, they knew it now. Hugh turned on her like a maddened beast. "I'll kill him for you."

Alarmed by the bloodshot eyes that glared so furiously, she said, "Nay, you won't."

"Aye, kill him."

Juliana didn't recognize the low male voice, choked and thick with hatred, that called from beyond. Her glance grazed the assemblage, but so many emotions existed on so many faces she couldn't tell who would incite such outrage. Felix stood beside the remains of his meal, eyes darting, head bobbing, trying to act as if he understood the situation. Sir Joseph sat gripping the table, shock bleaching his ruddy face. Sword drawn, Layamon stood between everyone and the door. Opposite him, Keir waited, tensed for action.

Who had called for Raymond's death?

Valeska and Dagna were disappearing into the undercroft, and in the background, her servants hugged each other, smiled and sighed with relief.

Relief? she wondered. Why relief? But she had no time to discover, for Hugh gestured extravagantly, and she tightened her grip on his fingers.

"Who would know?" Hugh persisted. "We'll tell the king he never arrived, or he died of the flux, or he hanged himself of melancholy."

"Who would know?" she repeated, the emphasis different when she said it. Raymond stepped back, out of her vision, but she couldn't watch him go. She could only keep her wary gaze on Hugh and wonder how this evening had so quickly turned into a farce. "Who would know? Only every dogsbody here. If a secret kept by three is no secret, what is a secret kept by thirty?"

"You were going to kill him," Hugh accused.

"Don't be a fool." She rubbed her forehead. She ached as if she'd been beaten. "I would never have been able to kill him."

"This knife—" He nudged it with his toe.

Raymond and Keir, Valeska and Dagna consulted together in a tight circle, and she wondered at Raymond's strategy. Surely any man who could plot so devious an infiltration into the home of his betrothed would have an agenda for every occurrence.

She said, "I'm not a knight, Hugh. I'm not a man. I don't hold life cheap, nor beat my servants to hear them cry, nor get a babe on some serving girl for fun. I wouldn't have killed him."

Insulted, Hugh drew himself up. "Because he's your lover."

"Don't be an ass. If he were my lover, everyone would know." She pointed. "The screen that separates my bed from the great hall allows no pleasures to go unheard, no sins to go unseen."

Hugh's sword dangled from his hand, a dejected symbol of his defeat. "There will be no sin when you have to wed him."

"Wed him?"

Lowering his voice, he queried, "Surely when he announced himself you must have realized you would have to wed him."

Oddly enough, she hadn't realized it. With her hand at her throat and the pulsing of blood beneath her fingers, she knew the fragility of her needs, her desires, her fears.

"Don't you feel trapped?" he taunted.

"Trapped?" She explored her emotions as she spoke. "I should, but I don't. Maybe tomorrow, when the immensity of my error will have lodged itself in my mind. For tonight, there is only humiliation."

"Think on it," Hugh urged.

"Why do you delight in this?" she asked. "I thought you were my friend."

"Your friend is not what I wish to be." Hugh caught her shoulder and pressed it until she winced.

The blade of a sword slipped between them, and as one they followed it with their gazes to its owner.

Raymond stood, balanced with the casual care of a fighting man.

"Let go of her," he said.

Hugh's hand crept from her shoulder, and as she rubbed the bruises he'd left, she demanded, "Where did you get that sword?"

Raymond never took his eyes from Hugh, urging him away from Juliana, but he answered her. "From the king."

"Nay, I meant"—he knew what she meant, but the castle builder had vanished, leaving an arrogant knight—"where did you store it in the castle?"

"Valeska is in charge of my armor. Dagna is in charge of Keir's." His gaze flashed her way, inviting her to join him in the humor. "They are our squires."

Juliana found she had no humor tonight, nor any night. "I was not aware of swords in my castle."

"If you had known of the swords," Raymond said, "you would have suspected my ruse."

What he admitted oppressed her, and she said bitterly, "Instead you perpetuated your deception without this poor tottyhead ever suspecting."

Valeska sidled close. "Oh, you suspected, my lady. Remember when you asked me about him? I was too sly for you, but you suspected."

"Aye, my lady." Dagna hovered just beyond Valeska's shoulder. "There's no need to berate yourself when you had so many enterprising folk working against you."

The two old ladies showed capacious grins as they jostled for positions as targets for her wrath, but Juliana was thinking too clearly for comfort. "Should I blame you, then, for my own stupidity in trusting this liar? Should I blame you for his conniving disloyalty?"

They drew back with little hisses of dismay, and

Valeska croaked, "Nay, my lady, that's not how it happened at all. He takes care of two old women who are no good to anyone. Look at him!"

"That's true, my lady." Dagna sang the same lyrics with a sweeter voice. "We're from a far land with no way to get home, but he feeds us and treats us like his family. And you—you're a kind lady who deserves a man who'll warm your bed, give you children, keep you safe. You could travel the world over and not find a man as fine as Raymond. Look at him."

Juliana didn't want to look at him. She avoided looking at him. Even now, when she knew how he'd deceived her with every step, he captivated her.

"Juliana." Raymond took her hand, threaded his fingers through hers. "Forgive me."

She looked at Hugh, but his brief frenzy had burned out. As he stared at their twined fingers, his face portrayed loneliness, laced with a resignation only habit could provide.

"Look at Raymond," Valeska said.

She looked at Felix, but the familiar sickness of the spirit had been distanced by new events and by a new man.

"Look at Raymond," Dagna insisted.

She looked at Sir Joseph, pale except for two red spots that burned over his thin cheekbones. For the first time in years, his malice was directed at someone else—at Raymond. But that malice was laced with a hearty respect, and Juliana didn't fear for Raymond.

Raymond was invincible.

"Look at Raymond," the old ladies crooned.

One glance at him trapped Juliana in his sorcery. He stood coiled beside her, all male beauty and wicked enchantment. Like the jewelled snake of Eden, he beguiled her until she forgot the pain and humiliation a man visited upon his woman. She forgot the reasons why a woman avoided taking a lover. She forgot that men demanded more than babes, were more unreasonable than babes. She remembered only the promise of pleasure. He made her wish to seek that pleasure. Like the end of a skein of yarn, he dangled fulfillment and she wanted to chase after it.

"Ooh, my lady," Valeska whispered, quivering with awe at the quiet passion that hummed in the air. "You'll make fine babes for us to rock."

"I will not!" Juliana said.

"But my lady—"

A gesture from Raymond stopped Valeska. He turned to Hugh. "Perhaps we should become acquainted. We will be neighbors."

Hugh nodded. "But first, you wouldn't be offended if *I* ask to see some proof of your identity."

"No need, Hugh," Juliana mocked. "My hindsight is excellent. He snuck onto my lands, prepared to abduct me, saw a perfidious way to insinuate himself into my household, and seized the opportunity. Isn't that right, Lord Raymond?"

"Hush, Juliana," Hugh said as Raymond withdraw a small object from the pouch on his belt and handed it over. Hugh examined it and, satisfied, pressed it into Juliana's hand. "Your intended's family seal. An old and famous one. Look on it well before you defy him."

She took it between two fingers and stared at the roaring bear depicted so graphically there. "I've seen it before. 'Twas stamped on every message this Count of Avraché sent me, commanding my presence for my wedding."

"Doesn't it frighten you?" Hugh demanded.

"Should it?" It was a marvelous bit of bravado, for she had been frightened before she ever gazed at the seal.

"Have you never heard of the strain of wild fighters in Lord Avraché's family who wear bearskins and transform themselves into berserkers?"

"That's enough." Raymond plucked the seal from her and dropped it into his pouch. "Those stories are naught but legends told by my ancestors to inspire panic in their enemies. Let us become acquainted now, Lord Holley, in a friendly manner." Taking Juliana's hand, he threaded his fingers through hers and started toward the fire.

Juliana tried to hang back, but he wouldn't release her hand. He tugged her forward until she complained. "I must supervise the clearing up."

"Oh, nay, my lady." Wrinkles overcame Dagna's face as she smiled. "We'll do that for you. Won't we, Valeska?"

And Valeska said, "With the help of your competent maid, Fayette, it will take no time at all."

Raymond again tugged at Juliana's hand. She twisted it, trying to loose her fingers until he warned, "I'll put my arm around your waist and bring you."

She yielded immediately, following, she thought, like some obedient ewe at the behest of the master ram. Only Raymond didn't resemble a ram, and she was no bleating ewe. "Your penitence was brief," she snapped.

"But sincere." He settled her on the bench by the fire, then despaired that her feet were roasting. She replied she would rather her spine bear the brunt of the heat, and turned her back to the fire. Her features were no longer exposed by the light, but she realized her error almost at once.

Raymond faced the fire. Raymond sat next to her.

By facing in a different direction, he could look at her any time he wished, and he wished to often. But he spoke to Hugh as if he were the host and Hugh the guest. "How came you to Lofts Castle now, so close to Christmastide and through the storms of winter?"

Juliana knew how hopeless her cause must be when Hugh answered with the courtesy due a lord. "I heard tales of the diggings about the castle, and couldn't imagine such madness."

"Such madness," Felix echoed.

"In such weather, who brought tales of my"—Raymond sounded stern—"construction?"

"A message from—" Felix began to say, but Hugh interrupted.

" 'Twas a message from a wandering troubadour, nothing more." Leaning forward, Hugh patted Juliana's shoulder. "And I wished to visit my old friend at Christmastide. Her wassail is the best in all of England."

"The best in England," Felix mimicked.

She tossed Hugh a weak smile, and fought as old memories and anxieties overwhelmed her. Her mouth quivered; she clenched her jaw to stiffen it.

But Raymond noticed, for he slipped a casual arm around the front of her waist and brought her close to him.

He didn't speak to her—her equanimity would have shattered if he did—but his hip met her hip, and he seemed comforted by the contact. It didn't comfort her, of course. No man's touch could comfort her. She really wanted to squirm away. The weight of his arm made her aware of each breath she took, and she concentrated so much on maintaining a slow, even rhythm, she forgot how upset she was. She couldn't summon any interest in the men's tales of tournaments long over and battles long gone, but the merriment of the servants impressed her. Hailing her maidservant, she asked, "Why are the servants singing so heartily?"

"Haven't ye noticed, m'lady?" Fayette grinned in pure delight. "Sir Joseph's snuck right out."

Juliana saw it was so. "He's been absent from the great hall before, and never have I heard so much mirth."

"Aye, m'lady, but he's not comin' back. Sir Joseph can't hurt ye no more."

Staggered by her answer, Juliana stammered, "Hurt me?"

"Did ye think we never noticed when he said those nasty things t' ye? An' clapperclawed ye time an' again?" Fayette hooked her thumb in her rope belt and jutted out her lip. "Made us right angry, he did, but what could we do? He was yer chief knight." Philanthropy forgotten, she added, "Besides, he can't hurt us no more, either."

"Hurt you?"

"He was always aslappin' an' abeatin' on th' servants, kinda sly-like." Fayette rubbed her behind in remembered injury.

Juliana blushed. She knew about Sir Joseph's rages, and she'd tried to force him to temper them, but hitherto none had complained. "I didn't know . . . I had hoped he wasn't so brutal."

"Ach, no use in complainin', m'lady. We knew there weren't nothin' ye could do t' th' ol' whoreson."

Juliana glared at the smiling maid. "I banished him."

"Aye, that ye did, but we didn't know if ye had th' strength t' force him t' go." Seemingly oblivious to Juliana's indignation, Fayette beamed at Raymond. "But now—Lord Raymond, *he'll* make him go. That

Sir Joseph'll have no chance against a sure-lance like Lord Raymond."

Guilt stabbed at Juliana. She'd been so weak, so occupied with her own problems, she hadn't even been able to control her own chief knight. Another good reason to wed Raymond. Another proof of her own ineffectiveness.

She glanced sideways at Raymond and found him watching her. Immediately her unruly emotions gained sway, and again she concentrated. She wanted no sobbing to disrupt the cadence of her breathing.

A cup presented itself beneath her nose, and a voice said, "My lady, I've brought you your favorite wine, well-strained."

Startled, Juliana took it from the beaming Valeska. She'd been focussed so intently on each inhale and exhale, she'd noticed nothing else.

"And I brought a wrap for your feet." Dagna laid it across Juliana's lap, hiding Raymond's arm and giving him, Juliana feared, tacit permission to caress her as a husband would. They had been betrothed by proxy, and to the servants, the old ladies, the men, the wedding ceremony was a formality. Performed on the steps of the church, it would give their children the shelter of legitimacy.

When those children would be conceived mattered to no one but Juliana.

To the two old ladies hovering over her, anticipating her every need as if she already carried the babe they desired, she whispered, "Go away."

They retreated, unoffended, still smiling.

Raymond murmured in her ear. "They want only your comfort, and are perhaps overzealous in their pursuit. Don't be angry."

"I don't punish servants for my own bad humor," she said stiffly.

"I never thought you did."

"And Sir Joseph learned better. He grew up at my father's side, and one of the first rules my father taught me was not to abuse my servants or my serfs or my villeins." She took a breath and wished she could stop talking. She stifled the yawn which struggled from her depths to the surface. The excitement, the fear, the anger of the evening had left her exhausted and unable to cope. She wanted to sleep. But Raymond still pressed close to her. When he spoke, his breath warmed her cheek. She saw his jewelled eyes gleam in the firelight. She absorbed the warmth of his body. Did he, like the rest of the castle, consider the proxy betrothal valid unto the day? Would he expect to join her on her bed?

The thought brought an odd flush to her cheeks. His arm seemed to toast the skin of her belly, and her skin itched beneath its weight. She pressed her thighs together to relieve the sense of pressure, but that only made it worse, and she lost control of her breathing— a double disadvantage.

Scornfully, she labelled this as youthful, immature, lacking in sense. Any woman who reached the mature age of eight-and-twenty should know the insanity of allowing such sensations to control her emotions.

She sipped the mulled wine and considered how she could remove herself from his grasp. Should she stand without explanation and leave? Should she excuse herself to supervise an already efficient household, or explain she must use the garderobe? Should she express concern for her exhausted daughters, check the pallet where they slept, then never return?

She didn't know. She was afraid she had become

the celebrated whore of Sir Joseph's ranting. When she looked at Hugh and Felix, she felt as if she rocked in a boat in a fierce storm. When she looked at Raymond, the waves calmed, the wind smelled fresh, and only Juliana and Raymond existed, alone on the sea.

Whatever his true feelings were at being condemned to marry her, he played the faithful lover well. Such kindness when none was required made her resent him all the more. She should hate him; it proved impossible. She found herself wishing she'd met him before, when she had known how to laugh. She'd never been a beauty, but at one time men had flocked to her side for a smile. In her imagination, she saw herself laced into a sky-blue cotte with a sun-yellow chainse peeping out. Men surrounded her, but none of them frightened her. They weren't important, for she was not only the lady of Lofts, but the wife of a great knight and the mother of brave daughters. Her girls explained they owed their courage to their mother's example. Her husband—

The support beneath her head gave way, and she blinked. A hand, broad, callused, hovered in the line of her vision. Raymond's hand. Without thinking, she placed hers in his grasp and let him swing her to her feet.

She stood swaying while he said, "Lord Hugh, Lord Felix, our acquaintance will no doubt prosper, but tonight, Lady Juliana is nodding. The servants are drooping, and your journey has made you wish to seek your own pallet. 'Tis time to sleep"—he wrapped an arm around her shoulder—"and we bid you good-night."

8

He hadn't even kissed her.

Juliana groaned as stripes of sunlight pressed on her eyelids. It couldn't be morning. Not yet. Not when so many ordeals faced her today.

It should have been the laughter she dreaded, the laughter directed at the gullible Lady Juliana. She curled into a little ball and dragged the pillow over her ear.

She did dread the laughter, and the merriment with which her household would prepare for their mistress's marriage. But more than that, she dreaded facing Lord Raymond. Last night he had been so kind, so apologetic, so completely a chivalrous knight. He had helped her climb, fully clothed, up on the bed. He'd sat on the covers and explained how the disastrous masquerade had come about, how he'd lied only to ease her fears, how he had become trapped in his disguise, and how he'd intended to reveal himself.

He'd been a bit vague about *when* he had intended to reveal himself, and he'd invited her to speak her thoughts. She'd wanted to. She'd wanted to badly, but every time she looked at him, she was struck by a sense of vertigo. She'd been imprisoned in this stony, thorn-edged tower for too long, and Raymond pushed her out on the ledge and was going to make her fall.

Every time she looked at his shaven chin with its newly revealed cleft, every time he leaned close and she inhaled the fresh-washed scent of him, every time she heard the determined rumble in his tone, she felt the surge of air in her face and saw the ground rushing up at her.

But he hadn't tried to kiss her. He hadn't even tried to join her under the covers. She was glad to put off that ordeal a little longer. She didn't mind that she was cowardly, and so stained by her disgrace he dreaded the marriage bed as much as she did.

"Why do you wish to wed her?"

Hugh's bass rumbled through the great hall, and she closed her eyes and snuggled into the feather mattress to shut him out. To shut the whole wretched day out.

Still loud, Hugh continued, "A man like you—"

Raymond interrupted quickly. "What do you mean, a man like me?"

The knights sounded as if they stood right beside the master bed, and she pulled the warm furs closer about her shoulders.

"A man like you," Hugh said stiffly, "has lived at court and all over the continent. You have the backing of the king. Why would you want to come to a provincial backwater in England to marry a woman like Juliana?"

"A woman like Juliana?" Raymond inquired.

"You've eyes to see." Juliana could almost imagine Hugh's shrug. "She's pretty enough, but she hasn't lived an exemplary life, and she doesn't own many lands, not when compared to what you're used to. She's jumpy and suspicious, and doesn't listen to a man when she should. Too much indulged by her father, I guess. When he rejected her, it struck her down and she became strong-willed and determined. And of course, she's a snivelling coward."

She stared at the wall. Sunlight beamed through the arrow slit and told her she'd slept too long. Morning mass was over, morning's meal cleaned up, morning work had commenced, and she still didn't want to face the consequences of last night's events.

Raymond sounded polite. "How can she be a snivelling coward and a strong-willed woman at the same time?"

"That's Juliana." Hugh's voice softened with affection. "She'll keep a man on his toes." He cleared his throat, deepened his voice. "But I don't understand why you want to wed her."

"Because the king commands it." Raymond's answer couldn't satisfy Hugh, but in a different tone, he asked, "What think you, Cuthbert? Can we build here?"

Ignoring the chill that struck at her skin, Juliana snuck an ear out from beneath the covers. Build what? Where? What mischief was this phony castle-builder making now, and why did he have her carpenter from the village here in the keep?

"Aye, m'lord." Cuthbert sounded sure, confident, pleased, and close. " 'Twill be a pleasant addition fer m'lady's comfort. An' yer own, o' course, when ye're wed."

Hugh sighed, loud and exasperated. "Raymond, if you would give me your attention."

"You have my attention." Raymond's voice dipped, became muffled.

Obviously piqued, Hugh said, "Lady Juliana is fragile, unused to the hearty ways of men. It has been suggested you would not realize her delicacy and perhaps use her ill."

"Who would suggest such a thing?"

Raymond sounded overloud to Juliana, but she lifted the pillow to hear the reply.

"It doesn't matter." Hugh sounded chagrined, a man who'd said the wrong thing and achieved the wrong results. "What matters is you and your station."

Raymond ignored that protestation with the arrogance of one born to power. "Last night you seemed easy enough in your mind about the marriage. What changed it so abruptly?"

Juliana heard a shuffling, and remembered how Hugh moved his feet when cornered. He denied Raymond's tacit accusation. "No one! No one changed my mind."

"I asked what changed your mind," Raymond reminded him, "not who."

"Nothing changed my mind." Hugh spoke too rapidly. "I just want to do the right thing for Juliana. Don't you like to do the right thing for the women you feel responsible for?"

In marked contrast, Raymond drawled as if his thoughts impeded his speech. "I do the right thing for the women I am responsible for."

"I feel the same responsibility a brother would feel for Juliana."

"Or a father?" Raymond said.

Hugh plunged on. "But you could easily persuade our noble sovereign to award you a new bride, and it would be advantageous for you to have a wife accustomed to the court's ways."

"You want her for yourself," Raymond accused.

"I want the best for Juliana," Hugh replied, stiff as any man whose secret has been revealed before all.

Raymond lowered his voice, made it intense and threatening. "Listen to me, Lord Hugh. Lady Juliana is mine. My woman, my heiress, my bride. No challenge shall go unanswered. Henry gave her to me, and she's mine."

What Hugh would have answered, Juliana never discovered. Such a blatant declaration in front of the whole room infuriated her, and she swept back the covers and prepared to leap up.

Raymond stood beside the bed, tall and broad and handsome as she feared. He spoke to her now, not Hugh. "We spent the night in a snowed-in hut all alone, and there I determined she was mine."

It was a lie, the worst kind of falsehood, one that stole her virtue and reduced her, once again, to status of fallen woman. She bounded up until they were nose to nose—and faltered. His gaze locked with hers and he smiled without warmth.

"Did we wake you, Lady Juliana?"

"What—?" She glanced around, noted in some lesser part of her mind that Hugh stood beside him, her screen had been removed, and on the dais beside her bed knelt her master carpenter. She wanted to attack Raymond for his blatant declaration, demand he explain, but she shrank from the confrontation. If she insisted he clear her name of wrongdoing, would Hugh tell him the truth? Would Felix come from his place by the fire to smirk with his red lips and strut like a little peacock? Would Sir Joseph—?

A quick survey of the great hall confounded her. Sir Joseph was still missing, but such a blessed state could not continue. Her whole life he'd been there, sneering, snitching, so rather than reply to either Raymond's question or claim, she asked, "Cuthbert, what are you doing?"

Cuthbert scrambled to his feet, bobbed his head, and

beamed. "M'lady, yer new lord cares only fer yer comfort an' th' comfort o' yer people. 'Tis honored I am t' offer ye congratulations on yer marriage. Honored."

"My thanks, Cuthbert." Confused, she shivered as the chill struck her.

"You're cold," Raymond said smoothly. "Let me warm you."

He picked up a fur and prepared to tuck it around her, but she snatched it from him and wrapped it around her hunched shoulders. "I'll do it." In a forced, but pleasant tone, she asked, "Cuthbert, do you have enough to keep you busy this cold winter?"

Cuthbert laughed heartily. "Ye jest, m'lady. This winter, me family will have th' extra they need fer true comfort." He swung his arm to slap her on the back, realized his error, blushed a painful red. Bowing, he retreated back to his straight edge.

With her eyes, she measured the marks he labored over. Scratched into the oaken floor, they marked an ample area around the bed and they puzzled her. Whatever was happening, she didn't like it. She knew she didn't like it, but when she looked up to Raymond, tall, and even taller on the dais, she opted for diplomacy. "My lord, what is your plan?"

He sat down next to her; that didn't make it better. His weight depressed the mattress, and she had to brace herself to keep from rolling into him. Now he was close enough for her to inhale his essence of smoky fires and sawn wood. He said, "Lofts's keep is badly lacking in the comforts essential for a lady's pleasure."

Her keep lacked comforts? She swept it with a glance. The long, narrow arrow slits let in light but kept out most of the cold. The fire burned continuously on a central tile hearth, and the smoke exited through louvers in the roof. Rushes covered the floor and the removable trestle tables were easily cleared to give work room. What more could a lady ask for? In discouraging tones, she said, "I've heard some castles have their fires close to the wall."

"I have seen it," he agreed.

She sniffed. "A foolish idea, to my mind. How can all the folk warm themselves?"

Raymond didn't act at all like a superior male who'd seen the world and all its wonders. "Some keeps have more than one hearth. Say, one against that wall"—he pointed to the far wall—"and one against this."

"What a mess that would be," she scoffed. "How can the smoke reach the peak of the roof without much meandering?"

"A hood is built above the hearth to collect the smoke." Raymond treated her concern seriously.

"I've done it myself," Hugh added, and flinched when Juliana glared. "It works well, and it seems to heat the stones. My keep is much warmer than this old pile of rock."

The disparagement in his tones irked her, and she turned her back on him and spoke to Raymond. "I have heard some ladies insist on a place to sit ringed in large windows to let the sun in."

"Aye, I have seen that," Raymond acknowledged.

"It saves the eyes of the sewing maids," Hugh said.

"Do you ruffle the covers with your sewing maids, now?" Juliana snapped, pushed by his championship of Raymond.

He snapped back, "You've got a saucy mouth for a lady, and you'll give Lord Raymond a disgust of you. Besides, what does it matter to you whom I ruffle the covers with?"

Juliana blushed, mortified at being so justly reprimanded and worried the mere mention of bed-time activities would give Raymond a taste for them. "So it saves the eyes of the sewing maids. 'Twould be a fine idea, but what of a siege? My master castle-builder—" She snapped her mouth shut. The devil could fly away with him before she'd quote him to himself.

Raymond didn't point out her unconscious error. "I told you any opening is a weakness in the defenses, but when larger windows are added, it is usual to add them in an upper storey, above the great hall, as part of a solar."

"A solar?"

"A place away from your family and retainers, with ample room for your chests and our bed," Raymond explained. "A place with windows that allow the sun to light your weaving."

She was horrified. "Sleeping in a separate room from the people of the castle? But—"

"When spring comes, we'll have the master builder construct a stone structure for a proper solar, but for now Cuthbert will build walls for a makeshift room." Raymond moved closer to her. "It will be an addition for your pleasure."

"An addition for my pleasure? Are you mad?" She gripped the covers to keep from sliding into him. "No members of my family have ever so separated themselves from their people. It will encourage sedition, a lack of loyalty."

"Your words are your father's," Hugh said.

She turned on him, her fists bunched. "What's wrong with that? My father was right."

Hugh planted his feet, put his hands on his waist, and challenged her. "About everything?"

She wanted to cry, "Aye!" but she dared not. Too well she remembered her father's coldness as he withdrew from her after her ordeal. She'd needed him badly then. He'd failed her, and she couldn't help but wonder if he'd betrayed her, too. Not even Sir Joseph's admission eased the pain of her beloved father's defection. Her gaze fell; she scraped the furs with her nails and wished they were Hugh's eyes. "Go away, Hugh," she ordered. "Just go away."

Big, brash, and offended, Hugh stomped toward the fire.

"He means well," Raymond said.

"I know, but he's been a trial to me."

"Is he the one who hurt you?" Raymond probed.

"Hurt me?" She laughed weakly. Was she concealing a secret Raymond had already discovered? "Hugh wouldn't hurt me. Not deliberately. Anyway, I've forgiven him."

Raymond moved closer again, and propelled by a conspiracy of feathers and gravity, she tumbled into him. "Shall I kill him for you?"

Shaken by the offer, she exclaimed, "Nay!"

"I would. I would kill any man who hurt you. Did you hear what I told Hugh?"

Raymond sounded sincere, but men were tricksters all. "I . . . when?"

"When we stood beside the bed."

Her gaze dropped to her fingers, frantically groping for an anchor among the furs.

His hand covered hers; he pried the nervous digits from the strands and cradled them. He stroked her palm, tallying each callus with little circles that tickled. "Valeska and Dagna taught me to read palms. Would you like me to read yours?"

"Nay." But she stared, fascinated, as he traced

the long crease curving around her thumb.

"They would tell you your life line betrays how hard you work." His half smile brought a dimple straying to his cheek. "Actually, of course, they would be looking at the evidence of the work. You have blisters on your fingertips. What causes those?"

"Weaving," she answered, hypnotized by the slow dance of his fingers across her palm.

"Weaving," he repeated. "The slow intertwining of thread to form one cloth. Like you and me, becoming one through the blessing of wedlock. I told Hugh you were mine. My woman, my heiress, my bride."

Her attention snapped away from his compelling touch and back to the conversation. What was he trying to accomplish with this intimate tête-à-tête? She should stay alert, aware, on guard. She had only to remember she'd outshouted her beloved father, outsmarted the men who would barter her. She could outmanuever this sham castle-builder, for what weapon had he that the others did not? On a sour note, she said, "I suspect my role of heiress is the one that appeals to you."

He lifted her hand to his mouth, kissed each fingertip, warmed them with his breath, and her discontent slipped away. With his tongue, he touched them, soothed them, and she stirred in a sudden onset of uneasy craving. It was a craving she'd not felt for many years. A dangerous craving, a craving, in any case, never fulfilled, but it made her realize the sham castle-builder did indeed carry another weapon no other man could wield.

"Originally, before I knew you, it was the only part of you that appealed to me," he said. His subtle torture of tongue and mouth halted. "But with the broad side of a log, you knocked sense into me."

She would be on her guard, she resolved. The castle

builder was attempting seduction. "I only hit your shoulder," she replied.

"Aye, and as the wind from its passing whistled in my ear, I heard my destiny call me."

She shouldn't ask. She knew she shouldn't, but his expression, both puckish and resolute, piqued her curiosity. "Destiny?"

"The people of the desert believe in destiny. They believe whatever happens was meant to happen and a man should pursue his destiny with vigor."

Curiosity woke in her, distracted her from his able enticement. She had forgotten his escape from the Saracens. The tale had been sung by a minstrel, and Raymond of Avraché had been hailed as a hero, larger than life. She disputed the existence of heroes. In her experience, men strutted about in a glut of masculine vanity quite out of proportion to their deeds. But of all the men she'd met, only of Raymond could she believe such tales of bravery and daring. "What else did you learn on Crusade?"

He hesitated so briefly no other person would have noticed. She did and wondered what it signified, but he drove inquisitiveness from her with a cheerful declaration. "That as my destiny, I shall pursue you with vigor."

She tried to close her hand against him.

He wouldn't allow it. Following one of the lines that ran sideways across her palm, he said, "Valeska would say you're passionate, for the line of your heart is deep and strong. I'll be the man to tap that passion, and I would be lying if I said I didn't look forward to it."

"Passion." She gave a fair imitation of Sir Joseph's snort. "There's no passion in me. I'd just as soon visit a surgeon."

He threw back his head and laughed, a great ringing laughter that brought the activity in the great hall to a standstill.

She shushed him indignantly. "It's true. The pleasure's all for the man, and, in my case, I'm paying the cost for it."

That stopped his laughter, and he inhaled sharply as if he'd been struck.

He stroked his cheek; she heard the rough sound of stubble against skin, and wanted to stroke it, too. She wanted to tell him not to fret, that she'd marry him and keep him safe, but the next moment she realized her sentiment was absurd.

As if the beaten boy had never existed, Raymond grinned to display all his fine white teeth and became again the handsome, overly confident seducer of women. "That's true," he acknowledged. "So if I'm the noble equivalent of a harlot, I must assure your continued patronage."

Color burned her cheeks, although whether from her misplaced sympathy or his outrageous sentiments, she didn't know. The man confused and bemused her. She wished she'd never met him. And she wished she believed her own rantings.

"How old was your husband when you married?"

Rubbing her fingers over her forehead, she answered absently, "My husband was in the summer of his fifteenth year." In her own mind, she'd gained respect for the way she handled Raymond—and herself—in the snowy hut. Something about her had convinced him to abandon his plot to force their marriage and to assume a false identity. There'd been no profit in it for him, although he seemed to revel in the manufacture of tools and the endless digging.

He pointed to a tiny line on her palm. "See, there is your first marriage. And he died?"

Absently, she answered. "In the winter of his eighteenth year." Even before she'd known Raymond's true identity, his unspoken support had endowed her with the strength to dismiss Sir Joseph. He'd given her back something she'd been missing for these three years. Her backbone, her father would say, but it was more than that. A healing had begun.

Passing his hand over hers, Raymond pondered the evidence of her palm. "There's the scar of your grief. No woman finds pleasure with a boy. They're quick and selfish. How many years ago was that?"

Challenging him, she leaned back. "You tell me."

He examined her hand, front and back and said, "It's about ten years."

Remembering, she said, "I told you." She thought he watched her closely, but when she inspected him his gaze was fixed on her palm.

"Surely your father wished you to wed again."

Her newfound confidence failed her. "Nay."

"Hugh would have wed you."

"Nay."

"Felix—"

"Nay!" She jerked her hand out of his with such force she hit herself in the chin. Graceless, she supposed, but symbolic. "I don't want to marry. Until my father died, the king was satisfied with my widowed state. Would God he'd never heard of my father's death."

She would have said more, but he watched her with such interest that speech failed her. She wondered when this man would tire of her tantrums and hit her. Or was his punishment more subtle? Was he, even now, punishing her with these endless questions? Did he know the truth?

Raymond cupped her chin. Beguiling her like the dark prince, he whispered, "You didn't come to court, even when I so ordered you. Even when the king so ordered you. What did you think to gain by postponing our wedding?"

Dazed and unthinking, she told him, "Things happen. A disease might have killed you, or you might have died in battle or tournament. . . ." What had sounded so logical before she knew him now sounded cold, murderous.

His hand tightened slightly. "And if that had happened, do you think the king would have allowed you with your prime lands to go unwed?"

"They aren't prime," she insisted. She didn't like the way his eyes narrowed, she didn't like the way he held her, but she knew he wouldn't hurt her. "They're small."

"They're important, as you well know. Any lands close to the border of the Welsh are important to keep back the tide of barbarians."

"Some women are allowed to remain single," she retorted.

He smiled without mirth. "If they petition the king with a payment for his pocket, and if he believes those lands aren't at risk for invasion. Do you have the gold to offer the king?"

She stared at him mutinously.

"If I had died—if I died even yet—think you the king wouldn't betroth you to yet another man?" He moved closer, and she tried to scramble back, but he placed his knee on her legs to keep her in place. "Pray for me," he recommended. "Pray for my good health. The next man might not be so timid in his quest to gain your bed nor so kind when he hears the rumors of your past."

He rose above her, set on intimidating her with his size, his nobility, his male aggression.

"Did you think I would welcome you with open arms?" she whispered.

He made no attempt to lower his voice. "I had hoped you would be reasonable, but if you will not, I have weapons you barely understand or know how to use. If it comes to war, my lady, I am a veteran of battle and you are only a soft and pliant flower, easily trampled."

"You tricked me."

"*You* tricked me. You made me a laughingstock of Henry's court with your feeble excuses."

"You don't understand," she cried, frustrated. "What weapon does a woman have against the man she takes to husband? I was protecting myself and my children."

"Your children?"

"Children of a previous marriage are effortlessly disposed of, if the new husband so chooses. Daughters can be dismissed into a convent, or even found dead of an accident."

"I wouldn't do that to your children!" he said.

"I didn't know who you were!" she flared back. "I've given you charge of my children, and you admirably fulfilled that charge, but that doesn't wipe clean your deception. Had I taken like advantage of you, you would have exacted a terrible revenge."

He looked thoughtful. "Perhaps."

Encouraged, she added, "I had no reason to distrust before, but now I do."

"Are you saying you trust me with your children but not yourself?"

Why was he amused? Defiantly, she said, "Aye."

He moved until his body almost touched hers. "What kind of mother would give her children into the hands of a man she didn't trust to care for herself?"

She leaned back until her neck strained. "It's not like that."

"I think you fool yourself. I think you've surrendered all to me, and you wait only my desire to present it."

His pleasure was some kind of trick, she thought resentfully, an illusion produced by this charlatan to touch her tender heart. In a flurry to defend herself, she said, "My trust is my own to bestow. My hand is the King's to bestow. Be satisfied with what you're given by your sovereign, and never think of what I offered you."

For an answer, he bent his head over her palm. He brushed his fingers over it until it tingled, then rubbed the center back and forth, back and forth until she demanded, "What are you doing?"

"I was observing your line of destiny."

"There's no line of destiny. You're making that up."

"Not at all. Not everyone has a line of destiny, but you do. See the line that cuts right up the middle."

She peered past his finger. "Aye."

"That's your line of destiny."

"And what does my line of destiny say?"

"It says only one thing." He lifted his head and gazed into her eyes. "Raymond and again, Raymond, all your life long."

9

Raymond stomped through the frozen puddles in the bailey, breaking the thin layer of ice with his boots and exalting in the crunch as each perfectly smooth surface shattered.

Juliana wouldn't come to marry the unknown lord called Raymond because she'd hoped he would die, eh? He'd made his displeasure clear to her all through the morning, all through the dinner, and even until she sharply invited him to go outside and do battle with a warrior more worthy than she.

As if there were such a warrior. She had him by the ballocks, and they ached until he could only snarl and wonder how she could wish death on the man whom the king, in all his regal wisdom, had bestowed on her. Of course, if a scaly monster had brought that merchant ship from Algiers to Normandy, Henry would have awarded Juliana to him. The king was first a statesman and diplomat, second a humanitarian. And Raymond did know of men who would dispose of girl-children with no more conscience than tomcats.

Yet the thought that Juliana had, all unknowing, wished his death made Raymond sore and angry.

And the way she'd acted when Cuthbert measured for the solar! As if she were the only one with the right to make decisions about her castle. He'd thought she would be thrilled about a place where she could keep her trunks, speak with her children—and a chance to consummate her marriage in privacy. Instead she'd quoted her father to him.

Raymond had heard little to admire about her father. In fact, he had begun to suspect her father was to blame for much of her distrust of men.

He kicked at a frozen chunk of mud and cursed when it failed to yield, then scowled fiercely enough to guarantee privacy in the midst of a teaming castle crew. Layamon walked toward him, then swerved away. Sir Joseph stood in the door of the stable speaking with Felix, but at Raymond's appearance he ducked inside. After one panicked glance, Felix scurried toward the keep. Keir never flinched, so Raymond scowled twice at him.

Keir seemed unfazed, and in fact he hailed Raymond. " 'Tis a gray day," he greeted Raymond. "I believe there will be snow before nightfall."

Raymond grunted.

Keir hefted a pickax, its head new and shiny, its handle smoothed by a patient workman. "Carry these picks to the men below. With this hard freeze, they'll need them."

"Can't some serf do your bidding?" Raymond asked in irritation.

"But you are going to the diggings," Keir pointed out, piling picks into Raymond's arms.

"I am?"

Keir glanced around the bailey. "You were going elsewhere?"

"I could have been," Raymond said righteously. "I could be visiting the men-at-arms or the stables."

"The *real* master castle-builder has gone down to view the destruction." At Raymond's glare, Keir corrected himself. "The construction."

"I'll take the picks," Raymond said, his arms already loaded.

As matter-of-fact as if he discussed the weather, Keir asked, "Have you got your apples caught in Lady Juliana's press?" He studied the frustration twisting Raymond's expression. "It's true, I see. In my opinion, you expect too much of that proud lady."

"Damn your opinion," Raymond snarled.

In no way did Keir indicate he'd heard. "Lady Juliana wouldn't wish to bed a man who made a fool of her, yet if I may offer some suggestions—"

"You may not," Raymond answered.

"Although you've humiliated her, still there is evidence she trusts you. That's a big concession from a woman as wary of men as she seems to be. As I noted in Tunis, you project an aura of reassurance that should prove an asset in this instance." Raymond grumbled, but Keir continued, "If you would woo her as gently as a maid, and treat her with respect, her mistrust will wane."

Raymond leaned forward until his nose almost touched Keir's. "I don't need advice on how to handle a mere woman."

"Please be careful," Keir advised. "The load of picks will shift, and if one should strike your foot, you'll be most unhappy."

"I am careful, I'm just telling you—"

One of the picks tumbled off the load in his arms, and Keir caught it. "One hopes you can handle your mere woman with more success," he said, straight-faced.

Raymond sucked in a gulp of cold air to retort and coughed with the shock to his lungs. When his eyes cleared, Keir had retreated into the smithy and shut the door in his face.

Damn Keir. Damn his expressionless, all-knowing face. Damn him for always being right. Raymond's very bones ached with desire. He didn't want to woo Juliana like a maid, he wanted to handle her like a woman. He'd dreamed of a passionate woman, a woman who would be giving and kind and love him unconditionally.

Juliana had fulfilled almost all his dreams, and her generosity made him all the more eager. She'd given him so much, but like a greedy boy he wanted it all. He wanted to taste her, pet her, let her envelop him in the body that had disturbed his sleep for too long.

And when he tried to righteously claim he would be gifting her with himself, his own humbled conceit made him ashamed. Perhaps he would be good for her: shoulder the defenses, remove Sir Joseph, keep her daughters safe. But always he taunted himself. Was he really man enough, was he really skilled enough to cure Juliana of her fears? And when they were joined, would he be able to keep the gaping darkness of his own soul from her?

The load of picks shifted, and he swayed with the changing weight. He didn't lose his balance. He never lost his balance, except with that sweet-faced widow.

Aye, damn Keir for his clearsightedness. And damn him, for he'd loaded Raymond with twice as many picks as he'd give any other man. Damn Keir and damn this *real* castle-builder.

"Lord Raymond? Lord Raymond!"

With a start, Raymond responded to the call.

"What?" he barked. He found himself standing on the drawbridge, arms full of pickaxes, glaring at the frozen trench and the workers who clustered around the fire. The king's castle-builder—the *real* castle-builder, Raymond thought spitefully—was screaming instructions and imprecations in French. Not surprisingly, the men, all of whom spoke English, stared with open mouths at—what was his name? Oh, aye. Papiol.

"Lord Raymond!" Tosti hailed him, gesturing wildly. "What's this strange fellow talkin' about? We can't understand a word."

No work was getting done, so Raymond slid down the slope until he reached the fire.

"Let me take those fer ye," Tosti said, soothing Raymond's pride. "Our new lord shouldn't be carryin' such things."

As the men removed pickaxes from Raymond's arms, he asked in English, "How did you know I was your new lord?"

"Well, ye weren't no castle builder, that's certain." Tosti nodded.

Raymond pointed at Papiol. "He's the king's castle-builder."

"May th' Madonna save us," Tosti said piously. "Is that what he's been ahowlin' about?"

With a grin, Raymond reached for his tool belt—and it wasn't there. Only his jewelled dagger, a present from Henry, remained around his waist. Inside the great hall, in the company of other knights, he'd felt foolish strapping on a tool belt. Out here, with the serfs shouting questions at him, he felt foolish carrying a ceremonial dagger.

Ah, well. It took a good sham castle-builder to put things to rights.

"My lord." In an excess of passion, Papiol pulled at his greasy brown hair. "These men are imbeciles. All Englishmen are imbeciles. They pretend they do not understand me, no matter how loud I shout."

"It's all right," Raymond soothed in French. "I'll speak to them."

"And look what they did." Papiol pointed a shaking finger at the trench. "They dug an immense hole in the middle of the winter. Of what use is this immense hole in the middle of the winter? Any fool knows castles are constructed in the summer. In the summer, I tell you."

Raymond's smile and his sense of superiority disappeared. "They seem to have done a good job preparing the foundation."

"Preparing the foundation?" Papiol was screaming again. "What foundation? 'Tis nothing but dirt!"

"But the foundation—"

"Must be dug in the summer." Papiol recollected to whom he spoke and explained in impassioned courtesy. "My lord, in summer we dig, we strike bedrock, we put up some of the wall, winter comes, we wait, summer comes, we put up the rest of the wall."

Incredulous, Raymond asked, "Two years for one wall?"

Papiol spread his hands in a fatalistic gesture. "It is the way."

"Well, the way should be changed. We'll finish digging the foundation now, and by the end of the summer we'll have the wall up."

Again Papiol forgot to whom he spoke. "But we cannot dig. The dirt is frozen solid."

Raymond paid no heed. "We'll have the wall up by spring. Tosti!"

Tosti leaped to attention.

In English, Raymond commanded, "The castle builder says he wants you to take those pickaxes and dig the hole deeper."

The men glanced doubtfully at Papiol. "The *real* castle-builder?" Tosti asked.

Raymond ignored Tosti's distrust. "We'll feed you well every day you come to work. At Christmastide, we'll have a feast for your families, too."

"Every day?" Tosti asked, agog.

"Every day," Raymond said. "We'll do the upper end of the wall now, and finish the lower end and the gatehouse in summer."

"Hey, th' twelve days will be a joyful time this year," Tosti yelled, and the men cheered. Shouldering their axes, they slithered into the trench. Only Tosti remained above ground, and he gazed down the river. "There's snow abrewin' in those clouds. Do we get fed if we can't work?"

Raymond had a vision of men struggling through snowdrifts to fill their bellies. "Stay home if the snow is too deep. The elves will not do the work while you're gone."

Tosti chuckled and headed down to join his friends. "Nay, I suppose they won't. Never been that lucky before."

Raymond threw his arm around the real master castle-builder and led him toward the castle. "The men want to keep digging," he confided.

"Idiots!" Papiol railed. "I am the king's master castle-builder. I have learned my craft through hard work, years of study, years of working with every trade. This is impossible, I tell you."

"Has it ever been tried?" Raymond asked.

"Never!"

"Then we don't know it's impossible, do we?" Cheerful, Raymond swung to greet Layamon. "What is it?"

Layamon's demeanor sobered him. "M'lord, riders approach th' castle."

"Riders?" Raymond was startled. "More guests?"

"Don't know, m'lord. Would ye like me t'raise th' drawbridge?"

"Allow me a look," Raymond said, bounding toward the ladder that led to the curtain wall. The party of riders was far off, racing toward the castle to beat the storm, and as Raymond leaned through the crenellations he said, "Quite a lot of company we've been having."

Layamon agreed. "Aye, m'lord, I've never seen th' like. Lord Felix and Lord Hugh just yesterday, the castle builder last evening, and now more folk arrivin'."

"Is it not Hugh's habit to visit at Christmastide?"

"Not his habit, m'lord, although he's been here once or twice. Nor is it Lord Felix's habit t' travel in th' winter." Layamon's lips curled scornfully. "Might muss his hair."

Layamon's unspoken skepticism bolstered Raymond's unease, and he remembered Hugh's odd behavior just this morning. What was he doing, trying to convince Raymond not to marry Juliana? Just the night before, Raymond had thought Hugh was, if not happy about the union, at least resigned. What worm had eaten at the man's mind and cocked it askew?

"How do you suppose," Raymond wondered, "rumors of my construction came to the attention of Hugh and Felix?"

Layamon pulled his ear. "'Tis almost a miracle,

m'lord. In th' summer in these parts, news passes from castle t' castle wi' th' freemen who drive their wares t' market an' back, an' th' minstrels wander from one place t' another, composing songs an' singin' them fer a loaf. But in winter—" He shook his head. " 'Specially this winter."

"Especially this winter?"

"It started so early wi' such a snowstorm—ye remember, m'lord. Still an' all, Lord Hugh could have come, but Lord Felix, too? Did they start th' journey together? Did they meet on th' road?"

"You're a suspicious man," Raymond said, and met Layamon's gaze.

Layamon nodded. "Aye, m'lord, there's some that'd say so."

Raymond laid his hand on Layamon's shoulder. "You're a fine commander. My lady Juliana chose wisely."

"Thank ye, m'lord. Should I be suspicious about this batch, do ye think?"

A rich band of horsemen, Raymond observed as they rode closer. Their banners flapped in the freshening breeze, and the women who rode in the middle drew up their hoods against the sudden flurry of snow. "That's no fighting troupe. I don't recognize . . ." Raymond squinted through the lowering clouds and frowned. "It can't be . . . ah, nay." He dropped his head into his hand. "My saints have surely deserted me today."

"Should I raise th' drawbridge, m'lord?"

When Raymond raised his head, he saw an eager Layamon. "No such luck," Raymond replied. "Those are my parents."

* * *

"The cream wool is fine, my lady. The finest I've ever seen." Valeska patted the balls of yarn stacked in the basket. " 'Twill make a beautiful cloth."

"Aye." Juliana's hand flew and her right foot tapped on the treadle of the loom. "It will."

"Your arm must be weary, my lady. Let me work on it a bit," Valeska said.

Smiling, Juliana shook her head.

"What will you make with it?" Dagna asked curiously.

"I don't know." From Juliana's left hand to right and back again, the shuttle travelled between the even threads of the warp. Quickly the threads of the warp crossed, catching fast the thread the shuttle left behind. " 'Tis too light a color for everyday use. I should have dyed it."

Valeska winked at Dagna. "Why didn't you?"

"I don't know." Juliana thumped the hand bar furiously, making enough noise to cover the sound of the old women's amused speculations. She did know, of course. So did everyone else. She was appalled by the state of Raymond's wardrobe. The king's cousin should be dressed in more than a ragged cloak, a cheap chainse, and worn hose. She provided a suit of clothes for every man, woman, and child on her land. Why shouldn't she provide one for Raymond?

She glanced sideways at the old women's smirking faces.

No reason, but everyone insisted on treating it as an event. Surreptitiously, she touched the fine cloth. This *was* beautiful, and she was being unusually stern about the quality, but a sleeveless cream-colored surcoat would accent Raymond's dark beauty. She imagined it worn over a long-sleeved and high-necked green tunic.

It would be fine.

That she had woven a cloth of just that green color last winter and put it away for some special garment was a fortunate coincidence. Even now, Fayette cut the green, smiling slyly all the while. The hand bar thumped, the treadle thudded, and she shut her ears to the sounds of the great hall. Bringing the shuttle back and forth again, she slammed the hand bar hard.

It resulted in a tight weave, she told herself with a righteous sniff.

A hand touched her neck. She looked up with an annoyed exclamation—and leaped backward from the florid face that peered at her.

"Juliana?" Felix bobbed up and down, filling her vision, touching her.

Her skin crawled as his fingers crept along her collarbone like some repulsive new insect, and she brushed him away. "Don't!"

He was too odorous, too greasy, too close. He was her worst nightmare, recurring to bring her down. But another hand, a supporting hand, touched her, and Valeska snapped, "What do you want with my mistress, little lord?"

The disrespect of it broke Juliana's obsessed stare, and as Felix reared back to slap the old woman, she snagged his wrist. "You're too free with those blows, Felix," she told him.

As Felix sputtered in shock, she tightened her grasp. Then the enormity of her challenge struck her, her fingers trembled, and she dropped them to her lap. Folding one hand over the other, she pressed her palms together. The strength of her own grip comforted her, gave her courage.

"She's disrespectful," he said.

"She's my personal maid." It wasn't an answer, nor the truth.

His eyebrows waggled, his nose twitched. "She's a witch."

"Who told you that?" Juliana asked sharply.

Felix shrugged, and his gaze shifted away from her. "Why did someone have to tell me? Why do you always treat me like a Looby Lumpkin? I have my own thoughts. Everyone always treats me like a Looby Lumpkin. I can see she's a witch." Waving his hands, he said, "She's . . . she's ugly."

"So are you," Valeska retorted.

Felix reached out again, but something stopped him. Valeska knew she had won, for she showed her three teeth in a grin.

Juliana didn't trust the old dame to keep her mouth shut, and besides, Dagna had taken her place at Juliana's other shoulder. Juliana gave Valeska a push. "Go now and assist Fayette with her sewing."

"Isn't she competent to cut your precious cloth?" Valeska teased.

"So she is," Juliana answered. "But you know Raymond's measurements."

Valeska touched the cream cloth on the loom. "Who will cut this?"

"I will." Juliana pushed her again. "Go."

Valeska walked away, cackling in her best witch imitation, and Felix made the sign to ward off the evil eye. "She really is a witch," he said in awe. He demanded of Juliana, "Is she a witch?"

Dagna's hostility rang in her melodious voice as her hand tightened on Juliana's back. "There are some in the castle who believe so."

"Aye." Felix edged around until he could watch Valeska. "Aye."

He fumbled with his cloak, smoothed his well-combed hair, while Juliana watched and meditated on the futility of it. Felix draped himself in the best materials, cut only in the most fashionable styles. He groomed himself meticulously, and constantly checked himself in the polished metal mirror that hung from a thong about his waist. Yet he was nothing but a bully rooster, a man to watch lest he do accidental harm.

Only the shabbiest clothing graced Raymond's figure, and he cared not whether he kept his hair trimmed. He shaved infrequently, and yet . . . and yet, that dark shadow on his chin made her wonder how it would feel on her skin. The too long locks swept rakishly across his shoulders, glistening like exotic silk. His clothing—well. Juliana glanced across the room at Valeska and Fayette. His clothing would soon do honor to a prince.

"I've had some thoughts on your marriage."

She jerked her attention to Felix. "What?"

"I've had some thoughts on your marriage," he repeated.

"*You've* had some thoughts?" she questioned. "Amazing."

"Aye." He bobbed in agreement. "I knew you'd want to hear them."

"I'd like to hear any thought of *yours*." Again Juliana emphasized her amazement; again Felix remained oblivious.

"This Lord Raymond is a bit odd." He leaned close to her to whisper, and the odor of him struck her. "There are rumors circulating about him."

"Rumors?" She leaned as far back as she could without tumbling off the bench. "Rumors don't interest me."

Oblivious to her discouragement, he blithely told her, "He was captured by the Saracens."

"Aye, while on Crusade, fighting to free Jerusalem from the Infidels. Have you never been moved to take up the cross?"

"Nay." He licked his palm and smoothed his eyebrows. "Nay."

"You wouldn't want to get rumpled."

"Exactly." He nodded.

Juliana blew a stream of air up her face to cool it. How could she mock a man who had no modesty, no sense of fallibility?

Still obtuse, Felix prattled, "They say Lord Raymond was enslaved for years."

Clenching the hand bar, Juliana stilled her irritation. She didn't approve of such gossip. Didn't really want to hear it. But she hungered to hear about Raymond, hungered for any scrap of his past, and so she said, "Years?"

"At least a year. And they say he mucked out the stables." Ever the busybody, Felix relished the gossip. He laughed in little snorts, and when he could contain himself, he delivered the wildest part of the tale. "They say he fought so fiercely, the Saracens soldered an iron collar around his neck."

Juliana forgot her troubles, her apprehensions, all the parts of herself. Instead she concentrated on Felix and his loathsome gossip, for something stirred in her. It wasn't true, of course. It couldn't be true, that a knight as proud and powerful as Raymond would be chained.

She looked at Dagna, but Dagna watched Felix without expression. Dagna wouldn't interfere with his recitation, but neither would she affirm it.

Low and gleeful, Felix said, "He went mad. Your

Lord Raymond went mad. They say he still goes mad if he's gainsaid. You know you made me hit you. I only hit you because you made me. What will your Lord Raymond do when you refuse him? He'll go mad. He'll foam at the mouth like a dog in midsummer, and you'll have no place to run." Felix grasped her upper arm with fingers that squeezed too tightly. "He's a berserker, I tell you."

Hand on pounding heart, she stared at him in frozen fascination. "Why are you telling me this?"

He sighed. "Because I want to be friends again. I'm warning you because I'm your friend. Let bygones be bygones."

"Is that all you think it takes? Just the words to heal the scar?"

"Nay," he assured her, ever eager to show his magnanimity. "I want to do more than just give you warning. I want to offer you sanctuary."

He leaned back, his hands tucked across his belly, the picture of a satisfied burgher, and she wondered if it were he who'd gone mad.

"Aye, Juliana, I offer you sanctuary. I'll rescue you and wed you myself." He swept her with his smug glance. "Surely you'd prefer me over a madman."

Quietly, but definitely, she replied, "Nay."

Undeterred, he swept on. "Surely you'd prefer a man who wants a mere duo of heirs from you." He held wide his arms. "Look at me! I'll spend most of my time in bed with my own pastry. That's Anne. Remember Anne?"

She nodded numbly.

"All you'll have to do is supervise the cooking and the cleaning, take care of the laundry and the, er"— he gestured at the loom—"the weaving."

"What an inducement," she whispered.

"I thought you'd appreciate it."

He sat his loathsome body down beside her. His hip touched hers, his arm wrapped around her waist—and she realized he no longer intimidated her. She'd never again cringe from his pompous threats, nor duck when he swung at her. He meant nothing. This ridiculous little man meant nothing. He offered marriage, and rather than run from him screaming, a grim mirth bubbled within her.

He said, "We could go to my castle."

Mouth skewed with distaste, she asked, "Do you believe this berserker, as you call him, would allow us to travel through the countryside with nary an attack?"

Unease touched his face. "We'd have to kill him."

"Kill the king's cousin?" His stupidity ground away at her, releasing irritation and some other emotion. She couldn't put a name to it, but her fists clenched. "Someone would hang for that. Who do you suppose it would be?"

"Well, not me," he said huffily.

He was so stupid. She couldn't help it. She laughed.

Unamused, Felix said, "You try to be so rational. You try to be a man."

"Nay, Felix," she corrected. "I don't lack for ambition."

Dagna chuckled, but Felix's face remained blank.

"You want someone like me," he said. "Not someone like Raymond who watches you and lusts after you day and night. He's an animal, they say, with ravenous appetites. They say—"

Unease touched Juliana. This donkey who called himself a man had less intelligence than her loom; so how could he be presenting such cogent reasons to end her betrothal? Unerringly he touched on her fears and her wishes, and Juliana cried out, "Who told you these things?"

He glanced around as if assassins lurked behind every oak column. "Just . . . a trustworthy person. He's always been my friend. And yours, too." His brown eyes squinted into hers. "He has your best interests at heart."

Hugh, she thought. Hugh had said these things. Her disappointment brought a bite to her tone. "Do you believe everything you hear?"

Again she unhinged him, and he reacted with irritation. "This cynicism of yours is not attractive. No knight will want you."

"Every time I express sentiments that deviate from those of a harlot or a mat"—she kicked at the rushes on the floor—"you say I'm unfeminine. Why would I want a man who's so dogmatic?"

His mouth hung open; he breathed through it noisily. "You . . . you act almost like a man."

"So do you, Felix. So do you."

She watched as the barb worked its way into his mind. When it struck the vital spot, and he understood at last, his eyes popped. Quick as a snake, he slapped at her, but she caught his hand, and he shrieked, "Bushbitch! Worthless daughter of Diabolus!"

Heads swerved, all chatter stopped.

Fear, anger, a sense of her own rightness gripped her, and as her emotions grappled with her good sense, he snatched her up. "I offered you marriage!" he yelled, and she heard the echo of that time long ago. "I would save you from your shame! And you refuse me. Refuse *me*. I'll show you what kind of man you trifle with. I'll show you."

He tried to wrap his arms around her, to push her head against his shoulder. He wanted to punish her with those tight-lipped asphyxiations he called kisses. Dagna leaped toward them, but rebellion exploded in Juliana. "Nay!" she screamed. Struggling to free her arm, she knocked Dagna away and cried, "He's mine."

"A quaint little castle." Isabel, Countess of Locheais, removed her riding gloves while sweeping her fine emerald gaze over the keep. "Quite quaint."

Geoffroi, Count of Locheais, placed his hands on his hips and squared his shoulders. "It certainly isn't what we're used to, is it, Raymond?"

Jerking his head, Raymond ordered the stable boys to tend to the horses. Careful to reveal no emotion, nothing which his parents could use against him, he answered. "Nothing about this place is what I'm used to, Father."

"I would say not. Looks paltry with the clouds all around and the snow drifting down. Doubt the wolves would bother to attack it." Geoffroi's face was sculpted with all the care of the creator and maintained with all the care of man. It drooped now in noble disdain. "Thought you and Henry were still close. Can't imagine him shipping you off to protect some shoddy little dab of a castle like this."

Raymond corrected him. "He sent me to succeed to this castle."

"Aye, when he told us where you were, we came straight away." Laying one long, straight finger on his cheek, Raymond's mother asked in elegant distress, "Tell me, *mon petit*, are you quarrelling with the king? Because I don't need to remind you that's not good for the family."

"Nay, Mother, you needn't remind me." Raymond smiled without mirth. "Henry and I are not quarrelling—or at least not much. He has granted me my dearest wish—properties and an income of my own."

His parents exchanged weighted glances, and as always they seemed to have planned their attack for every eventuality.

His mother was the chosen emissary this time. "But at what a price? You know we would have given you the income of Avraché when you were ready to assume the responsibility."

"When would that have been, Mother?"

Clasping her soft, pale hands together, she moaned. "But this . . . this marriage! To a nobody, a woman never even introduced to the king."

This time she refused to answer his question, Raymond noted. Next time, she would lie. He corrected, "Not to a nobody, Mother. To Juliana." Somehow her name lightened his heart, acted as a talisman against the poison of his parents.

"Juliana?" Geoffroi cocked an insolent brow. "Attractive bit of skirt?"

Raymond took a steady breath of frigid air. It never did any good to get angry with his parents. They were cold and manipulative, and when he lost his temper, he lost the tournament. But to hear his Juliana disparaged in such a way . . . "I doubt you're familiar with a woman like Juliana." He smiled back just as insolently, and his gaze slid to his mother. "She's a noble lady."

Again his parents consulted each other with their gazes. Geoffroi clapped him on the back. Isabel folded him in her scented embrace. *"Mon petit,"* she murmured. "Is she every mother's dream?"

"As you are every daughter-in-law's nightmare,"

Raymond answered, disengaging himself from the tangle of arms that clung like tentacles.

Isabel sputtered, surprised for once, but Raymond didn't pause to savor his victory. It had become important to reach Juliana's side, to protect her from these manipulating monsters who called themselves his parents.

"Wait, son!"

Raymond stopped with his back to his parents. "Father?"

"We have a little gift for you."

A little bribe, more like. Swivelling on his heel, Raymond murmured, "Indeed?"

Geoffroi thrust a heavy purse into Raymond's hand with barely a wince. "'Twill buy you a handsome outfit. You haven't been appearing before the king like that, have you?"

Spreading his arms wide, Raymond glanced down at himself, then cast an amused glance at his parents. "Not good for the family?" he mocked.

The derision missed Geoffroi. "The king might not approve. But the purse is filled with gold." His gaze lingered on the leather pouch. "Buy what you need."

Raymond balanced the purse. "Gold," he repeated. Gold, they thought, would erase his memory of past injustices and render him more amenable to their schemes. "I'll keep the gold—and buy Juliana a marriage gift." Ignoring their sputtering dismay, he indicated the wooden stairs that led to the second story which housed the great hall.

"Primitive." Geoffroi snorted. "Primitive."

Ignoring both his father's comment and his mother's curled lip, Raymond held the stairs steady as his parents climbed. When they stood perched on the landing, eyeing the unrailed space around them, Raymond bounded up. In an unkind grip, he held their arms and warned, "You'll not hurt Juliana, or you'll be dusting the dirt of the road off your rumps."

Beneath his hand, Geoffroi's pectorals tightened. "Now see here, boy—"

"I am not a boy." Raymond looked at his father's face, so similar to his own. "I'm not as heartless, or as treacherous, or as cunning as you." Geoffroi tried to interrupt, but Raymond raised his chin and Geoffroi stopped. "But I could be. I had, after all, the best tutors."

"Ah, Raymond." Isabel sounded unutterably sad, but a slight shake of Geoffroi's head halted her.

He sounded gruff and sincere when he said, "Our son's right, *ma cherie*. We've been dreadful parents, and if this lady is the wife he wants, why, we should help his suit in every way."

By which he meant, Raymond supposed, that they would have to sneak around to perform their dirty deeds. He didn't care. He'd surrounded Juliana with a cushion of devotion, and during those few times he would have to leave her side, his dear witches were more than a match for his parents. With a chilly smile, he opened the door and led them down the dark passage. "Juliana is a woman without guile. Her voice is ever low, her smile sweet and soft."

A shriek cut off his recital, and Raymond stopped to listen.

"What was that?" Isabel asked.

"One of my new daughters, possibly, playing with her puppy." He moved on, hugging his delight in his heart. "Did you know you were now a grandmother, Mother?"

From behind, a choking sound rewarded him. He'd stabbed her vanity—surely a major wound. Bland as new-cream pudding, he continued his lecture. "Juliana is gentle and kind. Wherever she goes, birds sing." Another shout echoed off the stones, closer this time. "Flowers blossom." He quickened his step. "The sun shines." This shout sounded angry. Raymond broke into a run and burst into the great hall.

Across the room, Juliana fought with a red-faced Felix. Raymond leaped toward her, but too late. With one mighty swing of her arm, she brought her open palm up under Felix's nose. Cartilage crunched, blood spurted.

Felix screamed and doubled over.

Gaping stupidly, Raymond stared at his bride as she cried, "Never touch me again, or not even your dog will recognize you!"

From behind Raymond came the encouraged voices of his parents.

"Gentle and kind?" Isabel cooed.

"Sweet and soft?" Geoffroi chuckled. "How like you, son, to describe your Valkyrie as a saint."

Juliana heard the voices. She didn't understand, or care. She could only stare at Felix, who screamed imprecations while the blood from his nose seeped between his fingers. Lifting her hands, she stared at them. They trembled. Bruised by the force of her blow, one throbbed to the beat of her heart.

Felix straightened, and his reddened eyes bulged as if he couldn't comprehend that she had been the instrument of his defeat.

She almost said, "I'm sorry," but she would have been lying. She was sorry he was hurt, but not sorry she had done it. Someone should have done it years ago.

She should have done it years ago.

A roar filled her ears. She was shoved back; she

realized Felix had sprung at her. Dagna caught him. Valeska joined the wrestling pair. Hugh arrived. They took hold of Felix, subdued him, sat on him. The women shouted words Juliana couldn't understand. Hugh's bass boomed, "Let me see it." They grappled with Felix, and Juliana's hysterical laugh bubbled up.

Felix feared to have them touch his nose.

Juliana wanted to snicker at his absurdity.

She wanted to cry at her own cowardice and laugh at her own bravery.

She felt sick, yet at the same time a sense of wonder gripped her.

She had defeated Felix.

She wanted to savor her victory, but her stomach churned. Closing her eyes, she held her breath. Someone caught at her. She opened her eyes—Raymond. Raymond, looking intense and questioning. Raymond—oh, God, she didn't want to vomit on Raymond. Pushing him aside, she headed outdoors. Another man veered into her path; she stepped aside to avoid him, but his face shocked her into temporary sanity.

It was Raymond's face. Raymond's face worn by an older man. Raymond's face with cold brown eyes. That was too much. With a wail, she fled the great hall.

10

"*You can't throw* Felix out. He can't ride with a broken nose."

Raymond ignored Juliana's tug on his arm. "He doesn't sit on his nose."

Digging her heels into the reeds that littered the floor, she slowed his angry march. "Felix is harmless."

He turned fiercely on his betrothed. "Then why did you hit him?"

"Oh . . ." She shuffled her feet and gazed at the beamed ceiling of the great hall. "Just to prove I could, I suppose."

"Prove to whom?"

She thought about that. "To me."

Something about her—her breathless glow, her amazement—softened him, and he bolstered his ire. "Then let me prove I can hit him, too."

" 'Tis unnecessary. I struck him in his weakest place."

"His nose?"

She grinned. "His vanity."

He laughed; he couldn't help it. "Bold woman, how you delight me."

Geoffroi agreed. "Bold indeed. To think you called her sweet and soft. I had forgotten your droll humor."

"Not Raymond, my dear," Isabel said. "He has no humor. He's depressingly earnest."

Raymond stiffened. Ever since their arrival this very afternoon, his parents had been shamelessly eavesdropping, poking and prodding at him and at Juliana like warriors circling to break a siege.

Juliana had been all that was gracious.

He had not. Juliana pushed him down onto a bench by the fire. "Let me get you some wine, my lord. 'Twill relax you."

"I don't want to relax. I want to show that twitching, moaning gazob what happens when he treats my woman poorly."

His voice rose, and she rubbed his shoulders. "I already showed him."

"Why did you show him?" he demanded. "Did he advise you against marrying me?"

Her startled expression answered him. He leaped to his feet and started toward the prostrate Felix, but Juliana caught him before he reached Felix's pallet. "Aren't you pleased with my response? Once I would have agreed I should not wed you."

He looked down at her, all rumpled and pleading, and his fury gave way to her wiles once more. "Aye, once you would have agreed. Have you then changed your mind about wedding the king's choice?"

"Did she pretend she didn't want you to whet your appetite?" Isabel asked.

"I've had the devil's own time convincing Juliana to wed me." Raymond snarled. "And now she's met my kinsfolk, she'll be doubly reluctant."

Isabel tittered. "How naive you are, son." To her

maid, she said, "Set up my embroidery frame here, close to the fire. There are drafts in this keep. You should put up tapestries, Juliana. Decorative, and so useful, too. I see you're constructing a solar. Most fashionable. All the best castles in Europe have them."

Juliana's hands dropped from Raymond's arm. "So I've heard."

Raymond rolled his eyes at Hugh, and Hugh buried his nose in his cup to contain his laughter. Keir, the coward, was nowhere to be found. Raymond said, "Juliana is like the wild rose, glorious in texture and scent."

Isabel sniffed. "The thorns are thick."

"I'm not a clumsy boy," Raymond answered. "I know how to pluck the rose." His parents exchanged glances over his head, but he tossed the purse of gold. It annoyed his father, he knew, to see his money treated so casually, and Raymond enjoyed the unique sensation of coins in his possession.

Never before had the great hall, with its central fire and its torches dipped in pitch, seemed anything less than welcoming. It had been an extension of Juliana; old-fashioned, none too comfortable, but his. Tonight the room overflowed with his parents, their pallets and furs and screens and retainers. The smoke irritated his eyes, the light flickered ominously, and the great hall reminded him of the netherworld.

But of course it would when this paternal devil and his dam came to call.

The unwieldy wooden contraption that supported Isabel's needlework was placed before her. Her maid threaded a needle and passed it to her mistress. Isabel dipped it into the delicate cloth and asked, "Juliana, where is your needlework?"

Juliana glanced up. "I don't do needlework."

"Don't do? . . ." Isabel cleared her throat. "I see."

Juliana answered Isabel's unspoken accusation of laziness. "I prefer weaving. I like to see the cloth take shape under my hands, and to plan the garment I will make from it."

Isabel smiled with chilly politeness. "How quaint. She sews, too."

"Weaving is less intricate." Juliana hugged Ella and Margery, who were waiting for her to kiss them goodnight. "With these children and the larger male children"—she looked pointedly at Hugh and at Raymond—"all clamoring for attention, weaving suits me."

"You consider my son a child?" Geoffroi picked his teeth with the golden toothpick his serving man had presented after the evening meal. "An insulting view from a woman, but nevertheless I must agree. He takes action thoughtlessly. Witness his disastrous foray to the Crusades."

Raymond's hands flexed in his lap, and the coins jiggled. "Father."

Geoffroi slapped his palm to his forehead. "Doesn't she know? Rest assured, son, I'll not tell her."

"Nothing could be shameful about taking up the cross to win back the Holy Land from the Infidels." Juliana patted her daughters and said, "Wish our guests a good-night."

Geoffroi waved the curtseying children away as he answered in a voice guaranteed to stir curiosity. "There's much you do not know."

Juliana refused to seize the bait offered so temptingly. "The basest slavery is ennobled when endured for our Lord's sake."

Raymond was amused by the almost painful disdain on his parents' faces. When he had first announced his intention to take the cross, they told him that only knights who sought riches and salvation joined the Crusades. With the cockiness of youth, Raymond had asked which of those he had a surfeit of. They'd been sour, but they were unable to promise him heaven and unwilling to release lands to his control. So he had gone to Tunis, and paid the toll with his courage. "My bride's piety is to be commended."

"She cooks well," Isabel said, obviously displeased with the direction of Raymond's thoughts. She, too, waved the courtesy of the children aside. "The meal was adequate, considering the supplies she works with." She turned to her husband. "We should give them a wedding gift of spices. Perhaps some peppercorns. They add such savor to the food, and mask that aged taste of the meat."

Juliana sat down at her loom as if she hadn't heard, and Raymond murmured, "Your frustration is showing, Mother."

"The food was hot," Geoffroi commented in his sonorous voice. "An amazing feat in this weather."

"Hot? Well, not hot, but not cold." Isabel considered Juliana, her head cocked to one side. "Not even in the king's palace does the meat arrive without being congealed in its juices. How do you do it?"

Picking up the shuttle, Juliana ran her hand over its smooth wood and admitted, "My kitchen is below stairs."

Isabel blinked. "Below stairs?"

"In the undercroft," Juliana clarified, her gaze on the web of cloth.

"In the undercroft? That's madness! What of fire?" Geoffroi asked.

Annoyance brought a sharp edge to Juliana's voice. "The fire is contained."

"Contained? Contained? I find it hard to believe this keep isn't a burned shell." Geoffroi lifted one foot as if he already felt the flames licking his toes.

Juliana looked up now, her lips set firmly. "The kitchen's been in the undercroft for two years now, and we've had no such incidents."

"No one has the kitchen in the undercroft," Isabel said.

"I do," Juliana said stubbornly.

"In noble castles, this isn't done."

That seemed to be Isabel's final word on the subject, but Geoffroi turned to his son. "You'll cure her of this lunacy, of course."

Raymond said, " 'Tis a woman's decision."

"A woman's decision?" Geoffroi seemed honestly scandalized. "When a fire from within could destroy a castle's ability to repulse attackers?"

Raymond swallowed his trepidation. "Not all can remain as it was during your youth."

"I see what it is. You're soft on the woman." Geoffroi bent his lips into a dictatorial smile. "Let me give you some advice. It never pays to be soft on a woman."

Raymond looked at his mother. She formed the other half of the iron tongs that pinched him, gripped him, threw him in the fires of hell, for money or prestige. "I'll remember that."

Unconvinced of his son's sincerity, Geoffroi leaned into the attack. "If you were a real man, you'd settle this matter right now."

The battle cry of manipulative fathers caught Raymond unprepared. He rose to his feet, primed to satisfy the masculine challenge even if he had to crush Juliana's pride to rubble. Only a small, eager voice saved him.

"Lord Raymond," squeaked Ella, "may we sit in your lap?"

He looked down at the two skinny, smiling children. Ella was blissfully unaware of the fire raging in him, and even Margery underestimated the danger. She watched him with grave eyes, waiting to see if he would accept the invitation to join her inner circle, not realizing she'd picked a moment of raging male ego to extend the invitation.

Juliana knew. "I yield!" she proclaimed. "The kitchen shall be as my lord commands. Only don't . . ." She clasped her hands in supplication. "My lord Raymond, I beg you, don't . . ."

He understood her plea. Don't hurt the children, she wanted to say, but she didn't want to suggest such violence within their hearing and destroy that newly forged trust between Raymond and the girls. With a smile that showed all his teeth, he reseated himself and patted his knees. "Sit," he invited. When the girls had settled themselves, and he'd wrapped an arm around each one of them, he said to Geoffroi, "You see? A simple matter, easily settled. Lady Juliana will do as I command—and I command the kitchen remain where it is." He ignored the huffs of indignation emanating from his father and asked Juliana, "If that is what you desire?"

Confused and overwhelmingly thankful, Juliana agreed, "Oh . . . aye."

For all that it was almost justified, her gratitude and the accompanying distrust it betrayed irked him.

Tucking her short cloak tighter around her shoulders, Isabel stepped into the breach. "Raymond, you know we only want the best for you. Now that we're here, we'll begin negotiations on your wedding contract and perhaps plan the day you can say your vows. 'Twill be a lengthy process, of course."

"The wedding date is set," Raymond said, the muscles of his neck straining as he tried to muffle his frustration.

His mother picked at her needlework. "For next spring, I presume?"

"Much might happen by spring," he answered.

"Aye." Geoffroi sheathed his toothpick with the flourish most men reserved for a sword. "Much."

The air hung heavy, and the unpremeditated words flew from Raymond's mouth. "We wed on the morning of Twelfth Night."

"Twelfth Night?" Ella cried.

"Only a fortnight away!" Margery said approvingly.

"What a Christmas this will be." Ella's eyes shone, and the two girls giggled together.

Juliana said not a word, but the hand bar thumped and the shuttle flew. Perhaps she hadn't heard—he could only pray that was the truth.

"Mon petit"—his mother drawled, and he hated it when she assumed that superior tone—"you were always so impetuous. Surely your bride doesn't wish to marry so soon."

Juliana didn't lift her head from the cream-colored wool stretched before her, but a hectic color rose up her neck and burned in her cheeks. "According to the king's command, we should have been wed a year ago last spring. So whenever we wed, 'twill be late."

Some of the tightness in Raymond's chest eased. Regardless of what she would say later, for tonight she supported him.

"Ah." His mother nodded, understanding. "So many girls long for the moment when they may unite with a great family and raise themselves to a higher station. Raymond has come to you, and your dreams are fulfilled."

"Mother."

Wrath exploded from Raymond, but Juliana waved him to silence. "It is my assessment that I am raising Raymond's station, since he comes quite without coin or land."

Raymond winced. A good parry, he acknowledged, but she hadn't pierced the thick armor that surrounded his parents. Only his pride had been wounded. In a battle between his parents and Juliana, he suspected, his pride might be fatally overcome.

"You want both an honored family name and title *and* riches?" Isabel tittered. "Greedy little thing, aren't you?"

"Not at all. His honored name and title are of no use to me. His only use is as a warrior, and for that he might as well be an itinerant knight."

Geoffroi smiled patronizingly. "My child, perhaps you don't understand. Raymond is the king's cousin."

"The king has many cousins," Juliana retorted, repeating what Raymond had told her.

"He's the king's *favorite* cousin. They ride together. They hunt together. Henry asks his advice on state matters and personal matters." Geoffroi walked to his son, threw his arm around him, and hugged him with the enthusiasm he displayed only for his most useful treasures. "Raymond is one of the most influential men of the court."

Geoffroi's patronizing tone visibly shook Juliana's composure. She sought Raymond's eyes, asked for the truth without words. Sheepish, he shrugged and spread out his hands, palms up.

"The king's dearest cousin?" Juliana said slowly, and Raymond's parents began reciting the greatest doings in the kingdom in a light, chatty tone that made them all the more corporeal.

"He's Queen Eleanor's cousin, too." Isabel lifted one eyebrow. "Didn't you know?"

She'd been ordering a great lord to build her wall? Numbed by embarrassment, Juliana shook her head.

"Eleanor of Aquitaine is a great woman, a powerful woman, a true statesman." Isabel clasped her hands to her slight bosom.

"Making a damn fuss about Henry's newest mistress, though," Geoffroi said. "Henry's gotten Eleanor with child again. What else could she desire?"

Raymond interposed, "War—if Henry doesn't show her some respect."

"War?" Geoffroi chuckled. "War? How could a woman hope to win against Henry, lord of half of France and all England?"

"She has sons."

"They're young," Geoffroi argued.

"They will grow." Raymond throttled the worst of his animosity. "The young king is twelve. He's vain and argumentative, and he hates his father. Richard is nine, and promises to be as great a warrior as Henry. He's Eleanor's favorite, and he hates his father. There's Geoffrey, who is eight. He's too intelligent to accept Henry's constant neglect, so he hates his father. If this child Eleanor carries is another boy, and Henry continues to treat their mother with such disrespect, he's planted the seeds for years of rebellion."

"The princes aren't ripe for rebellion," Geoffroi complained.

"Yet." The resentment, held by so tight a rein for so long, burst from Raymond. "Yet. Trust me, Father, I know how a lad feels about a derelict father. Henry's sons have the Angevin temperament, years of disregard to avenge, and their mother's resources with which to wage war. 'Tis a dangerous combination."

Geoffroi proved himself to be a diplomat of consummate skills—he changed the subject. "The nonsense with that sheriff's son wouldn't have occurred if Raymond had been at Henry's side."

Obviously shaken by the evidence of intimacies between royalty and her betrothed, Juliana stammered, "Do you mean the exile of the archbishop of Canterbury?"

"Some call him Thomas à Becket," Geoffroi said disdainfully. "He's just a commoner Henry raised to chancellor, then to archbishop, and an ungrateful commoner, too."

"I don't know about that, Father." Raymond's countenance tightened, and the resemblance between father and son became acute. "I thought Thomas a consummate statesman with a mind exceeding any in our age."

Geoffroi's handsome, aging face stiffened. "Both you and Henry have a dreadful tendency to weigh men on their merits rather than their titles. Don't you yet realize the nobility are naturally superior beings? God wills it so."

Raymond leaned forward, his hands on his knees. "The only time you express such pious opinions is when you're affirming your own preeminence."

Puffing out his chest, Geoffroi answered, "I am

the heir of one of the greatest families in Normandy and Maine. Your mother is the heir of one of the greatest families in Angoulême and Poitou. Our lands stretch for roods through hill and briar, through field and meadow. Do you imagine for a moment we are not superior to almost every living creature on this earth?"

Tongue in cheek, Raymond said, "Except the king, of course."

"Through us you are related to both the king and the queen." Geoffroi clasped his hands behind his back and paced to a place just outside the firelight. "I would not say we are superior to the king, of course, or to the queen, but our house has survived since time immemorial, while theirs is a young dynasty."

Dumbfounded by this flight of arrogance in his already unbearable father, Raymond could only stare.

In an inspired gesture, Isabel waved her needle. "You are the fruit of our loins, the most perfect product of a perfect union." She looked at Juliana, then dropped her head in sorrow. "Do you wonder that we wish only the best for you?"

A silence followed the extravagant claims. A silence broken by Ella's delighted exclamation. "That's why the king gave Raymond to Mama. He wanted only the best for him."

Margery nodded solemnly to Ella. "Aye, that's true. Can we call you Papa now?"

Ella, not to be outdone, flung her arms around Raymond's neck and placed a loud, smacking kiss on his cheek. "Can we?"

Raymond looked at Ella, a sparkling-eyed, mischievous sprite who welcomed him wholeheartedly. He looked at Margery, who understood too well what his parents meant but who abetted him with all the fervor at her youthful disposal. Disarmed by the homage so sincerely paid, he said, "I would be honored to be called Papa by you."

"We're your parents," Isabel objected. "*We're* the ones who love you."

"As the devil loves holy water." Raymond boosted the girls to their feet. "To sleep with you. Tomorrow will be a busy day."

Margery curtsied. "Aye, Papa."

Ella followed her lead. "God keep you 'til the morn, Papa."

Isabel cried, "You listen to those two cozening little—"

Geoffroi laid a ponderous hand on her shoulder, and Isabel snapped her mouth shut.

Dagna led the girls away. She would bed them down in a far corner and protect them from the impending battle, Raymond knew, and he blessed the hunchbacked woman with all his heart.

"You still have those witches with you, I see." Isabel's acid burned all the more for being earlier diverted.

"You recognize them, then, Mother?" Raymond asked. "Part of your majestic family?"

"How childish, *mon petit.*" The acid bubbled, and Isabel etched his soul with a threat. "If you insist on wedding"—she gestured at Juliana—"that, I'll strip you of the title of Avraché."

Raymond stood and held out his hand to Juliana. Braced for her rejection, he breathed easier when she came to him without hesitation, and he said, "You are asking me to defy the king's command."

Geoffroi dismissed that with a wave. "The king will change his command for enough coin."

"I can't believe you haven't tried that method already," Raymond protested incredulously.

With a regal toss of her head, Isabel said, "Henry has this piddling determination to see you wed. But if you asked him to free you . . ."

"Is that what you came here for? To convince me to abandon the freedom I have here and come back into slavery with you?" Raymond laughed harshly and shook his head. "You mock my intelligence, dear mother."

Geoffroi's lips curled back from his teeth. "If you marry into this uncivilized English family, you'll not be welcome on any of our lands. Not mine, nor your mother's."

Blind with rage and pain, Raymond turned his back and tugged Juliana toward the master bed. With only a slight hesitation, she followed him.

Breathing hard, Isabel delivered the final blow. "If you marry this harridan, I will give the lands of Avraché to the Church."

Pain vibrated from Raymond's heart, down his arm to where he and Juliana were linked. It leaped from his nerves to Juliana's and burrowed itself under her skin. He missed the step onto the dais. She caught him as he stumbled, and beneath her hand she felt his painful, indrawn breath. He faced his parents and declared, "Do as you will. I wed Lady Juliana on the morning of Twelfth Night before the church door."

"Raymond," Isabel wailed, disbelieving. "Raymond!"

Ignoring his mother, he called, "Valeska! I want a tub of snow. Juliana, pull the screen around the bed and shut them all out."

Gladly she did as he commanded, shutting out the sight of that wicked woman, that walking plague of a man. "How did you ever grow and flourish?" she mumbled.

"Lord Peter of Burke, who fostered me, must take the credit or the blame." He tried to smile. "Until I was knighted and of some function to my parents, they paid me no heed, for either good or ill." Perching one hip on the bed, he cast a mournful gaze about the room as if he were a man who had lost something he could never find. Like a man who had lost his title and his lands.

She crossed to his side in a rush and covered his hands with her own. "Will they really do it?"

His expression was grim. "Do you jest?"

Of course they would do it. One day in their company convinced her. She wanted to offer her own lands as recompense, but Raymond wasn't a child to be appeased with one toy when another had been removed. He was a man, and although he'd never talked about Avraché, she knew how her lands sustained her: with their seasons, their fertility, their everlasting beauty. They lived in her soul, and she didn't know if she could survive without them.

Raymond shrugged with a creditable imitation of detachment. "I have never had two coins in my pocket at the same time. What difference if I have neither cross nor pile now?"

Raymond needed her—for her lands, for her wealth—but he needed her. Her prosperity kept this handsome courtier shackled by her side, and she wondered at the tiny, embarrassing thrill of possession her selfishness engendered.

She sat beside Raymond. "Are you really the king's dearest adviser?"

Embarrassed, but honest, he answered, "Henry's

so bloody-minded, you understand. I'll tell him when he's a fool."

"You call the king a fool?" Pride, previously undiscovered, enveloped her.

Her Raymond did that.

Her Raymond. She jerked in dismay.

Only yesterday she'd believed herself to be the mistress of what Raymond called destiny. Only last night, she'd discovered the true identity of the man perched on her bed. She'd been furious, then horrified. Had she been surprised? Not really. At some point, she'd acknowledged Raymond's nobility, and the discovery had only reaffirmed her instincts. She'd been hurt. She'd been humiliated. She hadn't been surprised.

So when had she started thinking of him as "her Raymond"?

"Aye, I called him a fool, and quite vigorously, too." His lopsided grimace might have been a smile. "Perhaps marrying me isn't a good idea."

"I never thought it was," she snapped.

His laughter pealed out. Catching her chin in his fingers, he praised, "Excellent, lady! You vanquished that little bully this morning, and with one blow bought yourself a measure of freedom."

Remembering Sir Joseph, she said, "I would it were so easy."

"Even a long journey begins with one step."

"Do you think I was . . . brave?"

"Brave? To strike a man who'd trained, however inadequately, as a knight?" The very darkness around them complemented him, drawing his face in shadows and lines, and his voice rasped with the sincerity of his praise. "Brave is not nearly strong enough a word to describe you today. Savor your victory, and I will finish the business with Felix for you."

Juliana turned to see Valeska directing two sturdy lads to place the mounded tub against the head of the bed. "Ah. Valeska, many thanks. This will cure what ails me," Raymond said. The serving boys looked questioningly at their mistress, who shrugged in mystification.

Seemingly at ease with this madness of snow inside the already chilly castle, Valeska threw back the furs and laid a hot stone, wrapped in a cloth, at the foot of the bed. She covered it and nodded at Juliana. "That'll keep your legs warm, my lady." To Raymond, she said, "Your parents have commandeered the best places by the fire. Geoffroi told your little Lord Felix to stop moaning and holding his nose. Said any man who's been thrashed by a woman should have the decency to be embarrassed about it."

She grinned at Juliana, and Raymond visibly relaxed while kicking off his shoes. Untying the tapes that held his hose, he shook them down his legs and removed them. "You should call my father by his title, Valeska," Raymond said. "He'll knock you arsey-versey for disrespect."

"I don't respect him." Valeska picked up the hose.

"You can ill stand to lose more teeth, for my father is no respecter of age." Raymond removed his cloak and doublet, and Valeska took those, too.

His chainse was linen, worn thin with time, and hugging his chest like a lover's touch. When he turned, the outlines of some dreadful beating shone clearly though the thin material.

The serving boys gasped, and Valeska clicked her tongue in disgust. "Get on with you, you pudding-heads." The lads scurried around the edge of the screen, and she grumbled, "You would think they'd never seen a scar before." She confided to Juliana, "Although those whippings would have killed him without my herbs."

Raymond met Juliana's gaze with an ironic smile, and lifted the chainse away. The scars were dreadful; deep, ridged with white, and flecked with red. She saw now a scar circled his throat, and Felix's story returned to haunt her.

Could it be the mark of an iron collar? A protest rose in her. Could someone—an infidel—actually have chained this magnificent man?

She shivered, and he said, "Your eyes are as big as a sleepy child's. Snuggle down in the blankets. I'll join you after my bath."

Weariness and shock exaggerated her surprise. "Your bath?"

He nodded toward the tub of snow. "There's my bath."

"There's your bath," she repeated stupidly as he rubbed his chest. She couldn't take her eyes off the long slow strokes of his hand, and her own hand tingled as if she massaged the crinkled hairs.

Assured of her attention, he stripped down till he stood in nothing but his goosebumps. She didn't want to stare, but her eyes couldn't turn away from the body of her Raymond. All of him was brown, a legacy of his southern ancestors. All of him was big, a legacy of the Viking raiders who'd settled in Normandy. All of him was muscled, a legacy of his knightly training.

She glanced with quick embarrassment at Valeska, but Valeska had whisked away.

"I wouldn't do this tonight, but"—he plunged headfirst into the tub and scrubbed snow into his hair—"my parents make me feel dirty. I have dreamed of snow, white, pure, and cold, melting on me, cleansing me."

"I can understand that." She challenged him with the memory. "I felt used last night when the master castle-builder arrived."

"I have the cure." He started toward her with a handful of snow. "Would you wish to join me?"

"Nay!" she shrieked. "I'm not mad."

Halting an arm's length away, he grinned. "Do you forgive me for my grievous deception?"

He stood, so proud and unbowed, after shielding Juliana from his parents. What was her injured pride when those dreadful people sought, through any means, the hurt and humiliation of their own son, their heir?

In her hesitation, he lunged toward her; she hastily said, "I forgive you."

Packing the snow a little tighter in his fists, he teased her. "Goodness delights to forgive."

"I delight," she assured him.

"You are too good," he said mockingly.

"I know."

He lifted the snow threateningly, and she recoiled. With a laugh, he plastered it over his shoulders.

She shuddered violently as he wiped handfuls of the white stuff along his ribs and hips. Sliding fully clothed under the blankets, she closed her eyes against the sight of him, but contrary to her behest they popped open. Her gaze examined him and lingered. How thin her young husband had been! How easy to disdain masculine contact when temptation had never been offered! Wanting to distract herself before she lost all her pride, she asked, "Did you scold him about hurting Eleanor's pride?"

Arrested in mid stroke, he demanded, "What? Who?"

"The king. Did you scold him about hurting Eleanor's pride?"

"Oh." He dug out another handful of snow and scrubbed his thighs. His long, sleek, muscled thighs. "Aye, I scolded him."

She pressed her palms to her eyes until she saw colored stars. "Perhaps that's why he gave you such a poor castle to wed."

"You've been listening to my parents. Nay, there's no truth in that. Henry gave you to me long before he was displeased with me. This castle is important to the kingdom, and will sustain us well until I inherit from my—"

He said nothing else, she looked up, and he jerked his head, indicating the couple outside the screen. And once she had looked up, she couldn't again deny herself the sight of him. "Is your inheritance as large as they say?"

"Aye, for all the good that will do me. Can you see either of those two demons dying before they please?"

Restlessness afflicted her, and she fought the feather mattress to find a comfortable spot.

The long muscles of his thighs flexed, his toes curled, and his teeth chattered as he scoured himself. "Why do you display such consternation?"

"I . . . because you're taking a snow bath, of course."

"My people in Normandy brought this from the North long ago, and use it as a ritual cleansing before the great events of their lives. 'Twould refresh you, should you try it."

"May the sweet Virgin prevent it," she said with fervent piety.

He chuckled, a rich sound originating deep in his

chest. She'd grown to like this sound that warmed her with its vitality.

He shook the melting drops off and used his cloak to briskly rub himself dry. He came toward her, and she shrank back, threatened by his size, threatened by his nudity. He smelled like fresh air, like air she hadn't breathed for too long. She inhaled in a gasp.

"Scoot back," he ordered, pushing her to the wall, lifting the covers, and lying down.

The cold came in with him. The cold was him. His body begged for her heat from across the inches that separated them. She tucked the blankets tight around his neck, and scolded, "That was a mad thing to do. You're chilled."

They faced each other on the feather bolster. He was so handsome, he made her breath catch. Her lips parted. She wanted to taste him, to see if he tasted as glorious as he smelled, as he looked. She wanted to kiss him, but her courage evaporated when confronting a large obstacle.

Like Raymond.

He'd come to her bed because he wanted to prove to his parents the marriage lacked only the last of the vows. He was a lad, cocking his nose at authority and saying, "See? You can't touch me."

She knew that. But she also suspected he'd come to her because he wanted comfort. He'd been hurt by the people who should love him most and who cared the least, and the same lad who cocked his nose must have cried bitter tears about their indifference. All day she'd watched him do battle, and now she'd give him the comfort he wanted.

But at what price?

They were betrothed, they were alone in the master

bed, she'd have to touch him, and he'd like it. He'd consider it encouragement, and he'd seek the ultimate comfort from her. Could she give it? Just thinking about touching him made her breathe in an erratic fashion.

Once a coward, Sir Joseph would say, always a coward.

She shook thoughts of Sir Joseph away. Since he'd discovered Raymond's identity, she'd not seen him at the fire. He, and his taunts, were best forgotten. Or, even better, she could prove him wrong.

"For shame." She scolded Raymond in a wavering voice. "Foolish man, what if you catch a fever? What will I do then?"

"Dose me with potions?" he suggested.

"I have more faith in the power of prayer."

"Then I pray you come closer."

Beneath the blankets, her hand twitched and moved. It seemed to have a life of its own as it crept close to him. It settled on his waist; the cold of his flesh made it jerk back. He didn't move, watching her with his jewelled eyes, and her hand settled back at his waist. Like a treasure, his smile flashed free of his restraint, and he sat up and leaned over her.

He wanted her. In the hut, she'd feared it with the panic of a virgin. Now she feared it with the reservations of a woman. How could she, cursed by this nightmare that haunted her, satisfy a man who looked like stardust and moonbeams?

Her eyes hurt from holding them so wide, and when he leaned to touch his lips to hers, her eyes crossed. She didn't try to fight and scream, nor did she shudder with revulsion. She gave Raymond the same obedient response she'd given her husband so long ago, and for that she was thankful.

Raymond did not seem equally thankful. He kissed her cold, still lips for a moment, then flung himself back on the pillow.

She waited, but he made no further move and she asked, "Am I not to your liking?"

"Not to my—"

He folded his arms across his chest and made a sound like an offended boy. "Why do you hold your lips so tightly closed when I kiss you?"

"How else should I hold them?" She laughed a little. "Open?"

His arms slid apart, and his head swivelled toward her. " 'Tis the usual way."

Sitting up in one straight-backed move, she cried, "Say not so."

He seemed to be struggling with some emotion. Amusement, perhaps, or disbelief. " 'Tis the French way."

"The French eat snails, too," she replied tartly.

His chuckle was a seduction in itself. "Some French customs are more enjoyable than others."

She struggled, but vulgar curiosity won. "Do you kiss like that?"

He didn't answer her directly, only his lids drooped in sensuous remembrance. "French women kiss in that manner. French women are experts at kissing."

Raymond seemed like a dream she'd had once, a dream that had slipped away but had never been forgotten. If he were a dream, perhaps she could touch him without fear. Perhaps . . .

She put her hands to his neck, but he caught her before she could touch that ridged scar where an iron collar had dug a groove in his skin.

"Don't. I don't *like*"—his tone was too emphatic,

and he modulated it—"to be confined in any way."
Abashed, she bit her lip, but he placed her hands on
his chest and said, "Here, instead."

With a lopsided smile that couldn't mask his intensity,
he used her wrists to stir the hair that grew in a black
froth. It crinkled beneath her sensitive palms, a curious
texture and one that soothed and distracted her.

She wanted to kiss him.

She couldn't. No one had ever kissed her in the way
she'd seen the groom kissing the milkmaid. No one
had ever kissed her in a loverlike way. She'd shared
the kiss of peace with her father, her tenants, even her
husband—but this strange method he urged? Never.

Never was too long a time. Cautiously, she laid
herself against him lengthwise. He moved his arm to
wrap her in a hug. The sensation of his body against
hers wasn't intrusive or demanding, but gave the
impression of a tremendous patience, and that
patience lent her courage. Resting her cheek against
his, she whispered, "Sir Raymond."

"Lady Juliana?" he whispered back.

"Sir Raymond, this may sound rude or even
demanding. . . ." She couldn't do it. She couldn't do it.

"Demand what you wish."

He watched too closely. He saw too much. "It's
nothing." She tried to crawl off the top of him, but he
held her with his arm across her back.

"I am yours to command."

A simple phrase, much used by cavaliers, but when
spoken in his deep tones it convinced her.

"I'd like to kiss you."

"I would be . . . honored."

Honored? Honored wasn't what he wished to say,
she suspected. She wet her lips, wet them again, took

a breath, and swooped on him like a bird of prey. The impact shook her—and what should she do now?

Her panic eased as his cold lips layered themselves on hers. Although he let her kiss him, he expected to participate. A conundrum occurred to her. Was her own lack of participation the cause of his earlier vexation? He learned her in degrees, and she let him, encouraged him until his sweet breath entered her mouth. She tried to shut her lips against it, but he insisted in unspoken direction. She broke away with a gasp and stared wildly at him.

He touched his mouth with his finger. "Again," he suggested.

It wasn't so odd this time. She liked it this time. It made her move against his chest. When his tongue touched hers, she chased it out with her own, and he encouraged her with his own deep groan.

She jerked back, and stared at him.

His chest heaved as if he'd been exerting himself, and he reached for the ties on the side of her cotte. "What do you think of the French now?" He had her out of the garment in less time than it took to skin a peach, and his very expertise inhibited her. The linen of her chainse matched his in age and softness, and he must have seen her nipples through the gauze, for he took one in his mouth without fumbling or groping.

The heat of it flattened her like a runaway cart. When she opened her eyes, she was looking at the ceiling with handfuls of black hair clutched in her fingers. Life moved in her womb, but it wasn't the quickening of a child. It was the quickening of Juliana. It was lust, forbidden and absolutely delicious.

This clawing confusion of passion and fear, of desire and revulsion brought a little moan to her lips, and Raymond eased away. "You're sensitive. Don't be embarrassed. Tell me what you like."

"I don't like any—" she gasped as his thumb stroked her through the wet cloth "—any of it."

"I do recognize pleasure when I see it." He cupped her breast. "This is a symptom of arousal."

Her nipples puckered so tightly they ached, and her head whirled so swiftly it ached. She didn't understand these emotions Raymond plucked from her as easily as he would pluck the petals from a rose, but she did understand her own gripping dismay. "I'm cold."

"Aye." He blew on the wet cloth. "So you are."

Flushing, she pulled her chainse away from her chest and wished she had remained unresponsive. Too much had changed too rapidly, and her voice quavered as she confessed, "I don't know how to do this. I don't know how to satisfy a man who has . . . kissed so many French women."

His hands tightened briefly on her. "You've made an excellent start." Then he relaxed. "I would not have you believe I find you unattractive."

"Oh, nay!" She blushed. "You watch me, and I suspect . . . that is, I realize you will gladly perform your martial duties."

"Nor would I consider them duties," he said. "Still, your reluctance doesn't surprise me. Not when I think about it." He tugged on his earring. "Not that I like it. If I had known I would be unsatisfied, I would have saved that snow bath. This is my reward for thinking I'm irresistible."

He laid a hand against the side of her head and pushed it against him. She rebelled briefly, then yielded. Her cheek and ear rested in the hollow of his shoulder, and, by some magic, his skin had heated until it welcomed her with its warmth. He snuggled against the length of her, and she discovered he'd warmed in other ways, too. She found it daunting to be so close to an aroused man, yet equal parts of curiosity and that mercuric quickening made her fidget.

He clamped a hand on her hip. "Gently, my girl," he advised. "I've been watching you, wanting you since the day I took you to that snowbound hut, and celibacy is"—he laughed softly—"difficult. So we'll sleep now, and my pleasure will wait on your surrender."

Turning her until her stiff back made contact with his chest, he nestled them together like the cup of two spoons.

She couldn't resist asking. "What if I don't surrender?"

"I will do all in my power to bring you to rapture," he promised.

"But if I still don't?"

He sighed; his breath ruffled the wisps of hair on the back of her neck. "Then we shall make an end of it on our wedding night." His arm weighed across her hip. "Are we agreed?"

"You are too good," she said formally.

"I am," he said with equal formality and a great deal of conviction.

His hand lay too close to the bottom of her chainse. In a sudden flurry, she dragged the hem down to her knees.

"Are you through?" he asked.

She said nothing, rigid with suspense.

"Then go to sleep. No love tonight. No matter how you beg me."

11

"*I hear you heeded* my advice and eased your stone-ache."

Raymond glared at Keir. "How would you know? You failed to appear in the great hall last night."

Keir finished pounding a glowing plowshare and plunged it into water before he answered. "I've met your parents."

"So has Juliana, now," Raymond said gloomily.

"Will she still wed you?"

"On Twelfth Night."

Keir put his tools aside and wiped his hand on a cloth. "In a hurry?"

"I cannot let her get away from me." Raymond walked to the door of the smithy and grasped the frame with his hand. "I woke this morning and found her gone, and leaped up like any crazed man who thought he possessed a fairy."

"Did you find her?"

With a disgusted look at his friend, Raymond said, "She was packing Felix's nose in snow to slow the swelling. She didn't want me to know for fear I'd tear him into little bits."

"Did you?"

Raymond smiled an evil smile. "I made him think I would. He fled the hall most precipitously, and I think I'll find him and . . . suggest he leave Lofts Castle just as precipitously."

"Sir Joseph has been living in the stables. You might start your search there."

Raymond rolled around until his back rested against the wall. "What do you mean by that?"

"They're a cozy trio," Keir replied as he removed his leather apron and hung it on a peg. "An earl, a baron, and the puppet master who controls them both."

"An earl, a baron . . . are you saying Hugh is under the control of . . . ?" Keir watched Raymond steadily as he thought aloud. "Now Felix, I can believe, but Hugh . . . and a puppet master. Is that what you see when you look at Sir Joseph? Not an old knight, disgruntled at the power of which age has stripped him, but a man who pulls the strings?"

"I see what I see." Keir stepped outside and took a breath. "Look now."

Raymond stepped to Keir's side. Hugh stood before the open stable door, talking—arguing, mayhap—with someone just inside.

"From what I know of Hugh, he would not do harm to Juliana," Raymond argued, his gaze fixed on the stable.

"Not if he realized he was doing harm. But Sir Joseph is, I think, very intelligent, and Hugh—"

"Is not," Raymond finished. "Nay, Hugh's a blunt man. He could be manipulated."

"Felix—"

Raymond acknowledged Keir's unfinished sentence with a bark of a laugh. "Never an original thought, never a sign of wit or wisdom. But why would Sir Joseph tangle these men in such a wicked net? What does it profit him?"

"That I do not understand, but as you know, I'm often in the position to hear things."

"You're insufferably nosy," Raymond corrected. Keir said nothing else, and Raymond added, "A trait to which I've been indebted many times."

Keir dipped his head in acknowledgement. "I've been listening to the gossip of the stable boys. They've suffered since Sir Joseph moved in, and they've found a pleasant place to congregate in the smithy. It seems Sir Joseph spoke to both Hugh and Felix when they came to inspect their horses early yesterday morning." A stolid satisfaction spread over Keir's face. "He believes the stable boys are deaf, you ken."

"Ah," Raymond said. "Hugh tried to convince me not to wed Juliana, and Felix tried to convince Juliana not to wed me."

"More than that. Felix tried to convince Juliana to wed him rather than you."

"What?" Raymond's shout captured Hugh's attention. "I'll kill him."

Raymond started toward the stable, and Keir kept pace. "Kill him if you like, but I think you should know this is not the first time he's tried to convince her to wed."

Swinging at his friend, Raymond gathered a handful of Keir's shirt. "Tell me what you know."

"It will tear, Raymond, and Lady Juliana will be most distressed."

Raymond loosened his grip.

"I know but little. The stable boys—indeed, the

whole castle—labors under a conspiracy of silence out of respect for their lady. I only know her father tried to betroth her to Felix. She valiantly refused."

Remembering the hair that frothed around her shoulders, Raymond wondered, as he always had, why it was so short. Most women of Juliana's age had never cut their hair, and it curled around their thighs when released from their wimples. Hair was cut in case of life-threatening fever, or . . . as a Biblical revenge for wanton behavior. Slowly, he admitted, "I had begun to suspect something of the sort."

"That would account for her revulsion for the wedded state."

Raymond grinned. "As I would account for her renewed enthusiasm."

Keir swept Raymond from head to toe with his gaze. "Women are mysterious creatures. See your quarry peek around the door."

Raymond's smile turned savage and he shouted, "Stay!"

His long strides ate up the ground, but Hugh confronted him before he could reach the stables. "I must take my leave." Staring at the toe of his boot, Hugh added, "You may have surmised I have an affection for Juliana that transcends the affection of youthful companions."

"I had suspected," Raymond answered.

Hugh glanced toward the stable. "Juliana's marriage will be difficult for me to accept."

Seeing the head that bobbed outside the stable door, then bobbed within, then bobbed out again, Raymond took a few cautious steps while keeping his attention fixed on Hugh. " 'Twill be a difficult matter for Juliana to accept, that her dear friend leaves even as Christmastide begins. Does Felix accompany you?"

"He has other plans," Hugh replied.

Raymond pitched his voice to be heard in the stable. "Felix couldn't plan his way out of a whore's arms. He's so stupid." He took another few steps, still watching the dismayed Hugh. "That blow Lady Juliana landed to his nose could only improve his visage, so ugly is he. He's not a knight, he's a worm, the lowest thing I've seen since I shovelled shit from under a Saracen infidel's horse."

Felix popped out of the stable, ruffled up in indignation, and Raymond snatched him before reason could reassert itself. Grunting, Raymond lifted the round little man and glared into his eyes. "See? Here he comes out from under a good Christian horse."

"I'm not ugly," Felix shrieked.

Raymond threw back his head and bellowed with laughter. "Oh, aren't you? Wait until that pretty bandage comes off your face." He shook him until Felix grabbed at his nose. "It'll be warped as badly as your morals. In fact, I find myself desirous of shovelling your ugly self right down the garderobe shaft with the rest of the shit."

Off balance and incensed, Felix reached out, closed his pudgy fingers around Raymond's scarred throat, and squeezed. With the roar of a wounded bear, Raymond threw Felix through the open stable door. Blind, mad with a combination of fear and fury, he rushed at Felix, but mighty arms caught him and held him fast. He fought against the restraint, ranting in the foreign words he'd thought forgotten.

Keir and Hugh shouted. Felix squealed and crawled backward into the dark interior. Stable boys scattered. And one pair of eyes inside the stable gleamed and observed with relish.

* * *

"Lady Juliana? Lady Juliana?"

The call rang through the kitchen, echoing through the high beams and thinning in the great expanse of undercroft that lay beyond. Juliana turned in a slow circle to face the cook. "Did you call me?"

Valeska and Dagna exchanged concerned looks. "Nay, Lady Juliana, it was me," Dagna said, her contralto voice as soothing as if Juliana were a child. "Cook wants to know what to serve for the feast today."

"Ah. Spiced cheese with walnuts to start. Goose with prune sauce. That's a fine meat for Christmastide. Wassail, of course, and for the sweet . . ." Juliana stared into the fire that flamed in the fire pit. The coals, with delicate greed, ate the split oak logs. The spit stood ready to impale the meat. It reminded her of Raymond.

Raymond, warming her, tempting her. Every night she decided she would keep her wits about her. Every night he pressed those devastating kisses on her, touched her in places men never cared about, and charmed her out of her cotte. Once he'd even charmed her out of her chainse, much to her later embarrassment. "She needs a long spoon who sups with the devil," she murmured.

"Pardon, my lady, I didn't hear you."

Wondering why Dagna looked concerned, Juliana said, "I didn't speak."

"Of course you didn't." Valeska asked, "What about the feast?"

Juliana lifted her abstracted gaze to the withered woman. "What? Goose with prune sauce, I think. That's a good meat. And goose-neck pudding."

They waited while Juliana thought.

She wished she knew what he wanted. She had thought he was a simple man. She had thought he wanted his pleasure of her, but he reminded her of a river that flowed to the sea. Slow, steady, relentless: moving stones, rocks, boulders by the constant exertion of his will. If he couldn't push the boulder of her fear aside, he'd undermine it, slip around it, twirl about until she was so confused she didn't remember why she was afraid.

He'd accused her of tempting him; how dare he turn the tables so cruelly? How dare he wait for her to beg him, as if he were in no hurry? Oh, nay, he wanted more than just his pleasure of her.

The noises originating behind the screen convinced her servitors and his parents that marital activity occurred nightly, yet Raymond's increasingly short temper confused them. For while between the furs, he held himself under tight rein, never allowing himself a shred of satisfaction. He seemed delighted with her new knowledge, but watched her during the day in the manner of a starving man before the feast.

"The feast, my lady." Valeska shook Juliana's arm. "What do you wish for the sweet?"

Juliana snapped back to the present. "I told you. Plum-and-currant tart. And I want goose with prune sauce as the meat."

Mouth puckered, Valeska nodded. "As you wish, my lady. Many thanks for coming below to consult with us. We never expected such an indulgence from the woman who will soon be a bride."

"Nonsense. I'll be a bride in eight days—"

"Six," Dagna said.

Juliana glared. "But that doesn't mean I'm not capable of handling all my duties. That's why I'm down here. To—" To avoid Raymond. The servants had complained—politely, and, of course, erroneously—that Juliana was distracted.

And if she was distracted, the fault rested with Raymond. With the eagerness of a new scholar, she'd learned the lessons he taught. How to kiss, how to touch. Where to touch, and more important, where not to touch.

The depths of him frightened her, yet lured her, and as long as she followed his rules, he brought her close to satisfaction, stopping her just short of some exotic release. Like a ripe plum's, her skin felt close to bursting. Her fingers failed to shut properly, and she frequently dropped things. "And I talk to myself," she said aloud.

"My lady?" As Juliana wafted away, Dagna dug a malicious elbow into her cohort's side. "I always thought the kitchen was the warmest room in this castle. It would seem that half-finished solar is warmer."

Vaguely, Juliana wondered what they were cackling about, but the question didn't occupy her long as she ascended the spiral stairway leading to the great hall. Since the night she'd met the real castle-builder, her life had been knocked askew. She'd grown tired of seeing smirks on the faces of every servant. She'd grown tired of the endless wedding preparations and the endless Christmas celebrations. She'd grown tired of the constant inner turmoil and the breathless physical desire.

Perhaps she was just tired from lack of sleep.

Her inattention earned her a collision with somebody who stepped out of the deep shadows onto the landing. "Pardon"—she stared and her mouth dried—"me."

"Lady Juliana." Sir Joseph purred. "Such a surprise. I haven't seen you alone since your betrothed revealed himself."

Caught in the crossroads between up and down, between the bustle of the kitchen and the business of the great hall, between the light of the torches and the light of the sun, Juliana didn't understand how the shadows smoothed the wrinkles and the liver spots from Sir Joseph's face and returned his youth. But she did understand her wariness. If Sir Joseph had come to wish her well, he'd have done it before an audience.

Pitching her voice low to avoid eavesdroppers, she said, "You no longer sit at your place by the fire."

He smiled and created a pocket of tantalizing evil in the darkness. He, too, spoke almost in a whisper, but the stealth seemed a part of him and not an aberration. "When Lord Felix and Lord Hugh fled, even before the first celebration of this joyous season, I was without acquaintances in the keep. Even your noble Lord Raymond seemed abashed at their rapid leave-taking."

She shifted from one foot to the other. "He wished, no doubt, for the chance to bid them farewell, but I believe Felix felt constrained to leave before"— she straightened her shoulders, narrowed her eyes, and tried to looked menacing—"before I broke more than his nose."

As always, as usual, he sneered at her pretensions. "You give yourself too much credit for your puny blow. 'Twas not your insanity that warned Felix away, but the insanity of the man who some would call your husband."

A frisson of unease shivered up her spine, and something about Sir Joseph and his glistening eyes reminded her about the long, winding stone stairway behind her, unprotected by any handrail. "Did my Raymond strike Felix? He threatened to, for he believes a man shouldn't intimidate a woman." She watched Sir Joseph closely. "He believes it's a sign of degeneracy."

"Degeneracy." Sir Joseph was seized by a fit of silent laughter, made all the more menacing by his true amusement. "Degeneracy. Lord Raymond complains of degeneracy in another. He who embodies all that the demons of hell would celebrate."

Shock kept her still. Such an accusation rang of witch hunts and warlock burnings. The fear of such devilish manifestations was bred into her, and into everyone who lived at one with the Catholic Church. No one was too mighty to be brought down by such a rumor. She whispered, "I do think your scurrilous soul welcomes wrongs."

"Nay, my lady"—her title sounded like ridicule on his lips—"I come to you to right a wrong. You accuse Lord Felix of degeneracy with righteous vehemence, when you fornicate with a madman, one who uses human form to disguise the vicious wolf who preys on his victims."

"You jest."

"Lord Felix doesn't think so, nor does Lord Hugh. Your lord tried to kill Lord Felix."

"Why?"

"Why? For merely touching his neck." She was jolted, and he saw it. With delicious relish, he described the scene in the bailey, telling her, "It took two men and the stables boys to tear him away."

"That scarcely makes him a demon."

"You didn't see him. Teeth bared, hands curled into claws, eyes red, an unrecognizable voice shrieking inhuman curses." Sir Joseph's smooth voice brought a chilling terror to the tale. "'Twas a transformation, my lady, all the more frightening for the sunlight that shone as he completed it."

Sickened, she demanded, "Are you calling Lord Raymond a werewolf?"

"I would be a fool to say such a thing about the man who holds my life in his hands. Nay, my lady, I simply seek to warn you of the horror awaiting you." His long, thin, white hands gleamed as he drew his dark robes around him. "Who knows when the dementia will take him again? When he fights? When he drinks? Or in the excitement of the marriage bed?"

He withdrew with swift and silent assurance, leaving her staring at the stone walls with her arms coiled around her waist and her hands gripping the cloth of her cotte. The trust Raymond had worked so hard to earn now seemed cheap. The courage she had struggled to obtain now seemed impetuous. With diabolical skill, Sir Joseph had probed her vulnerabilities, validated the rumors Felix had called to her attention, and twisted the knife of distrust deep into her mind. She knew what he'd done; she knew her own folly in listening, but although she ignored the wound, it throbbed and bled.

Creeping out of the stairwell, she assured herself Sir Joseph had disappeared from the great hall. Nor was Raymond within, and she squelched the bubble of relief that rose in her. She was foolish to allow the words of an old and bitter man to influence her, but, like a wicked spider, he had woven a web about her, skillfully using her own doubts to poison her dreams.

"Fayette," she called, heading toward a bench by the sunny arrow slit. "Bring me the embroidery."

Fayette hurried forward, unwrapping the fine cream-colored cloth. Juliana herself had cut the finished cloth into a surcoat for Raymond, then supervised the sewing by her maid. The tunic, already finished, would cover his arms and fall to his calves in a sweep of dark green wool. The sleeveless surcoat was cut to reach the knee, and would contrast with the green tunic at neck, arm, and hem. It was elegant in its simplicity, but with needle and matching green thread Juliana added the finishing touches. Whenever Raymond was absent, she worked surreptitiously on a vine of ivy leaves twined about the wide neck. On the morning of Twelfth Night, she thought, she would give it to him. He'd be amazed, he'd gather her to his bosom, press one of those kisses on her, they'd tumble onto the bed, and—what would happen? Would they find joy in each other? Or would Raymond turn into a beast, satisfied with nothing less than her torment and death? Was that the reason he had been so restrained in their bed? Because when he let himself go, he turned into a monster of the netherworld?

"My lady? My lady!" Fayette shook Juliana's shoulder urgently. "Lord Raymond is entering the hall."

"What?" Juliana stared as Raymond swept into the room, but he looked nothing like the werewolf of Sir Joseph's warning. Big and broad and so alive he sparkled, he dragged a lad of perhaps fifteen years behind him and headed straight toward her.

Shoving the surcoat at Fayette, she demanded, "Take this. Why didn't you warn me sooner?" She smoothed her skirt, tucked a strand of hair into her braid, then stood with a smile. "My lord."

"Ah, Juliana." Raymond's answering smile pleasured

her, and some of her caution slipped away. "Allow me to present the newest addition to our household. This is Denys."

Juliana's mood swung from relief to dismay. "An addition to our household?"

"William of Miraval sent him as a present, for he knew of my dire need for fighting men. Denys has impressed me so with his abilities, I have made him my new squire." With a friendly hand on his shoulder, Raymond pushed the gangly youth forward.

Denys tugged at his drooping hose and, in a voice that changed octaves, said, "My lady, I offer you my undying service."

Dumbfounded, Juliana observed the boy. His hair, not blond, not brown, looked as if some maddened sparrow had made its nest therein. His long, thin nose dripped, a fine fuzz decorated his chin, and his watery blue eyes gazed worshipfully at her. He reminded her of someone, although she didn't know whom, and her mood swung again—to anger.

"He looks forward to your welcome," Raymond said, hinting.

Her welcome? What welcome? For almost three years, she had supervised the comings and goings of servants and men-at-arms in Lofts Castle. She'd stayed informed of the movements of every villein, every serf. It had been important, for it had meant security. Now an important member had been introduced into her household without her consent. She'd have to feed this youth, teach him manners, tend the inevitable wounds he would receive as he completed his training. And she was being treated like some trifling woman with no reason to care about the matters on her own lands.

She managed a small smile. "Denys, are you hungry?"

Raymond looked startled at this unconventional welcome, but she had read Denys correctly. "Aye, my lady. I'm always hungry."

"Fayette will fetch you bread and cheese. 'Twill keep you until today's feast." His clumsy bow looked more like a curtsey, his sleeves were too short for his arms. "If I might have the pleasure of your company, my lord? In here," she commanded, leading him to the passage above the kitchen stairs.

No one stood there. Sir Joseph's presence did not linger among the shadows, and anger swept away her caution.

"Juliana—"

"What do you mean, bringing that boy in without my permission?" Raymond stiffened, but she didn't notice. "A youth from some presumptuous lord."

"William of Miraval is my friend." The chill in Raymond's voice penetrated her anger, but did not douse it.

She thrust out her chin. "William of Miraval probably wished to rid himself of a small thief or liar."

Raymond glanced through the doorway as though to assure himself they spoke of the same person. "*That* lad?"

Juliana glanced, too. She saw a colt of a boy, all arms and legs, smiling with fervent appreciation at her maid. He wiped his nose on his sleeve and plunged into the cup of mead like a horse drinking water after a hard ride, and with a shock she realized whom he resembled. He had the look, God help her, of her first husband. Too thin, eager to please, without personality or charm.

Raymond explained, "In the letter Denys brought with him, William says the lad's lady mother came to his wife and begged succor. Saura is known for her good works, and she did all she could, but 'twas too late. The lady expired of a combination of starvation and consumption, and Denys took it badly—very badly. His father had gambled away his lands and his wife's dower, then killed himself. At the death of his mother, Denys swore a great many foolish things."

She hardly heard Raymond speak, so bound up in her own misgivings was she. Was that why she had rejected Denys so vehemently? Not because of pride but because he recalled the boy she'd married and lost after such a long, painful illness? The memories of Millard contained a confusion of love, exasperation, and distress. She'd thought she had put him behind her, but how could she forget the father of her children?

Raymond seemed impervious to her confusion. "Denys swore he'd have wealth once more, regardless of the price to himself. William and Saura took him into their family and trained him, and the desperation has faded. They sent him to me because . . ."

He flushed, and with a shock she realized young Denys meant more to him than a simple squire, also. Raymond wanted Denys fervently. "Why did they send him to you?"

"Because at his age, I also was without support of parents or wealth. They thought I could help him. Also, I owe it to Lord Peter."

"You owe him? You owe Lord Peter?"

"Lord Peter of Burke. He's William's father, and he fostered me. He taught me honor and dignity and leadership. That code of conduct saved my life. And Denys needs someone to help him learn the refinements of a knight's art."

A smile quivered at the corners of his mouth, but her suspicions couldn't stop her from asking, "Such as?"

"Such as removing your metal gauntlets before peeing in freezing weather."

She stared at him; he stared at her. She tried to control it, but couldn't. She burst into laughter.

He waited until the first explosion of merriment had subsided, then took her hand and pressed it onto his chest. "Juliana, the lad has a good heart. He's had bad times, but together, you and I can make a man of him. Don't make me send him away."

Her laughter faded. Beneath her palm, his heart beat a strong and steady rhythm, his chest rose and fell. His flesh warmed hers, his smile lulled her, and she realized he, too, wove a web. Sir Joseph's web had trapped her in the sticky threads of suspicion. Raymond's web gathered her close and wrapped her in seduction. "Nay, don't send him away," she said reluctantly.

"There's my girl," he said, and kissed her hand again as if that would put all to rights.

Her hostility bounded loose. "Patronizing ass," she hissed. "You don't understand at all."

Like any oaf of a man, he looked confused. "Understand what?"

She jerked her hand free. "My life is no longer my own. My body is no longer my own. My castle is no longer my own."

Anger flickered in his face, and too late she thought of caution. Crowding her against the wall, he held her with a hand on cheek and chin and pressed a hard kiss on her lips. Reservations were swept away as her desire leaped to meet his. Eager moans erupted from her, and he answered with a hum of frustration. When he dragged his mouth from hers, he said, "Your life and body and castle are no longer your own because you are mine. Remember that." He swooped on her and kissed her once more. "Remember that."

He flung himself away, and Juliana shouted, "You are a wart on the nose of my existence."

She didn't wait to see if he would turn back. Plunging down the stairs, she found herself in the kitchen, facing the cowering cook and two unimpressed old gypsies. Raymond's retreating footsteps rang clearly down the stairs, and Juliana drew herself up. "You heard everything?"

"Aye, with Sir Joseph and with Raymond, and we're sore disappointed in you." Valeska's eyes drooped like a hunting hound's. Braced for a lecture on a docile woman's rightful place, Juliana staggered backward when Valeska said to Dagna, "We'll have to teach this little one the correct way to curse."

Dagna's disappointment sounded, if anything, deeper than her friend's. "That we will. You'd not get any respect in my country for such pallid oaths."

"Nor mine." Valeska moved close to flank Juliana's right side. "For instance, m'lady, a wart is an ugly thing, but a blister is uglier."

"A carbuncle is uglier yet again," Dagna chimed in, taking a station at Juliana's left side so that Juliana swivelled her head from side to side, up and down, trying to follow the conversation.

"True. You are so clever, sister." Valeska waved a gnarled finger. "So, m'lady, we'll call Raymond a carbuncle. Then we must decide the most disgusting place for a carbuncle. A nose isn't disgusting."

Dagna interrupted. "Unless—"

Valeska pointed that finger, and Dagna stopped. "Not normally. A nose is not normally a disgusting place. So perhaps you'll want to call Raymond a carbuncle on the foot of your existence."

"Personally, I like the term carbuncle on the ass of your existence, but one wonders what he would have to do to develop a carbuncle there." Dagna clucked and shook her head.

"True. And I thought we should ease Lady Juliana into the art of swearing. If she's been satisfied with calling men mere warts—"

"Stop!" Juliana covered her ears with her hands. "Stop! This is stupid! This is trivial. You're making a fuss about nothing. Why would anyone make a fuss about such a trivial—" She heard what she was saying and stopped. In each suspiciously naive face, she read a message.

"Sometimes—" Valeska began.

"—we make a fuss about trivial things—" Dagna continued.

"—to conceal or reveal our true feelings," Valeska finished.

Juliana found herself backing away from those too clever eyes, from that too clever observation. The old women never moved, only watched her avidly until she twirled and ran toward the wine cellar. There she stayed until all her fears, her frustrations, her unhappiness had congealed into one big lump, and she swore she'd avoid Raymond and his squire and all the complications they had brought to her life.

12

Don't touch me, Juliana prayed. *Just don't come near me.* The singing of the drunken villagers washed over her while she concentrated on her invocation. Far too close for comfort, the object of her plea sat mounted on his big black horse. His cloak fluttered, revealing the tunic and cream-colored surcoat that had been his wedding apparel.

She would not soon forget the triumph in his eyes when he found it spread out on the bed. He had watched her as she stammered that it was a gift, a suit of clothing like the clothing she gave her servants.

He hadn't believed her. He'd touched the tight weave of the tunic, examined the fine embroidery of the leaves, and he'd accepted her surrender, although she hadn't offered it.

Now his black hair rippled, shiny in glints of moonlight. He looked like the spirit of winter watching the night's festivities. Watching, too, his wife with a regard that spoke too clearly his intention.

Please don't touch me.

"M'lady, will ye pour th' cider on Apple Tree Man? In yer newly wedded state, 'twould be extra good luck t'

have *ye* do th' honors. Mayhap th' apples next year will
be as sweet as ye are." Tosti blushed at his own temerity.

"Oh, ho, the lady has a little admirer," Geoffroi
shouted. Tottering on his horse, he laughed unkindly,
and Isabel giggled with the high-pitched nasal
sound of a woman far gone with drink. The master
castle-builder smiled fatuously, overcome with the
abundance of wine. Tosti glared, offended by the taunt,
yet unable to retaliate. Refusing to leave the festivities
until the last pleasure had been wrung from them, the
noble folk had insisted on accompanying them down to
the orchard. Through the stark moonlight they had
ridden, drinking from the pitcher of wassail until
they stayed on their saddles more from the kindness
of their steeds than from their own skill.

Ignoring the swirl of frigid wind that rattled the
branches, Juliana smiled at Tosti kindly. To herself,
she said, *That's right, Tosti, stand between us. Block
me from his very gaze.* Aloud, she said, "Of course.
One of my sweetest duties is the blessing of the trees
on Twelfth Night."

About to dismount from her gentle mare, she
cringed when Tosti's father said, "His lordship be
pourin' th' cider, too. Just as newly wedded."

Tosti snorted. "They can't both pour th' cider,
Dad, we've only th' one ceremonial cup."

"Both pour," Salisbury insisted, his mouth puckered into a wrinkled knot. "Wish Apple Tree Man
wes-hâl, an' off t' home t' drink th' night away."

Raymond moved his horse close to Juliana's.
"*Wes-hâl?*"

Tosti explained the English tradition to the new
lord. "*Wes-hâl* means good health. Wassail is th'
drink we make, o' cider an' spices, beat together an'

bobbin' wi' apples." He smacked his lips and winked. "With that we toast th' apple trees an' give them thanks fer their bounty. Makes th' spirit in th' tree want t' give us more next year."

"Then Lady Juliana and I would be honored to toast the tree together. We wish the best for the village. Isn't that correct, Juliana?"

Raymond's voice dipped deep and husky when he spoke her name, and the sound transported her back to nights filled with scarlet passion.

The fright Sir Joseph had given her had been for naught. There had been no worry when Raymond touched her. And touched her. When darkness hid them, one from the other, those magic hands found her. No longer did he allow veils between them. Every night he pulled her chainse from her. Every night they lay with all their skin touching until there were no secrets but the ultimate one.

Sometimes, when the delight was over, she'd strain to see his face. Sometimes she could imagine his flesh melting away, his beauty transformed, torn from him by some evil pact with the devil. Mostly, though, she knew the reason she feared him was his blatant claim of possession, and his methods of enforcing it.

The withholding of pleasure, she'd found, was as agonizing as the application of pain.

Dismounting before Raymond could come and help her, she hit the frozen ground so hard tingles jarred her ankles. At once he stood beside her. Stripping away his gloves, he shoved them in his pocket. Before she could object, he took her hands and her gloves followed his.

She squeaked, " 'Tis cold."

He ignored her, demanding, "The cup." Salisbury

placed it in his outstretched palm. Raymond handed it to Juliana, and as she wrapped her hand around it, he wrapped his hand around hers. The carved surface bit into her flesh. His palm rested directly against the back of her hand. Spreading her fingers, each of his fingers entwined with each of hers, he effectively trapped her.

The serfs laughed and jostled, unaware of the cataclysm shaking Juliana. The noble folk drank ale with no care to the morrow. Juliana produced a sickly grin as Tosti poured the wassail from the pitcher into the cup.

"Now what?" Raymond asked, moving behind her.

Resisting the urge to protect her tender neck by tugging her hat down, she said, "We pour it on the soil around the tree and onto the trunk."

Tosti looked appalled at this evidence of forgetfulness in his lady. "Don't forget, m'lady, t' dip th' branches in it first."

Soft against her ear, Raymond imitated the man's dialect. "Nay, m'lady, don't forget that."

She snapped her head around, glaring, but he stood solid and solemn. Never removing his hand from hers, he led her to the closest branch and together they dipped the tip in the wassail. The villagers were singing again, louder this time, and she said, "This will wake the tree from the long sleep of winter."

He tilted his head as a particularly loud verse assaulted them. "I suspect it will."

They moved to another branch, repeated the ritual. "This will prepare it for spring, for the rebirth of life."

"The tree?"

What did he mean? She turned in his arms. Enclosed by a golden cocoon, she felt isolated from the world. The singing washed over her, but she could hear only Raymond's voice. Grubby bodies jostled close, but she could breathe only the scent of Raymond. The stars glittered in the black sky, blindingly bright, but she could see only the stars in Raymond's eyes.

She backed away from him; he held her with his free arm around her waist. "The tree," he said, reminding her.

Abruptly, the roar of humanity invaded her senses. She tried to hurry, but, shackled at hand and waist, she could not. She could only pray again, but now her prayer begged, *Just let me finish without humiliating myself.* Disgusted, she admitted she didn't know what she wanted. Him, of course. But she was frightened.

Of a man! A man whom she'd never seen raise his hand in anger.

And of an animal act that meant nothing in the final tally.

Yet no matter how she snorted and champed at her own foolishness, she still feared. And wanted. God, how she wanted.

When they at last gave the cup back to Tosti, she sighed with such gusty relief the wind groaned in envy.

Raymond smiled at her. She turned to stone. He smiled more, and she stood helpless, unable to move until he turned his back to speak to Salisbury. She was very much afraid he still smiled.

Streaming away toward the village, the serfs shouted their pleasure to the skies. The castle servants, too, followed along. "M'lady? Help you?" Salisbury formed a cup with his hand and boosted her into the saddle, then touched her knee. She looked down at the toothless man, and he said, "Brave woman. Told ye so three winters ago. Braver than a man. Don't forget."

Thankful that the taciturn tracker had made the

effort to encourage her, she agreed, "I'll remember."

She looked for Raymond and found him moving among her villagers, praising their celebration. She ought to join him, but he was so anxious to be lord; let him handle the responsibilities. Ignoring the inner voice that taunted, *coward*, she said quietly, "I'm going back to the keep now."

Salisbury looked at her, then at Raymond. "Won't help," he advised, and she doggedly ignored him.

At her back, the wind urged her on as she plunged toward the castle. Anxious for his stable, her horse moved willingly along the woodland path. Her hands hurt, cold and bare, so as she slowed she tucked one inside her cloak. She moved far ahead of the others, for she heard no sound of tack behind her. No doubt Isabel and Geoffroi delayed Raymond. No doubt she'd be in bed, pretending sleep, when Raymond slid between the covers.

But wait. The soft thud of hooves came to her ears. Only one horse? She turned in the saddle and looked. Behind her rode a man clad in a black cloak, raven hair flowing behind. Beneath his dark brows, she imagined she could see the stars of his eyes. The spirit of winter pursued her, and like a silly girl she wanted to run. Run in a panic until he caught her, brought her to earth. In her loins, a thrum of excitement made her question her own mind. What did she want?

The black stallion reined in beside her, and she called her horse to halt. Raymond panted slightly, his hair askew from his ride. "Juliana, your gloves."

They dangled from his hands, and she snatched at them. Jerking them back, he demanded, "Hold out your hands."

She stared at the gloves with longing, but did as she was told. His touch failed to create the tumult she feared; her fingers were so cold they were almost numb. Quiet and demure as if she'd never experienced his brand of desperate passion, she said, "You've outstripped the others."

"The others aren't coming."

Her calm fell away, and she slewed around to examine the bare path behind. "Why not?"

"My parents found themselves in the midst of the celebration and they rode along to the village."

"You mean the villagers trapped their horses and they had no choice."

He lifted his brows at the contempt in her voice. "They drank deep, but it's not for me to curb them. Besides, I wished to speak with you."

Again, that place inside her gave a little jump. Casual, she rested her chin in her palm, but that was awkward. She crossed her arms on her chest, but he watched where her hands rested. She clutched the pommel of the saddle. "Oh?"

"Do you avoid me, my lady?"

"Avoid you?" She made a sound of amusement, and moved her hands to her waist. "How could I avoid you?"

"I've wished to speak to you these many days, yet it seems you're always busy when awake."

She was nervous, he noticed, and that pleased him. He'd just spent a miserable six days of his life, and all because Juliana couldn't accept one deprived youth into her castle. She'd pretended to be kind to Denys. She'd fed him and helped him learn his duties and introduced him to her children, but she could scarcely stand to look at him. All because Raymond had dared to bring the lad without her permission. The pettiness of it irked and surprised him. He had never thought Juliana would be so uncaring of a youth under her supervision.

Well, tonight he would finish the lessons he had begun, and she would forget all her masculine pretensions. She would stop looking to her lands for security and start looking to him.

She picked up the reins and encouraged the horse to walk. "I can't imagine what makes you think so. What did you wish to speak of?"

"Bartonhale," he said flatly.

That got her attention. No more feigning she didn't see him or hear him, no more polite little inquiries about his health: now she focussed on him like an archer on a target. "What about Bartonhale?"

"It needs a new castellan."

Troubled, she said, "We're sending—"

"Sir Joseph. Exactly. Sending a disgruntled knight to a rich demesne with no supervision."

"I know." She sighed. "But what can be done? There's no one—"

He interrupted her. "There's Keir."

"Keir? He's not one of my men!"

"Nay, he's one of mine. All of your men are now mine."

He saw her uneasiness fly under the tide of fury. "Then all of your men are now mine."

This was their wedding night. He should be soothing her fears, proving she could trust him, not infuriating her with his rightful claims. But the promise of her white-hot body didn't allow for wisdom or logic, and he taunted her. "I will permit you to say so."

She stopped her horse, but he continued on, ignoring

her with the languid ease of a courtier. She asked, "What gives you the right to treat me this way?"

Without turning, he said, "The priest. The vows. The Church. The law. You're mine now."

She galloped up behind him and pulled across his path. "What are you going to do with me now that you've got me?" she taunted back. "You, who have no family, no burdens? I come with lands you covet, true, but I also come with children and servants and villeins and all of them will want a piece of you. All of them will hold you accountable for the filling of their bellies, for their shelter and their safety, for their very happiness. What are you going to do with all those obligations, nobleman?"

Her aim left him breathless with admiration. She put aside her own misery and targeted with unerring precision the subjects that troubled him—which placed her just where he wanted. "I am a nobleman, trained since my birth to handle the responsibilities of large estates. When I pledged myself in marriage, I pledged myself to your people and your children—and you." He caught her reins in his hand. "If you don't trust me to discharge my responsibilities, then I will have to teach you to trust me"—he allowed desire to heat his gaze, and she fumbled for control of her palfrey—"starting tonight."

He saw the moment reality overcame her rage. Her fingers trembled and her voice quavered. "Tonight? You mean you'll come to me in anger?"

"In anger?" With a rasp of laughter, he said, " 'Tis not anger between us, my lady. I have secrets I would share with you, as you will share yours with me."

Her indrawn breath alerted him; he'd said something that worried her beyond the natural caution of a woman with her mate.

"Your secrets . . . frighten me."

Peering into her stricken face, he wondered at her thoughts. The tender, new-shaven flesh of his chin would be pleasing for a woman. His body, his skills had pleased her. They'd proven that time and again. So why, when he asserted they would share the ultimate secret, why now did she cringe from him as if he were a beast?

Anger and impatience rocked him. Hadn't he done enough to win her trust? He said, "I've been patient with you. I've allowed you to keep your chaste bed. I've wooed you slowly. But it's clear to me I've made a mistake. You mistake tolerance for weakness. My lady, it's time to show you who will be the father of your sons." He emphasized the plurality of the word, and pushed her palfrey forward. "Go to the keep now, and I'll start your lessons."

Her hand slapped down on her mount's neck, and the horse sprang forward. She knew a shortcut, if only he didn't follow too closely.

He didn't. He sat watching her ride away.

Anger was a safe substitute for despair, and throughout the wild ride along the narrow path she shouted her rage to the elements. How dare he act as if her lands were his to dispense? How dare he threaten her with himself, raising the unwanted specter of Sir Joseph's warning?

Abandoning her horse to the one stable hand, Juliana stormed away. She flung back the door to the keep, and it smacked the wall with a satisfying thud. Did Raymond think he could control her with his intimidation? She stomped on each stone leading to the great hall. She put her hand on the handle of the door, and it swung open with a force that pulled her with it. She stumbled in, not understanding until she saw *him* towering above her. "You dare?" she cried. "You chased me here?"

Raymond gleamed with his triumph. "Nay, my lady, I led the way. Do you think that puny animal you ride could beat my horse?"

"Of course not. Anything you do is better than anything I do." She slid out of her cloak and flung it in a great, bat-wing swish across the empty room. "Of course you ride better than I."

"You little witch. You reproach me for the puny things I can do?"

"What can't you do? You take over my castle, charming my servants and my villeins until they don't remember who their lady is. You bring in a strange youth and make him a squire. Do you think I don't know that Layamon comes to you for his orders?"

He reared back like a stallion affronted by a gentle mare. "Would you have me leave you to sink beneath the burden?"

"Why can't you just sit around on your rump like the other men? Why can't you leave the running of my lands to *me*?"

"It's winter. Surely you don't expect me to loaf until spring?"

"That's just what I expect. Why must you poke your nose where it's not wanted? Why don't you behave like other men?"

Grabbing her shoulders, he lifted her to her toes, leaned down until they were nose to nose. "If I behaved like other men, my darling, you'd be letting out the waists of your dresses. You'd be thrashing beneath me, not moaning in your sleep when you dream of me."

"You conceited ass. You think I dream of *you*?"

He smiled, but it was only a display of teeth. "Don't you?"

"Nay, I—" With horror, she realized he'd trapped her, for she couldn't tell him of what she did dream.

He brought her closer, crooning. "Don't you? Don't you dream of me?"

His breath, scented with apple and spice, fanned her face. His eyes, green jewels of light, teased her. All along her body, contact brought heat of his body, produced heat in her own. "Raymond." Her lips moved without a sound, but he heard, for he lifted her with an arm at her shoulders and one under her knees.

Behind his head, she saw the beams of the ceiling whirl and rush aside, saw the casement as he entered the solar. He tossed her on the bed and feathers rushed up to envelop her. Struggling against the plush restraint, she heard him shut the new-hung door. Propped on her elbows, she watched as he discarded the surcoat and tunic. Opening his breeches, he paced toward her and she saw that the waiting was over.

Enclosed in the room, once so large, now shrinking, she never thought of denial. She never thought of her lands or her secrets or his transformation. She never thought at all. Instinct, blind and trusting, cocooned her against fear as he climbed on the bed, pushed her cotte to her waist, settled himself between her already open legs. His hands on her bare skin sent a thrill through her. She'd have him at last.

Without a hitch, he moved inside her. His groan shook the rafters. Her cry echoed without restraint. They'd waited so long, she ached. She moved against him, trying to ease the engorgement of her tissues; he kept her still with his hands on her hips.

Savage, fiery, he thrust against her. Furious, she

smacked his shoulder, wanting to respond with her own fire. He grunted beneath her attack, bent close against her neck, nuzzled her. She dug her heels into the mattress, lifted herself to him, and in a simultaneous burst, they climaxed.

Sinking down together, they panted like two of the king's runners. He tried to lift himself off her; she pulled him back down.

"I'll crush you," he protested without vehemence.

"Nay."

"Should we remove our clothes?"

"Aye." She wasn't quiescent as she should be. Her sensitive skin burned with an unquenched fire. Inside her, little trills of sensation rippled as her body tried to find more of the long-awaited sensations.

Still encased in her, he detected it; noticed the heat of her skin and the restless movement of her legs. For the first time in six tense days, he chuckled. "For a woman who doesn't want me, you're proving insatiable."

"Shut up."

The silk of her leg rubbed up the back of his, soothing him as she abused him. "I'm only a man," he said, but by slow stages, her fever transferred itself to him. He pushed her hat off her head, sought the lacing of her gown with his fingers.

Watching him, her lashes shaded her eyes in unconscious coquetry.

"I'll love you only until I'm exhausted," he warned.

"That should prove satisfactory."

The way she said it made him feel invincible, and he half groaned, half laughed. This promised to be a long night.

13

Pickaxes thumped in an uneven rhythm, and the usual bustle in the bailey was absent. Raymond threw a genial arm around Keir as they watched the Twelfth Night revelers trail in, pale with the morning's payment for last night's sport. "Sad to watch, aren't they?"

"Even the stoutest clutch their stomachs when they drink too deep," Keir said. He looked at Raymond from toe to head. "You, however, do not seem to suffer from this complaint."

Raymond puffed out his chest. "Married life agrees with me."

"Lady Juliana complied with your desire for consummation?"

Remembering only the night filled with scarlet emotions and not the wild conflict preceding it, Raymond said in astonishment, "Aye, certainly she did."

"I had surmised," Keir said delicately, "that the Lady Juliana had reservations about the final act."

Raymond felt too good to pay the observation any heed. "Perhaps at one time she did. But her objections were easily overcome."

"Easily?" Keir repeated the word, tasted the word, then shook his head. "Then why, even though you shared her bed, have you been like a badger in love with a porcupine these last weeks?"

With a great burst of laughter, Raymond bellowed, "You jest."

As solemn as Raymond was jolly, Keir said, "I never jest."

"Juliana . . ." How to explain Juliana to Keir? She purred like a kitten when petted, never seeming to get enough of the caresses he lavished on her. Her astonishment at her own response expressed itself in little squeaks and moans, and once he'd distinctly heard the whisper, "To hell with Saint Wilfrid's needle."

He'd laughed at that, reminding her they were wed and she was indeed a chaste woman. Her grip had tightened on him then, and the words had faded away. Aye, he'd cured her ills with the application of wedded bliss, and he looked forward to the next treatment with unbridled eagerness.

Raymond couldn't explain Juliana to Keir, he realized, and instead waved a dismissive hand. "Women are easily handled."

"Easily," Keir repeated, expressing his reservations with one raised eyebrow.

Raymond turned away from the gate and wandered toward the keep. "A woman's needs are minor. Not like a *man's* needs."

Keir kept pace with him. "I would hesitate to agree with such an assessment. A woman's problems tend to be of an emotional nature. Women wish to be loved by their mates and by their families, to be respected in the community. When a man has what he considers to be problems, they are usually of a physical nature."

Impatient with such nonsense, Raymond demanded, "Such as?"

Keir looked him right in the eye. "Such as which corner to piss in."

"You're the porcupine, man. Are you trying to tell me something?"

"Only that I believe your scheme for the disposition of Bartonhale Castle has caused strife between you and Lady Juliana."

"Nonsense!" Raymond clapped his hand on Keir's shoulder. "Who better than you to take over the management of my second estate?"

"No one better," Keir said with a fine irony.

"Juliana gladly gives up her responsibilities to me. If at first she seemed reluctant, 'twas because she didn't know me."

But actually, they'd settled nothing last night. Their mating had been cataclysmic, but he wasn't fool enough to think he'd diddled her brains away. In the broad light of day, she would wish to lift each and every one of her burdens again, and she would balk as he relieved her of them. "The woman," he said to himself, "doesn't know what's good for her."

Keir shook Raymond. "Perhaps I should not have interrupted your orgy of self-congratulation, but I did wish you to realize the pitfalls of your new status. Still, you should never doubt you are good for Lady Juliana. She is like a wounded bird in your hand, sometimes frantic to escape, sometimes complying with your desire to help, and you should not yield to her entreaties to let her go. She cannot be healed except with your restraint."

"You're a deep one, my friend, but—"

The door of the keep slammed back and a frantic

cry interrupted Raymond. "Fire. Fire!" Fayette dragged Ella and Margery out by the arm, and screamed again, "Fire!"

Raymond broke into a run, Keir by his side. Catching the girls around their waists as they descended the ladder, Raymond asked, "What fire?"

"In th' kitchen," Fayette said.

"In the kitchen," Raymond repeated.

Above him on the landing, Denys cried, "Is Margery hurt?"

"Get out of the way, lad," Raymond commanded. "The girls are unharmed, but my Juliana—" He bounded up the steps.

Before he could enter the keep, Papiol dashed out shrieking, "Fire! We are all going to burn. Fire!"

Raymond shoved the quivering wreck of a castle builder aside and sprinted through the great hall and down the spiral staircase. Shrieks and shouted imprecations resonated against the stones, and he met two boys with buckets coming up. "Is it out?" he asked.

"Aye, m'lord. 'Tis out, but 'tis merry hell down there."

Merry hell? What did the lad mean? As Raymond rounded the last corner, he stopped so abruptly Keir rammed into his back, knocking him down a few steps. Merry hell, indeed.

Every servant who should have been above was below, waving his arms against the smoke so that the massive room looked filled with crazed windmills. Every one of them was talking, giving his version of the incident or lamenting the cleanup. His parents stood on overturned kettles, craning their heads to watch the madness. Sir Joseph leaned against the stone in the corner, watching the mania and laughing softly. Layamon strode back and forth, trying to herd the servants back up the stairs and succeeding only in moving them from side to side. The cook stood loudly weeping amid the soaked ruin of her kitchen, while Juliana, blackened with soot and wet from head to toe, stood patting the cook's back and speaking into her ear.

Raymond's gaze settled on the evidence of the greatest damage. Juliana's skirt had been burned to her knee. Her hand was wrapped in a white cloth, and pain pressed a hard line between her brows. "The kitchen must be moved to the bailey," he muttered.

"Raymond!"

His mother's screech made him close one eye against the misery of the shrill note.

"Raymond, we were almost burned in our beds." Isabel jumped off her kettle and flailed her way through the crowd.

Geoffroi joined them, pressing so close Raymond backed up a few steps to gain the advantage of height. "A terrible tragedy, narrowly averted by my own quick thinking."

"Your father told everyone to come down and lie on the fire," Isabel said gushingly. "And such a surge there was to obey."

Layamon waved from across the room and shouted, "'Twas not so bad. Only a bit of an escape from the pit, if you follow my meaning."

Geoffroi glared. "I told you softness to a woman would avail you nothing. A real man would—"

"Get out!" Raymond bellowed. The noise abruptly died, and he jumped off the steps onto the wet floor. His foot went out from under him; he regained his balance and his fury seethed all the more. "Get out!" His finger swept the room. "Unless you have a reason to be here, get out."

The first rush of servants to the stairway was like the foam that tipped a wave. Behind the first rush came the force, pushing up and up, catching his protesting parents and dragging them in the midst of the swell. Sir Joseph was carried along, negotiating the currents with jabs of his ever-present stick. In an amazingly short time, the room stood empty, save Keir, Layamon, the cook, and Juliana. Raymond stood with his wet feet in the largest puddle and demanded, "What happened?"

Layamon squatted beside the rock-built fire pit in the middle of the floor. The oven for baking bread swelled out from one side. The other side, a wall with a single thickness of stone, had crumbled away. Layamon pushed the rubble with his finger. "Was the fire too hot, woman?"

The cook wailed, "Not more than any other time."

Keir squatted beside Layamon. He, too, stirred the rubble, then the charred remains of the wood. The acrid odor of wet charcoal rose, and he grasped the end of a log and pulled it out. "A large log."

"Sent down in a load an' shoved in by me new kitchen boy. He don't know much about fires, yet." The woman mopped her face on her damp apron, leaving streaks of soot on the broad, fair face. "Still, I'll always maintain it shouldn't have popped th' end out like that."

"Before I allowed this kitchen to be used, we tested the strength of the fire pit and oven, again and again. I don't understand how it could have crumbled," Juliana said. She leaned against the oven with a weary wince that brought Raymond's wrath bubbling up.

"Not often enough," he roared. In two strides he reached her side and reached for her hand. She jerked it back, but he glared until she extended it. Gently, he unwrapped it. The back was only dirty, but the palm was reddened in random splotches, and a blister had formed. The cook hovered, craning her neck to see over his shoulder, and he directed, "Bring a clean bucket of water."

As the woman hurried away, Raymond lifted the charred area of Juliana's skirt. With her free hand, she slapped at him. "There's nothing there but a few singed places. 'Twas my hand I set down in the embers."

With awesome patience, he asked, "And why did you do that, my lady?"

"Because in the rush to put out the fire, someone pushed me down." She sounded cross. "If that blasted boy hadn't come into the great hall yelling about the fire, Cook would have had it extinguished with no problem."

"Here ye are, m'lord." With a thump, Cook placed the bucket beside his shoe. Straightening, she looked for a cloth to dry her hands. She settled for her own sleeves, muttering, "Fools don't know how t' aim fer th' fire. But m'lady's right, I would've had th' fire out. M'lady insists we keep th' full buckets on hand, an' I could've done it."

Raymond brought the bucket up and Juliana plunged her hand in. "It's cold," she said. Her shoulders relaxed. "It feels good."

Glancing down at the men, Raymond asked, "What caused it?"

"Maybe . . ." Keir paused doubtfully. "Maybe fire stress to the stones."

Layamon stood and shook out his knees. "Maybe."

"We'll move the kitchen out to the bailey at once." Raymond indicated the oven with a wave of his hand. "If we start on the fire pit immediately—"

"Nay." Juliana's voice was flat.

Raymond froze, his arm uplifted. "What?"

"Nay. The kitchen stays where it is." Juliana swept her loosened hair back from her face. "We'll bring the master castle-builder in to look at this."

"Ha!" Raymond said, remembering Papiol's blanched face.

Juliana ignored him. "Maybe he'll have some ideas why the wall failed, and how to fix it so it doesn't fail again. Next time—"

"Next time?" Raymond rumbled.

"Next time we bring a new boy into the kitchen, we'll drill him on what to do in case of fire, so he doesn't run squawking up the stairs and rouse the entire castle."

Juliana's exasperation was obvious, but not nearly as deep as Raymond's aggravation. "After this demonstration of the dangers of a fire in the undercroft, you would leave it here?"

"Nothing happened," Juliana answered patiently. "When I designed the kitchen, I took good care to put the fire away from anything that would burn. If you'd look around, you'd see most of the damage was done by the panicked rampage of the idiots above stairs."

He did look, and it was true.

Juliana continued persuasively, "The well is down here. As Cook says, I insist buckets of water be kept ready at all times."

She lifted her hand from the bucket and examined it. With her other hand, she explored the injuries, and

Raymond was reminded of the night before. Of her soft hands exploring him. And he knew one of those soft hands would be aching for days to come. "We'll move the kitchen outside," he said.

She didn't lift her head. "Nay, we won't."

"Aye, we will."

"Do you think"—she exploded, her voice rising—"I would allow my children to stay in a place where there is any danger? Even I am not so stubborn."

His voice rose, matched hers, exceeded hers. "And even I am not so shortsighted as to allow you to continue with this madness."

"This is not your concern." She stopped, gulped in breath, and regulated her tone. "I am trying to say this is a woman's concern."

He didn't bother to regulate his tone. "You are my concern." He was roaring again, and he didn't care. "Everything that happens here is my concern."

She shouted back. "Not in the kitchen."

From the corners of his eyes, he saw the observers stepping back, but he didn't care. This damned woman—*his* damned woman—was arguing with him. "Not in the kitchen? Where else? Not in the garden, not in the bailey, not in the great hall, not with your children, not with the defense? What is my concern?"

Juliana, too, seemed to realize she'd overstepped her boundaries, and she sounded subdued when she said, "Well, the kitchen's not your concern."

Cold reality prodded him; hot anger burned him. "Is the defense of your castles my concern?"

She squirmed under his considering gaze. "Aye. Well, aye, that's a manly concern."

"Then you will be pleased to know I've informed

my trusted knight Keir the castle at Bartonhale is his to maintain as our castellan." He watched the red color ebb up her neck, up her cheeks, to her forehead. "I've also decided to give you permission to keep the kitchen in the undercroft."

He turned away, letting his cloak swirl around him in a grand gesture, and stalked toward the stairs. A moment before it hit, he heard a swoosh, and then the water from her bucket plastered his back. He dodged none too soon, for the bucket itself followed, and like the cold north wind he swept back to her for retribution.

She didn't cower. She held out her face for his slap, and he smashed his mouth on hers. With her mouth already open in a surprised gasp, it took no more than a second to remind her of the night's passion. He locked their lips together, locked their bodies together, leaned her back against the rounded oven, and groaned when she wrapped her legs around his waist. When he lifted his head, he looked at the enraptured face that rested in the crook of his elbow. "Listen to me, and mark this well." Her eyes flew open, and she watched him warily. "I do not hit women or any other simpletons. When you displease me, I will treat you thus, and leave you dissatisfied. Remember that, when next you rouse my anger."

He lowered her to her feet and headed toward the stairway once more.

As he knew she would, she drawled, "If that is my punishment, I will displease you often."

His cape did not swirl so well when wet, but he turned with a competent flourish and said, "Swear not so, lady mine. First you should find out what I do when I am pleased."

* * *

That smile. All flashing white teeth, tanned and dimpled cheeks, eyebrows cocked at a quizzical angle. His smile. A taunting smile, as if he knew she would be tempted to please him, just for an introduction to those delights he promised her.

As if there could be more delights than the ones he had taught last night.

Taking care not to break the heat blister on her palm, Juliana folded the tightly woven brown cloth in half and spread it over the trestle she'd set up by the arrow slit.

"Th' tunic first, m'lady?" Fayette asked.

Juliana nodded absently, and Fayette laid Raymond's ragged old tunic over the cloth to use as a guide. With a rough chunk of chalk, she outlined it, then whipped it away. "There ye be, m'lady. All ready fer yer cuttin'."

He was lying. He had to be lying. There could be nothing he hadn't done to her in bed. . . . But a niggling bit of curiosity kept her wondering, and a smile tugged at her mouth. No demon, he. Sir Joseph had lied about that, too. All through the night, she knew Raymond had retained his manly form. She knew, because she'd explored every bit of him and found him to be quite human. Or perhaps more than human, with his stamina and his expertise.

Fayette knelt beside the chest which held the woolen materials, dyed and packed with camphor to keep out the moths. "Will ye be wantin' t' cut th' cloak next?"

"Bring the scarlet for that. 'Twill look elegant with his new surcoat, yet 'twill be serviceable enough for everyday wear."

"Aye." Fayette winked in saucy appreciation. "An' 'twill make him up pretty, him wi' that dark skin an' hair."

"I suppose it will." Untying her scissors from her belt, Juliana tested the edge. "I hadn't thought about it." Fayette's coughs sounded suspiciously like laughter, but Juliana ignored her. Keir—who really seemed to know his smithing—had offered to sharpen them. She jerked her finger back and sucked the tiny cut. It seemed he had done as he had promised.

Keir.

That bit of betrayal ached like a sore tooth. While she wanted—needed—someone of trustworthy character to take over the care of Bartonhale, nothing could sweeten the fact that Raymond had given the position to Keir without her permission.

The scissors bit into the cloth with a snap.

Her permission.

He didn't need her permission. By every law in England and France and Aquitaine, by every law in the known world, the disposition of her lands now rested in his hands. And though they were competent and caring hands, the years on her own had taught her much, and she wasn't ready to give up control. There was no safety in dependence.

"Well done, m'lady." Fayette whisked the tunic away and handed Juliana the bundle of scarlet cloth. "I'll have th' sewin' maids start on it at once."

"Have them finish it by tonight," Juliana instructed. "Lord Raymond is in rags. Until he moved his trunk in with mine, I had not realized . . ." That his shabby dress wasn't merely male carelessness. She'd been horrified to discover he owned only the clothes on his back.

"Aye, 'tis a shame." Fayette cast a dark look at the well-clad Geoffroi and Isabel where they sat, heads together, by the fire. "Smell like rotten meat, they do."

Juliana didn't answer. What could she say? She couldn't approve such criticism of the maid's betters, yet she would not reprimand Fayette. With a flip of her wrists, she spread the thick wool on the table, looking up only when Fayette whispered, "God help ye, m'lady," and moved swiftly away.

Isabel stood beside the table and with a bitter kindness that could turn sweet milk to curds, she asked, "Are you talking to yourself, my dear?" Not waiting for an answer, she sat on the tall stool her maid had provided. "I've been hearing the most interesting rumors about you."

Juliana snipped the scissors and watched the flash of the blades in the sunlight. Should the cloak close with a string tie around the neck, or should she create a more elaborate yoke? With the yoke, she could attach a hood for warmth, but from what she'd seen of Raymond, he preferred to grab a hat and jam it on before leaving the keep. Or to go about bareheaded. She frowned. Although she'd reprimanded him, still he forgot, and just this afternoon she'd had to chase him clear to the door with his hat.

"Well might you frown." Piqued at being ignored, Isabel sounded a little sharper. "I know the whole story of your escapade three years ago."

A string tie was the simplest, Juliana decided, and would therefore be Raymond's choice. A string tie it would be. Having distanced herself from Isabel's blatant cruelty, she answered, "No one knows the whole story."

"Enough of it to condemn you, and even if you were to deny every word"—Isabel lifted one brow, but Juliana refused to justify her silence or her behavior—"there is still the matter of your reputation."

"My—"

"Which is in shreds."

"You have been busy." Juliana tightened the cloth and walked her fingers across it as a measurement. "To whom have you been speaking?"

Isabel waved an airy hand. "Everyone."

"I can hardly believe *everyone* has the bad taste to talk to you."

"Such sharpness is not attractive in such a young woman." Isabel turned Juliana's face to the light. "But you're not too young, are you?"

"I'm getting older all the time," Juliana said drily. "Why don't you tell me what you want, and then I'll tell you to go to the edge of the earth and drop off?"

Isabel tittered, not at all offended. "Go to the edge of the earth and drop off. How amusing. You have a witty tongue, my dear. I suspect you would do well at court. It's almost a shame Raymond can't keep you."

"Ah, so we come to it." Juliana tried to be as sophisticated—or at least as uncaring—as Isabel. "Why can't Raymond keep me?"

A swift change of masks, and Isabel became the caring, commiserating bearer of bad news. "We told you before. Raymond is the only heir of a great house. He can't have a woman like you as his wife. No matter how carefully you hid them, no matter how firmly he quashed them, the rumors would overwhelm you. He'd have to banish you or be banished with you." With a sob in her voice, she said, "And you know how honorable Raymond is. He'd insist on being banished with you. He would spend the rest of his life in this provincial backwater. The king would be without his greatest counselor. The kingdom would suffer."

"All because of insignificant me," Juliana finished. She distrusted the smile that curved Isabel's reddened lips.

"You doubt me."

"Not at all. Everything you imagine may come to pass. But I didn't want to marry your Raymond." Juliana set the scissors and began to cut a straight line guided by the weft. "Why should I care what happens to him?"

Isabel tapped one curved nail on the table. "Look at what you're doing."

Juliana glanced at the scarlet material that seemed so significant to Isabel. "Cutting?"

"Cutting what?" Isabel demanded impatiently.

Still puzzled, Juliana said, "Cutting a cloak?"

Isabel leaned over the table. "For whom?"

"For Raymond."

"What kind of clothes?"

Now Juliana understood, and the scissors began their trek across the material again. "Everyday clothes."

Isabel tossed her well-coiffed head in triumph. "One can easily understand the import of that."

Deliberately stupid, Juliana asked, "You're offended because you think I shouldn't have Raymond work?"

"Nay, nay." Isabel slapped her hand on the cloth just ahead of the scissors, and Juliana jolted to a halt. "You're making clothes for Raymond because you've conceived an affection for him."

Juliana stared at the thin, aristocratic fingers so close to her own.

Scornfully, Isabel continued, "One of those sickening, all-consuming affections like Queen Eleanor's troubadours sing about. I thought nothing of it when you made him that fine outfit—and it was fine, my dear. If you should ever desire a position in court, I'm sure I'd be glad to recommend you as seamstress to her majesty."

"My thanks," Juliana said with a sarcasm that eluded Isabel.

"Where was I?" With cupped hand on forehead, Isabel thought. "Ah, the clothes. Well, of course I understood when you made Raymond that princely tunic and surcoat, but these everyday clothes betray you."

Juliana did not have to feign puzzlement now.

"My dear, I myself kept Raymond's court clothes in excellent condition, for of what use is a son except to further the family's ambitions? And if he doesn't embody wealth and power, how can he gain further wealth and power? It's part of the image, you see."

Juliana did see, and it sickened her. "You believe I made Raymond fine clothes so he could go to court and gain new honors from King Henry. But you believe I make him everyday clothes—"

"Why, to keep him warm." Isabel braced both hands, leaned across the table, and smiled fatuously. "'Tis obvious by the thickness of the material, the generosity of the cut."

"Perhaps," Juliana offered, "I only wish to assure myself he'll not sicken and die, thus ruining my chances for advancement."

Unable to conceive of any ambition other than her own, Isabel agreed. "Possibly, but there's a passion between you, both in bed and in battle."

"That's lust."

"Ah, is it lust that makes you gaze on him when you think he's not looking? Is it lust that brings the color to your cheeks when he glances up and catches you? Is it lust that makes you hum while you weave, and is it lust that makes you run after him with a wool cap when he goes out into the cold?"

A longing, previously undetected, called itself to Juliana's attention. It centered itself in her chest, quite unlike the other longing Raymond had called up, but still she insisted, "It's lust. I don't wish to lose so skilled a bed partner."

"Your actions bespeak a greater emotion. Doesn't your breast ache with it?"

Juliana's hand flew to her chest like a guilty confession, and she mumbled, "Lust." But this was a pain of the heart.

"You love him. Confess it."

The scarlet cloth, lit by the strip of sunlight, burned Juliana's eyes. Isabel's hands were spread like a spider's legs across her cloth. The scissors flashed temptation, and Juliana yielded. With an unsteady laugh, she cut through the material, chasing Isabel's hands backward until Isabel gave a shriek of pain.

"You cut me!"

"Aye. I did." As Isabel sprang across the room to Geoffroi, Juliana reeled away from the trestle table and fought her way outside. Standing on the platform outside, she took big breaths of the fresh, cold air and looked over her bailey. Like iron to a lodestone, her gaze found Raymond. He held her palfrey for young Denys, patiently showing him the ways of a horse.

His ragged brown cloak could not detract from his aura of masculine glory, and although he laughed the wind whipped the sound away. He was strong and brave, kind and clever, and too loyal for his own good. Juliana put her hand to her chest. The ache now burned like unshed tears. "I do love him. And I'm going to make him hate me."

14

Juliana had been the image of the perfect woman all night. Her voice had never risen with excitement. She'd never laughed aloud. She took extra pains to ensure that the young squire, Denys, was well fed, slept on a pallet, and had a blanket. She moved with grace, dealt patiently with servants, and refrained from pointing out the superiority of the supper Cook had prepared on her makeshift fire in her undercroft kitchen.

The entire castle was worried.

What had dampened her vivacity? Raymond leaned his elbows on his knees and watched her as she moved from torch to torch, removing them from the sconces on the wall and giving them to Layamon to extinguish. "Is she really so offended that I gave you Bartonhale Castle?" he murmured.

"I tried to warn you," Keir said. "You look out over the lands and see the place where you will put down your roots. She looks out over the lands and sees her home."

Raymond glanced at Keir. His usual imperturbable friend had a slight pucker between his brows—a sure sign of agitation. Raymond said, "I'll convince her 'twas my own blundering that disgruntled her."

"Do so," Keir advised. He stood and stretched. "You have ways to sweeten her disposition I do not, and I would prefer that if the lady is angry, she is angry at you."

Slyly pleased, Raymond chuckled. "A bit in love with her, aren't you?"

Keir looked right at him. "Aren't we all?"

He left Raymond with a half smile on his face. "Oh, aye," Raymond whispered. "Aren't we all."

He welcomed it, this sweet emotion for a woman. So long ago he'd seen her, captured her, then found himself captivated. He hadn't liked it, hadn't liked the softness she engendered in him. He'd seen it as another manifestation of his monstrous cowardice, but now he wondered . . . was it only the recognition of one kindred soul for another?

One by one, the servants found their places among the reeds or on pallets, rolled themselves into their rugs, and closed their eyes. The usual banter was absent tonight; they all experienced the strain of living with an unhappy mistress. Rather than retreating to the solar, Juliana pulled a bench closer to the fire and sat down. Her back was to Raymond—deliberately, he was sure. A man, when he was angry, would roar and bluster. A woman took refuge in silence until like a chastised dog the man came to beg pardon. Raymond stood, checked to make sure his tail was firmly tucked between his legs, and went to ease her manner toward his friend. If not . . . well, perhaps he could lure her to their bed and bribe her with love. He smiled at his body's immediate response. He'd bribe her, regardless. Casually, he wandered over to rest his hand on her shoulder. "Come to bed."

She shrugged in a rude attempt to dislodge him. "I'm not sleepy."

Raymond considered her. True, she didn't sound sleepy. She didn't sound angry, either, or offended, or any of the ways he'd expected her to sound. She sounded frightened.

Frightened. That he would beat her about the scene in the kitchen? About Keir? Hunched over the fire, cradling her bandaged hand, she watched the embers as if they would speak to her if she waited long enough.

With his toe, he shoved at the figures sprawled around the hearth and they rolled obediently away. He perched on the other end of the bench, as far from her as she could wish. "I'm not sleepy, either." Stretching out his hands to the flames, he said, "This reminds me of our first night together."

"Two moons ago. So much has changed since then." She sounded distracted. "So much remains the same."

He watched her rub the scar on her cheek, and thought he understood her thoughts. Words were his tools, and he picked them with the care of a master craftsman. "You thought I would force my will on you."

A shudder shook her, and she lifted her gaze to his. The despair he'd suspected, the shame and fear, filled her eyes. He scooted closer, lifted his arm to wrap it around her shoulders, but she cried, "Don't touch me!" Glancing around at the wrapped figures around them, she lowered her voice, but her intensity did not diminish. "You don't want to touch me."

What a statement! He suffered when he didn't touch her. He sweated, struggled with demons while he waited to touch her. Joining in the dance of love each night had not eased him. It had only made him aware of his needs, of his growing sense of possession, and of how delightfully she danced to his music. Cautiously, he said, "I like to touch you."

"Nay." She shook her head. The copper-colored hair flew around her shoulders, and she couldn't seem to stop. "You wouldn't want to if you knew."

He exhaled in a long, comprehensive breath. So—this wasn't about the day's events. He gripped the edge of the bench with his hands and tested her. "I want to apologize about Keir."

Her fevered gaze found his. "Keir?"

"My knight. Your new castellan."

"Oh." She waved a dismissive hand. "Keir. Why do you distract me? This is of no moment now. I have a confession to make."

He swept a strand of hair off her cheek to prove he *could* touch her, and when he leaned back she looked at him as if he were dead to her. Unable to find adequate words, he crooned, "My lady love, don't hurt yourself so."

Her hand pressed the place above her heart, and her head drooped. She seemed to be listening to some dirge inside herself. Whatever swept the hope from her life and the joy from her face was so terrible—so she believed—he wouldn't long for her once he knew it. And for some reason, she had decided he should know now. He didn't hesitate. Voice rough with smoke, but luxuriant with compassion, he said, "Secrets are a burden on the soul. Tell me yours, and I'll carry half the burden."

She made a sound in her throat, half snort, half sob, and all skepticism. "No one wants a woman like me," she answered. "Certainly not a man like you. The king's kinsman, heir to a noble title and fortune."

"Ah." He drew out the breath. "You've been talking to my parents."

"Your mother. Isabel." She choked on the name. "She's a dreadful woman."

"Surely an understatement."

"But she knows the truth of matters."

"Such as how I should live my life?" Her stricken face forced him to take a grip on himself. "Isabel knows the truth of nothing."

"She knows what you don't know."

He took a breath and took a chance. "About your rape?"

Her anguish wasn't pretty, and he could no longer restrain himself. He snatched her close against his chest, wrapped her in a hug so tight she couldn't escape. He murmured, "You see? I did know, and it doesn't matter."

She fought her way out of his arms as if they were instruments of torture, not protection. "You don't know anything."

Heads lifted off the floor, and he propelled them away with one sweep of his hand. "Tell me."

"You've been asking questions." She wrapped her shawl closer in a self-protective gesture. "Just like your mother."

Setting his teeth, he refused to answer.

Her accusing gaze wavered, then dropped. "Nay, you wouldn't ask questions. Who told you the rumors?"

"You did."

Her gaze snapped back to his. "Nay. That is . . . did I talk in my sleep?"

"We haven't been sleeping enough for you to talk," Raymond said, taking her hand. He stroked the rough knuckles, watching as his thumb dipped into the hollows and scaled the peaks. "You dropped clues, my girl, bits of a puzzle to piece together. At first, I thought you had taken some inappropriate lover to your bed and been caught. But then I thought—would a secure woman ever strike a man as you struck Felix?"

"You've taught Margery to strike," Juliana mumbled.

"*Taught* her. Women are so imbued with gentle qualities, they must be *taught* to defend themselves." He gripped her wrist until she looked up at him. "Who taught you?"

"No one."

"Exactly. No one. So some hard experience taught you. When Sir Joseph taunted you, threatened you with such violence, and expected you to cower, it became too clear."

"Sir Joseph," she said with loathing. "You knew because of Sir Joseph."

" 'Twas not all Sir Joseph." Catching a handful of her glittering hair, he said, "This told me."

She froze.

"Someone cut it, didn't they?" The firelight painted a false color on her face, now white and strained. "Sir Joseph?" he asked, knowing it to be false.

"Nay." She formed the word with her lips, but no sound escaped her.

It sounded like a guess, but he already knew the truth. "Your father. He cut it so all the world could read the sign of your shame."

Tears filled her eyes and overflowed in silent, wrenching agony. Her intense whisper sliced through the sighs of the sleepers, the crackle of flame. "But I *wasn't* raped."

Taken aback, Raymond studied her.

Her trembling chin firmed, her hand squeezed his so hard his knuckles popped. "I fought so hard, and I escaped unscathed, but the truth didn't matter. Only what appeared to be the truth mattered. My father wouldn't listen to me. I told him and told him. He said he didn't believe me. He said it was my fault I was taken. He said it was my fault anyone wanted to take me, because I dressed attractively and smiled at the men. He said it was my fault I was hurt, and he told me I had to marry . . . had to marry."

"Felix?"

She turned on him in something like rage. "Aye, Felix! Do you know *everything*?"

"Not everything. Not nearly enough. Not soon enough. If I'd known before he left . . . let me kill him," he said.

"Nay!" Horror bathed her in stark shades of white skin and red cheeks. "He's not worth going to confession for."

Any other time, he would have laughed at her succinct summing up. " 'Tis a sin I'd carry lightly on my soul."

"I might as well blame Sir Joseph's staff for striking me when Sir Joseph swings it."

"You believe Felix is an instrument of some greater authority?"

"My father had wanted me to wed Felix, and I had refused."

"Your father." Raymond condemned the man by his very tone.

"He could have forced me. He could have locked me up and beat me until I agreed, but then he would have had to tend to my children. The servants would have been unhappy, and they would have burned his dinner, let the fire go out, and made his life a misery. And I would have been angry at him. It would have been uncomfortable for him, and he was a man who liked his comforts. So it would have been easier . . ." She rocked back and forth, holding her belly as if it ached. "I think sometimes my father conspired . . ."

She took a deep, quivering breath, fighting to keep the tears at bay. "Father said his reputation would be repaired if I wed."

"Your father's reputation?" he asked ironically, hiding the rage that made him want to rail at a dead man.

Here was the anguish Raymond saw. It wasn't a rape that destroyed Juliana, nor the violence she'd been subjected to. It was her father's betrayal, and the suspicion of a yet greater betrayal. She knew her father had wanted her to marry Felix. She knew he believed she had been raped and his subsequent humiliation of her had etched her soul.

But had her father been the driving force behind her kidnapping? Had he encouraged Felix to rape her and thus force her to wed? Could he have ignored her anguish and pain to enforce his will? It seemed a sly, sideways method of coercing his only daughter, but Raymond had heard nothing to admire of the man.

With a show of fierceness, she said, "Aye, *his* reputation." Then her vehemence faded. "When I wouldn't wed Felix, he hacked off my hair with his knife so he would remember, every time he saw me, my shame."

Raymond's heart misgave him, for he comprehended more than he would say. He, too, had been subjected to the greatest indignities a person could

sustain, and found his survival instinct too powerful.
He'd compromised his religion, his upbringing, his
principles. Her confession tempted him, made him want
to tell her of his own guilt, but he couldn't. His iniquity
was so much greater than hers, she would eventually
come to despise him—and her disgust would wound him
beyond reparation. As a sop to his conscience, he pushed
his hair behind his ear and turned it toward the fire. His
glittering earring drew her gaze, and he asked, "Haven't
you ever wondered why I wear this?"

Her hand lifted, reached in a slow and almost
reverent manner, touched the beaten gold.

"'Twas one of my master's whims, to have all his
slaves marked with one large loop in the ear."

"It's so large. Didn't it hurt when they put it in?"

"All the marks of slavery hurt, and I still bear them
all. I'll bear them as penance forever." He ran his fingertips along the edges of her shimmering hair. "So
you see, your father didn't understand shame. *We*
understand shame."

She touched her hair as if assuring herself it had
grown, and he was satisfied he'd formed another link
in the chain that bound them together.

Their hands brushed, and she subsided. "Papa
invited Felix back to the castle after he attacked me."

"Why do you still let him visit?"

"Felix never seemed to realize how heinously he'd
behaved. And"—she hesitated—"I was haunted. I
always wondered if it was my fault that he kidnapped me. What if I did entice him without realizing it?"

Guilt had been forced into her soul as surely as the
gold had been forced into his ear, and he said sharply,
"You didn't. Don't even think such a thing. And

you'll not have to face him again." He looked down at his fists. "I suspect Felix now realizes his welcome has worn thin."

"I don't know what kind of fury transformed you. I don't even care. I can only thank you for removing him from my life."

She sounded breathless, almost afraid, but her gratitude shone from her blue eyes. Raymond realized she'd heard about his frenzied attack on Felix. " 'Twasn't hard to intimidate the little maggot into leaving."

She brightened. "Is that what you did? Did you intimidate him?"

"I certainly did."

"Good, because Papa made me wait on him as if I were a servant. He wanted to impress me with my sin. *My* sin." She mourned, "My own father wouldn't believe me."

"I do."

She stared as if she didn't understand.

"I believe you."

"You can't believe me." With a wealth of bitterness, she said, "I'm only a woman, one of Eve's descendants. Men can't be trusted to know their own minds around me. Men aren't accountable for their actions, for I tempt them."

"I've heard that before. 'Tis nothing but a specious reasoning for men who are too weak to control their urges." He patted his own shoulder. "You forget, I've been on the receiving end of a log."

Her laugh was sharp and hysterical. "I wasn't so clever when . . . when that stupid ass kidnapped me. I fought him, and he kept saying, 'This isn't how it's supposed to go.' He beat me until I lost consciousness. When I woke I was alone, and I escaped." She pointed a finger at him as if he'd argued. "But I wasn't raped while I was unconscious."

The rage Raymond felt for her father didn't ease, it only compounded, piled on top of that he felt for Felix. "Was that the argument they used to try and force you to wed him?"

She didn't answer directly. "When a man takes a woman, he leaves evidence—proof that makes a woman count the days until her next monthly flux. There was no evidence. I wasn't raped, and I was glad. Foolish of me, I know, for it shouldn't matter. I'd already been degraded, treated as if my tears and my pain were worthless. But I didn't want to be used as if I were a bucket for his waste."

"It wouldn't matter to me. It matters that you were hurt and unhappy. It matters you've lost your faith in those who should protect you."

"Sir Joseph never believed me when I said I wasn't violated. He insisted I should be grateful I wasn't killed as well."

"Sir Joseph has a lot to answer for," Raymond said grimly. He wanted to shout and beat his chest, and his anger grew with his restraint. All he could do now was soothe her wounded spirit. "But Sir Joseph is not important. You are my wife. You fulfill my every dream. Nothing you do can send me away. Even if you'd been raped, I would not abandon you."

Recalling her mission, she said, "But you must. The king—"

"Does very well without me."

"The queen—"

"Will come to see me if she desires."

"England—"

"Can sink below the waves. As long as I'm with you, I won't care." Bringing his lips close to hers, he gentled her with one soft kiss.

"You can't—"

Another kiss, soft as a spring breeze.

"There's no sense—"

He used his tongue.

With her uninjured hand, she pushed him away. "That's not likely to discourage me from arguing."

She sounded almost normal; brisk, impatient, humorous. His sigh of relief was silent, but heartfelt. Chuckling, he lifted her fingers to his mouth. He ran the edge of his teeth along her knuckles and said, "Come with me. I'll see if I can discourage you from arguing."

"Nothing's settled," she warned, but she allowed him to tug her to her feet.

He led her to the solar lit only by the night candle and thrust her through the door. "Stay here," he said.

The silence in the little room was awesome, and Juliana hugged herself as she waited. She'd failed to drive Raymond away, and she found herself unable to work up any repentance.

So he'd known, and he hadn't judged her lacking. He'd married her, treated her with honor. How odd she felt, like a babe, free of guilt and bitterness, willing to be pleased with the face of her loved one.

Loved one. She closed her eyes and hugged the thought. The aching place in her chest had been transformed. The tightness had eased. She could take a deep breath, could laugh aloud with no restraint. Lifting herself on her toes, she twirled through the reeds like a rosy cherub. Dust rose beneath her feet, and she decided to decree a castle cleaning tomorrow.

Tomorrow, the old would be swept away, and all would be new and clean. She flung herself on the bed and deliberately messed the covers, finding as much pleasure in her infraction as any child.

"Now there's a picture." Raymond's grin was wicked.

She asked in alarm, "What are you carrying?"

From beneath his cape, he pulled two buckets, heaped with snow.

Her euphoria died—almost. Lifting both her hands in firm denial, she said, "Nay."

He grinned even wider, shedding his cape and surcoat, pulled a linen towel from his shoulder, and laid it on the bed. "But you trust me."

"Trust *you*?" She raised her wary gaze to him.

He flirted with her like a lad with a maid. "You do trust me. Don't you?"

Bracing herself against his charm, she answered sternly, "As much as I trust any man."

"That's a start, then." He stepped closer and started unwrapping her as briskly as a mother with a child.

He allowed no struggling, giving her a swat on the rear when she protested, "But I trust my dogs more."

"What an unscrupulous tongue you have," he teased. "You try to drive me away when I plan only the best for you."

"You're thinking of giving me one of those snow baths." She held her breath, hoping he would deny it.

He did not.

"I won't do it," she whispered. She hadn't impressed him. Indeed, she hadn't impressed herself with such a weak objection, for she wasn't sure she did object. Raymond had taken such pleasure in it. She remembered how he'd worshipped the snow, frolicked in it, had made it look like child's play. A snow bath seemed somehow symbolic, a baptism for her soul.

Standing at attention, she put her arms straight down at her sides. "You have my permission," she said grandly.

He seemed to take that for granted. As he disrobed her, he said, "You'll like it." Her short cape flew into the corner, her shoes clattered after them. "These snow baths are a tradition my ancestors brought from the north to cleanse the spirit and the body." Her cotte wrapped around the bedpost. Her hose he flung at the ceiling; one caught on a beam and hung there like some bizarre decoration. Her chainse he tucked under the covers. "For the morning," he said. Then he stripped himself, and she no longer noticed the chill of the air. Something about the sight of his brown muscular body prepared her for warmth.

He moved her away from the bed to stand next to the buckets and plunged his hands into the mounds of soft snow.

Second thoughts struck her, and she cried, "Raymond?"

"Trust me," he said.

Those might be his last words, she thought. Then she thought no more. Cold punched her so hard she screamed. He piled snow on her shoulders. She swung her fist and connected with nothing, but the force of it turned her in a half circle.

He scrubbed her back. She tried to scamper away, but he caught her wrist, swung her around, and her chest met a handful of snow.

She lost her breath and couldn't scream again. He washed her arms. He spoke, but she couldn't hear him. He scrubbed the skin away, so only nerves were exposed. He knelt before her. She would kick him.

She couldn't move her legs. He stood up, said brightly, "Almost done," and with a handful of soft snow, washed her face.

She kicked him.

"Ooh." Those tortuous hands left her, and he leaned over with a grimace of pain. "If you were a little faster, we'd have no children."

"Well, here." She scooped up snow. "Let me cure the pain." He jumped aside, but not quite fast enough. His bellow shook the rafters as she rubbed him with an intimate handful of snow.

"You wretched child." His eyes gleamed as she skipped away. "Do you think you can get away with that?"

Flinging her arms wide, she asked, "What are you going to do? Throw snow at me?"

He picked up a cloth. "Nay. I'm going to dry you."

"Why does that sound like a threat?" she said, wondering aloud. He grinned and reached for her. She rounded the corner of the bed. "Now, Raymond." He stalked toward her. "Now, you deserved it."

"And you deserve this."

She shrieked when he caught her and flung her on the furs. Pouncing on her, he straddled her and began the chore of drying her. Slowly. With great precision and a concentrated attention to parts of her body he deemed important.

When he had finished, she wasn't cold anymore. Flames licked at her—or was that his tongue? "You make me want too much," she said.

"Not too much." The rich timbre of his promise pleasured her ear. "I'll give you everything you desire, then give you more."

Her hands tangled in his hair; she held his head as if he would try to escape. He didn't try. He acceded to her when she leaned into him.

"I like your hair," he said. "I like the thickness. I like the length."

Her gaze clung to his as he salved old wounds.

He lifted a strand to his lips. "It's the color of copper, alive in the candlelight. Look."

He spread her locks across his chest, and she looked. The black of his hair mingled with the red of hers, and she agreed. It was alive. She was alive. And she would love him even when their hair had turned to gray.

In slow increments he moved her back down to him. "Warm me. Warm me with your hands."

Her hands. With care, she loosened them from his hair and brought them along his arms. "You're so handsome," she murmured. Inane words for the emotion that stoked the fire deep inside her. He *was* handsome, but she would have loved him if he'd been an old man or an elf from the woods. He'd given her everything. He'd been lover and friend, mate and adversary, and out of gratitude, she would be bold. She rubbed up, down, and the ripple of his muscles made her explore further.

He watched her from half-closed eyes. When she hesitated, too unsure to go on, he imitated her. He rubbed up and down her arms, worked his way across to her chest. His fingers circled her nipples. "I'll kiss you here."

She blurted, "With your mouth open?"

"I promise."

The arousal she'd experienced the first time she ever saw him had never faded completely. His words, his touch brought it back to painful intensity. Lifting, he sucked her breast into his mouth. His tongue tormented already tender skin. She shivered and chewed her lower lip. Waves of heat, waves of cold crashed around her. His breath puffed beside her breast.

"Tell me what you like," he demanded.

He'd wanted to know that before, and she'd denied liking anything. Now, buffeted by the maelstrom of sensation, she didn't answer. His hands stopped; his mouth no longer shredded her faculties.

"Tell me what you like. Or I can make suggestions."

"Please." She'd waited too long for this. "Please."

"Your legs are so long." He stroked her buttocks, her thighs. "Wrap them around me. Hold me close."

Selfconsciousness returned as she snaked her leg over him.

"This way, lady of my heart. Turn this way." Grasping her ankles, he pulled himself deep into her embrace, and turned so they rested on their sides. Confused, she struggled to lie on her back, but he restrained her.

With light touches, he explored her.

She didn't know what she liked, what she relished, what she wanted. She strained away from her own responses, but he followed her, relentless. "Is it the light touch you enjoy? Or is it the massage of my palm?"

She whimpered as he used the heel of his hand against the bones of her hips.

"I pray you tell me. How can I know without your words?"

His teasing swirled with undercurrents, dark as the sea on a moonless night, and she didn't know how to navigate. She could only clutch his waist and plead with her gaze.

"Is this what you want?" His finger tickled her curls, slipped into the folds of flesh.

A moan rose from her, unstoppable, and she could hardly see him for the heat wavering in the air between them. Moving in reflex, her body undulated against his, but still he murmured and caressed. She reached for him.

He laughed a tortured laugh and caught her wrist. "Do you want me inside of you?"

"Aye." She took a breath. "Now."

"My lady, whatever you want, I'll do."

He should have sounded subservient; he did not. Yet he moved into her at once.

It forced her attention, made her aware of more than her desire. To some women, this act created more than satiation; it created emotions.

She was such a woman, and she wanted to give him everything, love him until they were one.

To some men, this act symbolized more than release; it symbolized possession.

Raymond was such a man. He observed her with such rapt satisfaction she knew a stab of fear. What did he expect from this mating?

Then he moved, and she forgot to wonder. They were the still axis of a twirling sphere. All things centered on them; all things rotated around them. Her awareness wound so tight she twisted and sobbed, fighting to free herself. He held her close, restrained her, encouraged her, until with a silent moan she spasmed. She flew out into the sphere, dissolved, became one with him.

"I will never betray you," he vowed. "Nor you me."

"Never," she whispered.

Triumphant, he rose on his elbow, locked his eyes with hers, and poured his seed into her body.

15

A shriek of outrage pierced the solar door and woke Juliana in the half-light before dawn.

"Bartonhale is mine!"

Sir Joseph? In the great hall? At this hour? She blinked and tried to gather her wits.

"You can't send this overgrown mute with me to Bartonhale! I've been the castellan of Bartonhale for years."

Raymond's measured tones interrupted. "Keir will check the accounting and give you your just reward."

"Are you accusing me of stealing the profits?" Sir Joseph screeched.

"Not at all." Raymond's voice sounded clipped now. "Why would you think I've accused you of such a heinous vice?"

In the pause that followed, Juliana groped for her chainse. Donning it and the clothes piled neatly atop the furs, she staggered into the great hall. Four figures were silhouetted against the fire. Raymond sat on a bench, back to the flames. Layamon and Keir flanked him, and Sir Joseph faced the tribunal.

"You did not accuse me of thievery, of course, my

lord." He tottered dramatically. "But I'm an old man, leaving the place where I've lived and served most of my life. I reserve the right to worry about the future of Lofts"—he glared at Layamon—"especially when I'm uncertain about its leadership."

"Of whose judgment do you complain?" Raymond asked. "Lady Juliana's, for appointing Layamon, or mine, for allowing her to?"

"I did not complain about anyone's judgment," Sir Joseph said sharply. Keir put his hand to his knife, and Sir Joseph added, "My lord."

From where Juliana stood, clad in shadows, she could see the defensiveness that tightened Sir Joseph's features. His bushy white eyebrows shadowed, but could not hide, the craftiness of his bulging blue eyes. He leaned on his stick, pretending he depended on its stout strength.

Or perhaps he didn't pretend. He'd carried the staff for years, using it for intimidation or to emphasize his age. But through those years, he'd grown old, although she'd not truly realized it. After all, he'd always been a presence in her life. When she was a young child and her mother still lived, he'd been a shadowy figure hovering in the background. Later, he'd been the one her father turned to for companionship. She'd tried to please her widowed father, and learned she must please Sir Joseph, too. Only after her young husband died had Sir Joseph stepped forward as an enemy.

And when she'd been kidnapped! She closed her eyes and pressed her fist to her stomach. She'd never forgive him for encouraging her father in his actions.

She opened her eyes when Sir Joseph said, "As a man who's watched Juliana grow up, I would warn you about the defects in her character. She was ever a sly, lying creature, given to unbefitting mirth and pagan celebrations of nature. Watch her, my lord. Watch her closely."

"Or what?" Raymond asked.

Sir Joseph raised one finger and in the voice of a prophet said, "Or you'll find yourself wearing the horns of cuckoldry."

Raymond chuckled.

With a swish of robes, Sir Joseph turned on him. "She seeks to hold her lands in unwomanly possession, and she refuses counsel generously given. If any man thinks he can take control of her property, she'll soon break him. Beware, my lord, beware, or you'll be a victim, like her first husband, or die of a broken heart, like her father."

Before Juliana could leap forward in indignation, Keir asked, "Is it your contention she killed her husband?"

"Much is not known," Sir Joseph answered.

"Or that she broke her father's heart?" Keir insisted.

"It was a lamentable day when he died," Sir Joseph intoned.

Infuriated, Juliana cried out, but Layamon cried louder, and his indignation overrode hers. " 'Tisn't true. None o' it's true!"

"We know it's not, Layamon," Raymond soothed, but Layamon would speak his piece.

"Her husband died o' th' wastin' sickness. He wouldn't have lived so long if Lady Juliana hadn't nursed him tenderly. An' 'twas a shame, a *shame* that m'lady's father was so lackin' in affection, was so concerned wi' his bloated pride, that he treated her as he did. M'lady's mother must have turned in her grave, t' see that happy woman destroyed by her own father."

Shocked, Juliana said, "That's enough, Layamon."

The men swung around as she moved into the light. "Don't talk about my father in such a manner."

"As you wish, m'lady." Layamon subsided, but he muttered, "But 'tis all true."

Juliana ignored his outburst, saying to Sir Joseph, "I don't know what I've done to deserve such contempt from you."

"You're nothing but a Looby Lumpkin, so stupid you can't see the nose before your face." Sir Joseph sucked his lower lip into the gap left by his rotting teeth, then spat. "I've groveled to you my whole life, and this is what I've come to? Exile to a lowly position in a paltry castle?"

Keir's calm tones interjected, "I do not believe Bartonhale is a paltry castle, nor have you been exiled to a lowly position. My experience as a castellan is untested, and I would profit from your help. If you consent to—"

With eyes still bent to Juliana, Sir Joseph took a step forward. "Everyone heard you screeching last night. Did you finally find a man who could satisfy your voracious appetites? Does he know you're a bloodsucker who uses men, then drains the life from them?"

The guilt inside her relaxed. She was exiling an old man from his home, but he'd brought it on himself, and she'd never allow him to intimidate her daughters the way he had intimidated her.

But her refusal to answer infuriated him. His staff clicked on the floor as he paced nearer. Raymond rose from his bench, but halted at her shake of the head. Sir Joseph whispered, "You pretended to be too good for the local lords, waiting and baiting your trap for bigger game. So you have him, your mighty lord, and may you find pleasure in each other."

In a husky, early morning voice, Juliana replied, "My thanks, good man."

Her condescension broke his feeble control. "Rolling in the grass like a green skirt. Like a whore!"

Without thought or repentance, she kicked the staff out from underneath him, and he stumbled forward. "You are a carbuncle on the ass of my existence," she declared in ringing tones. "Get you hence to Bartonhale before I forget our shared blood and throw you into the street like the turd you are."

Sir Joseph regained his balance and started toward her. Raymond, Keir, and Layamon rushed forward, but somehow Denys was there before them. In a voice cracking with youthful zeal, he proclaimed, "Go away. Remove your evil self from here."

Juliana gaped at Denys, perplexed by this unexpected defense, but Sir Joseph recognized the youth. He bent toward him and coaxed, "Stand aside, boy. This is between me and the woman."

"Nay!" Denys's fervor seemed all the more excessive for its incongruity. "You shall not touch her."

Valeska slipped in front of Sir Joseph. "The lad's right."

Dagna, too, pressed close. "Get thee gone, old man. Your time is done."

Craning his skinny neck, Sir Joseph tried to see beyond the women, but he hadn't the courage to raise his stick to them.

Raymond took his arm in a punishing grip. "A cart awaits your departure."

"A cart?" Sir Joseph cried. "I'm a knight. I would ride!"

"Nay," Raymond said. "We wouldn't want you to lose your way to Bartonhale."

Sir Joseph drew himself up and shook Raymond off. "I'll not lose my way. You'll not be rid of me so easily."

As he stumped off, Denys said, "He's the devil." His young eyes burned with a fever he could only have caught from Sir Joseph, and he wrapped Juliana in a hug. "He's been talking to me, tempting me, offering me things that aren't his to offer, or mine to have."

Caught by surprise, Juliana struggled to handle the emotion his long arms and skinny chest roused in her. Once she'd had a husband who hugged her thus, but Denys's hug imitated that of a son for his mother. His head burrowed into her shoulder, and he sought comfort from despair. Patting him gingerly on the back, she said, "He's gone now. Put him behind you."

"Aye." Denys unwound himself from her. He wasn't even embarrassed, didn't even seem to realize the inappropriateness of his action. Obviously dazed by the morning's events, he said, "I'll put temptation behind me." He glanced around the great hall, now stirring with excitement, and his gaze rested on Margery and Ella. "I *will* put temptation behind me."

"Aye, that you will, lad." Valeska took a grip on his arm. "You can start after you break your fast. There's bread and cheese awaiting, and good ale and new milk. Lady Julian has commanded we put some meat on those bones, and Lord Raymond says you'll not sit a destrier until you weigh at least nine stone. Defending her ladyship is hungry work, eh?"

Denys's starved young face lit up at the mention of food, and he trudged toward the trestle table with many a backward glance at Juliana.

Dagna waggled her heavy eyebrows. "The lad follows

where his belly leads. I'd best bring food up from the kitchen."

Raymond winked at Juliana. "'Strewth, you've found a new champion."

"It seems I have," she agreed, and tried to contain the upsurge of affection the youth's thin arms and fervent defense had aroused in her. She'd tried to keep aloof from him and the memories he brought back, comforting herself with the excuse that she saw to his clothes and his belly and that was enough. But he'd watched her as she braided Ella's hair, as she showed Margery how to sew, and when she tucked the girls into bed and kissed them good-night, and his gaze revealed a lad starved for motherly affection. She'd tried to keep her heart closed to him, but she'd have to be a monster not to appreciate the courage he'd displayed for her.

Raymond grinned, obviously aware she'd been won over. "Young Denys is a good lad, eh, Juliana?"

Before she could answer, Keir interposed, "A good lad, but crippled by his upbringing. You will teach him the meaning of honor, will you not, Raymond?"

Startled, Raymond studied his friend. "Lord Peter said honor couldn't be taught, it had to be shown, and even then the results depended on the pupil."

Keir nodded toward the breakfasting Denys. "He is an apt pupil, I think, and not only to those things which are virtuous. He has been shown that virtue is sometimes difficult, and he is impatient."

"Really?" Raymond drew the word out. "Are you ready? I'll walk you down, and we can discuss what you know."

"I must take my leave of Lady Juliana," Keir answered.

He said it without visible emotion, but she blushed as Raymond looked meaningfully at Denys, then at Keir. Bowing in a deep obeisance and backing away, he called, "Tell her all your secrets, Keir."

Keir cocked his head. "I have no secrets."

"Then you'll have none to tell," Raymond replied.

Keir's puzzled expression brought a gurgle of laughter from Juliana. His face cleared, and he said, "He's not always intelligible, but I find him a good man." Putting his hand on her arm, he steered her toward the arrow slit overlooking the bailey. "I thought we could watch as the servants pack for my trip to Bartonhale."

A ludicrous suggestion, for the sun had not yet done more than create purple in the sky, but Juliana knew Keir would not make a ludicrous suggestion without good reason. He wanted to speak with her, and she acceded with an inclination of the head.

His forefinger and thumb clasped her wrist like a bracelet. Not for the first time, she noticed those fingers were the only remaining whole digits on his right hand. The other three fingers had been cut down to the first joint. She flinched in empathy, then flinched again, for she didn't want anything in common with the stolid man for whom her husband had usurped her authority.

He adjusted his steps to hers. "Before I leave, my lady, I wish to thank you for your generous welcome to me."

She suspected him of sarcasm, then acquitted him. Sarcasm required a sense of iniquity which she doubted Keir harbored, or even understood. "I would that I had done more."

"A woman in your circumstances cannot be too

careful, and I saw your occasional lapses of courtesy as merely the instinctive reaction of a woman to a male stranger. Would that all women were as wise as you."

"Would that all men were as astute as *you*," she answered cautiously.

He inclined his head. " 'Tis true, I fear. Most men prefer to use their sword and shield as a substitute for intelligence, and by the time they discover God gave them brains, they totter on the edge of the grave."

"Some not even then," she said, thinking of her father. When they reached the arrow loop, she found she *could* see. The serfs had lit a bonfire for light and warmth, and she picked Raymond out of the figures who hurried past. She smiled when she heard his voice bellow a command, and saw the servants scurry to load the carts as he ordered.

"When a younger man does make use of his faculties, he finds greatness." Keir sounded sad. "Raymond is such a man, and his greatness is the result of a painful maturation. He cut my fingers off."

Her gaze flew to his.

"To free me from bondage." He flexed his hand. "I thanked him, but he cried."

"Cried?" Had she spoken aloud? Did it matter? Keir seemed to hear what she couldn't say.

"You have no doubt surmised Raymond and I were together in Tunis." He braced that mutilated hand on the sill where she could see it. Indeed, she couldn't look away from it. "We had never met each other before we stood on the auction block together. Our master liked to buy good, strong Christian knights and subjugate them to the most humiliating labor."

"Was Raymond a blacksmith like you?"

"For Raymond to be a blacksmith, he would have had to cooperate with the training process." As unemotional as the statement was, it released a wealth of information—about Raymond, and about Keir, too.

"He would not . . . cooperate, then?"

Keir's head turned in a slow arc. His jaw clenched, his eyes flashed, and with a shock, Juliana realized he was an attractive man. She'd just never seen it. Never seen it because of Raymond, and the enchantment he'd woven around her. Keir turned back to the arrow slit, and her awareness of him dwindled.

"He spat on me—literally—because I chose to become a blacksmith."

A half smile played on Keir's lips, but incredulous, she whispered, "Raymond *spat* on you?"

"He was as hard a man as I had ever met. He preferred death to association with the Infidels. What Raymond didn't realize," he said gently, "was that death was preferable to the methods they used to break recalcitrant knights. Our master showed Raymond the way of things."

"He beat him."

"With a great deal of pleasure," Keir said. The mutilated hand flexed on the sill. "In the end, I wished they would break Raymond, just to end the constant bloodletting. I cauterized his deepest wounds, you see."

Shamed curiosity drove her to ask, "What broke him?"

Keir shook his head in self-admonishment. "I talk too much."

"You do not!" she cried.

"I should go below and do a final check on the supplies we are taking."

Desperate for this last information, she asked, "Why did he cry?"

He hesitated. "Are you referring to the moment when he cut off my fingers? Raymond organized our escape. It was successful because of its daring, and it was daring because of Raymond." Meticulous to a fault, he asked, "You've heard we stole a Saracen ship and sailed it to Normandy?"

"Aye. Aye, I have, so go on."

"During the escape, I was caught in a chain on the docks. It tightened on my fingers, and while I could have pulled them off, I feared I would leave much of the inner workings of my hand. So I requested Raymond take a knife and remove the crushed parts. I had crafted the knife, but it was not as sharp as it could have been—"

She shuddered.

"—for we had used it to saw through ropes and to pick locks. Although I was phlegmatic during the amputation, Raymond found he had no vocation for surgery."

Emboldened by his commentary, she picked up his hand and examined it.

He suffered her touch without flinching. "The king's surgeon had to saw off some bone splinters, for Raymond wasn't able to break them off cleanly."

In recognition of his fortitude, she clasped his hand in both of hers.

"Raymond rescued eight Christian knights, four Christian sailors, and two old women—Valeska and Dagna—without loss of life. He brought a laden Infidel ship into a Christian port. Some of my fingers seemed a small sacrifice for my freedom, but he still mourns their loss. This is muddled thinking, and quite a change in his disposition at the time of his capture. Yet the imprisonment changed me, also. Before I was imprisoned, I never found a man I considered worthy of my service."

"And now?"

"I would lay down my life for Raymond." His chin jutted out, bold and stubborn, as he made his demand. "The captivity fired Raymond, made him the man that he is. But it also placed a burden on his soul. I am not a man given to unwarranted sentiment, but I wish Raymond to be happy. Not just satisfied, not just pleased with his situation—happy." He turned her hand in his, bowed over it, and walked away.

She leaned into the arrow slit and waited. Keir appeared and went to Raymond without hesitation. Raymond pointed to the carts, piled with provisions, and at the sturdy work horses harnessed to the carts. Juliana's eyes narrowed when Raymond pulled a small bag from inside his cloak and handed it to Keir. He gestured, giving instructions clearly involving the wall, the keep and, she suspected, her. Money? she wondered. Whose money? Where did he get it? And why was he sending it with Keir?

Yet Raymond and Keir proceeded with their business without answering her queries. Keir stood while Raymond embraced him, as Raymond gestured to the war-horse, a destrier stallion, the finest in her stable, and at the saddle and bridle it wore. Clearly, he was presenting it to Keir—clearly, he'd done it without her permission.

Yesterday, she might have accused him of thievery. Today, she sighed as she considered her situation. It hadn't changed, not really. The conflict between Raymond and her hadn't been resolved. He still imagined he was lord of all of her lands. She still knew her word was law. But somehow, during the night, the balance had changed. Somehow he'd spoken to her with his body, inviting her to join him, be one with him. He'd insinuated that together they were greater than apart. Together they would do more than maintain the lands, they would expand them—and expand their family, too. They would become a great family, one of the greatest in England. She made a face as she remembered his mother's insistence. And of course, in France.

But somehow, this morning, it wasn't the lands or the family that seemed important. She stuck her feet out from under her cotte and looked at them. Newborn feet. She wiggled them. They worked the same as yesterday, looked the same as yesterday, but they were newborn.

She couldn't resist sticking out her hands. They, too, looked the same as yesterday, worked the same as yesterday, but they were newborn. They weren't the same as yesterday.

Could it be *she* wasn't the same as yesterday? That a few simple words—and a snow bath, and an exhaustive loving—had created a new woman? When she'd gathered herself together, seeking all the parts of her she'd given away, all the parts of her he'd taken, she had found she was different. Whole, but different.

A timid hand touched her shoulder. A timid voice said, "My lady?"

The new and different Juliana faced Denys, and she smiled at him without the selfconsciousness that had marred their other meetings.

He realized she'd changed somehow; he tilted his head like a bird and studied her from his bright eyes. Thinking he had been too bold, he dropped his gaze and blushed. "My lady, I wanted to thank you"—his voice squeaked, and he sheepishly lowered it—"for your kindness to me. You've treated me like one of your family"—it squeaked again, and he blushed even brighter—"and I wish I were worthy."

She leaned against the long sill of the arrow slit and took his hand. "You are worthy to be one of my family."

He glowed. "Do you really believe that?"

"Anyone who has the courage to stand up to Sir Joseph has gained my respect." At the mention of Sir Joseph, he cast her an anguished glance, and she urged him on. "Tell me what troubles you."

"Lord Raymond talks about honor. Do you know much about honor?"

She brushed one scraggly brownish lock out of his eyes and thought how she should reply, and her silence made him rush into speech.

"Because Lord Raymond says it's a way of life. He says Lord Peter told him that if a man is to be honorable, he must think honorable thoughts as well as do honorable deeds."

"That's true," she agreed. "But sometimes honor is easier for a lord to maintain than for a woman or, say, a youth. A lord has only to obey the king and his laws. A woman or a youth counts for little with the king or his laws, and so ofttimes our needs drive us where they don't a lord."

He nodded, and his cowlicks flapped. "It just doesn't seem fair sometimes."

"So if you were afraid of Sir Joseph in your mind,

but stood up to him in your body, it doesn't mean your actions were for naught."

"Oh." Squeezing her hand, he mumbled, "Sometimes I steal bread from the table."

At last she saw the direction of his reasoning. Gently, wanting to reassure him, she suggested, "Because you're hungry?"

"Because I might get hungry."

The specter of starvation hung about the lanky youth, tugging at her sympathies. "If I told you to take as much bread from my table as you wish, then it wouldn't be stealing."

He brightened, then his face dropped again. "But in my heart it would be stealing, and Lord Raymond says a knight must be pure at heart, too."

Disgusted with her pedantic husband, Juliana tugged Denys's hand until he stood beside her, then wrapped her arm around his stiff back. "You are so young that purity of heart is yours without even trying."

He broke away from her and stood, chest heaving, glaring from teary eyes. "Nay, it's not. I want to kill my father for what he did to my mother and me, and the priest says I'll go to hell. I want to hurt all the people who refused to help my mother, and Lord Raymond says a knight shouldn't concern himself with petty vengeances. I'll never be like Lord Raymond, so strong and noble. He's got Lofts Castle and Bartonhale Castle, all because he's the greatest warrior King Henry has. He's got you for his wife and Margery and Ella for his children, all because he's honorable in mind and soul. I can't ever be honorable like that! I can't."

She reached for him, but he turned and ran blindly for the door. Her heart ached for the lad who had set his goals impossibly high, and she hoped her honorable, noble ass of a husband didn't tumble off Denys's pedestal too soon or with too big a crash.

As Raymond stood shivering on the drawbridge to wave Keir off, he whistled the tune his sailors had taught him on the merry journey back to Normandy. He'd done it. He'd given Juliana succor and released none of his own secrets. It had been difficult last night, but he'd throttled the impulse to ease Juliana's embarrassment by revealing his own. After all, what would that gain either of them? His transgression opened like an abyss, so wide he could never cross it or fill it in. He could only cover it and hope Juliana never suspected its presence—and hope, too, the edges did not crumble beneath his feet. Thus far, he'd been successful beyond his hopes.

Deep in his soul, he knew a tiny, penitent elation that he'd gotten Keir off to Bartonhale before his friend blurted out the truth.

Raymond glanced up at the arrow slit where Keir and Juliana had stood to say good-bye. He *hoped* Keir hadn't blurted out the truth. Keir had interesting insights into moral character, and he believed in setting things to rights regardless of the hapless victim's protests. That was why Raymond had roused the entire castle to dispatch Keir before dawn, giving as an excuse the blanket of cold that had settled over the land. It had driven the clouds away, yet maintained the piles of snow in the corners of the bailey. It had frozen the mud of the road into ruts and made travel possible. And it wouldn't break, the farmers told him, until spring puffed in. So he'd urged Keir to go while he could, and to take Sir Joseph with him.

With few words, Raymond had sketched the outline of Sir Joseph's evil and suggested, in the mildest tone, that Keir watch Sir Joseph. He hadn't said—not aloud—that he would like to see Sir Joseph dangling from a post at the crossroads, but Keir knew. Keir was an honest man, more honest than Raymond thought always necessary, but he seemed positive Sir Joseph would prove his misdeeds.

Raymond also suggested that once Keir had settled in his new home he prepare to attack a neighboring castle. Lord Felix, Raymond assumed, would benefit from a lesson. Keir reminded him that such private wars were not encouraged by the king, and even Henry's cousin would be severely fined for such an infraction of the king's peace.

Raymond only smiled, so wide and hard his jaw popped. "Lord Felix needs an operation," he said. "To remove a troublesome part of his body. Once it is done, he'll have no more trouble from me, and he'll give no more trouble to my lady."

"Ah." Keir nodded solemnly. "Then of course I see the sense in assisting you with the surgery."

Aye, Raymond was glad Keir had gone, but he would miss him. He was even gladder he'd given Keir the pride of Juliana's stables. The destrier was a reward, an apology, and a pledge of friendship ever-lasting.

Hauling up a basket filled with chunks of frozen mud, Tosti spotted him and shouted, "M'lord!" Tosti waded over the uneven ground to reach Raymond's side. "M'lord, we've dug so deep we feel th' flames o' hell. Do ye think we should stop?"

"Are you on bedrock?" Raymond asked as he slid over and peered in the trench. A dozen diggers panted and stomped to show the hardness of the ground. "But is it bedrock?" he insisted.

" 'Tis stiff enough t' be."

Raymond examined a chunk of the solid stuff, and the dark soil showed particles of stone. "Gravel," he said admiringly. "I believe you've got it."

With a leap into the air, Tosti crowed. " 'Tis deep enough, lads. Halt wi' yer diggin'."

Raymond scratched his stubbled cheek. "Maybe just a little deeper," he said. Tosti halted his dance. "Might as well dig until the stone arrives."

" 'Tis here." Tosti gestured toward the shadow of the wall.

Raymond strode toward the sandstone blocks. "Why didn't anyone tell me?"

"Th' castle builder was here when it started arrivin' yestermorn, an' he screamed an' jumped around like th' lunatic foreigner he is." Too clearly, Tosti's expression showed his opinion of the hapless Papiol. "So he said, in that gibberish o' his, t' put it there, an' we did. Mayhap we should have called ye, m'lord, but wi' yer parents an' yer weddin' an' all th' ruckus—"

Raymond fingered the cuts on the stone. "No matter. Papiol didn't think it would arrive until spring. This shows what determination can do."

"Aye, m'lord. Th' quarry men said they started fer th' castle as soon—"

"As the ground froze." Raymond smiled.

"Aye. An' look, here comes more." A cart, heavily laden and pulled by oxen, labored up the road. " 'Twill be comin' th' rest o' th' week, I suppose."

"Dig at least until midday," Raymond said. "Then we should be through the gravel and down to bedrock."

cheeks, freshly washed, shone with a rosy blush. Her hair, unbound, still sparked with color, and unwillingly beguiled, he asked, "Why not?"

"Because the priest would assign you penance for years."

"It might be worth it."

"The penance would probably be"—she tapped her chin and thought—"sexual abstinence."

His indignation collapsed. "You have saved my father's life. I won't murder him. But for a penny—" He swung on his parents and shouted, "Why do you want to end a marriage sanctioned by the king?"

"Henry only sent you here for his own selfish reasons," Isabel said.

"To care for his Welsh concerns," Geoffroi added.

"He's always in need of coin," Isabel continued.

"And if we pay him, he'll get over his irritation at having his plans thwarted," Geoffroi concluded.

In falsely shocked tones, Isabel said, "Raymond, she cavorted with that man."

Raymond's hands bunched into white-knuckled fists.

"I don't know why we didn't think of it before," Geoffroi enthused. "Lady Juliana was shamed before the whole country."

"Think of the priest," Juliana said, rubbing Raymond's arm up and down, trying to soothe the biceps that clustered.

"Most important, her father wanted her to marry him," Isabel said. "He arranged for the priest to call banns on Sundays and holy days."

"And it is rumored he had a betrothal drawn up," Geoffroi added.

Juliana's massage stopped, then jerked into motion

again, but a tranquil smile still curved her lips. "It was never drawn up. I wouldn't agree to it."

"Of course you would say that." Isabel's lips pursed in a contemptuous moue.

"Did the marriage pledges take place on the church steps?" Raymond prodded.

Juliana seemed to struggle with speech, and at last said, "They did not," in smooth, well-modulated tones.

Raymond threaded his fingers through hers and put his other arm around her. "Then the banns and the betrothal served no purpose."

"But they did," Geoffroi said. "Don't you see? A betrothal is as binding as a marriage . . . almost, and we can declare previous union bonded by previous consummation."

"Nay," Raymond answered.

The hand in Raymond's tightened in sudden, painful tension, and she stiffened in pain and rage. "Annul our marriage? It's impossible."

Smug as a priest on the first day of Lent, Geoffroi smiled. "What's the use of being related to the pope if we can't get a simple annulment?"

Juliana's chin dropped. She took long breaths to recover her equilibrium, and when she raised her head she'd made a momentous decision. Calm and smiling, she said to Raymond, "I won't let you hurt them. But you can throw them out."

16

Juliana shaded her eyes against the sharp winter sun and watched as Geoffroi, Isabel, and all of their entourage followed the winding road down the hill. They were bound for the coast, to catch the next ship that crossed the channel, and she couldn't work up regret at their going. Beside her, Raymond dusted his hands in excessive satisfaction, and she said, "May I ask you one thing?"

He beamed at her. "As you wish."

"Are you really related to the pope?"

His smile disappeared, and he grumbled, "The Prophet Mohammed is my uncle, Charlemagne is my brother, Saint Thomas Aquinas is my godfather, and the apostle John is a dear friend."

Juliana laughed at his droll expression, and Raymond said, "It's my turn to ask a question. Why did you say you shared blood lines with Sir Joseph?"

Juliana forgot the pope in a rush of embarrassment. Clasping her hands behind her back, she whistled once in a short, sharp exhalation. "Oh, didn't you know? He's my uncle."

"Nay, I didn't know." He mimicked her fake innocence. "Why didn't you tell me?"

"Well." Abashed, she laughed a little. "He's not the sort of relative to brag about. He's the eldest son of my grandfather by a serf."

"He's a bastard?"

"Of course, or he would have been heir to my lands."

His eyes were watchful. "Let's see, Sir Joseph is your uncle . . . so there was never any chance of a marriage between the two of you."

Shocked, she cried, "Oh, nay, that's ridiculous."

"'Tis not so ridiculous. At your father's death, Sir Joseph had domination over the castle."

She shuddered in disgust. "Don't speak of such a thing. 'Twould have been a dreadful sin. Why, when the king sent word he'd given me to . . ." She stammered to a halt.

"Aye?" he encouraged.

"To a member of his court—"

"Tactful," Raymond approved.

"Sir Joseph supported my decision to avoid the marriage."

"Your chief man-at-arms urged you to defy the king? Did you believe he did that in your best interest?"

"I . . . never thought . . ."

"I guessed that. Your uncle has much to answer for."

"He was tender about his birth, although 'tis no shame. One hundred years ago William conquered England, and he was a bastard, also."

"I know," Raymond answered. "He was my cousin."

She opened her mouth, reconsidered, and shut it.

She didn't want to know if her husband was truly related to the first Norman king of England.

Raymond grinned at her caution. Hands on her waist, he picked her up and lifted her until their faces were level. She kicked at him, careful not to inflict serious damage, as he teased, "We'll work most assiduously until we have another legitimate heir for our lands. Do you not look forward to that, Lady Juliana?"

"Put me down," she commanded in a grand manner, and he slid her down his body in a long, slow tease. The breath stopped in her lungs, and, ever a warrior, he leaned closer to take advantage of her weakness.

His hand stroked the vein in her throat, a vein that leaped at his touch. "Let us go to bed."

"'Tis daylight."

"The better to see you."

"There's work to be done."

"It will keep."

"The castle builder."

Taken aback, he repeated, "The castle builder?"

"The real castle-builder," she clarified. "Listen."

Raymond listened, and heard the shrill babble of Poitevin French from the trench below. Exasperated, he asked, "What is that madman screaming about now?"

"I don't know." She pointed down the hill. "But I think you're about to find out."

Papiol and Tosti were storming toward them, shouting in different languages and making gestures that crudely translated their messages.

Papiol, with his high voice and arrogant manner, spoke in his rapid French. "My lord, this imbecile has at last broken his head. Do you know what he wants to do? Do you know?"

"What's he tellin' ye?" The flushed Tosti bunched

his fists. "Can't he speak a decent language like th' rest o' us?"

Revealing an understanding he forswore, Papiol spat out the words, "You stupid Englishman. French is the only civilized language in the world. Poitevins are the only civilized people in the world."

Tosti, too, divulged a comprehension he denied, and in a broken French he'd previously disclaimed, asked, "Can ye speak English?"

Papiol lifted one finger and posed nobly. "Never!"

With a beatific smile, Tosti asked, "Well, how does it feel t' be stupider than an Englishman? Huh? Huh?"

Raymond wheeled away, overcome with a sudden onslaught of laughter. Papiol sputtered, and Tosti danced like a fighter in a circle around him.

"That's enough," Juliana said sharply. "This is my wall we're discussing, not some trifling matter which can be dismissed by laughter and insult."

Raymond subdued his amusement. "Lady Juliana is correct." He pointed at Papiol. "Now, what has disturbed you?"

Gathering the shreds of his dignity, Papiol declared, "This dolt has sabotaged the curtain wall, my lord. Without consulting me, the king's master castlebuilder, this peasant has ordered the digging stopped."

Tosti threw up his arms in disgust.

"'Twas on my order—" Raymond began to say.

While at the same time, Papiol said, "He claims he acted on your order."

They stopped and stared at each other. Papiol's consternation was palpable as he exclaimed, "My lord, this is not possible! There must be a strong foundation for a strong wall, and this trench is neither deep enough nor has it reached an underlayer

of rock. As I told you, in the spring the digging will
be easy, and the wall will be—"

"Finished before then," Raymond said smoothly.

Papiol pleaded, "My lord, you must listen."

"Nay, you listen." Raymond leaned down until he
stood face to face with Papiol. "You claimed no more
digging could be done in the winter, but I proved you
wrong. You claimed the building stone could not
arrive in winter, but I proved you wrong. Why should
I believe you about this?"

Papiol wrung his hands. "Perhaps I made some
miscalculations, but my lord, about this there is no
mistake."

"What will happen?" Juliana asked.

Papiol shifted his attention to her. "The wall will
not stand without an adequate foundation."

"So as soon as I put the wall up, it will fall down?"
Raymond asked, skepticism ringing in his tones.

"Not immediately, but *oui*, it will fall down." In an
excess of frenetic emotion, Papiol fell to his knees and
raised his clasped hands high. "Please, my lord, you must
believe me." When Raymond turned his head away, he
walked on his knees to Juliana. "My lady, this curtain
wall cannot be depended upon. Perhaps in battle,
perhaps one day without cause, it will collapse."

Troubled, Juliana glanced at Raymond. "He *is* the
king's master castle-builder."

Raymond folded his arms across his chest. " 'Tis
your keep. Do what you think is best." Her doubts
didn't truly offend him, but he was a man with a
mission. He knew the process of castle building
could be refined; he knew he was the man to refine it,
and he experienced no compunction at using unfair
tactics to sway Juliana for the chance to prove it.

Walking to the end of the drawbridge, she looked out on the work in progress, then over the sweep of her lands. "This is important to me. I want a wall twelve paces wide, with two arrow slits in each merlon and a tower on either end."

Raymond strode to her and grasped her hands. "'Twill be the safest castle in the west of England."

"I want the safest castle in England."

"So shall it be. I have made it my goal to protect you and all that is yours. You have given me so much, and I have given you so little. Let me build your wall."

Her nostrils glowed with the cold, and wisps of hair escaped the scarf that bound her head. With an inquiring tilt of her head, she weighed his sincerity against her fears, and he waited, tense with anticipation, for the results. It seemed the sun would dip below the horizon before she answered, but at last she said, "It will be as you say. Build the wall."

He marvelled at the trust she'd placed in him. Not a complete trust, for she strode into the keep before she could change her mind. But from the woman who'd knocked him arsey-versey the first time she'd met him, this declaration was greater than any he'd hoped for.

"My lord." Papiol still knelt on the frozen ground, an agonized frown puckering his forehead. "My lord, what have you decided?"

"We'll build the wall."

"After the hole has been dug deeper?" Papiol asked hopefully.

"Immediately."

Papiol dropped his head into his hands and rocked back and forth. "This is madness. If you insist on proceeding with this plan, I cannot in conscience remain here. My reputation would suffer. Although I dread the voyage across the sea in the winter, I would leave, and so I beg of you—"

His perturbation seemed so sincere that, for a moment, Raymond doubted his own judgment. The castle builder lacked the arrogant disdain he'd shown, and he was, after all, the king's master castle-builder. Maybe, just maybe . . .

"Ye heard th' master." Tosti sneered. "Get ye gone. Ye're nothin' but a pompous bladder filled wi' th' air o' a flatulent cow."

All Papiol's candor disappeared as he leaped to his feet. Venom hissed from him in a stream of French. "Son of a pig! Worthless bird-turd! You know less than nothing. You insult the king's master castle-builder with your mere presence."

"Yah, yah," Tosti chanted.

The absurd little man ruffled up like a capon, and Raymond ignored the pang which his inexperience presented him. Papiol had probably bought the position of master castle-builder from Henry. "Do what you must, Papiol," he said, "and I will do what I must."

Tosti smirked and strolled away, strutting like a peacock, but Raymond's lingering doubts convinced him to say in English, "Dig the foundation just a little deeper, Tosti."

Tosti whipped around and glared, but Papiol didn't understand or notice, and Raymond didn't care. His own sneaking, gloating pleasure embarrassed him, yet it couldn't be denied. When Juliana's curtain wall was finished and she surveyed her mighty bulwark against intruders, she would know only one man was responsible, and that one man was Raymond.

Her gratitude would be worth any amount of work and worry, and would surely bring him forever into the golden inner circle of Margery, Ella, and Juliana.

Papiol begged. "My lord, please reconsider."

"If you hurry, you could cross the channel with my parents and save yourself the agony of trying to engage a passage by yourself," Raymond said.

"Your parents?" Papiol looked stricken. "You would send me with your parents?"

"They'll travel directly to Henry's court," Raymond assured him.

"I would like to go there directly, my lord," Papiol said faintly, "but for the matter of the fire in the kitchen."

Raymond swung to stand before Papiol. "What do my parents have to do with the fire in the kitchen?"

Distressed, with tears in his eyes, Papiol said, "I know nothing, my lord, but you did ask me to examine the fire pit with a view of making it safer. Somehow the mortar around some of the stones had been scraped away."

"Are you sure?"

"In no way could it have been removed and scattered without a man's help." For all of his disclaimers, Papiol looked and sounded very positive.

"What has that to do with my father?" Raymond asked.

Papiol looked up at the sky, down at the ground, anywhere but at Raymond. "My lord, your parents arrived in the kitchen almost before the fire took place. They were smug and most vocal in their criticism of your bride." He shivered and wrapped his velvet, fur-trimmed cloak close around him. "It's getting colder, don't you think, my lord?"

Raymond drove toward the truth. "So you think my father arranged the trouble?"

"I would not accuse so lofty a nobleman of such deception," Papiol answered.

"Nay, you had best not." In sooth, Raymond realized Papiol intended no insult. "You're right, it is getting colder. Spend another night here, and I'll send you after my parents tomorrow. You'll not have to travel with them except on the ship, and can separate immediately upon landing in Calais. We'll pay you the wage we owe you, plus your travelling expenses for your trouble."

"Many thanks, my lord." Papiol bowed and wandered toward the keep, a pathetic yet dignified figure.

Raymond didn't notice. His mind was bound by this newest horror. Had his parents tampered with the fire in the kitchen in hopes the keep would burn to the ground? They would have lost everything—or would they? None of their clothing and household equipment had been unpacked. Such a fire would have lost them nothing, and gained them all.

Raymond stared out at the lands stretched before him, and found them appealing—but not as appealing as the lady who awaited him inside the keep. What was the last thing his father had said before riding for Henry's court—and perhaps for the Vatican? "We would do anything to end your marriage. Anything."

Aloud, he answered his father's vow. "And I will do anything to keep my marriage. Anything."

"Surrender, knave." Raymond pressed the point of his sword against the Adam's apple of the trembling Denys.

Denys tried to nod his head, and Raymond pulled the sword back. "Nay, Denys, when steel is pressed close against you, it is imperative you do not move. Signify your agreement with a single, 'Aye,' briskly given. That way 'tis clear that though you are defeated in fact, you are not in mind." He sheathed his sword and extended a hand to the youth on the ground. "Come, let's go or Lady Juliana will give us nothing but old bread and sour wine."

Trembling with fatigue, Denys allowed Raymond to hoist him to his feet. With a despair only too obvious, he asked, "Will I ever defeat you, my lord?"

"Not soon, I hope." Raymond flung his cloak around his shoulders, then picked up Denys's cloak. "When you practice sword work in the cold," he lectured, "make sure you warm yourself afterward."

Denys wiped beads of sweat off his forehead. "I am warm, my lord."

Raymond glanced around in satisfaction. The bite of winter had eased as Ash Wednesday approached, and now on this, Saint David's day, the temperature encouraged the first flurries of work that presaged spring. All around them, kettles of water were boiling with lemon balm. Women from the village stood over them with huge paddles, stirring the winter's scum off the bed covers. Juliana had threatened that before Easter everyone would have to strip to the skin and have their clothes boiled, but that dreaded day could be ignored for now. For now, Juliana flew around the castle with her hair pulled back in a kerchief, directing operations with a snap that had the serving women praising her renewed spirit at the same time they bemoaned their duties.

Raymond wrapped Denys in his cloak. "Nevertheless, you should wear this. You've improved these last weeks, but until you fill out and develop the muscles of a man, you haven't the weight to put behind your blows."

"Then of what use is this daily practice?" Denys asked, picking up his sword off the chilly earth.

Intent on soothing Denys's wounded pride, Raymond answered, "You're a good sparring partner for me."

"For you?" The youth's eyes widened. "Lord William of Miraval said you're the best warrior in France."

Raymond roared with laughter. "But not in England, eh?" He laughed again. "William is ever aware of his own greatness."

"He is a great warrior, isn't he?" Denys asked wistfully, trudging toward the keep, dragging his shield.

"Don't do that. You should take care of your weapons. Here, let me take it for you." Raymond hoisted the shield on his shoulder with his own. "William is indeed a great warrior, and I was his sparring partner just as you are mine." He ran a judicious eye over Denys. "I was smaller than you by two stone, and had not your strength of arm until my seventeenth year."

Denys beamed and straightened his skinny shoulders.

"Watch your belly. It takes a long time to die from a belly wound, and 'tis an unpleasant death."

Denys laid hands on his flat stomach.

"And don't be afraid to sweep under my guard. That's why we wrap the swords in cloth. You're smaller and weaker, so you must take advantage where you find it."

"How odd," Denys mused. "That's what Sir Joseph told me."

"Sir Joseph?" Raymond bent his critical gaze on his protégé. "When did you speak to Sir Joseph?"

Denys flushed guiltily. "He, ah, he sought me out the first night I came and discussed my, ah, mother. My prospects."

Raymond squelched his first impulse, which was to give the youth a scolding. Denys's valiant defense of Juliana lingered in his mind, and he contented himself with an austere, "Seeking the advantage is the only thing Sir Joseph and I agree about."

"Aye, my lord." Unhappy with even that mild reprimand, Denys scuffled the dirt. "I try not to think about what he said."

"He was a mischief maker," Raymond said.

"Oh, nay! More than that," Denys insisted. "He was an evil man."

Disturbed, although he didn't really understand why, Raymond answered, "Perhaps so, but he's gone now." Denys raised his gaze, and it burned with a fervor Raymond had seen only recently. Had seen, but couldn't recall.

"Thank Saint Sebastian for that."

"Papa!"

Raymond looked up to the second-story platform that led into the keep.

Margery waved at him. "Papa, Mother says to come in right now or she'll serve you stale bread and sour wine for supper."

Raymond grinned and nudged Denys. "What did I tell you?"

Denys didn't answer, and Raymond was surprised to see a look of hunger on Denys's face as he gazed at Margery. Raymond felt the first stirrings of fatherly indignation, strong and fresh. Margery was a child, eleven years old, almost too young to marry. How dare this young pup stare at her as if she were a woman?

"Tell her we'll be there soon," Raymond called, and grabbed Denys by the nape of the neck. Denys squawked, but hurried along with Raymond until they reached the horse trough. Then he balked, but too late. Raymond plunged him in, headfirst, let him go, and backed away as the youth flung himself out. Hands on hips, Raymond spread himself in his most imposing stance and said, "Don't even think about Margery."

Shocked by the water, shocked by Raymond's accusation, Denys didn't try to pretend ignorance. "My . . . my lord," he stammered. " 'Tis not my intention . . . 'twas never my intention. . . ."

And Raymond's paternal affection for Margery sank under in a wave of kinship with the mortified Denys. For all the wealth of his parents, Raymond had been just as poor as Denys. With the humiliations of his own impoverished youth heavy on his mind, he removed his cloak and briskly rubbed Denys's hair. "Face life realistically. You have no prospects. When you're knighted, you'll become a mercenary, following the tournaments and the wars. Use the serving maids—there are many who've been eying you. But Margery's a maiden of good family."

Stung, Denys cried, "I'm of good family, too."

"I know you are, but you're poor, orphaned, and landless." Raymond could feel the heat of humiliation burning off of Denys, and he wished he knew of some other way to break the brutal truth to the boy. He did not. "Margery is beyond your reach. Stay away from her. Stay . . . away . . . from her."

17

So annoyed he scarcely moved his mouth to speak, Raymond said, "She's trifling with that youth again."

"Who's trifling with a youth?" Juliana left the basket she was packing with bread and cheese and moved to the arrow loop where Raymond stood. In the bailey below them, Margery stood talking to Denys, and Juliana smiled. "She's honing her womanly skills on him."

"She shouldn't do that."

"She has to learn sometime. I learned myself once. I remember how merry it was, how innocent." She looked at him, a mixture of sadness and spirit in her face. "If Margery must learn the ways of a maid with a man, I'd rather she did so under my eye. Denys is safe."

With grim amusement, Raymond questioned her. "Safe? No youth of that age is safe."

"*He* is." Juliana squeezed his arm. "Haven't you noticed? He's in love with her."

"I've noticed," he said forbiddingly. "She's too young for that type of attention."

"That sounds fatherly," she teased.

He stiffened even further. "I think I'm feeling fatherly."

She patted his arm. "Good, because Margery's in love with you."

His annoyance cycled into rage, and he roared, "What? I thought you said she was practicing her womanly wiles on Denys."

Startled by his ferocity, she said, "He's in love with her. She's in love with you. 'Tis nothing but lamb love, the result of spring and youth together. I know if we ignore their infatuations, they will fade. He'll hear her screaming at her sister. She'll see you scratching your belly in the morning. This kind of love is crushed by the first signs of reality. The worst thing we could do is challenge them about it. That would change an infatuation to a crusade, and you know how fervent young people are about crusades."

She returned to her basket, and Raymond wondered if his guilt showed. He *had* challenged Denys about his infatuation. He had thought Denys would take his admonishment with the same good sense he'd shown with all of Raymond's admonishments. But the young man's affections seemed different from his fighting abilities—or perhaps Denys considered Raymond an expert at arms but not at love. Whatever the reason, Denys was now cool, thoughtful, and given to watching Margery with a calculation that made Raymond all the more dubious. "Juliana," he said. "Are you at ease about this expedition?"

"Well." She shrugged. " 'Tis only a trip into my own woods to pick Lent lilies and gather the first greens. Layamon and his men will stay here to watch from the walls. Valeska and Dagna remain within the keep to wait for our return. You'll be with the girls and me, and we're taking the castle serving folk. They've got stone fever from staring at these walls. So I'm as much at ease as I can be, and I have to go out sometime."

"I don't want you to be afraid."

Crossing to him in a rush, she flung her arms around his waist. "You're a wonderful man."

He wrapped her in his grasp. "So I am," he agreed. Laying his cheek on the top of her head, he gathered comfort from her the way steel gathers strength from a forge.

Once he'd been a wanderer, never knowing the comforts of love, and he scorned them as a fairy tale. Then Henry had given her to him, and all unknowing, she'd begun to break away the shell that had held him prisoner since his release from Tunis. She'd maddened him by refusing to accept their marriage, and he'd been determined to defeat the unknown Lady of Lofts.

He'd challenged her, and she'd seemed to yield. He'd thought he won a battle, only to discover her strength and courage had defeated him—and she didn't even know it. She'd taken the lonely, wandering man who'd forced his way into her life and given him a home, a family, and a love that would outlast his very soul. His forebodings slipped away, and he straightened. "Stop loitering, woman. There's something in the woods I want to show you."

She lifted her shining face to his. "What is that?"

"Something you'll like very much," he promised with a leer.

"Aye, spring has a way of making everything grow, doesn't it?"

Juliana gazed at her folk with a bone-deep satisfaction. Their appetites were satisfied, they had picked the greens, and now they sprawled about the woodland grove, entertaining each other with songs, dancing, and feats of daring. Tosti sat nearby, flirting with the female servants. Restless Denys leaned against a tree.

Drunk with spring fever, Fayette and two of the maids stood before the castle servants and sang a bawdy tune about the mating habits of birds, skunks, and other woodland creatures. "To hear them tell it," Raymond murmured to Juliana as she packed the remains of the meal away, "the animals cavort about in one long debauch."

Juliana answered, "The singers just wish to inspire their swains, I trow."

"Fayette's a fine figure of a woman." Raymond tucked his knee up to his chest and propped his arm up on it. "Her swains should need no inspiration."

Smacking his arm with her fist, she chided him. "You're supposed to notice."

"How could I help it? The first night I arrived here, you practically threw her into my arms. I had to see what I was rejecting."

She'd forgotten that, and she mumbled something, not even she knew what.

"But I wanted only the best." He pulled her, struggling, onto his lap. "So I held out for you."

The people around them grinned and nudged each other, and Tosti called, "Just 'cause you own th' tree, doesn't mean ye can't look at them other apples, eh, m'lord?"

Juliana intercepted a glance of masculine tribute passing between Raymond and Tosti, and lifted her head off Raymond's arm. "I'll take no more insolence from you, Tosti." She turned swiftly to catch Raymond's grin. "Nor from you, my lord."

Before she'd realized it, he'd lifted her near and, using the most devious of weapons, wrested her resentment away. Her eyelids weighed too much to lift when he finally raised his mouth, and she wondered if the laughter and amazement that filled the grove were for her or for the performance before them.

"I think," he said into her ear, "you'd better look at this one. 'Tis Margery and Ella, performing the most extraordinary feats of acrobatics."

She sprang erect and stared at her daughters. Someone had stretched a taut rope between two sturdy tree trunks, and Ella—her Ella!—strolled across it. Well, not strolled, exactly. Crept would be a better word, but regardless, the child was standing up and, putting heel to toe, moving across the rope. Raymond clapped his hand over Juliana's mouth before she could scream a protest. Only then did she notice Margery stood below, juggling three shrivelled apples—while eating one of them. She slumped against Raymond.

The castle folk were silent, too, straining to watch with an intensity that told Juliana how much they wanted the girls to succeed. Once, Ella wavered and would have fallen off if she hadn't grabbed a convenient branch. Once, Margery dropped her half-eaten apple, but before she leaned to pick it up—while still juggling the other two—she said, "Almost dropped that one."

Everyone laughed in one explosive gasp, and Raymond removed his hand from Juliana's face. Ella reached the other side, jumped the five feet to the ground, and the ensuing applause saved him from a reply. Juliana applauded more enthusiastically than anyone, and welcomed a hug from each of her beaming children. "Well done, dearlings! I was thrilled. Now run along and play. We've had enough entertainment for the day."

"Let's play hoodsman bluff," Tosti proposed, and a chorus of argument greeted him. Eventually, he organized a ball game, and Juliana turned on Raymond again.

"Who taught my children such skills?"

"Valeska and Dagna." Raymond spread his hands in an innocent gesture. "Haven't you deduced who those old women are?"

She shook her head.

"Camp followers tagged along after our Crusade to the Holy Land. So did anyone with a taste for adventure. Wandering tailors, priests, cooks, leeches . . . and entertainers of every shape and color. They came from every country. They played music, the strangest sort of tunes. They sang in the strangest sort of languages. And"—he tapped her forehead—"they performed acrobatics and juggled."

"Ah." Juliana understood now. "When the Crusaders were captured—"

"Aye. Every tailor, priest, cook, and entertainer was sold, just as I was. Valeska and Dagna were slaves, valued for their entertainment and their healing arts, and they wisely preserved the skin on their backs while I squandered mine. They kept me alive, although I cursed them for it."

"So you helped Valeska and Dagna escape in gratitude for their gift of life."

He looked amazed, then amused. "Not at all. We needed them to scale the Saracens' walls for us and secure our ropes. We needed them to attach the ropes from the dock to the ship. They helped *us* escape."

Juliana stared with open mouth until Raymond pushed it shut with a finger under her jaw. "I'll have to treat them with greater respect," she said. "Right after I do them a violence for teaching my children such hazardous games."

A yawn caught her unaware, and he suggested, "Lie down and rest." He patted his lap, and she eyed it with interest. He shook his head at her in reproof. "Rest, I said."

With a disappointed moue, she settled her head on his thighs, shut her eyes, and dozed until Raymond dangled a daffodil above her nose. The scent, rich with the earth's promise of spring, woke her. She opened her eyes, and the vivid yellow petals hung so close she could see every velvet vein. He touched it to her lips, and she could taste the sweetness of its caress. "Mm." She sighed and asked, unnecessarily, "Did I sleep?"

Raymond laughed. "Aye, that you did. 'Twill be dark soon, so we must leave."

She hated to go. The trees above them had leafed out, it seemed, even as she slept, but not even the beauty of the trees could compare with Raymond's face. She raised her hand to his cheek; he caught it and kissed the palm, then each one of the fingers.

"Only one more thing could make this day perfect," he told her in a husky whisper that reminded her of beds and sweaty bodies. "Privacy."

"Tonight," she promised.

"Aye. Tonight." He stood, stretched, and called the servants.

They came running to shoulder their packs, and Ella arrived on Fayette's sturdy shoulders, crying, "Where's Margery? She promised she'd play with me, and she didn't."

"She's here somewhere." Frowning, Juliana looked around. "Although I don't see her. Has anyone seen Margery?"

The servants murmured and shook their heads; then Fayette said, "Last I saw her, she was talkin' t' Denys."

"Denys?" Raymond roared, "Where's Denys?"

"Raymond." Juliana took his arm and shook it. "We'll find them. They've probably just strayed—"

"Search the woods," Raymond instructed. "See what you can find."

His urgency scattered the servants, and he shouted after them, "Be back here before full dark." He peered down at Juliana, and in the light of the dying day his skin appeared gray. Furrows lined his brow, and for the first time since she'd known him, he looked all of his thirty-five years.

Alarmed now, she asked, "What is it you fear?"

"They're alone. It's going to be dark soon. There are wolves and boars in those woods."

"Tell me the truth," she demanded.

"I took Denys to task for worshipping Margery from afar, and the lad resented it. I'm afraid—"

"Sweet Mother of God." Juliana interrupted him, remembering her conversation with Denys, remembering his unadulterated hero worship of Raymond. "You fell off the pedestal."

"What?"

"He thought he could never be as noble as you. He thought he was hopeless. So why not do his worst and . . . abduct Margery?" She read the confirmation in Raymond's face, and pushed her rising panic down. "He won't hurt her," she said, as much to reassure herself as Raymond. "He's a good youth, he's just misguided."

"He's a love-crazed, land-crazed youth," he said. "He has taken her for his own gain. I'm sure of it. I knew there was something wrong, something he wasn't telling me, but I was too distracted—"

She put out her hand and grasped his. "This isn't your fault."

"Whose, then? My responsibility is the safety of everyone on your desmesnes. Especially the safety of our children."

Our children, he called them. *Our* children. She dashed a tear off her cheek. "Perhaps my fault. You warned me she shouldn't practice her lures on him, but I thought he was safe."

"My fault," he insisted.

"We'll share the fault."

"Share it, be damned." He started toward his horse. "I'm going after them, and I won't be back until I find them."

She caught him and said, "You can't track at night. You're no huntsman. You'll confuse the tracks if you go galloping through the trees. We'll send Tosti."

"Tosti?" Flabbergasted, Raymond asked, "What do you want that dirt digger for?"

If Juliana could have smiled, she would have. "He's my tracker. He comes from a long line of trackers. His father . . . his father found me after I escaped from my abductor, patched me up, and took me to meet my own father. Tosti and his father will find Margery, you'll see."

"I remember," Raymond said slowly, doubtfully. "But—"

Tosti came forward as if he'd been waiting for the call. The spritely fool had disappeared, and in his place stood a responsible man, aware of his value to the demesne. "M'lady, do ye want me t' start after them at once?"

"Of course," Raymond snapped.

Juliana lifted a hand. "Do what you need to. If you wish to have your father—"

Tosti cinched up his belt. " 'Tis more than twice as fast wi' me father, an' I've already sent one o' th' village folk back fer him."

"Good," Juliana approved. "Salisbury's got the instincts of a hunting hound."

"Aye, if not th' hound's stamina. Not anymore, anyways. We'll start tonight, m'lady." Tosti squinted at the sky. "Moon's close t' full."

"I'll come with you," Raymond said decidedly.

"Nay, m'lord, if ye please." Tosti seemed to be begging. "Leave it t' those wot know wot they're doin'."

"I can help," Raymond insisted.

"M'lord, I must speak th' truth. Ye'd be in our way." Without apparent thought to their different stations, Tosti patted Raymond's shoulder. "Ye don't do th' trackin', an' we won't do th' fightin'."

Raymond clearly struggled, but at last he nodded.

"When you've found the trail, send a message to us. We'll go back to Lofts and prepare to travel. If you find Margery"—Juliana drew a breath—"send word to us as quickly as you can."

*   *   *

"What do you mean, we can't go?" As Valeska helped Raymond don the chain-link hauberk that protected his chest and back, her booming voice broke the funereal silence of the great hall. "We always go with you."

Raymond rubbed his eyes, sandy from lack of sleep. No one in the castle had slept all the night through, and now the old women were taxing him with their displeasure. "I'll go faster if I go alone."

"I'm going with you," Juliana said.

He swore in languages he thought he'd forgotten.

"Don't use those heathen tongues on me. I'm going with you."

He stared at his wife. She looked better than any woman who'd passed such a night had the right to look. All night long, they had lain in bed, shoulder to shoulder, so alone they might not have been together. When Salisbury arrived, they came to their feet without a word, dressed and ready to go.

The toothless old man spoke to Raymond. "Didn't find yer daughter or th' youth. Found an area showed signs o' a fight." He stood before the fire, twisting his hat in his hand. "Two roods from th' place where th' castle folk ate. Proved th' little lady didn't know his plan. M'son's waitin' there." Again he twisted his hat, and turned his head toward Juliana. He looked through her and spoke to the air, but the reassurance was for her. "Couldn't see no signs o' blood."

Raymond glanced at Juliana, and he died inside.

His gentle wife looked hard and determined, like a commander who faced battle alone. He had betrayed her trust, and he knew what she knew— she no longer depended on him. Last evening's sharing of the fault had been pretty words, no more, for if she willingly left the safety of her castle walls despite her own ferocious fears, it could mean nothing less than the total collapse of her belief in him.

And after all, why else had she needed him? She had children, she had properties, she had food and clothing and servants. He wasn't worth much as a husband, but he'd thought to ingratiate himself by giving her unconditional security.

He'd failed.

Yet now he had the chance, not to redeem himself, but to offer reparation, and he'd not allow anyone to get in his way. As he buckled on his sword, he repeated, "No one's going with me to search for Margery."

Juliana said, "Valeska, Dagna, I want you to remain for Ella. She's come to depend on you, and when she wakes she'll be wild if she's alone."

"Layamon represents security," Dagna argued.

"He'll be patrolling the walls with his men." Conjuring a threat from thin air, Raymond warned, "Someone may hear of Margery's plight and seize the chance to attack Lofts Castle. That's why you must stay within the keep."

Clearly uncomfortable with the presence of females, Salisbury added, "Rough terrain. No delicate castle women."

Valeska snorted. "Delicate." She looked at Dagna. "I'm flattered, sister, aren't you?"

Made patient through weariness, Raymond said, "You'd slow me down."

"I won't," Juliana said.

"You aren't coming." Raymond was adamant.

"I am."

A man's resolution, Raymond found, was for naught when placed beside a mother's anxiety. The night had not yet yielded to the sun when they rode over the drawbridge. The ride was silent, broken only when Raymond said, with some surprise, "Why Juliana, you have no hunting dogs."

"Nay. My father did not hunt in his last years. They cost to feed, so he sold them and I never replaced them." They had left the road and entered the woods before she thought to say, "We'll get more this summer for your hunting."

A sop, he thought, to keep her noble, useless husband entertained. "They would be useful *today*," he said.

She agreed. "All the more reason to acquire them."

When they reached the glade where the struggle had taken place, no one was there. Stopping his horse just outside the circle of trampled grass, Raymond asked Salisbury, "Where is he?"

"Don't know. Gone on ahead."

"In the dark?" Raymond said, but Juliana shushed him.

The old tracker looked worried. As the light had improved, he examined the ground. "Strange markin's," he said with a frown. "Someone here after I left. Lotta someones. On horses."

"What kind of horses?" Raymond frowned. "Farm horses?"

"Big horses. Knights' horses. Seen th' print o' this one afore." He got on his knees beside a mark almost invisible to Raymond. "From m'lady's stables."

"You've made a mistake," Juliana told him. "No one left the castle last night. It couldn't be from my stables."

He peered at it again. "M'lady's," he insisted. Putting his face close against the ground, he sniffed.

Like a hound, he followed his nose around the ground until Raymond demanded, "What are you doing?"

"Blood."

Brief and terse, but the one word galvanized the mounted couple.

"Whose?"

"Where?"

"New." The old man prowled along, sniffing, stiffening with alarm. "Not here last night. Wish m'son was here. Good snout. Good wi' tracks." He quivered when he found something. "Holy Mother. Lookee this."

He held a rope knotted with two bloody knots, and Raymond loosened the knife at his belt. Chills crept up his spine; he felt as if some malevolent presence watched from the surrounding trees. He slid out of his saddle as Salisbury crawled into the bushes, and Juliana swung her leg over and landed beside him.

Catching his arm, she said, "Nay, you don't." She didn't speak aloud, but whispered as if the atmosphere affected her, also. "You're not following him and leaving me alone in this eerie place."

He wanted to tell her that this was why he hadn't wanted her to leave the castle. He couldn't concentrate on the business at hand when he must worry about her, but reproaches were too late. She was here and frightened, and quite right when she said she couldn't be left in a glade that had proved to be a menace to someone. To Tosti? "Come, then."

Bent almost double, they trailed Salisbury through the underbrush. A thin strand of blood led them, and Raymond thought he could smell it, too. Smell blood, or fear, or both.

Salisbury muttered as he scrabbled through the bushes. "Bad smell. Bad feeling. Wish Tosti—"

He broke off with a gasp. Raymond leaped forward. One horrified glance verified that the body stretched out on the green moss was, indeed, Tosti. Looming over Juliana to block her view, Raymond instructed, "Don't look. Go back to the clearing."

A keening rose from Salisbury, wild and forlorn, and she tried to push her way forward. "I've got to help."

Raymond pushed her. "Tosti's been tortured."

She began, "Salisbury—"

"Salisbury wouldn't want you to see him like this." She wavered, and he pressed his advantage. "I'll do what must be done. Go back."

It went against her instincts, but she did as instructed. Salisbury had been good to her once, treating her with the care of a mother, and she owed him that same care. But Raymond was right. Salisbury would not appreciate her seeing him in his weakness; he was a man to whom weakness was an embarrassment. That explained why he seldom spoke to her; the memory of her collapse and his own compassion mortified him.

But now the knotted rope gained new significance in light of Raymond's revelation. If the murderer had wrapped the rope around Tosti's head and tightened it with those knots over his eyes—she grabbed a branch and swayed. Bile tasted sour on her tongue, and she whispered, "Margery."

There were murderers abroad, and her daughter blundered lost through the woods with a skinny youth. Imitating Salisbury, she searched the edge of the clearing, looking for tracks made by two children.

She couldn't find them. Only trampled grass and

broken bushes that signalled the passage of a troop of horsemen. "Raymond," she screamed. "Raymond!"

He came dashing out of the underbrush with Salisbury on his heels and found her mounted on her palfrey. "They're going after my Margery. We've got to go."

"Aye, you've got to go," he agreed, his mouth set in a grim line. "Back to the castle. When we started, we were seeking a boy and a girl. Now we'll be following a troop of warriors. We don't know what Tosti told them before he died, but I would guess the warriors will take Margery and Denys for ransom."

She leaned from her horse. "You don't understand. I'm her mother. I'm not going back."

"Someone has to fetch Layamon," Raymond said sharply. "I can't defeat this troop single-handed and without the weapons I need."

A sound argument backed by Raymond's gimlet gaze dented Juliana's certainty. Someone did indeed need to go for help.

"I'll go." Salisbury looked right at her, acknowledging her for the first time and expressing himself so even Raymond understood without difficulty. "Ye go wi' th' knight, m'lady. Get yer child outa their hands. Men that'll do such t' a man such as Tosti'll do worse t' a helpless girl."

Raymond's breath hissed through his teeth. "Tosti must be buried."

The old man met his gaze. "Tosti'll not go anywhere. Take m'lady. I'll go fer Layamon."

Exasperation exploded from Raymond. "Damn it, Salisbury, she's a woman. She shouldn't ride into battle."

Salisbury met Raymond's gaze. "She's strong. Ye trust in her, m'lord."

Raymond's eyes narrowed, then his expression went blank, and he carefully spaced his words. "If my lady wishes to ride on with me, then of course she must go. However, she must do as I tell her for her own protection."

"I will," Juliana said.

"Let us go, then."

Salisbury pointed at the broken shrubbery. "Easy path. An' m'lady?"

"Aye?"

He came to her and pulled a dagger from his belt. Weighing it in his hand, he said, "Not a pretty knife. Made it meself. Hew wood an' cut rope an' slice a man's liver t' hash." He handed it up. "Take it. Use it fer me, fer Tosti."

"We will avenge his murder." It was a prayer and a vow.

Tears glinted in Salisbury's eyes. He looked down at his shoes and dabbed his nose with his sleeve. "Yer daughter's strong, too."

Tucking the knife into her belt, she hurried to catch Raymond. They followed the trail of slashed foliage and horse droppings. The brown of winter still clung close to the earth, while high above them, the leaves of spring were making their appearance. The forest floor exhaled a damp, mossy scent as the morning became afternoon, and Juliana's tension grew. Her neck ached from bending to avoid branches. Her eyes ached from holding them wide, sure that if she so much as blinked, she'd miss something important, some clue that would lead them to Margery.

She wanted to speak to Raymond, to ask him what

he thought, where they were going, what his plans were, but the stony cast of his face blocked the words in her throat. His resentment slashed her with the force of a gale wind, snatching her breath and her warmth, and she was sorry for it, but she wouldn't turn back. She'd walked in Margery's shoes. The longing for home, the anger, pain, and embarrassment Margery must be experiencing formed part of Juliana.

Raymond stopped in a clearing where an abandoned hut stood. "We'll eat a hasty meal here," he said.

"Should we stop? I thought we were closing in on them."

Without a glance at her, he said, "We'll need food to fight this battle."

Grudgingly, she nodded and dismounted. Loosening the bag that held the food, she rummaged in it while he searched the area. When he hoisted one sturdy branch on his shoulder, she couldn't restrain her curiosity. "Of what purpose is that?"

He smiled, and she eyed the savage gleam of his teeth uneasily. "Believing our expedition was a peaceful one, I brought only a sword. I take this as another weapon." He leaned it against the wall of the hut. "Is there a bucket?"

She stared. "A bucket?"

"I hate to eat with hands so recently stained with blood. If you could fetch me water from the brook, I would wash."

"Oh." She bit her lip on the suggestion he walk to the brook and wash himself. After all, Raymond had the right to act as helpless as any horse's ass of a man when he chose. "I don't see a bucket."

"Maybe there's one inside." Rubbing his fingers

together, he frowned. "'Tis a shame when I carry such proof of Tosti's death."

The sadness in him roused her guilt, and she volunteered, "I'll go see if I can find you a bucket."

"As you wish."

He sounded so meek, she scrutinized him, but he was removing the extra bags from his destrier and she couldn't see his face. The door of the hut opened with a creak, and she peered into the dark interior cautiously. Sunlight, filtered by leaves, entered through the door. One shuttered window put a feeble stripe against the wall, and she could see that whoever had left this place had stripped it except for a pile of wood left for weary travellers. "There's nothing in here," she called.

"Surely they left a bucket in a corner."

He sounded closer, but when she glanced over her shoulder it seemed the horse had moved and he with it. Raymond was tightening the girths of the saddle, preparing for battle.

"I don't see one." Stepping inside, she wrinkled her nose at the musty odor. "Plenty of cobwebs and dust—" She squinted and started forward. "Wait. You may be in luck."

At the door, his shadow blocked the light. "I know I am, my lady."

She whirled on her heel, but too late. The door shut with a wholesome snap, and she heard the thump as he wedged the log against the wood.

18

Juliana ran at the door of the little hut, clubbing with her shoulder, and from the other side of the barrier, she heard, "Good English construction, good English oak. Farewell, my lady. I'll be back for you when the fighting is over."

"Raymond!" She struck the wood with her palm, but no one answered her. Running to the little window, she shook the shutters and peered through the crack that ran vertically between them. She could see him, preparing to mount his destrier, and shouted, "Raymond, you'll not succeed with this."

Satisfaction surged through her veins when he turned from his horse and started back toward the hut. He'd seen the error of his ways; he would release her. Too late she realized her mistake. Picking up another stout stick, he used it as a crossbar. She heard it thunk into the brackets that kept the shutters closed in windy weather. Standing on tiptoes, she met Raymond's eye peeking through the upper end of the crack. His dry voice informed her, "You have my gratitude, my lady, for reminding me to secure the window."

Cursing with words she'd forgotten since becoming

a parent, she fell back and tried to think of an escape. But not yet. Not now. It had been her mistake to show him her likely escape route. Now she had to discover another. The jingle of Raymond's reins sounded like betrayal to her, and she ran to the window once more.

He was going. Leaving with a salute to her—or the hut—leaving her alone and half mad with worry. As he rode away, she gnawed at her knuckles and listened to the scuttle of some woodland rodent in the corner. It firmed her resolve to escape, and to escape before nightfall. Her eyes had adjusted to the dimness, and she made a slow circuit of the room. Exploring the wall around the door revealed an area where the mud had broken away from the woven frame of the wall. She scratched more of it away, but the woven wood beneath the mud held firm. With a smirk, she pulled Salisbury's dagger from her belt—"It'll hew wood, m'lady"—and went to work.

At last she sat down on the soft dirt floor and flexed her fingers. The dagger *would* hew wood, but not fast enough for her needs.

The thatch roof sagged; she jumped up and smacked it with her knuckles, bringing a shower of dry grass and dust down on her. Coughing, she went to the bucket and carried it to the low place. Climbing on it, she tugged on the sturdy cross timbers, releasing another shower and clogging her lungs, but bringing her no closer to the out-of-doors.

Dragging herself to the window for fresh air, she reflected grimly on her situation. She was locked in a filthy hut with no food or drink. Night was coming on. No one knew where she was except for one foolhardy knight who was riding into a battle against uncounted foes armed only with a small sword.

Sniffling, she wiped her nose on her sleeve. How could Raymond have done this to her?

Raymond, who was facing death. And her daughter, who had been kidnapped, probably twice, and faced unknown horrors alone.

Who had taken Margery? Why had they taken her? For ransom, or was this a repeat of Juliana's abduction? Was this the result of a collision of the stars, or the culmination of some malevolent design?

Again she made a circuit of the hut. The sagging roof proved secure, and no small holes had opened in the walls in the short time she'd mourned her freedom. She stopped by the woodpile. Raymond had suggested he would use a log for a weapon, and she'd imagined some small, efficient battering ram. Was it possible? Could she smash through the door?

Reaching down, she selected a stout length of wood and hefted it in her arms, then dropped it with a cry and sprang back.

She'd found the source of the spiderwebs.

Controlling her shudders, she gingerly picked it up again, hoping the impact had dislodged most of the residents.

Except for the one that crawled up her sleeve, making her loose her grip once more, the log seemed uninhabited—and well suited for her needs.

"Stout English oak," she muttered. "To counter stout English oak." Puzzling about which end to ram with and which end to hold got her no closer to her goal, so after randomly deciding the wide end should meet the obstacle, she gripped it in her slippery fingers and ran at the door.

The log met the door and the blow knocked her backward. The log was wrenched from her arms; she stumbled over the top of it and fell so hard it knocked the breath from her. When she could whimper, she whimpered. When she could speak, she said raspingly, "The door will not yield."

A chatter from the resident rodent seemed like agreement.

Rubbing the place on her ribs where the log had bruised them, she dragged herself to her feet. "My mistake," she said aloud, "was not trying the door before I assaulted it. Perhaps . . ." She staggered to the window and shook the shutters. She could not see even a shiver in the gap between them, but something did rattle. Something. She shook them again, watching the line of sunlight for movement. The stick Raymond had placed pressed tight against the shutters—the line remained stable, but somewhere in the window frame something was loose.

She smiled, her first real smile for a full day.

This was it. Rubbing her scraped palms together, she searched for her battering ram and hoisted it up again. She hesitated, then put it on her other side. Might as well be evenly bruised, she reasoned. She backed herself clear to the other side of the hut, took a breath, started forward—

And stopped. That fall had been brutal and confidence-reducing. Some part of her quivered at a repeat of the pain. Some cowardly bit of her mind suggested she was better here in the dark with the rodents than in the midst of a battlefield where she could be raped, mutilated, murdered.

The battering ram—nay, it wasn't a battering ram, it was only a log—sagged in her arms. Tears dribbled down her cheeks, and defeat beat through her veins. She shouldn't have come. She wouldn't have come, either, but for Salisbury. What was it the old tracker had said? "She's strong. Ye trust in her, m'lord."

He respected her, and she respected his opinion. But even he wouldn't expect her to overcome such odds. Nay, he wouldn't. He wouldn't.

Devil fly away with him. He would.

Lifting the ram once more, she placed it against her side. She held it steady with her hands and took good, deep breaths of good English air. That would combat the strength of the shutters. Aye, it would.

Aiming at the place where the crossbar rested, she glared at the window, pawed the ground, and charged with all her might.

The log hit square on her target. The end met the shutters, held firm by the crossbar, and the entire frame, shutters, crossbar, and brackets flew out of the window, and Juliana flew out behind them.

Salisbury hung on to Layamon's sleeve and gasped in agony. His heart swelled nigh to bursting; his head throbbed with the rhythm of his rushing blood.

"Hold up, ol' man," Layamon urged. "Wot happened? Is it m'lord an' lady?"

Salisbury nodded. "Tosti . . . dead. Troop o' men . . . murdered him. M'lord . . . after th' girl."

"Where's m'lady?" Layamon looked out to the road.

"Went . . . too. Gave her . . . me dagger. Keep her safe."

"Ye gave m'lady a dagger, an' that'll keep her safe?" Layamon shook Salisbury. "Are ye daft, man? No lady knows how t' use a dagger."

Salisbury pulled himself erect. "She'll learn."

Swinging on his heel, Layamon said, "I have no time
t' argue wi' ye, ye ol' fool. I must . . ." His brow knit.

Swaying, Salisbury whispered, "Go after . . . m'lady."
His vision clouded, and he collapsed in the dirt.

Juliana's hips struck the wall; she somersaulted in
the air, smacking her head on the side of the hut and
landing with an audible *wump.* As she slowly recovered
her senses, her first emotion was amazement, then
triumph. She was outside.

She lay panting beside the shutters. Her palms
were well paved with gravel. Her chin had acquired a
scrape. Her elbows were bruised.

Once more she gained her feet, spreading her
arms wide to heaven, but a glance to the west cut her
celebration short. She hadn't escaped to get lost in
the woods at night. And how quickly could she move
without a horse? She would soon find out. But first . . .

But first she had to eat, for her head still spun, and
the pain of her scrapes and bruises made her almost
nauseous. Spring greens dotted the woods, and with a
little searching she could provide herself with . . .
with the bags Raymond had left hanging over a stump
at the edge of the clearing. She rubbed her eyes. How
odd—it was almost as if they were waiting for her.
She stumbled to her knees beside them and opened
them with greedy fingers. One loaf of bread was missing,
one hunk of cheese, and a skin of wine. He'd taken
what he needed and unloaded the rest. To ease his
horse's burden, she supposed, and was thankful for
the consideration, no matter how accidental.

The food put heart back into her, and she started
down the path marked with the passage of many

horses. Walking, she assured herself, would keep her bruised muscles from stiffening, and a horse wouldn't be an advantage in the woodlands, anyway. She rubbed the bump on her head and sighed.

Rounding the first corner, she kept her gaze on her feet and concentrated on putting one foot in front of the other. A whinny interrupted her meditations; she froze. Had she wandered close to the battle without realizing? Had a knight, posted as guard, seen her? At once she saw the horse, minus a rider, and jumped into the bushes. But before the creature could whinny again, she jumped back out. She stared and said aloud, "You're my horse."

Her horse. Her palfrey. Left staked to a tether beside the path and munching grass while waiting for her to arrive. She circled the animal and asked incredulously, "What are you doing here? Raymond abandoned you?"

She didn't believe that. Raymond's reverence for armor was only slightly less than his reverence for horses. His steed made him a knight, and he never forgot it. So—"He left you for me to find, didn't he? He thought I would escape."

Her aches miraculously eased, soothed by the recognition that Raymond hadn't left her to molder in that hut. Raymond had faith in her, a faith as strong as Salibury's. Maybe he wanted her to miss the battle but was anxious for her to follow.

She squinted at the sun, still dipping only halfway down to the horizon, and queried the absent Raymond, "You didn't think I'd escape so soon, did you?"

Her saddle had been placed over a log. Although she hadn't done it for years, she could saddle a horse, and she put her back into the job. As she mounted, she hesitated. She should go back for the food bags. No doubt she would want for food before this journey was over. But she couldn't spare even those few moments. She had to get to Margery and Raymond, and her sense of urgency grew.

On the path, she kept a keen eye out for signs of passage. Once she thought she heard an animal shriek, and shriek again, but the woods deadened the sound, and she could not tell from whence it came. She had suspected the troop of horsemen was close when Raymond locked her in the hut. Soon, too soon, she found the evidence.

A sunlit meadow beckoned her just ahead. On its outskirts, hoofprints proved the presence of horses. A thread of white wool had caught on a branch; she removed it and fingered it. She couldn't prove its origin, of course, but she recognized local wool, and she noted its fineness.

Hers? Nay, it couldn't be, but her palfrey stirred as if she'd transmitted her uneasiness. She paused among the debris and looked out into the clearing.

She could see no one, but the grass had been trampled as if a battle had been fought here—and she feared one had. Listening, she heard the birds calling in their chirpy springtime manner and determined the hazard had moved on. She urged her horse into the meadow, moving slowly, looking for signs she could read.

And she found one, but only one.

In the shade of a yew, the dark, still body of a youth rested without moving.

With a gasp, she urged her horse toward him. At the sound of the cantering hooves, the body moved as if jerked by strings. Arms rose, then fell. Juliana jumped to the ground and ran to him.

It was Denys. He had no visible wounds, no marks of sword or mace, but the color and texture of his skin looked like those of a fowl, plucked and left for weeks untended.

"Don't step . . . on me," he whispered.

"I won't." She touched his forehead.

His lids fluttered open; his eyes focussed with difficulty. He cried, "My lady! Forgive. Forgive . . ."

"Of course." Glancing around, she found the brook that gave life to the meadow, and pulled off her kerchief. She wet it and wiped his thin face.

It seemed to revive him, for he sucked in a difficult breath. "Don't promise forgiveness . . . until you know . . ."

"Until I know what you've done? I do know. You were stupid and greedy, but you could hardly have realized—"

"Stupid. Took Margery . . . because Satan himself . . . tempted . . ." Tears sprang to his eyes. "My mother . . . I'll never see my mother . . . because I sinned. . . ."

Wetting her kerchief again, she let him suck the moisture. When he seemed to have trouble swallowing, she tried to lift his head.

He screamed.

She sprang away, horrified, and more horrified when he babbled, "Sorry. No courage. No knight . . . after all."

Cautiously, she took his cold, clammy hand, but that provoked no outcry. "Where are you hurt?"

His deep, quivering sigh frightened her, made her wonder if it would be his last. "Rode over me."

Lifting his chainse, she began whispering the prayers for the dead. Hoof marks crisscrossed his chest, marking it as clearly as they marked the virgin forest floor. It looked as if someone had stood their horse above the lad and danced for pleasure. She credited youthful strength and a merciful Providence for the life still lingering in him, and she said, soothingly, "You'll be with your mother again. She awaits you on the other side."

His head flopped from side to side. "Mother . . . good. Honest. Taught me . . . better."

"Mothers forgive all. I promise you"—she perjured her own soul, perhaps, but she had to ease this boy's death—"she'll forgive you."

His gaze clung to hers, absorbing her reassurance eagerly. Then the light went out, and he said, "Sir Joseph. Sir Joseph . . . Satan."

Comprehension came slowly, unwillingly. "*Sir Joseph* told you to abduct Margery?"

A faint nod answered her.

"Because she's an heiress?"

An even fainter nod.

Now the full anguish swept her, and she cried, "Where's Margery?"

"Sir Joseph."

She sat back on her heels, her hands pressed to her mouth.

"With mercenaries . . . he took. I stabbed . . . him in the leg. His horse . . ."

"His horse did this to you?"

"He laughed. Raymond . . ."

Her fear grew weightier with his every labored word. "Raymond?"

"She said . . . he'd come." As he spoke, he seemed to shrink. "He did. He fought . . ."

She spaced her words, enunciated clearly, wanted no confusion in this greatest of queries. "Is . . . he . . . dead?"

"Nay. Still fighting . . ." In a gigantic effort, the last

and greatest he would make, he pointed toward the end of the meadow.

"He still fought when last you saw him?"

"Not killing him. Sir Joseph said . . ."

"Not to kill him? Why? So that Sir Joseph could torture him?" She rose in a fury. She would go after her daughter. She would save Margery from the cruel hands of this bastard uncle.

She would go after her husband. She would save—

Before she could take her first step, a faint murmur stopped her. "God go . . . with you."

She froze.

She didn't want to look down. She'd forgotten about Denys, and she didn't want to be reminded. She didn't want to see him.

But she *could* see him, see his face floating in the tears of her conscience.

Hopeless young eyes faced a pitiable death, alone in a wood. Every fiber of her soul wanted to run to her child, to her husband, but . . . what if this was her child? What if Margery was dying like this? Juliana would want somebody to stay. To help. To comfort.

What the consequences of remaining would be to Margery, to Raymond, she didn't dare consider. She sank back down again. "Why? Tell me why you listened to that . . . to Satan."

"Riches in a dowry. Waiting for me. Margery . . . only a woman. Resigned."

"And you believed that? Of *Margery*?"

"Stupid. She told me." He sighed. "Already knew it. Never . . . touched her."

She bit back the several pithy comments that hovered on her tongue.

"Only . . . so poor. Starved. Kicked . . . like a cur." Tears built in his eyes, and he pleaded for understanding. "Mother . . . died."

Against her will, her outrage dissipated, and she brought more water.

She dripped it into his mouth, but even the exertion of swallowing seemed too much. When he quit, exhausted, she settled herself beside him and soothed his face with the cloth. "I've done stupid things, too. I avoided marriage with Raymond, because I was afraid and because Sir Joseph urged me not to wed."

"Satan," he whispered, his voice a thin thread of pain.

"His fine schemes are woven into the web of my life." Oh, God, it was true. Sir Joseph had manipulated her, and her voice wobbled as she continued, "You and I, you see, have much in common. We're battered souls who met with an evildoer and succumbed to his lures."

"Not you." She almost couldn't hear him. "Not your fault."

"Aye, it is." The responsibility for this disaster sat squarely on her shoulders, and she said, "If I hadn't been such a coward about Sir Joseph, this would never have happened."

"My fault."

"Nay. If I had been more gracious to you—"

"Always gracious." Denys's voice was stronger with a spurt of indignation.

"I could have been better." Wretched, she said, "I will make you a promise. Because I'm older and wiser, and have more than"—she swallowed—"more than a little responsibility for this disaster, I'll take your sin as mine."

His dull eyes fixed on her with something like hope.

"I'll do penance for it all my days, according to the priest's justice." The priest would scream about that promise, she knew, but willingly she would take his admonitions. "In this way, your soul will be free."

"*My* sin," he whispered frantically. "No penance."

"You've done your penance today," she answered.

Denys closed his eyes while Juliana held his hand. She thought he had slipped from consciousness, but as the afternoon shadows lengthened, he opened them again. His lips moved, but he had no more breath. "Aye." Aye, he would let her take the sin. Then, "Gracious thanks."

Tears clouded her eyes as she gazed on the racked body of the youth. A refrain sang in her mind. "Margery. Margery." Fainter, but sharper, "Raymond."

She wished Denys would die to ease his torment, and knew that, in truth, she wished he would die so she could ease her own torment by action. So odd a death vigil, she thought, sitting here with the warm spring sun on her face and the birds singing all around. Released from winter's spell, life sprang from the ground in crocuses and dandelions, and whispered to her with a zephyr's breath.

He whispered, too, "Go," but his blinking eyes told his bleak and lonely tale.

Although her heart misgave her, she said, "Nay. I'll stay."

His pallor grew, and as the sun sank behind the trees and the last light disappeared from the meadow, he whispered, "Mother," and died.

Juliana had thought she would leap to her feet with his dying breath; instead she held his hand as it grew cold and wept for the lad who had no one else to weep for him.

19

Layamon pumped Keir's hand and cried, "How did ye know t' come? Margery an' Denys have disappeared. M'lord an' Lady are chasin' a troop o' mercenaries. Lady Margery's been abducted!"

With a vigor and emotion that plainly shocked Layamon, the travel-weary Keir swore a collection of international oaths that put plain English oaths to shame. "I know all about the mercenaries," he barked. "They originated at Bartonhale under the command of the man I was supposed to watch. How long ago did Raymond and Juliana leave?"

Layamon straightened his spine to its greatest tension. "Early this mornin'!"

Keir looked at the setting sun and swore again.

"Salisbury came arunnin' at noon, half dead wi' excitement, squawkin' that a troupe o' men had killed Tosti an' m'lord an' lady were goin' after them, an' we were t' come at once."

Keir's features froze. "Why haven't you left?"

Scraping his toe in the dirt, Layamon blushed. "I haven't ever put together an expedition such as this one before. I guess there's some things I don't know how t' do."

Keir flexed his hands in frustration, but knew he couldn't—mustn't—berate the man-at-arms for inexperience. "Come inside with me. I must eat, and there I'll give my orders. Prepare the fastest steed in the stables for me."

Bewildered, Layamon glanced about the bailey. "But sir! When ye left for Bartonhale, ye took th' fastest horse we had, yet ye return on as sorry a nag as I've ever seen. Wot happened?"

Layamon shrank as Keir turned on him, savage where he was normally stolid. "It was stolen by the same thief who will kill your lord and lady if I don't find them at once."

Layamon stared after him with open mouth, then turned to the stable boy. "Prepare Anglais fer Sir Keir. He rides tonight."

Juliana trembled when the unearthly scream echoed again. She didn't know which way to flee. The almost full moon cast ghost-white shadows in the midnight woods, and she was lost.

"Lost in more ways than one," she said aloud, then hushed as the great silence swallowed her voice. A silence broken only by those eerie shrieks that drove her hither and yon.

Peering through the trees, she could see a clearing all silver with moonlight, and turned her horse toward it. There she could take her bearings from the stars. The approach to the clearing was easy, and as she examined the foliage, she realized she had found the trail of Sir Joseph's mercenary troupe. She should be glad, but instead she trembled.

Oh, God, she was afraid. Stupid, spineless Juliana was afraid.

She didn't want to be tortured like Tosti. She didn't want to die like Denys. But she did want her Margery back. She would help her Raymond. And Raymond was never, ever afraid.

Squaring her shoulders, lifting her chin, she pretended courage and moved toward the clearing—and she heard it, a scream of anger and pain. A shriek that blinded her, made her fall, made her cry.

When it finally died away, she found herself far back in the woods. Her palfrey danced in twitches and shudders. Her skin crawled as if she'd been tied to an ant pile.

Who was out there? What was out there?

Dull and clumsy with fear, she dismounted and crept toward the clearing. Her breath came in uneven whooshes of sound, then it stopped—even as her heart stopped.

In the center of the clearing, three large bodies lay sprawled, their arms outflung in death's supplication. She rushed forward, calling, "Raymond!" tripped on a tree root, and plunged full length onto the ground.

It knocked sense back into her. Guardedly, she lifted her head.

A fire pit still glowed beside the bodies, offering a share of earthly warmth to those evermore unheedful of it. One body still wore a helmet that glinted in the moonlight, but even from the distance Juliana could see the dent that crushed it into his forehead. The others wore nothing. They had been stripped by the carrion crows that were their travelling companions.

Mercenaries. These were the mercenaries of whom Denys had spoken, and some great calamity had come on them.

A calamity called Raymond?

She got up slowly, but caution arrived too late. Nothing moved except the trickle of smoke, pale and ghostly as it lifted toward the star-studded heavens.

Sidling along in the shadow of the trees, her eyes moved back and forth, back and forth. Her feet crunched branches and dead leaves, regardless of her care. Her hands swung first before her, then behind, trying to anticipate any attack. She swept the clearing with her gaze, trying to see into the darkness—then one of the shadows moved.

Something—someone—stooped against a mighty oak. It looked like a hunchback, bent and twisted. She crept toward it, but it didn't move.

It was a man. She could see the glint of the chain-mail hauberk that protected his chest.

It was . . . it looked like . . .

"Raymond?" she asked.

The stooped creature straightened with a jingle of iron.

It *was* Raymond, haggard and marked by battle, but Raymond nevertheless. She started forward at a run. His eyes glittered in the dark. He panted and snorted, and when she reached him, he leaped at her and screamed that terrible scream.

Valeska caught the reins of Keir's destrier, and as the stallion leaped and pawed, she hung on with a strength unimagined in her aged frame. "You'll take us, Keir."

Keir tried to calm the war-horse and insisted, "You'll slow me down."

"Raymond will have need of us," Valeska cried.

"Nay!" He jerked the reins to release them from her grip; Anglais reared. Valeska went flying, and though Keir watched anxiously he wasn't surprised when she did a flip in the air and landed on her feet. Taking advantage of their distance, he called, "I'll send word as soon as I can."

Valeska muttered Slavic maledictions that boded ill for the continuity of Keir's line as she watched him ride out of the bailey. Returning to Ella and Dagna in the shadow of the keep, she said, " 'Tis the evil one, Sir Joseph, who's wrought such havoc with our people. Keir leaves without us. Layamon prepares to ride without a thought."

Ella demanded, "When are you leaving?" The two old crones looked at their charge, then exchanged glances, and two slow, wicked smiles broke over their faces.

Juliana found herself huddled on the ground some distance from the madman at the tree. Her fingers plugged her ears; she shivered with a palsy.

With all the pent-up despair of a condemned prisoner, Raymond shrieked again. She felt as if her heart had been ripped out and left bleeding on the ground. This was terror, the terror of a woman who approaches her lover to find he has become the devil's spawn.

The scream came again and again, louder and louder. She didn't know how he forced that noise from his throat, and she cringed even as the horror receded.

"Raymond?" she whispered.

He said nothing. He did not move, although even her thin voice reverberated through the silent woods.

Slowly, with many a nervous glance behind, she sat up. Pulling her knees up under her chin, she rested it there and watched the creature who watched her.

Oh, it was Raymond, but Raymond as she'd never seen him. His sleeves and breeches hung in shreds. His hair hung in tangled thread before his eyes. His lips were swollen. And his eyes never blinked.

Mad. Bewitched. She didn't know what had happened to Raymond, but she was afraid. Afraid she couldn't help him, and she had to help him. He was her love, the man who'd given her freedom and passion, and she would not—could not—abandon him.

Standing, she balanced herself as carefully as if she stood on Ella's high rope and sidled toward Raymond. She moved, then stopped, moved, then stopped. "Sweet Raymond," she crooned, and her voice shook.

Huddling back against the trunk, he showed his teeth in a snarl.

She stopped. He calmed. And she stared, unaware of the tears that dripped down her cheeks. "Oh, my dear Raymond."

Like some evil darkness that ate at his skin, an iron collar circled his throat. The man who could not accept even an affectionate hug about his neck had been collared and chained like a dog—or a Saracen slave.

Well had Sir Joseph chosen his revenge.

The fear which shamed her faded under the sharp prod of pity. With every step, she murmured soothing nonsense, sang bits of French cradle songs, trying to charm Raymond as she would charm a bird to her hand.

No acknowledgment lit his face. He neither recognized her nor his name.

Slipping around him, she noted that the short chain was connected to a bolt driven deep into the oak. She saw that his hands, too, were restrained, wrapped around the tree trunk behind his back. Restive, he moved his arms, and she heard the clank of iron, saw the chain, about ten stout links long, biting into the bark.

When she emerged from behind the tree, his renewed tumult moved her to murmur, "I didn't leave you." Dredging her mind for ways to hypnotize the beast, she approached him, moving slowly and deliberately. "I couldn't leave you." Extending her hands, fingers spread, she showed him her palms. "I have nothing here except a caress for you. Would you let me give it to you?"

He no longer showed his teeth. The dark eyes still glinted, but he blinked as if confused.

"Blessed Raymond, husband of mine, please let me help you." She wanted to touch him, but courage deserted her again. But he looked so like Denys— wounded, abandoned—she couldn't hesitate. "Please," she whispered again. With a tension that made her arms ache, she lifted them. He didn't move, didn't breathe. He seemed to be waiting, and when she placed her open palms on his chest, he sighed. One long, alleviating exhale, and he collapsed against the tree.

She found she'd been holding her breath, too, and released it in a sigh of relief. "Raymond." Sliding her palms around to his back, she whispered, "Raymond. I have no snow with which to bring you to your senses, so I will bathe you in kisses and dry you with hugs, and you'll be mine forever more." She leaned against him. The iron of his hauberk pricked her cheek, and beneath it she heard his strong heart slowing to a normal beat.

"Juliana?" He tried to enfold her in his arms, but

the chain caught him, and every muscle in his body spasmed in fury.

"Don't . . ." Compassion caught her by the throat, and she could scarcely whisper, "Don't hurt yourself more." She lifted her head and looked at him. Through the plethora of swellings and cuts that marred his perfect visage, she thought she saw tears; she knew she saw terror.

"Juliana." His voice sounded as if it had been scraped by a dull knife. "How did you find me?"

"I followed the trail of bodies."

"They've got Margery."

"I know."

"I couldn't stop them."

"No man could have done more."

"If I could have slain that swine, Joseph"—he gasped a little—"you didn't know, but 'tis Sir Joseph who has her."

She bit her lip against the audible agony of his voice. His recitation seemed to have exhausted him, for he slipped further down the tree. To curb his rapid, guilty admissions, she said, "Aye. Denys told me who took her."

"The youth?"

"Is dead."

"Another failure." He moaned. "Another . . ."

His knees gave way. He slithered down before she could restrain him. The collar and chain caught him; he gagged and choked while, frantic, she tried to lift him. At last he raised himself, and blood, warm and sticky, fell in droplets onto her head.

A fit of shaking took them both, and when he could speak, he said, "I am so tired. I just want to sit down, and I can't. I can't sit down. I'm so"—his body strained away from the tree—"tired."

"Lean on me, then. You're light as Saint Luke's bird."

"Saint Luke's bird is an ox," he said suspiciously.

"So it is." He tried to pull himself up, but she pushed her body hard against his. "You've supported me for every moment you've known me. This is a small settlement on a big debt." She tightened her grip on his ribs. "Lean on me."

Released by her succor from the chain's coercion, he slowly relaxed. He tested her strength in bits, easing onto her like the slow flow of honey in December. Tilting his head back, he seemed to slip away—to find himself again, she hoped.

Braced beneath him, she took his weight. Her joints creaked, her muscles groaned, but she rejoiced in the trust he placed in her. How long they stood there, welded together by his need and her strength, she did not know. She only knew the moon's light had touched her face when Raymond stiffened and opened his eyes.

"Listen."

Straining, she heard it, too. The thunder of a horse's hooves.

"He's coming fast," she said. "How can he ride so in such a tangle of forest?"

"The road lies just beyond the trees," he answered, hoarsely. "Sir Joseph wished for me to be discovered in my dishonor, taunted and ridiculed like any common felon."

"Do you wish me to stop the rider?"

If alarm could have freed him, he would be unshackled. "Nay! 'Tis most likely an enemy, and I fear for you. Hide in yonder trees and don't come out unless the horseman proves to be a friend."

Indignation shot through her, stiffening her spine. "I will not."

"You'll do as you're directed."

"The last time I did as directed I found myself locked in a filthy, spider-ridden hut." Pulling the dagger Salisbury had given her from her belt, she shifted to shield Raymond from the road. Over her shoulder, she said, "Accept my protection or be damned to you."

The horse was almost upon them, travelling at a madman's pace, and Raymond said urgently, "I am already damned, so I beg of you, don't subject me to this torture."

Ignoring him, she tensed for a fight, but the great white horse flew past, then reined in so abruptly it pawed the air.

"Keir!" Raymond shouted, while at the same time Keir roared, "Raymond!"

Rolling out of the saddle, Keir tossed the reins to Juliana and ran to the tree. Juliana thought he would simply smash Raymond against the trunk in an exuberance of sentiment, but he pulled up short. His brief flare of emotion vanished without a trace. As he walked around the tree, he became Keir again, observing Raymond's dilemma without expression. Completing the circuit, he looked Raymond in the eye. "I see I should have brought my smithery."

"Would that we had time," Raymond answered. "But I have a plan."

"And will I like this plan?" Keir asked.

"Likely not, but I have no other." Raymond stood tall; taller, Juliana thought, than ever before. "Take your battle-ax and chop through my chains."

Keir cleared his throat. "A battle-ax is not a woodman's ax, and even if it was, the chains are iron. The chances for success are slim."

Raymond answered him without a tremor. "What other chances are there?"

"Raymond, nay, he could slip off the chain or miss." Juliana tried to come forward, but the destrier dragged her back. "We'll get a blacksmith here from the castle, and you'll be free."

"By tomorrow? And what will happen to our daughter by then?"

Tying the reins to a branch, she tried to think of another way, but his relentless, damaged voice pursued her.

"Do you believe Sir Joseph took her as a kindly gesture? Even now, she might be suffering the fate of Tosti or—" At her whimper, he said, "We have no choice, and Juliana—"

Her aggrieved gaze sought his.

"I cannot remain within these chains, not even for your peace of mind."

She could see it was true. The shadowed eyes were sane now, but he held the skin of civilization over his gaping wound by strength of will alone.

"Go on, stroll up the road and leave Keir to his labor."

She found Keir beside her. The edge of his short-handled battle-ax glittered cold in the moonlight, and he swung his arm as if loosening the muscles. She asked him, "What if you chop off his hand?"

It sounded like an accusation, and Raymond answered before Keir could. "Then at last I will understand his assertion that the loss of his fingers was a small price for freedom."

Wheeling around, Juliana stalked into the darkness under the trees, seeking her neglected palfrey, but Raymond's stark question stopped her.

"How did you come so soon?"

He was speaking to Keir, she realized, and she waited, too, to hear the answer. The chains clattered as Keir replied, "Not so soon. Not soon enough. I did not know the extent of Sir Joseph's villainy until the steward at Bartonhale imprisoned me."

Juliana turned with a cry. "Imprisoned you?"

Keir examined the chain and bolt that held Raymond to the tree. "Sir Joseph has an interesting power over the minds of the people he influences. Your steward, my lady, believed Sir Joseph to be a demon."

Remembering Denys, Juliana didn't exclaim in surprise.

"Since your father's death, he has worked for Sir Joseph—out of fear, I assure you—cheating you out of your due and turning it over, without a murmur, to Sir Joseph." Keir sighed. "Raymond, I believe 'tis best to chop the bolt out of the wood."

"Out of oak?" Juliana cried. "Are you mad? English oak is—"

"Stout, eh, Juliana?" Raymond's teeth gleamed, but his grin looked more grim than amused.

"Impossible to cut when wet or dry," she replied, exasperated.

Ignoring her, Raymond advised, "Try not to trim my hair."

Keir hefted the ax. "Duck down."

As the shiny edge rose, so did Juliana's fear. The ax hovered above Raymond's head, descended, bit into the bark around the bolt. Mesmerized, she watched as Keir struggled to remove it from the tough wood and lifted it again. Falling to her knees in an agony of anticipation, she pressed her palms to her eyes.

It couldn't detract from the thump of the ax, Keir's grunts of exertion, Raymond's indrawn breath when decapitation threatened. "That was close, my friend," he said, and without volition, Juliana's hands fell away.

Keir stood and panted. "Damn short-handled ax. No precision. No stroke behind it."

"But 'tis the best of Spain's fine metals, meant for cutting into armor," Raymond comforted him. " 'Twill make short work of the chain."

"Wrong shape for wood," Keir complained. "I rode to Lofts Castle immediately on my escape. Layamon and the men-at-arms are close behind me. If you would wait until their arrival—"

"I will not allow them to see me so disgraced," Raymond said steadily.

Silence reigned in the clearing as Juliana and Keir absorbed Raymond's resolution. At last, Keir bowed his head. "As you wish. But cutting off a man's head is a more serious matter than cutting off his fingers."

"You won't cut off my head," Raymond said.

"Aye, and what's an ear or chunk of scalp?" Keir muttered.

Raymond obviously saw no sense in encouraging such dismal reflections, and turned the subject. "How did you escape from Lofts?"

"I convinced the steward he would do well to worry about the devil himself and ignore the rebellious demon."

Curiosity unclogged Juliana's throat. "The devil himself?"

"Me," Keir said, and watched with no visible interest when Raymond released a crack of laughter.

"How did you convince him of that?"

"He is not an astute man, and Valeska and Dagna had taught me a few of their more impressive tricks."

Even Juliana smiled at that.

"Keir, if you're through puffing," Raymond said, "I'd like you to finish me up."

Juliana didn't care for the phrasing, but the conversation had helped her achieve a measure of resignation, and she ducked her head into her hands again. Too, Keir had given her much to think about, and she concentrated on Sir Joseph's perfidy while the ax pounded and hewed.

"There!" Raymond announced as the bolt fell. "I told you you could do it."

"So you did." Keir's triumph wasn't as boisterous as Raymond's, and Juliana, while she rejoiced, understood why.

The oak had been easy when compared with the stout length of chain that bound Raymond's shackled wrists.

Juliana expected Raymond to sit, giving in to the exhaustion that had sucked the iron from his soul. But nay—with the release of his neck, he shuffled around the tree so his hands were visible in the moonlight. He called urgently, "Can you see where they connected the chain? I fought hard, and even when they put the coal to my hauberk, I would not cooperate. I hope that marred their work."

Keir lifted the chain, examined it with his fingers and stooped to scrutinize it. Juliana saw as Keir drooped and pushed his hair back from his forehead. Steadily he answered, "The cuffs are strong. The weak link in this chain is here"—he rattled it—"close to your hand."

"Then swing your ax true," Raymond answered. "Better you should cut off my head than my hands, for my hands will wreak vengeance on Sir Joseph."

"Your head is only good for butting down stone walls," Keir said wryly. "Sit down. Make fists, and stretch that chain as taut as you can."

Raymond obeyed. Keir leaned his rear against the tree, braced his feet and raised the ax. "Wait!" Juliana yelled.

Keir froze. "My lady?"

"Why are you doing it like that? You can't see as well as if you faced him."

"It gives me the power I need behind my swing. As for sight"—he lifted the ax again—"there's not much chain to see, anyway."

She wanted to close her eyes against the impact, but a horrible fascination held her. The ax struck the chain squarely, sending sparks as it skidded across a link and caught. The jolt sent Keir spinning away, the ax flying out of his hand. Juliana ducked, but it landed nowhere near her, and Raymond said impatiently, "Try again."

Flexing his hands, Keir grimaced at Juliana.

Her voice trembled as she said, "Wait, Raymond. Keir hurt himself."

"I can't wait," Raymond insisted. "There are riders approaching."

Putting her head to the ground, Juliana listened and heard it—the rumble of hooves. She nodded at Keir, and Keir picked up the ax. Positioning himself with care, he eyed the chain steadily, practiced his blow, then brought the ax down with a mighty clang. The ax sank into the wood. The severed chain whipped the air as Raymond brought his hands around. Keir and Juliana stared at the ax, both held by an unbearable suspense.

They shuddered when Raymond's voice broke. "You did it. You did it!" He staggered around the side of the tree, fists raised to the heavens.

"Your fingers!" Juliana cried. "What happened to your fingers?"

He stared as if she were mad, then opened his hands.

His fingers were there, all ten of them.

Keir lay over on the grass. Juliana put her head between her knees. Raymond laughed, too long and too hard.

And that was how Valeska and Dagna found them.

20

Fixing her gimlet eye on them, Valeska queried, "For this we rode until our old bones ached? To find you making merry?"

Juliana and Keir lifted their heads and glared; Raymond laughed harder.

Dagna looked at Valeska with disgust. "Let us go and rescue Margery from Lord Felix."

"Felix?" Juliana scrambled to her feet. "Why do you say Felix?"

"Because this is the road to Moncestus Castle," Dagna answered.

Juliana shook her head. "It can't be. He can't be in league with—"

Raymond reached out to her, but the jangle of chains acted like a dash of North Sea water. How much comfort could she derive from him? From a man shackled, body and soul, to old terrors?

She didn't see—or pretended not to see—his gesture. Dashing into the woods, she returned on her palfrey, her mouth hard, her chin set. "Let's ride."

Raymond sighed. "Would God I had my destrier."

And remembering, he said to Keir, "I thought the mount Sir Joseph rode appeared familiar."

Keir coughed, looking as embarrassed as that iron man could look, and indicated his steed. "Take this one. 'Tis yours, anyway."

" 'Tis my lady's," Raymond corrected, but he mounted immediately, not trusting Juliana to wait for them.

Valeska slid from the saddle. "I'll ride with Dagna, Keir can have my stallion, but first—" She presented Raymond with his arms. His long sword, his short sword, and his mace. Reverently, she lifted his shield off the leather straps that held it and presented it with a flourish.

Upon the shield stood an upright bear, claw and fang exposed to inspire dread and intimidation. Raymond gazed on the fearsome representation, then rested his hand on Valeska's head for a brief moment. "Thanks to you, my faithful squire."

The moon, sinking toward the horizon, deserted them among the tall trees, then shone its flat light over the ruts and mud that formed the road to Moncestus Castle. Juliana pushed ahead, setting a gallop that left the others jostling for position. Without a word, Raymond set off after her, the war-horse moving with a sweet ease of muscle that made him want to race. He wanted to face the chill, grip sword and shield, ride into battle with a bellow that carried terror on the wind.

But he couldn't. Until they rescued Margery, he was the leader, the arbiter of good sense. Renouncing the appetite for warfare and vengeance, he overtook Juliana, cutting her off with ease.

When she whipped her head around, he rebuked, "We'll not arrive soon if you fall and break your neck." To relieve the pressure on his collar, he shifted the bolt and its accompanying hunk of oak in his hand. "Keep a steady pace."

She set her chin, but nodded. As her palfrey settled into a slow canter, she said grudgingly, "Good advice."

"If hard to follow," he added, urging Anglais along the road beside her. As the horses picked their way with a steady rhythm, it freed Raymond's mind to meditate on the fate of Margery. His fingers tightened on the reins, and Anglais leaped forward.

"Keep a steady pace," Juliana said, clearly smarting from his reprimand, but he refused to relinquish the hard-won control on himself.

"As you say, my lady." He was proud of his steady tone, but Juliana didn't seem to notice it.

Her gaze kept sliding to his handful of metal and wood. She began to speak, stopped, then blurted, "Doesn't the weight of the chain bother you?"

In sooth, he'd scarcely noticed it. He'd worn heavier shackles for less purpose, but his sideways glance caught her puckered mouth, her grim brow.

The collar repulsed her.

Of course. What did he expect? To him, the demeaning collar could be borne as long as liberty accompanied it. For so many days and months in Tunisia, he'd been shackled tight.

No movement, no freedom. Muscles dissolving, disintegrating. Youth and power lost forever.

That had driven him mad. That had broken him. Broken him twice—once in a hot dungeon in Tunisia. Once in a cool forest in England.

He had too many memories of the snivelling creature he had become in Tunisia, and almost no memory of the howling beast he had become in England.

But Juliana remembered. She wanted security, and the sight of his shackles proved she couldn't trust him to give it to her.

He found himself stopped in the middle of the road, his chest heaving, his heart twisting as he tried to deal with the pain. Keir and the women circled around him, and Juliana pressed her horse against his.

Her cool hands touched his cheeks. She sounded fierce when she asked, "Is it your neck? Your wrists? Did they hurt you inside?"

Her copper hair, like bits of flame, warmed her pale face. Her eyes gazed at him with such a genuine appearance of concern he believed it for one sweet moment. "Hurt me?"

"Inside," she insisted. "Did Sir Joseph and his men—"

The name jolted him back to reality. Of course she was concerned; she needed him, not as a husband, but as a warrior. "Nay! Not Sir Joseph. He hasn't hurt me."

"Then why do you have such an expression on your face?"

Her hands tormented him, smoothing his hair, touching his ears, seeking injury where her vision might have failed her. He wished he could move away, but the lash of pleasure bound him. Hoarse with distress, he stammered, "The pain of . . . of the fetters is not great, but Keir will remove them."

Raymond suspected Keir understood more than he would say, for he, too, watched him oddly. "My ax is still back in the tree. I could not retrieve it, and it would do no one any good if I did. The first blow to the chain notched the edge. I hate to think what devastation the second blow wrought."

"If there's any danger, I don't want you to try and

remove them," Juliana said. "I only thought they must . . . hurt you."

Raymond marvelled at her ability to be polite after the agonies she'd been through and before the struggle she faced. She was a lady, from the tip of her nose to her dainty toes, and he wanted to keep her. He'd never wanted anything so much in his life, nor had he realized his own strength until he smiled politely and said, "I can't fight like this."

"Nay, you would be much impaired," Dagna agreed. "Try yon peasant hut. They will have an ax."

Raymond swerved off the road and pounded on the door. The quaking serf responded to his snapped request for a wood ax and a chopping block, and with ax in hand, Keir again approached Raymond. This time, Raymond knelt beside the chopping block, the bolt dangling off the other side. "Break it close to my head," Raymond commanded.

"Don't hurt him," Juliana said at the same time.

"Close," Raymond demanded, and closed his eyes.

The ax whistled past his ear; the noise as the chain broke assaulted his hearing, and he shook his head to clear it. Keir was speaking, and Raymond asked, "What? What?"

"That had better be close enough." Keir handed the notched ax, together with some coins, to the serf. "I'm not doing it again."

Raymond fingered the links that still hung from the iron collar, then tucked them in his chainse where the sight of them would no longer offend his lady. Holding out his left arm, he indicated the chain, half again the length of his hand. "This must go."

"Nay!" Juliana cried.

"Nay," Keir said.

"It must go," Raymond insisted. "It, too, will hinder my fighting."

Keir tucked his thumbs into his belt. "With your skills, that is most unlikely. What is likely is the amputation of your hand, which truly would hinder your fighting." Dismissing the subject, he turned away to his horse.

Brooding, Raymond weighed the chain, and Juliana said brightly, " 'Twill serve to remind you of my claims on you." She pretended it was a jest, but he felt she'd slapped his face, especially when she added, "Many men claim their wives are a shackle. You have proof."

He bent his mind toward this last service he would provide for Juliana. For his wife, the center of that loving, golden circle. The proof that every fairy tale was true.

Lunacy.

Juliana's teeth chattered as Moncestus Castle towered above her. Silent and menacing, it absorbed the early-morning light like a hole dug straight to hell. The crenellated battlements looked like an old man's teeth, jagged with rot and corruption. She hadn't realized how much she feared every stone, every turret and gate. In that massive structure, her trust, her faith, her life had been destroyed, and only after much strife had she rebuilt any of it. Now, again, she stood before Moncestus Castle, and she wanted to crumple into a ball and sob.

But Margery was in there. Had been carried in there last night by Sir Joseph. For Margery, Juliana would storm the battlements single-handedly.

She didn't have to do that. Layamon and his men had ridden up not long after their arrival, prepared—nay, anxious—for a siege. But they had no time for a siege, so Raymond told them. A siege meant months of sitting, of waiting for the enemy inside to yield from hunger or thirst. And this enemy held a precious hostage inside.

Everyone stood just out of arrow range. Raymond remained with Juliana, clad in his hauberk and encased in a warrior's intensity. As if her mere presence upset his concentration, he paid her little heed, and she jumped when he snapped, "How do we get in?"

Juliana looked around. He was speaking to her. "Get in?"

He turned his green eyes on her. "You got out. How do we get in?"

"Ah." Swift embarrassment swept her, and she carefully hoarded the details. "I only escaped from the keep. To escape from the bailey, I just walked across the open drawbridge. 'Twas daylight and I just . . . walked across."

"The drawbridge is closed," Raymond answered, quite as if he expected her to remedy that.

She shot him a question as reply. "Where are the patrols on the walls?"

"I don't know." Again he swept the battlements with his gaze. "Very interesting. Very puzzling. I wonder who's in command."

"Not Felix," she said.

"Nay. Probably not Felix. So if we get through these walls"—Raymond pointed with his dagger—"you can get us in the keep."

"I . . . aye, most likely I can." With a droll and horrible humor, she said, "I doubt that way has been plugged."

Raymond turned to Valeska and Dagna. "Can you open the drawbridge?"

Dagna's blue eyes flashed. Valeska sparkled with life as she announced, "You know we can."

Raymond lifted his shield and held it over his head. Keir did the same, and with the women they crept close to the walls.

Nothing moved. No attempt was made at defense, and the troop stirred and muttered.

Everyone watched curiously as Keir threaded a rope through the quarrel of a crossbow, tied it into a noose, and shot it high above the vertical stone spikes set into the merlons. The first shot slithered back down the wall, but the second caught a finial, and Keir set the noose with a jerk.

Still no one stirred on the walls, and the strain of such unusual stillness intimidated the company.

"Notch your bows," Raymond called to the men-at-arms. "If you see a head peek over the battlements, shoot it and don't fail me."

"Aye, m'lord," Layamon said.

Juliana gaped as the crones grasped the rope and, one after the other, began a nimble ascent of the wall. Raymond and Keir ran back to watch as the old women reached the top and pulled themselves up slowly.

Nothing.

The old women disappeared over the edge, then reappeared and waved. Raymond stood, hands on hips, and told Juliana, "If they don't meet with any patrols—and I don't understand why they haven't—they'll use the rope to enter the gatehouse and lower the drawbridge."

"What if Sir Joseph attacks them?"

A smile, obscurely pleased, touched Raymond's mouth. "He'd better send his mercenaries, for those two women terrify your uncle—and that doesn't displease me. He will pay for his atrocities."

She grasped his arm. "You don't think he'll kill Margery?"

"He tried to kill you."

She protested spontaneously. "Nay, say not so."

"Did he not? He is rotten with envy." As he watched the battlements, he asked, "Why do you think he abused you? Why do you think he threatened you?"

"He never envied me," she protested hotly. "From the time I was a child, he told me how the greatest woman is less than the lowest man, how the pain of childbirth was God's punishment for the original sin."

"He sneered at you for being a woman." Raymond nodded. "A woman, his kin, yet set above him by an accident of birth."

"My father said"—she wanted to make him understand how impossible this was—"My father said Sir Joseph would care for my lands well, for he was tied to them by blood."

"So he did, expecting that someday, somehow, he would have those lands for his own."

"The inheritance wasn't his for the taking should I die and even if my daughters died," she explained, trying to make clear the easily understood facts. "If there were no legitimate heirs to be found, the lands would revert to the king. You know that."

"I do. And so did—does—Sir Joseph. But he was reared during the dark years of King Stephen's reign, when men made their own laws and no one bade them nay. He could not steal the lands when your father lived—at least, not by force, so he stealthily consulted with Felix until he convinced that weak man to take you as a bride."

She could scarcely credit her own hearing. "You think Sir Joseph planned my abduction?" Her voice rose in hopeful disbelief. "Not my father? 'Twas Sir Joseph?"

"Your father was guilty of no more than being a

feeble pawn who said and did as others planned."
Raymond's distaste for such stupidity rang clear. "He
did not conspire against you."

In the darkest corners of her soul, she'd been convinced her father had betrayed her. So convinced, she'd
been afraid to examine the facts, then bruised herself on
the lock she put on the information. Now, *now* Raymond
insisted her father was guiltless of all but rank and total
stupidity. "I always knew my father blew hither and yon,
hot and cold, according to the opinions of others, but"—
she looked toward the walls, and in her estimation, they
had shrunk to normal size—"I didn't want to know he'd
deliberately allowed me to be seized."

"Such a weight lifted from your shoulders," Raymond
said, teasing.

She smiled, releasing the lock and allowing the
good memories of her father to flood her mind. "Love
allows for much."

"Too much."

He blenched as if he'd sliced himself on his own
sharp words, and she knew he was remembering his
weakness and mortification at the tree. She would
have comforted him with a touch, but his dignity
rejected sympathy before it was offered. Instead, she
said, "Sir Joseph could have killed me after my father
died and taken control through my daughters."

"He probably tried, but you are surrounded by loyal
servants—and King Henry is firmly in control. If it is
proved, the law frowns on the murder of one's liege."
He turned a cold, still face to her, but his eyes looked
right through her. "As you told me once when we were
discussing your distaste for the unknown husband the
king had picked for you—daughters can be dismissed
into a convent, or even found dead of an accident."

Anguish struck her, destroying her early exaltation. In a hoarse whisper, she asked, "Who better to arrange such accidents? I put my children at risk."

"You didn't know."

"I am the head of my family, and I failed to control my uncle."

"I am the head of your family now, and my failure overshadows yours." He pointed to the drawbridge. "Look."

The drawbridge started down slowly, creaking on its chains, then the weight of the planks took over, and it smashed to the ground. Juliana jerked and blinked, torn from the unassailable pain of obligation by the need for action.

Raymond winced and started forward. "Don't go under the portcullis until I say so. If those two women don't firmly secure it, we could be pierced by the falling steel points launched by our own allies."

Layamon laughed in ragged amusement, but Keir refused to move from his place just outside arrow range. "Aye, you test it, Raymond."

"It is my duty," Raymond answered without a smile, and crossed the drawbridge. He met Dagna, who shivered and made a sign back toward the castle—a sign to ward off the evil eye. Her sweet voice carried when she whispered, " 'Tis the castle of the damned. There are dead men-at-arms, propped at their stations, and the keep is shut tighter than a drum."

Juliana's men-at-arms murmured and shuffled their feet, infected by Dagna's solemn warning, but Juliana would not allow them to falter now. She strode toward the drawbridge, her skirts flapping around her ankles, and after a moment of hesitation, all the soldiers marched in, baited by the desire to appear brave in their lady's eyes.

"Are they even in there?" Keir asked, and as if in answer an arrow flew past his head and landed in the dirt.

Raymond pulled Juliana to him and raised his shield over them. As more arrows flew from the keep and everyone ran to the shelter of the stable, he answered, "Aye, they're in there."

Layamon crouched against the wall. "Why didn't they post a patrol on the walls?"

"They didn't think we'd arrive yet, or"—Raymond stroked his stubbled chin—"Sir Joseph hasn't the control over them he would like. Mercenaries won't sit out in the cold when there's a warm fire and cold ale inside."

"Money hasn't the strength loyalty commands." Keir cast a meaningful glance at Raymond, then supervised the men-at-arms and their dispersal around the keep.

To Juliana, Raymond said, "Now you must tell me how you escaped three years ago, and why they allowed you to walk out of the bailey."

She didn't want to tell him. Three years ago, few people had comprehended the desperation that drove her to escape through an unthinkable route. When she'd told her father, thinking it would make him believe, make him understand, he'd been repulsed, seeing it as another reason to spurn her.

If not for Salisbury, the man who'd found her, and his quiet commendation, she might have killed herself for shame. She'd never told anyone, never thought she'd have to tell anyone, but now—"Oh, Margery." She sighed and checked to see no one stood close. Taking Raymond by the wrist, she tugged him around the corner of the stable and pointed. "See the privy shaft? It leads straight up to the garderobe just off the great hall."

Stricken, Raymond stared at the stinking cesspit, then shook his head. With a mockery aimed more at himself than at her, he said, "And I just scrubbed the horse shit from under my nails."

Arms and legs splayed, like a spider climbing a rocky web, Juliana ascended the garderobe shaft toward the round of light shining down from above. It probably was the gullet of hell, but right now it looked like the gate of heaven. The fear of once more setting foot in the great hall of Moncestus, the fear of finding her daughter raped, or worse, dragged at her as she climbed the shaft. It pressed her down, made her weight grow and her courage shrink.

But Raymond kept close behind her, helping her, catching her when she slipped. As she neared the top, he propped her up with his shoulder beneath her rear and his hands cupping her foot. "Jump out as fast as you can," he advised. "Don't hesitate to draw your knife. Is it tucked in your sleeve?"

Peeking down, the sight of him braced against the sides of the tube and the long descent below struck another blow to her spirit. She tried to answer, but her teeth chattered, so she contented herself with an unseen nod.

"When the fight begins"—he now sounded like a lord directing a frightened servant—"you are to avoid me and the mercenaries. Do you understand why?"

It should be easy, but it wasn't. She had to think about it, grope for the reasoning. "Because you'll not be able to swing your sword if I stand near."

Even when she said it, she hardly knew if it was the truth, but his murmur of assent warmed her. "Then you find Margery."

Shivering with equal parts of resolution and terror, she gulped, trying to bring saliva to a suddenly dry throat. "As you say."

"You're to free her if possible. If not, you're to stand guard over her, protect her in case the battle swings in her direction." He nudged her upward. "On three," he said. "One—"

She inched her arms out of the hole.

"Two—"

She grabbed the edge of the seat.

"Three."

He boosted, she pulled, and she found herself lying on her stomach on the slab of stone, half in, half out of the murky shaft. She shot a suspicious glance around the earth closet, but no one stood in its close confines. From the head of the hall, she heard the clank of cups on a wooden trestle table and the rumble of men's voices. They weren't close, and, heartened, she slithered the rest of the way out and stood with her hand on her knife as Raymond tried to exit the privy shaft.

But what was easy for her proved difficult for him. The narrow hole held his broad shoulders hostage, and he struggled to bring out one arm and shoulder, then his head. He worked to free it, his forehead scraping on the pebbled seat, but despite almost-silent curses, he could not.

And someone approached. She heard the discouraged shuffle, and casting desperate glances at the door, she grasped Raymond's hand and pulled. He grunted when his head popped out, then groaned as he, too, heard the footsteps.

Juliana drew her knife and moved to the wall next to the entrance.

Raymond fought to bring his other shoulder out but knew this would defeat him.

The blade shook in Juliana's hand, and she stared with the wide-eyed valor of a squire facing his first blooding.

"For Margery," Raymond whispered, and the blade steadied a little.

A short, ruddy-faced man with a crooked nose stepped through the opening; she lifted the knife and struck at him, then turned the blade at the last moment.

"Felix!" she screamed in a whisper.

Felix jumped like a frightened rabbit and drew his knife with a skill Juliana could not match.

"Felix!" Raymond scrambled to climb out of the wretched hole. "Nay, Felix."

Swinging wildly around, Felix watched as Raymond freed himself and set his feet to the floor. "What are you doing here?" the hapless man sputtered. "How did you get here?"

Raymond reached for the knife, but Felix stumbled back, arms flailing, into the great hall. A burst of raucous laughter from the far end greeted his arrival, and Felix glanced toward the unseen side of the hall with fear and loathing.

Then he looked back at Raymond, and never had Raymond regretted his own hasty words and blows as he did now. He said quietly, "Felix, you'll not hold my foolishness against me, now will you?"

Felix tucked his chin close to his chest and examined Raymond as he would examine a maggot.

" 'Twas cruel on my part to beat a man so much smaller and less skillful than I." Raymond touched his earring, symbol of his slavery, and found comfort in the indestructible gold. "I've regretted it ever since."

Felix's head began to nod to some insistent, belligerent rhythm, and in desperation, Raymond said, "I know Sir Joseph has an influence on weak minds, but you can't be held responsible for . . ." Somehow this didn't sound as conciliatory as he wished, and he blurted, "All that will be forgotten if you throw in your lot with me."

Glaring out from under his brows, Felix turned to call the hooting mercenaries.

Juliana tossed a disgusted glance at Raymond and stepped forward, hands on hips. "Felix, don't make me sorry I didn't stab you."

"Juliana," Raymond groaned, but she paid him no heed.

She pointed to the place before her. "Felix, you get in here right now."

Felix wavered, and in her best motherly voice, she insisted, "Right now."

To Raymond's surprise, Felix shuffled into the garderobe, but he stood with his back to the entrance, as far away from Raymond as possible.

"What have you done with my daughter?" Juliana asked in a furious whisper.

"I didn't do anything!" Felix whispered back. "Sir Joseph brought her here, all trussed up, and threw her in the corner, and told me that's what I should have done with you. Like it was my fault you escaped."

Raymond spaced his words with grim vigor. "Have you used Margery ill?"

Primming his mouth, Felix said, "Nay." He interrupted Raymond's sigh of relief with, "I haven't used her at all. I tell you, I had nothing to do with this."

Juliana grasped his arm, her fingers digging into the flesh. "In the name of Saint Wilfrid, Felix, tell me true. Is Margery alive and unharmed?"

Quite as if she were the stupid one, Felix said, "Aye. I told you, she's trussed and in the corner. Of course"—he shuffled his feet—"I don't know how much longer she'll stay there. The mercenaries are drinking me out of ale and the way Sir Joseph keeps knotting that noose makes me wonder . . . would he hang her out a window?"

Juliana started toward the entrance, but Raymond grabbed her elbow and told Felix, "He killed all your men-at-arms. They're dead at their posts. What do *you* think he'll do?"

Felix's lower lip trembled. "He said he was my friend, but when I let him in, he ordered my men killed. His mercenaries have been using my serving girls and beating my menservants. Sir Joseph gave me advice before, but—"

"What kind of friend tells you to abduct your neighbor and force yourself on her?" Raymond snapped.

"I didn't get to rape her, and I didn't kill her," Felix snapped back. "She didn't cooperate. Sir Joseph said she'd be glad to spread her legs for me. But she resisted, and I had to hurt her." His little eyes squinted as he tried to look beyond the words to the truth. "I thought he wanted to help us, but now I suspect—"

His voice broke. A look of astonishment spread over his face. Staggering, he grunted like a slaughtered hog, and the point of a sword showed through his chest and pointed at them. Raymond's battle instinct returned with a snap. Shoving Juliana into the corner, he drew his sword.

Felix hung on the blade for an interminable

moment, the light leaving his widened eyes. Juliana cried aloud. The sword left Felix with a jerk, his body collapsed, and they stared right into the frigid blue eyes of Sir Joseph. He clutched his staff in one knobby fist, a dripping sword in the other, and he smiled as he pronounced, "He was a weak vessel, unworthy to be my representative."

Raymond's short sword rose and pointed at Sir Joseph. Sir Joseph pointed his much longer sword at Raymond. His gaze swept Raymond, and he sniffed with every appearance of appreciation. "This reminds me," he said, "of the stories circulated of your experiences with the tail end of a Tunisian horse."

"It's true," Raymond agreed, staring at Sir Joseph meaningfully. "I do know the best way to dispose of shit."

The bright red of fury spread across Sir Joseph's veined face, and he said in a shrill voice, "I chained you before, and this time I'll hang you out to watch you choke with your widow and that brat."

Raymond leaped over the top of Felix and into the great hall, but Sir Joseph jumped back with an agility that belied his age. The slash of Raymond's sword cut his staff down to a stub. Raymond drove at Sir Joseph, hoping to end the battle immediately, but the table crashed as eight partially armed mercenaries swarmed around. Before he could finish Sir Joseph, he found himself facing a battery of weapons held by men whose dishabille told of their unpreparedness.

"'Tis th' berserker," one man murmured, his fingers touching the fresh scab earned in his previous skirmish with Raymond. "He's come, just as he promised."

With a snarl, Sir Joseph turned on him. "It took half an army to release him, and they're waiting below to slit your throat, so you'd better swing that mace you're so proud of and put an end to him."

The mercenary, a common soldier, seemed unconvinced. He eyed Raymond with a caution that spoke eloquently of their previous conflict.

Then Juliana walked out and took her place at Raymond's side.

With gasps of pleasure and gap-toothed grins, the mercenaries surveyed her.

"A woman," the mace-wielder marvelled. Running his hand through his hair, he said, "An' no one will tell us nay on this one."

A cruel smile curved the mouth of the one mercenary who stood fully armed and at the ready. "See that iron collar around th' neck of Lord Garderobe? I locked it there, an' he'll die wi' it on."

Sir Joseph said, "You put it on under my command, you little piss-cutter, and it is I who will pay you, and pay you well when you have fulfilled your vows to me." The knight flushed at the reminder, and Sir Joseph leaned toward Raymond. "When your flesh, my lord, is worm's meat, still that collar will remain to embrace the bones of your neck and weigh your unmanly soul."

For Raymond, the reminder of his own destruction served as an agonizing prod. He'd failed to beat these men before. He'd killed his share, but these had come in waves, incited by their captain, and they'd defeated him.

What would happen if he failed now?

Answering Raymond's unspoken question, the knight looked at Juliana as if she were an houri clothed only in the seven veils. "I get her first, lads, then we'll all have a go, eh?"

The calm of desperation enveloped Raymond; the calm before the storm. "Juliana?"

She sounded breathless, disoriented with fear. "Aye?"

"I'm going to take these arseworms out." The captain's chuckle replied, but Raymond paid no attention. "I want you to do as I told you. Do you remember what I told you?"

"Aye. . . ." She remembered. Her teeth chattered, but she remembered. She must rescue Margery. She had only to avoid Sir Joseph and above all, stay away from Raymond.

Stay away from Raymond.

But how? She darted a desperate glance around. Cups and trenchers from the spilled table littered the floor. Bows and arrows had been abandoned where they dropped. Servants had fled. There was no place to hide, no exit in easy reach, and in the near corner a pile of cloth quivered.

Margery?

She clamped her mouth shut over her instinctive call. She wanted no one to remember Margery.

Sir Joseph stood well back as the circle of mercenaries drew close. Beside her, she heard Raymond take a breath. Then another. Slow and deep, he breathed in the essence of incipient battle, and, as he breathed, he seemed to suck away the courage, the skill, the very mass of his attackers. Before Juliana's eyes, the mercenaries shrank, their valor shrivelling before Raymond.

And Raymond—oh, God, Raymond seemed to grow in height, in muscle, in the merciless determination of an animal whose family is threatened. In the faces of the mercenaries, she saw dread, and remembered her own terror in the meadow when she believed Raymond to be a demon or a bear. Slowly, slowly, she turned her head and looked on him.

A bear's strength and agility. The relentlessness of a badger, the cold indifference of an adder. An eagle's swiftness and cruelty.

He was all those things, yet still a man. With a cry, she fled his side, straight through the line of mesmerized soldiers. Toward Sir Joseph.

Behind them, battle cries and the hiss of steel told of the battle joined, and she couldn't halt herself as Sir Joseph rushed to intercept her. She rammed into him even as she struggled to unsheathe the knife. The blade flashed with black sparks, but before she could wield it, he grabbed her wrist.

Grinding the bones together, he hissed, "You slut. You'll die for me and all the lands will be mine. Just as I always dreamed."

She struggled to keep her clasp on the hilt. "You can't kill enough people to take my lands."

"Perhaps not, but you, poor thing, will die, regardless of the final results. You and your children."

For my daughter, she thought. For my Margery. She tried to knee him in the groin, but his cloak rendered her ineffectual. Remembering the slap that had broken Felix's nose, she lunged for his face, but he remembered it, too, and grabbed her arm away with a painful twist. With both her hands captive, he put the point to his own stomach. "You're so close, but your strength is the strength of a woman, and no woman will ever be stronger than I am."

Seeking to stab with words if she could not stab in fact, she stated, "I am your lady. Let me go."

His blue eyes, so like her own in color, erupted with hatred. Steeped in the bitter brew of his resentment, he began to turn the knife on her.

Using all her strength, she pushed it back at him.

Their gazes locked as her youthful power fought his seasoned skill, but the outcome could be foreseen.

She would die on her own knife, for sometime she would not be able to turn the knife away. But not yet. Not yet.

She struggled, turned the point to him again—and he jerked, stumbled forward, fell with his weight on her. The blade, held rigid by his own grip on her, pierced the cloth of his cotte. His skin halted the point, then it wrenched in with a sickening thrust. As it sank to the hilt, his mouth dropped open and he sighed. "How?" His grip on her wrists loosened, and she snatched her hands away as he swayed.

Behind him tottered Margery, the impetus to his self-impalement. Her feet were tied, her hands were tied, a rag stuffed her mouth, but her eyes—like Sir Joseph's, like her mother's—blazed with a blue fire. Without the support of her two feet, she toppled.

The blade Juliana needed to cut Margery's bonds lay buried in Sir Joseph's bowels. She didn't want to touch the corpse, but the loathing that crawled through her veins was less than her love for Margery. Grasping the hilt, she jerked the blade free of its sheath.

Blood splattered her, the obscene shouts of the mercenaries assaulted her ears; from Raymond she heard nothing. But he still stood, she knew, for she heard the chain rattling, the thick cut of iron into flesh, a skull crack as it struck the stones.

Catching Margery under the arms, Juliana dragged her to a corner, removed the rag from her mouth, and huddled there with the taste of death thick on the air.

21

Raymond let the madness flow over him again, the madness that had spewed from him while he was chained. Lifted from the plain fury of fighting to a plateau above, he killed with complete, silent concentration, and the mercenaries were no match for him. The chain that dangled from his wrist disarmed the blades and broke bones. His short sword danced to the tune of death. Swinging the chain like an extension of his arm, he wrapped it around a mace and sent it flying, then with another heave broke the bones in the hand that wielded it. The mercenary looked at his mangled fingers, then staggered away, screaming, "The berserker will kill us all. Retreat! Retreat."

The weakened circle around Raymond wavered, and Raymond whipped his chain around. Spitting teeth, three panicked mercenaries ran, but one held his ground. "He's going to kill us anyway, lads. May as well go brave."

Raymond smiled at the armorless soldier, tasting conquest, strong and sweet. The soldier smiled back—with a little too much humor, and Raymond stiffened with alarm. Too late, he realized another mercenary stood behind him. A rope flew past his face and jerked around his neck. The familiar panic twisted his guts as the rope tightened and a voice murmured in his ear, "Like before, isn't it?"

But it wasn't like before. This wasn't the Saracen. It was only an impoverished knight forced to kill for his living. The mercenary descending on him with sword bared was no exotic torture master, but a common peasant who had abandoned the plow.

A roar exploded past the blockage of Raymond's battered throat. As the daunted mercenary captain dragged at the rope, Raymond plunged like a maddened bull and tossed him over his shoulders, into the oncoming blade.

With a shriek, the peasant picked up his arm, amputated at the elbow, and fled. The knight rose, unharmed, saved by his armor, and fled. And tasting victory, true victory, once more, Raymond chased them.

As Juliana sawed through the ropes binding Margery's feet and wrists, the cessation of noise broke her concentration. Facing the room warily, she found Raymond was gone. The mercenaries were gone. A few bodies stirred and groaned, but nothing else moved. "Where are they?" she whispered, and jumped when Margery answered in a normal voice.

"Papa chased them out." Fiercely, she added, "He was killing them all."

"Oh." Still reacting to the violence, the fury, Juliana put her hand to her thumping heart. All she could do was ask, "Did they hurt you?"

"They didn't rape me, if that's what you mean." Margery's hug contradicted the callousness in her tone. Juliana stroked her daughter's hair, and together they shuddered. When Margery spoke again, her voice had softened. "They argued so much, they hardly knew I was there."

"We'll say a prayer to Saint Mary, for she watched over you," Juliana said.

"I have to go on a pilgrimage to Ripon Cathedral," Margery mumbled. "I swore if I left here unharmed, I would go there and give thanks to Saint Wilfrid for the preservation of my virginity and myself."

"Then so you shall," Juliana said. "We have men outside the keep. Raymond is probably even now admitting them, and we'll"—she looked at Sir Joseph's bloody body and trembled—"see if we can find the keys on Sir Joseph to free Raymond from his bonds." She didn't want to. Not really. That one corpse held more fear for her than all the living mercenaries in the troop. But to observe Raymond's pleasure as she unlocked his collar . . . maybe he'd forgive her for her failures and her fears. And if he didn't, she'd still have his pleasure to remember. "I'll just take the knife," she said, falsely cheerful, "and look for those keys."

Margery seemed to hear more than Juliana said. "Mother, if you're afraid . . ."

"Afraid?" Juliana scurried forward on her hands and knees. "Why should I be afraid?" Halfway to the body sprawled in broken splendor across the stones, she stopped.

Sir Joseph was dead.

She'd put the knife in his gut herself. She could see his lips were blue. Blotches of red burned in his

cheeks, but the rest of his skin looked like parchment.
So he was dead. He lay unmoving. She came close and
leaned over him, watching for signs of consciousness.
A flicker of his eyelid, a twitch of his mouth, some
sign of life.

Nothing.

"He *is* dead," she whispered.

The words had hardly left her mouth when his
hand flashed up and caught her wrist.

The pain, immediate, intense, made her drop the
knife onto his chest, and he snatched it up. The fear,
immediate, intense, swept her into its familiar
embrace. Sir Joseph's eyes opened, their eyes locked,
and the square of his mouth smiled horribly. "You
stupid woman."

He said it as if it were the most obscene epithet he
could imagine. Margery leaped forward, but he shifted
around and lifted the point of the knife under
Juliana's chin.

"Don't, Margery. Oh, sweet Mary, please don't
come near him." Juliana twisted her wrist in his
grasp.

"That prick from your knife couldn't kill me." He
raised himself on his elbow, crushing her hand
beneath his, while Raymond's feet thumped on the
stairway. That horrible square smile shone again in
Sir Joseph's skinny face.

Raymond charged through the door, crying, "How
is Margery?" and skidded to a stop with a rattle of
chains. "Juliana."

Her name sounded like a prayer on his lips, but
Juliana did not dare remove her gaze from Sir
Joseph's. Her whole world was shackled with blue
eyes, blue flames, a fanaticism that sucked her in and

wouldn't let her go. Triumph blazed in his blue orbs, yet in the rank odor of his breath, she smelled his death warrant. His intestine had been pierced—a grievous injury, but slow to kill. "You're dying," she said.

"And I wish company." He caught her shoulder before she could scramble away and hoisted himself to his feet. Using only the tip of the knife as an urging, he pressed it against her tender throat and commanded, "Get up, Juliana. Get up."

She wanted to swallow; she feared to swallow. She feared to move, and feared not to. Tucking her feet under her, she rose stiffly, and she heard Raymond suck in his breath at her clumsiness. Sir Joseph stepped close against her, and his free hand caressed her chin.

"Put her away from you," Raymond commanded, smooth and urgent.

"Why should I?" Sir Joseph asked.

Chilled by the call of death, Sir Joseph's papery skin repulsed her. Yet nothing could make her insensible to the contempt in Raymond's voice, and she flinched when he said, "She's a woman, inadequate and lowly, not a fit shield for you to hide behind."

Sir Joseph threatened, "She's a fit sheath for my knife."

"'Tis Salisbury's knife," she murmured, and thought longingly of the old tracker. He had faith in her, more faith than she had in herself. "I'm your kinswoman," she said. "You don't want my blood on your soul."

He blinked at her, and she was momentarily released from his mania.

But he captured her again with a piercing stare, and

when he sniggered something inside her shrivelled. "What a feeble sentimentalist you must believe me to be. If you weren't my kinswoman, I wouldn't care if you lived or died. I've dreamt of your murder most of my life." He circled her and warned, "Keep yourself in my view, Lord Raymond, or I will cut all your hopes of saving your wife."

Raymond spoke from beside Margery. " 'Strewth, what matter? If you kill my wife, I have another at hand."

Three people stared at him in various degrees of distrust.

"Papa, how can you say such a thing?" Margery whispered.

Blotted with blood, still Raymond's countenance shone with grim humor. "Does Sir Joseph think he is the only one who takes advantage of another's gullibility?"

His words were as knives, sharper than the blade at Juliana's throat, more deadly for they sliced her heart. She looked at his face, still handsome despite its injuries; at his form, so noble in its shape. She saw the disdain for her, the way his hand caressed Margery's head, and she realized there was no help to be had from him.

She was betrayed.

If she was going to outlast Sir Joseph, she would have to outthink him.

Sir Joseph laughed, a burst of noise that ended in a painful hiccup, and saluted Raymond. "I should have known a man raised by such parents would understand treachery."

Wiping the blood off his sword with his cloak, Raymond asked, "My parents? Did you help them with the kitchen fire?"

Sir Joseph's hand shook in a seizure of palsy, and Juliana's ears buzzed as she imagined that sharp edge slicing her windpipe. "You are astute," he commended. "For all her look of delicacy, this one doesn't die easily, but she's stupid. Stupid as her father. He never suspected me, not even when I urged a siege on Felix's castle."

Juliana's heart beat heavily, pulsing through the veins in her neck. Her breath rasped at her throat, making her aware of the fragility of her existence. But she had to survive. What did she wish to teach her daughter about survival? Juliana had to use strategy and intelligence and all the characteristics she wished for Margery. So she took advantage of Sir Joseph's conceit. "No doubt you had a daring plan, so tell me—why besiege Felix if he had taken me?"

Sir Joseph tried to speak, then faltered; staggered slightly, but caught himself.

Raymond answered for him. "Sir Joseph is canny. He urged a siege because you would die, and your father, too, I trow. But I am not your father, and I will not die here, for I am not your father."

She listened to the repetition, and listened to the meaning. He was assuring her he wouldn't betray her, and she blinked tears of relief away. "Nay, you're not my father, are you? He was a weak man, one who listened to a counselor who'd sold his soul"—she looked again at Sir Joseph—"to the devil."

Guilt and terror twisted the aging face, and he whispered, "Aye, I think I did sell my soul to the devil. But I'll not pay the price, not when I haven't had the pleasure of my reward. You'll die with me, and I'll clasp your heel and fly to heaven in your draft."

As she stared at that livid face, smelled the odor of aging body and envy, something happened inside her. The mechanism that remembered terror, created fear, sent her scurrying inside her castle at the first hazard, snapped—from overuse, she guessed.

She was no longer a coward, forcing bravery from herself—she *was* brave. "You're not going to kill me," she said, and with swift impatience, she jabbed her elbow in his gut.

He staggered backward and, with a yell, Raymond threw his short sword. It whistled through the air, whipping through the flesh of Sir Joseph's throat. It severed the windpipe, the spinal cord. The body, already empty of its soul, catapulted across to land on the hearth.

Raymond sprang after the sword, grabbed Juliana by the shoulders and shouted, "Why did you let him near you? You could have been killed!"

"Don't touch my mother. Don't touch my mother." Margery pulled on him and sobbed.

Head down, hands over her ears, Juliana ordered, "Stop!"

Silence descended, and she looked up. To Margery, she said, "Raymond will not hurt me. He said those things to disarm Sir Joseph." To Raymond, she said, "I wanted the keys off his belt. I wanted to unlock your shackles."

With a snarl that showed sharp teeth, Raymond tugged at the iron collar at his throat. "Couldn't you have borne the disgrace of this for a few more moments? Did you have to risk getting yourself killed for a key?"

Margery sobbed again, the soft crying of a woman who had left childhood behind, and Juliana gathered her in a hug. From the doorway, Valeska called,

"Come to us, child. We'll take you away from this pestilence."

With a final hug, Juliana pushed her daughter toward the old ladies who peered in the door.

Layamon stood at the door next, fumbling with his jerkin. "Is there aught I can do fer ye, m'lord?"

"Secure the castle against wolves. We'll leave it empty, for any who pass and have the ballocks to enter this damnable house may take it." Raymond went to Sir Joseph and jerked the body off the hearth. Cutting the keys from the belt, he returned to Juliana and pressed them into her hand. "Unlock me, then."

The ring was heavy with keys, large and unwieldy. Keys to Lofts, keys to Bartonhale, keys that Sir Joseph should not have had in his possession. And somewhere the keys to the shackles. Selecting the smallest key, she fit it into the handcuff with the short chain. It fit, but the cuff wasn't easy to open. "I'm sorry I was stupid. I just wanted to free you."

"You believed me, didn't you?"

His bitterness was so palpable she could almost taste it. "Believed you?"

The cuff clicked open and fell to the floor with a thunk. He rubbed the flesh beneath it and said, "You believed I would betray you. Let him kill you. Marry your daughter."

"I . . ." She took his other hand in hers. From this cuff hung the chain which he'd used as such an effective weapon, and he winced when she pressed the key inside it. "Does that hurt you?"

"You hurt me."

"I believed you." Staring into his eyes, she willed him to vindicate her. "For just a moment. It was madness, but—"

"Open the cuff."

His bleak expression frightened her, as did the way he watched her, and she struggled to obey him. When the iron separated, she gasped. The skin beneath had been flayed away by the weight of the chain as he had wielded it in his vicious attacks on the mercenaries. Guilt consumed her, and she touched the flesh with shaking fingers. "Raymond . . ."

He no longer bore any resemblance to an eagle or a bear or a wolf. He looked simply tired and sad. "I wanted you to know. No real man would ever betray you. Remember that when you remember me."

"Remember you?" she repeated, alarmed.

"You want me to go, and I understand. I'll leave you Keir for your protection."

The bleakness of his face frightened her. "Go where?"

"Perhaps we can get the annulment my parents talked about." He rubbed his forehead with the palm of his hand.

Still dazed with shock, she repeated, "You want an annulment?"

"Don't! Don't pretend you want this disastrous marriage."

"Disastrous? Because I believed for one moment you had betrayed me? Nay, Raymond, 'twas only a momentary insanity."

"Whose insanity? 'Twas not your insanity that created a chained beast who knew not reason or"—he wanted to say love, but he could not—"or kindness."

"'Twas Sir Joseph's insanity that created that beast."

"Nay, for the beast came from within me. Even now it lives within me. Doesn't that frighten you?

Won't you always wonder if the beast will leap out of me to rip your heart out?" She tried to deny it, but he wouldn't listen. "You don't trust me—for good reason. So I'm leaving you."

She managed to say only, "By God's teeth, you'll stay."

Wrapped in his own misery, he paid her no heed. "You want a man to protect you. Of what other use am I to you?"

"Do you believe me to be so shallow? If all I needed was a man to protect me, I'd . . . marry Layamon."

Her imitation of anguish and indignation would have invoked pride in any performer, Raymond thought. "You couldn't marry Layamon. He's not a lord, nor even a knight. Now I . . . I am a lord fitting of your station, but not of your spirit. I've given you nothing of value."

"Nothing of . . . what do you consider value?"

So she wanted to do the right thing by him. He'd saved her daughter, he was her husband. Her sense of duty was gratifying, but not what he wanted. Not at all. "Something you can touch or taste or smell."

"Not security? Not pleasure in bed? Not courage? Not"—she tapped her chest—"not myself back?"

His neck hurt from the collar. His wounds, inflicted by the mercenaries and previously undetected, made themselves known. He felt old. "Too many truths have been discarded today, too many convictions overset. I'm not the man you believed me to be."

"You are everything I believed you to be."

It was the most brilliant, cutting insult he'd ever heard, and he responded with a roar. She flinched at his fury but held her ground as he asked, "Do you know what drove me to insanity out there by the tree?"

"Your collar. You don't like to be confined"—she swallowed with visible difficulty—"around your neck."

Low and clear, driven by inner pain, he said, "Let me tell you what caused that insanity. I stood for months in a dungeon, but not a dungeon like we have. Oh, nay. This one was hot and dry, dusty with the desert winds. A necklace of iron choked my neck, sturdy bracelets held my wrists close to my head." Lifting his hands, he demonstrated. "Pressed against the slimy wall, my raw back attracted scores of vermin. I was worm's meat—"

She pressed the back of her hands against her mouth, but he wrestled them away.

"Aye, listen to me. I was worm's meat even before my death. But even that wasn't as bad as the occasional flashes of light. That light announced the arrival of my heathen master—my tormentor. Food was pressed between my teeth. Water forced down my throat. My eyes were made so sensitive from the dark I couldn't even glare defiance.

"And he had a voice, a smooth, kind, drawling voice that offered slavery as if it were salvation." He no longer burned with pain. Now he was cold, cold and filled with a loathing for himself. "He broke me. Rather than remaining true to the things holy to me, I crumpled like a weakling, like a child, like a—"

"Woman? Like me?"

He tugged at the iron collar, wishing he could tear it from him. "If every man had your courage, we'd have never lost the Holy Land."

"Pretty words to wrap a cruel accusation."

He heard only the bitterness; he knew not at whom it was directed.

She continued. "You say you crumpled like a weakling, but I don't remember that. I remember the raging beast and how I tamed it. Then you brought it out again, here"—her sweep of the hand indicated the carnage around them—"and controlled it. You used it to protect me. That's what I remember."

Her eloquence swayed him. Oh, aye, it did, but this was temptation too sweet to be real, and he denied it, and her. "You deserve better than me, so I will do what is right for you. I will remove myself from your life." He moved toward the door, wondering why his joints didn't creak.

With a speed he would never have attributed to her, she stepped between him and the door, and tapped his chest. "You are forgetting one thing."

"My lady?"

"Let me remind you, my lord. You dismissed the king's master castle-builder and said you would build me a curtain wall. By all that's holy, you mighty Crusader, you'll not renege on your promise. You are bound to me until you finish the curtain wall."

22

"Oh, Mother, look at Lofts Castle," Margery said, her voice full of awe.

Juliana pulled her palfrey to a halt, wiped the rain out of her eyes, and stared. The hope she didn't know she had cherished sank. The shorter end of the curtain wall rose from the mud, finished except for the crenellations and finials. She should be rejoicing to see it standing after so brief a time, but if her men continued to perform such construction miracles, Raymond would be here only through the summer—if that long.

So much for her feeble attempt to keep him by her side while they mended the fabric of their marriage.

Their disastrous marriage, he had called it. Juliana squeezed her eyes shut as she remembered the tactful way he'd tried to tell her of her inadequacies. Of her cowardice and how it had destroyed him. She hadn't wanted to listen, for then he would be alone, and she would be alone.

But after riding two miserable days in the mud and rain, she realized they couldn't be more alone than they were right then. Their solitude, even though they were together, made her heart hurt, and her hand crept to her chest to press the ache.

In a dreamy voice, Margery said, "The first thing I'm going to do is change into dry clothes."

"I'm goin' t' have a hot meal," Layamon said.

Keir's stoicism faded a little as he gazed at the long slits of light shining from the keep. "I'll rest my weary limbs close to the fire."

"This spring drizzle has settled into my bones," Valeska said. "Do you look forward to your own bed, Raymond?"

Raymond only grunted, and Juliana winced.

Before her, Margery wiggled like a fish. "Look, Mother," she shouted, pointing. "There's Ella."

A tiny figure stood on the battlements, waving with both hands, and Juliana found tears springing to her eyes. She wanted to hold her younger daughter. She wanted to gain comfort from her family. She wanted to change into her own clothes, sleep in her own bed. Most of all, she wanted to love Raymond, and that would never happen again. The drawbridge crept down and touched the earth in front of them, and Juliana took her place at the head of the procession. She wanted to ride in with a flourish, but she was so tired, so discouraged, she could only plod.

"Mother," Ella shrieked, and flew down the stairs.

Juliana hurriedly prepared to dismount and greet her daughter with all the affection in her heart.

"Papa!" Ella shrieked again, and launched herself at Raymond.

He caught her, astonishment written plain on his haggard features, and she wrapped her arms around him in sheer exuberance.

"Oh, Papa, I knew you'd save Margery." Ella

plastered wet kisses across his cheek. "I knew you'd save her."

A smile, rusty from disuse, lifted first one side of his mouth, then the other. "Did you now, imp?"

"Aye. What else are papas for, but to keep their children safe?" she asked ingenuously.

Raymond's gaze swivelled to meet Juliana's; for one moment, they stared at each other in helpless agony.

But Ella interrupted them. "Margery, did you have an adventure?"

Margery slid out of the saddle onto the ground and bounded toward the embracing pair. "A great adventure," she boasted.

Looking down from her perch, Ella demanded, "Were you scared?"

"Nay. At least"—Margery's gusto faded, leaving a prematurely wise girl—"Denys is dead, and I liked him very much."

"Even after he abducted you?" Ella asked.

"Well, he was just a boy. Boys aren't very smart." Tears trickled from Margery's eyes, but she lifted her face and pretended they were rain. She tugged at Ella's leg, and Raymond let the child slide to the ground. "Come on," Margery said, grabbing her sister's arm. "I'll tell you."

Watching the family she'd labored to create, realizing it would soon disintegrate, Juliana swallowed the envy and tears that clogged her throat. The horse moved restively beneath her, smelling oats and a warm stable. Again she prepared to dismount, but Ella halted with a jerk and ran back to Juliana. Glad that Ella had at last remembered her mother, Juliana leaned down to caress her child. Ella wrapped her arms around Juliana's knee in such an enthusiastic manner she clearly had great news. "Mother, it's been so exciting! You wouldn't believe who has arrived."

Rain dripped onto Juliana's shoulders, wetting the already soaked material of her cloak, but it couldn't cool her surge of anger at such a breach of security. "Who?" she asked frostily.

"Ella," Margery nagged. "You can talk to Mother anytime."

Ella glanced at Margery, glanced at Juliana, and shrugged. "They'll tell you," she decided, and raced to Margery.

Juliana glared at Layamon, who looked harried and guilty. "I told th' men no one was t' enter while we were gone. No one. M'lady, I'll discipline them 'til they scream."

The door to the keep banged open, and Hugh stepped out on the landing. "Thank God you've come at last!" he roared, and descended the ladder.

"Of course." Juliana sighed with relief. "They would let Hugh in."

Valeska and Dagna tugged at her foot, and Valeska said, "We're going inside to see what damage those foolish maids have done in our absence."

"They were competent before your arrival," Juliana said.

"Your standards were low," Valeska returned.

Dagna grinned. "We'll warm the water for your bath, my lady. Is there anything else you desire?"

"Warm the covers on my bed," Juliana instructed. "I have dreamt of a feather mattress too long."

"Aye." Valeska winked and leaned closer. "Perhaps your use of the mattress will heal the wound between you and the master."

Juliana's doubts must have shown clearly on her face, for Dagna said comfortingly, "Time is on your side, my lady, and he cannot leave you when you have guests to entertain, now can he?"

Their wicked cackling rumbled, and, appealing for mercy, Juliana opened her hands to the heavens. The sudden cessation of their laughter brought her gaze back down to earth, and there, at the shoulder of her horse, stood Salisbury. He didn't speak, but she knew what he wanted. "The man who killed your son is dead."

"Did *ye* kill him?" Salisbury demanded.

"Raymond did," she said.

At the same time, Raymond said, "She did."

Startled, Juliana looked at Raymond, and he looked at her.

"We did," he decided.

"Knew that." Salisbury spat on the ground. "Rot in hell."

Juliana fumbled at her belt and extended Salisbury's knife. "Here. I used it to hew wood and cut rope and slice a man's liver to hash, just as you instructed."

Salisbury grinned, and all his gums shone pink. "Keep it. Assures yer lord's fidelity."

He hobbled off through the mud, and Hugh, who stood nearby, whistled. "I'd keep myself well away from *that* knife, Raymond."

As Juliana tucked it back in her belt, Raymond agreed. "I will."

Smoothing his few wisps of hair off of his forehead, Hugh said, "I suppose Felix is dead, too."

Juliana nodded.

"I suspected . . . but I liked the stupid fool."

Legs astride, Raymond said, "If you'd killed him when he first made trouble for Lady Juliana, we wouldn't have had this situation to deal with now."

"I couldn't kill Felix for snatching Juliana. After all, she's only a woman." But Hugh looked uncertain, and he veered away after the children. "I'll get the story from the girls." Turning, he pressed his fists to his hips. "Do you know what a strain it's been entertaining your guests?"

"What guests?" Juliana queried. Hugh didn't hear her, or ignored her, and wearily, she slid out of the saddle into Raymond's waiting arms.

Funny, how he wanted to avoid her, yet tried ever to ease her way.

No doubt he didn't wish it, but his warmth permeated her soggy clothing and brought a surge of heat to her skin. Especially her cheeks. "Your courtesy is appreciated," she said.

Looking everywhere but at her, he replied, "You are ever welcome."

Abruptly, unable to stop herself, she said, "You look dreadful." And he did. Rain dripped from his nose and subdued his thick, glossy hair so that it hung in strings around his throat. His tanned face was gray with fatigue, and his lips were blue with chill. Bruises blackened one high cheekbone. A sword had slashed his chin in a vertical line, and another crossed that wound to form an X. The edges looked puckered and red, painfully matched by another cut high into his hairline above his ear. He had his cloak pulled close around his neck, but when they had unlocked his collar, she'd seen the mangled flesh and bruised muscles of his throat.

Juliana wanted to tend him, pamper him, treat him like a king. He'd never looked so good to her as when he looked this bad. Her fingers hovered close to his face.

With a tender twist to his lips, he murmured, "You do not look well yourself."

She wanted to swoon. The way he'd spoken, she heard only a generous compliment. "Really?"

"Aye." His hand rose close to her face, and they stood poised, looking at each other, almost touching.

"Raymond!"

The roar of an aggressive male voice made them both jump. Their hands dropped, they turned guiltily.

A grizzled knight strode toward them. "Raymond, you crazed warrior!"

Juliana flinched at the tactless comment, but delight mixed with amazement spread across Raymond's face. Stepping out, he extended his arms and hollered, "Lord Peter, you blessed tyrant, how did you get here?"

Juliana flinched again, but Lord Peter laughed loud and long. The men wrapped each other in a bear hug, but when Lord Peter caught sight of Juliana's woebegone face, he called an abrupt halt to the masculine alliance. "Ah, Raymond." He poked Raymond in the ribs. "Is this your bride?"

Raymond cleared his throat and flashed one beseeching glance at Juliana. *Don't involve him in our troubles.* Taking her hand, he presented it to Lord Peter and said formally, "Aye. Aye, this is Juliana."

Lord Peter beamed. "Did you hear the world of pride in this man's voice? He's leg-shackled for sure." The muscled warrior spread his arms wide. "May I embrace the lady who captured Raymond's heart at last?"

Blushing so vigorously her ears burned, Juliana submitted to a hearty hug. When Lord Peter turned her face up, he studied her through eyes surprisingly astute and nodded, well pleased. "Ah, and you love him, too. He deserves the best, does my lad Raymond." As he released her, he grinned at Raymond. "You wouldn't have had a chance if she'd met me first."

"Aye, for that would have given her such a distaste for men she would have never recovered enough to see my superior qualities."

Raymond pushed Lord Peter's shoulder; Lord Peter pounded Raymond's back and said, "It's about time you got here. It's been raining and everyone is bored and we've used every indoor game ever imagined, and in the circumstances, that wasn't enough." He broke off and asked, "Is that my friend Keir I see dismounting from that mighty destrier?"

Keir responded with a solemn, "I am Keir, and this is indeed a mighty destrier." Lord Peter's great strides took him to the destrier's side, and he ran his hands over the horse as Keir explained, "This is the horse Lady Juliana and Raymond presented to me, but he was most rudely stolen, and I have only just recovered him."

"He seems to be none the worse for his adventure," Lord Peter said.

"He could ride farther." Keir rubbed his own back. "I could not. So if you will excuse me, I will tend to my mount"—his gaze wandered toward the children romping outside the smithy—"and inspect the work of the new blacksmith."

"Miss the girls, do you?" Lord Peter slapped Keir's back. "Well do I comprehend that. I've been gone from my wee grandchildren only a week, and already I wonder what mischief they've gotten into."

Keir looked puzzled. "Is it common, then, to miss a child when separated from it?"

A grin split Lord Peter's gray beard. "Quite common, and it's just as common to wish you were gone when you're around them."

Lifting his brows, Keir said, "It is illogical, but my emotions are similar to your description."

"Did William and Saura not come, then?" Raymond asked, disappointment in his voice.

"Saura's breeding again, and though she would have come, William forbade it." Lord Peter exchanged a grin with Raymond. "The woman leads him around by the nose, except when it comes to her safety."

"Think you it be a boy this time?"

Lord Peter raised his hands. "I told Saura one boy couldn't be as much trouble as the five girls they have now, but will she listen?"

"Is Maud home with her?"

"She'll not leave her lamb now," Lord Peter said, then turned to Juliana. "Raymond didn't tell you, but I'm Lord Peter of Burke."

Juliana couldn't help but smile. "I know."

"Has Raymond told you about me?" he asked, then said earnestly, "Don't believe a word of it. I'm actually a very pleasant fellow."

"Nay, nay." Juliana faced him. "Raymond has spoken of you in only glowing terms." Seeing the amusement that tugged at his mouth, hearing Raymond's chuckle, she realized she'd been hoaxed by a master. Relaxing, she said, "Raymond claims you are his dearest mentor. I bid you belated welcome to Lofts Castle. Would that we had been here when you arrived."

Lord Peter sobered and drew himself up. "Aye, would that you had been here."

The pleasure of the company faded as Juliana and Raymond caught the mood. Not realizing the rapport they betrayed, they exchanged concerned glances before Raymond asked, "What is it, Lord Peter? What news?"

"I don't know how to tell you. . . ." Lord Peter trailed off, clearly at a loss for words. "What I'm trying to say is that all things must pass, and we must take comfort in the knowledge that God forgives. . . ." He took a deep breath, and it sounded like fortification against adversity.

Raymond looked wildly at Lord Peter. "Are the Scots over the border? Have the Crusaders lost the Holy Land? Is Henry ill? Damn it, tell us!"

Putting his hands behind his back, Lord Peter rocked on his heels. "It is nothing so clear-cut as that. That is, death is clear-cut, but . . ."

"Tell us," Raymond said from between clenched teeth.

Raising his head, Lord Peter looked straight at Raymond. "Your parents are dead."

Juliana gasped at the sad tidings so plainly put. But as Raymond said nothing, did nothing, she realized the source of Lord Peter's uneasiness.

Raymond did not love his parents. The grief she'd experienced upon learning of her own parents' passing did not seize Raymond. As he stood there immobile, it wasn't evident what he thought, or what emotions boiled in him.

"My parents are dead," he repeated at last. "How did this happen?"

"Winter is no time to take a ship across the channel, and the wreckage of a ship has been washing up against the cliffs. The fisherfolk identified it . . ."

"As my parents' vessel?" Raymond wrung out a lock of hair that dripped in his face. To Juliana, he said, "These last two days, I've taken comfort in the thought the rain has washed away the reminders of the cesspit."

It seemed an aside, but Juliana understood. This was a break from the heavy atmosphere of unhappiness surrounding every evidence of mortality, and from the guilt surrounding these deaths. "I, too, have been glad for the rain," she agreed. "It's cleansing, like a baptism."

Whistling tunelessly, Raymond stared up at the weeping sky. "It's very odd. My parents have been there all my life. They have tormented me, controlled me, made me so angry I have screamed like an ale-wife. I hated them, but Juliana taught me there were worse things than unloving parents."

Dumbfounded, Juliana queried, "I did?"

"Aye, you did. 'Tis worse to have a father who loves you, yet lacks the strength of character to support you through your travails. 'Tis worse to have a father you love, yet who's so weak you suspect him of betraying you. To put that aside took real fortitude." He sighed and rubbed his fingers together to warm them. "So my parents have left this world, and I find I no longer hate them. Nor is there a shred of grief in my soul. There's nothing but pity for them." He surveyed the bailey. His gaze rested on Margery and Ella outside the smithy with Keir and Hugh, then roamed the lands through the open gate. He smiled. "They had not a tenth of the riches I have found."

He looked at Juliana, and she plucked the thought from his mind. *The riches I will renounce.* Aloud, he asked, "Shall we go in?"

They stepped into a great hall overflowing with women. Some Juliana recognized, some she didn't. Some were serving maids. Others appeared to be noblewomen. Julian gaped at the swirl of activity, noting it circled around one aristocratic lady seated at her sewing frame. For one mad moment, Juliana thought it was Raymond's mother, returned from the dead, but Raymond disabused her with a pleased exclamation. "Eleanor!"

The lady rose and came toward him with arms extended. "Cousin."

Juliana glanced at Lord Peter for guidance. He paid her no heed but stepped back a respectful distance. Raymond went hastily down on one knee.

"Oh, Raymond." The lady called Eleanor pounded Raymond on the shoulder. "No ceremony with me. Stand up."

Raymond did as ordered, embracing the lady with equal parts enthusiasm and respect. "When facing a monarch, I find it's best to assume an attitude of meekness until I discover if I'm still in favor."

"You are ever in favor with your queen."

As their banter penetrated her weary mind and Juliana grasped that Eleanor of Aquitaine, former queen of France, present queen of England, and duchess in her own right, honored her home, she sank to her knees—although whether from respect or amazement, she couldn't say.

With an arm around her shoulder, Raymond turned to face Juliana. "May I have the honor of presenting my wife, Lady Juliana of Lofts?"

This was indeed the queen the troubadours sang of. Her countenance disclosed the relationship about which Geoffroi bragged, but her beauty surpassed Isabel's. The overweening pride that marred Raymond's parents was absent in Eleanor. She had no need to remind those around her of her status. She was the living embodiment of romance, intelligence, and life—and she knew it.

Assessing Juliana with one shrewd glance, she held out her hand. "Stand, cousin. You'll not be on ceremony with me."

Juliana took the hand almost reverently and came to her feet. "I never dreamed of this honor," she stammered.

Eleanor pulled a wry face. "Didn't Raymond warn you I'd visit?"

Wordless, Juliana shook her head.

"Shame on him." Waggling an authoritarian finger, Eleanor said, "Raymond is my favorite cousin, and he's Henry's, too, when Henry is in his right mind."

"How is the king?" Raymond asked, leading Eleanor back to her stool.

With a moue, Eleanor admitted, "I don't know. I gave birth to another of his sons at Christmastide, and he has expressed his gratitude by staying as far away from me as possible."

"My congratulations, Madam, on another healthy son."

Raymond's deep voice made the plaudit sound like a benediction, but Eleanor rolled her eyes. "He's a mewling babe, and I cannot like him."

"Because of the circumstances of his birth?" Raymond asked.

"No doubt, although I don't emulate the Madonna at the best of times. I'm a good queen, a good duchess, a lusty wife, a fair poet, and a beauty." Her smile mocked herself and the lines which life had etched on her face. "I don't have time to be a good mother, too." Her fingers fluttered. "Although I'm a better mother than Henry is father. Henry's well, I'm sure. When is Henry ever ill?"

Raymond captured her restless hand. "He is never ill."

Gazing at Raymond, Eleanor said, "You have the look of him sometimes, especially in your rages."

Raymond dropped her hand. "Henry froths at the mouth when he rages, Madam."

"Aye, so he does."

Juliana suddenly saw Raymond's earlier transformation from gentle knight to raging beast in a less sinister light, and almost laughed aloud. King Henry's paroxysms were legendary. While in the grip of one of his rages, gossip claimed, he rolled on the ground, chewed the furniture, and banged his head, and all fled from him.

A family characteristic? The justification for the bellicose bear on the family arms? Perhaps. Juliana had reason to be grateful for that bear.

Lifting her needle, Eleanor then gave permission to those around her to be seated. Her ladies-in-waiting sank back onto their designated benches. Raymond indicated the bench directly in front of Eleanor, and Juliana sat. He propped his foot up beside her and leaned his elbow against his knee. Juliana decided he did it to avoid making contact with her.

"Sit, Raymond," Eleanor commanded.

"Nay, Madam. I have been sitting on a horse for two days, and have no need to place my arse on any hard surface for a long time."

"You're crude."

"I'm sore."

A smile played around Eleanor's mouth, and she seemed not at all offended by Raymond's bluntness. Dipping her needle into her work, she said smoothly, "Regardless of our differences, in one thing Henry and I are agreed. We are glad, Lady Juliana, of your marriage to Raymond. It had been much on our minds at court, especially when you did not come when summoned."

Eleanor's lightning glance destroyed Juliana's composure, and she shifted on the bench. Before Juliana could draft an excuse, Eleanor continued, "Our cousin Raymond is a treasure who has set many a maiden's heart beating faster. But more important than that, he is a mighty warrior."

"I do know that," Juliana said.

"Aye." Eleanor examined Raymond's battered face as if she'd just noticed its injuries. "You've just had a demonstration."

Juliana looked on him, too, and she wanted to cry at the damage to his handsome face. But she couldn't keep the pride from her tone when she said, "He saved my daughter."

"All the more reason for you to cease any resistance you have to this union." The whip snapped in Eleanor's voice, and Juliana tried to protest. Eleanor raised one long, pale hand. "It is the king's will, and mine, that the borderlands of Wales be in secure hands, and the hands we chose were Raymond's. Is that clear?"

Observing the grim brackets around Raymond's mouth, Juliana remembered his fervent determination to end their marriage. She wanted, so badly, to use the queen's command as a way to chain Raymond to her side. But she knew how he hated chains, and she couldn't be so selfish as to keep him when he wanted to go. "My queen—" she began, but Raymond's heavy hand on her shoulder cut her off.

"It is clear to both of us," he answered, stiff with pride.

Eleanor flicked a glance at them, seeing below the surface. But she approved his acquiescence with a biting, "How wise you are, as befitting the count and countess of Locheais."

Juliana wet her lips. "Madam?"

"The count and countess—" Eleanor broke off. "I'm sorry, Raymond. I assumed Lord Peter had told you of the drownings of your parents."

"He did," Raymond replied.

Faintly puzzled, Eleanor said, "I won't insult you by offering my condolences. I know what you thought of them, and rightly so. But you do assume your father's title. You're heir to all his lands and your mother's, too." She invited his smile with her own grin. "A preposterous amount of money and land. When I wage war on Henry, I'll know whom to approach for a loan."

"When you wage war with Henry—" Raymond began, but stopped when Juliana half rose in her chair.

"You're wealthy," she said to him accusingly.

"Well . . . aye."

She sounded witless, she knew, but she couldn't help it. "And you don't need my lands."

"Henry needs them," Raymond joked. Seeing the panic on her face, he sobered. "You always knew I would eventually inherit."

Still stupid with shock, she said, "Avraché will be yours still, for your mother—"

"Had no time to give it to the Church," he agreed.

Regaining control, she tried to smile, tried to be glad for him. "How marvelous for you. You'll have your home back."

"My home?" He shook his head. "Nay, Avraché was never my home. I was raised there, but—"

"But you were so upset when your mother threatened to take it from you," Juliana burst out.

"Well, aye, I would be. They had promised for years to give it to me to use as income, and in one vindictive move my mother tried to strip me of even so minute an amount." To Eleanor, he said, "Isabel wanted to give Avraché to the Church."

"Henry would never allow that," Eleanor snapped.

"Perhaps I could endow an abbey there in her memory?"

Eleanor considered, then concurred. "As I have endowed the abbey of Fontevrault. A kind idea, for if the nuns must pray for Isabel's soul every day, she will surely pass from purgatory before this millennium is through."

"So soon?" Raymond asked ironically.

"God's time is not of this world." Eleanor's rebuke possessed every evidence of piety, but she scarcely drew breath before she changed subjects. "Where is my master castle-builder? I sent him to Lady Juliana to build her a new curtain wall. Where is he?"

"Your master castle-builder?" Straightening to his full height, Raymond hooted. "That midget apprentice is *your* master castle-builder?"

With a gracious inclination of the head, she affirmed, "He is."

Throwing back his head, straightening his shoulders, Raymond declared, "He didn't believe we could dig a foundation in the cold, he didn't believe we could raise a wall in the wet, and he was dismissed and sent to—"

It struck Juliana at the same time it struck Raymond. "May God rest his soul," she said. "You sent him to set sail with your parents."

From the shadows beyond the fire, there was a sudden movement, a bold flash of color, and Papiol stood before them, arms outstretched. "Behold, your master castle-builder, safe from the arms of the salty sea!"

23

Unable to believe this reincarnation of his nemesis, Raymond stared, as, like a well-feathered rooster, Papiol strutted back and forth. He praised the ox-drawn cart that had taken him to the harbor too late to board the ship. He praised Lord Peter and Maud for giving him succor in his extremity. He praised *le bon Dieu* for bringing the queen of England to their magnificent castle where she would find him, and praised the queen of England for her continued patronage, and praised the maid who'd warmed his bed last night.

His praise, in fact, extended over the whole world—except to Raymond. And Papiol's sentiments, Raymond reflected, were wholly reciprocated.

As Papiol wore himself out, Eleanor said, "You have a very odd look on your face, Raymond. Does your arse still bother you?"

Raymond met her amused gaze. "The pain in my arse is growing by leaps and bounds."

Eleanor laughed heartily and waved a dismissive hand. "You and your lady are creating a rather large puddle on the floor. Go and do whatever's necessary to make yourselves presentable." Juliana made her obeisance and left with alacrity, but Eleanor caught Raymond's sleeve. Lowering her voice, she said, "I received the message and the gold you sent from Keir, and I brought the bride gift you requested. It's most unusual, and most unattractive."

Raymond had almost forgotten the bride gift, and he refused to yield to the inquisitiveness twinkling in Eleanor's eyes. "Good."

"You'll not satisfy my curiosity?" she appealed. "After I dragged it all this way?"

"You don't have to know everything, Eleanor."

She tilted her head back. "That's true, but I do know an unhappy couple when I see one. Is there anything I can do? We—Henry and I—meant this union to be reward for you, not a trial. I'll talk to Juliana if you wish."

"Nay!" he barked. Then, collecting himself, "Nay. The fault is mine."

Pressing her ringed fingers against his, she offered, "Let me help if I can. Sometimes a royal word is worth all the frantic activity of men."

Raymond indicated Papiol with a jerk of his head. "You've done too much already." Eleanor laughed again, but it was true. More than returning Papiol, Eleanor had given him a reprieve from exile.

Although his honor demanded he immediately leave Juliana, he couldn't, for the queen visited. He couldn't seek an annulment, for the king demanded he retain Juliana's lands. He would remain her husband, and even if he moved his official residence to Barton-hale and she stayed at Lofts, he would still have to meet with her at Christmastide and Easter, at harvest accounting and at Midsummer . . . what pleasure he would find in the touch of her hand!

What agony he would endure while away from her.

So it was a painful reprieve, but a reprieve nonetheless.

Eleanor interrupted his harsh reflections. "I'm occupying your nuptial bed, but there is no other in this castle. If I might give you some advice—have another bed built for visiting royalty."

Staring at her, Raymond scarcely believed his good luck. He didn't have to share Juliana's bed tonight? He didn't have to curb his needs and fight her allure? "Another reprieve," he whispered.

"What?"

Collecting himself, he bowed over her hand. "Thank you for your advice, Eleanor. I will certainly think about building a new bed."

As he strode away, she murmured, "Funny. That sounded as if he told me to tend to my needle."

"The sun is out." Keir stood in the doorway of the great hall, and proclaimed again, "The sun is out!"

The call reverberated through the great hall, bounced off the cold stone, and betrayed how desperately tired the occupants were of staring at the walls of the keep.

Margery and Ella threw themselves at Keir, begging, "Can we go outside? Can we? Can we?"

Keir's hand lingered on their bright heads. "You'll have to ask your father," he said, then came to kneel before the queen. "You ordered I inform you at the first sign of sun, and so I do."

"Gracious thanks, good Keir." Raising her voice, she demanded imperiously, "I wish to be entertained. Out of doors."

" 'Tis a quagmire out there," Raymond warned, holding off the clamoring children and eyeing the mud splattered well above Keir's knee.

"We'll make mudpies," Eleanor countered, rising to her feet. "We'll look at that wall of yours, and you can present your bride with her gift."

"Bride gift, bride gift," Ella chanted, and alarmed, Raymond glanced about.

"Juliana's down in the kitchen, ordering the noon meal. Royalty are such a drain on the resources when they visit, I'm afraid we must move on soon. Did you really think I'd so lost my senses as to reveal your present?"

The days inside had worn away Raymond's patience also, and it was all he could do to say, "Not at all, Eleanor."

Eleanor lifted her finger, and a lady-in-waiting came running with her cape. "You must give her the gift before I leave. I wish to observe her reaction."

"As you wish, Eleanor."

"I should order your head removed for your excessively polite insolence"—she leaned closer and examined his face—"but you look so thin and worn I'll attribute it to lack of sleep and excuse you."

"I thank you, Eleanor."

As she swirled the cape around her shoulders, she lifted one inquiring brow. "But if you can't sleep when half the hall separates you and your wife, how will you sleep when you share the same bed?"

His teeth clicked together for a wide, false smile. "Sometimes, Eleanor, you're a damned annoying woman."

She returned the smile with equal vehemence. "So Henry says." Lifting her hands, she called, "Attention!

We are going outside to christen the curtain wall of Lofts Castle."

From the corner of his eye, Raymond saw Juliana step out of the stairwell. She paused as if amazed, and he had the chance to feast his eyes.

She, too, looked thin and tired, worn by the demands of a royal household on the lady of the castle. When she hadn't been on her knees, doing penance for some sin, she'd been running from the kitchen to the larder to the wine cellar, ordering the entertainment—she depended heavily on Valeska and Dagna and their acrobatic skills—and organizing games. On their first night home, the queen's minstrel sang an epic ballad about a Crusader hero. As he sang, it became clear the hero was Raymond, and Raymond had cringed beneath the approbation of the court.

Juliana had stood to applaud the song, presented the minstrel with a fine woolen cape, and now, every night, the minstrel sang that damned song.

Raymond had seen Juliana consulting with the minstrel, and he suspected her interference, but what could he do? The court seemed to adore having a hero in their midst. The ladies-in-waiting hung on him, and one, bolder than the rest, had offered her services.

That was when he'd discovered Juliana had gelded him.

He didn't want just anyone. He wanted Juliana.

Now, unaware of her crime, she pushed the wisps of hair off her forehead slowly and listened to Eleanor.

"Keir, would you arrange seating for me and the other noble ladies?"

Keir bowed. "With pleasure, Madame." He snapped his fingers at Margery and Ella. "Do you want to come with me?"

They jumped at him, and he slung Ella on his back. "Hugh, you take Margery," Keir commanded, and grumbling good-naturedly, Hugh did.

"We'll bring down a cask of . . . what do you think, Raymond, wine or ale?"

Eleanor made the decision herself. "A cask of both. We'll have a party." Catching sight of her confused hostess, she said, "Eh, Juliana? A party to celebrate your wall. Do you have a gold cup we can use for the ceremony?"

"Nay, Madame, but there is the ceremonial cup we use at Christmastide to wish Apple Tree Man *wes-hâl.*"

Eleanor looked delighted. "That will do nicely."

Juliana nodded to Fayette. "Please fetch it."

"Aye, m'lady, but"—Fayette hesitated—"do ye think Apple Tree Man'll like us usin' his cup this way?"

Eleanor blinked. "We won't tell him."

Juliana agreed, adding, "'Twill be good to get away from"—she glanced at Raymond—"the great hall."

Irritated by lack of sleep, by constant arousal, he drew himself up and snarled, "I'll go pick out the wine."

"Fine," she said.

"Fine," he said.

Lord Peter hastened up and stepped between them. "I'll go with you, Raymond, to help you carry the casks."

"Fine," Raymond repeated, and grabbed a torch from the wall.

They trod the steps to the wine cellar, and Lord Peter said, "It's dark down here. Almost as dark as the inside of a woman's mind. They're strange creatures, aren't they?"

"Women are foolish creatures." Raymond unlocked

the door and slammed it against the wall. "Is Maud ever foolish?"

"Frequently, especially when she claims I'm foolish. What kind of wine do you wish?"

"The kind that mixes best with mud." Raymond placed the torch into a sconce and squinted, sightless, at the markings on the casks. "Doesn't she understand we have to remain wed? The queen has insisted. Our children expect it."

"So you will stay."

"Nay! I mean, aye. But even if I want her, dream of her . . ." He opened a tap and splashed ale in his face trying to dissipate the effects of his dreams. ". . . brood over her, I can't force myself on her. She saw me chained and humiliated. She despises me. She saw me mad with the fighting frenzy not once, but twice. She fears me."

From the doorway came Juliana's indignant voice. "You dolt." She advanced into the room. "You idiotic gazob. How dare you think I despise you because you were chained?"

Raymond found himself unsurprised. Something in the ether—a sudden warmth, a tingling—had warned him of her presence. Leaning back against the cool stones, he put his head back and visualized, once more, the scene in the moonlit meadow. "I saw the look on your face when Keir freed me. I thought you were going to vomit."

Lord Peter interjected, "I would vomit myself, to see you so abused."

"I wasn't repulsed that you were chained," she denied. "I was frightened that Keir would kill you with that ax. Tosti had been tortured to death. Denys had died as I watched over him. There were dead mercenaries by the fire. Death was all around me. But once I realized who was chained to the tree, I wasn't afraid. Finding you was the only luck I'd had that day."

"You were afraid."

"Not for *me*. I knew you'd never hurt me. I was afraid I wouldn't be able to help you." She sniffled, and her voice choked. "I didn't know how to help you. But I came to you, petted you, talked to you"— sobs began to punctuate her words, and she shook with each one—"and I only despised . . . the man who had abused you. I was . . . so afraid I'd lose you . . . I only tried to help . . . and you've hated me for it ever since."

She whirled and ran, leaving an uncomfortable silence, a silence that was finally broken by Raymond. "She thinks I hate her because she helped me?" he said incredulously. He cleared his throat. "As I said, women are foolish." But his voice lacked conviction.

Perched on an upturned cask, Lord Peter suggested, "Why don't you tell her you don't hate her?"

Juliana dragged her toe on each tread as she climbed the stairs. She didn't want to go christen the wall. She didn't want to feign laughter, make conversation, or be pleasant to that woman who wanted to take Raymond to her bed. She didn't want to do anything but curl up in a corner and cry.

Valeska and Dagna thought that time was on her side. But it wasn't. Every day, Raymond grew farther away from her. As she'd run to the larder, to the kitchen, to the cellars, she'd been able to think of naught save Raymond. The way he smiled, his easy banter with the queen, his way with her children. She loved everything about him—and he thought she despised him? That she feared him?

"Juliana!"

The queen's voice made her start guiltily.

"Come out of the stairwell and prepare yourself."

"Aye, Madame." Juliana scrubbed at her face, hoping to erase the signs of tears. When she stepped into the great hall, it was virtually empty. The queen stood by the fire, Valeska and Dagna were packing bread and cheese in several large baskets—but all the servants, the ladies, and the knights of the queen's household had vanished.

The queen's imperious voice tore Juliana from her reflections. "Are you ready to go outside? Come, come, you must not keep royalty waiting."

Juliana could never tell whether Eleanor poked fun at herself or was in earnest, and she hurried to do as directed. As she sat to put on her overshoes, the queen asked, "Did you make Raymond realize what an ass he's being?"

Relieved to find her feelings shared, Juliana asked, "Do you think he's being an ass, too?"

"I do," Valeska chimed, "He reminds me of . . . a knight I once knew. He always did what he thought was best for me and never asked me what I thought. Men are jackasses, one and all."

"What happened to your knight?" Juliana asked.

"I left him. I'll have no man telling me what to do." Valeska covered the basket with a cloth and grinned. "The Saracens cured me of that."

Eleanor, in her best royal voice, said, "Lady Juliana can't leave Raymond. She has to remain wed."

Juliana nodded. "Exactly. It's for the good of the realm. He's now wealthy, he could live at court among royalty—among his relatives—and the reason he wanted my lands no longer exists—"

"How does that alter the matter?" Eleanor inquired. "Once he had the blessing of the Church on your union, he could do anything he wished with your possessions, and you would have had little recourse."

Juliana tugged on her wooden overshoes. She knew that. Only . . . she'd come to depend on her wealth as a way to keep Raymond close. To find herself married to one of the greatest and wealthiest peers of the realm . . . well, it fed her insecurities. "Why did he stay, then? Why did he garner the affection of my daughters? Why did he make me love him?"

As Juliana fumbled with a cloth to wipe her nose, Dagna said, "I do not claim to understand the superior workings of a man's mind—"

Eleanor snorted.

"—but perhaps he's stayed for the pleasure of your company."

"Then why can't he stand to be in the same room with me?" Juliana jutted her chin. "Huh?"

"Because he's an ass," the queen pronounced.

Tears filled Juliana's eyes again. "He's not an ass. He's wonderful, and I will wither and die without him."

"Tell him that." Eleanor surveyed the watery Juliana as she shook her head, and insisted, "Tell him. It is your queen's command."

Juliana fought her way through the crowd to the doorway and stepped out of the keep. A sea of mud glinted in the bright, new-washed day, and she warned, "I don't know, Madame, this looks treacherous."

"Good," Eleanor said robustly. "I need some excitement. I'll go first."

Clambering down the ladder, she put her foot on the ground—and sank, and sank. "I suggest removing your overshoes, and your shoes, too." With an expression of delicious disgust, she put her other foot down. She saw Papiol trying to sneak back into the keep and, in her most authoritive voice, ordered, "All of you."

With resigned sighs, and a few squeaks from Papiol, the court sat down and removed their shoes. Barefooted, Juliana watched as the queen, dressed in the finest wools, held her cotte high and began to negotiate the slippery bailey.

"Mama! Mama!"

Margery and Ella stood at the drawbridge, their skirts trussed up, waving madly. "Come see your wall! Come see the seats we made you!"

Juliana waved back with considerably less enthusiasm, then descended into the mud. Cold as last night's lamprey pudding, it slithered between her toes. She sank halfway to her knees, and when she lifted her foot out to take a step, the mud released her reluctantly. The sucking sound it made embarrassed her, and the lady-in-waiting who followed close behind her exclaimed, "I know knights who sound daintier after a supper of pease porridge."

Juliana laughed.

She couldn't help it. She was outside for the first time in days, the sun shone warm on her shoulders, and every time she lifted her foot that dreadful, mortifying, funny noise erupted from the mud. Ahead of her strode the queen. Behind her in a long line stretched Eleanor's courtiers, dressed in fine clothes, speaking fine French, and as each one of them lifted a foot, it sounded like a vulgar digestive noise. It always brought forth the same response.

They laughed.

They laughed and tripped, held on to each other and laughed. They laughed at Papiol, trying to tiptoe as he muttered a dialogue with himself. They laughed until Raymond roared from the keep, "What are you doing?"

Turning, Juliana waved at him as he stood with a cask under each arm and his eyes wide. "We're obeying the queen's orders. Come on, it's fun!"

She didn't wait, but followed the queen across the drawbridge and down the hill to the low hedge of stone blocks Keir had placed as a bench. Shaped in the elegant curve of a Roman amphitheater, it faced the curtain wall and provided seating for the court. The queen took the highest block, of course, and as the courtiers straggled down they filled in, jostling for position. They cheered when Lord Peter appeared, and they cheered louder when Raymond appeared, holding the two casks.

They were ready to be entertained.

"Keir, take the ale and tap the cask," the queen commanded. "Raymond, put the wine close on that low section of wall, and since you did the wall, you'll do the christening."

Raymond nodded, knowing full well what was to come and dreading it.

"Juliana will help you." Eleanor made shooing motions toward the construction and stage-whispered to Raymond, "The bride gift is up there."

Juliana glanced at the half circle of grins, then at Raymond. Clearly dubious, she took the cup and started up the steep hill. Raymond followed, and he groaned at the whispers and giggles that broke out behind them.

Taking advantage of her smaller steps, he passed her on the slope and placed the cask on the wall.

He'd ordered the bride gift when he was determined to make their marriage a true one. When he was hopeful of winning her love. He'd dreamed of presenting it to her in private, when she could express her appreciation properly. But everything had gone wrong, and now he had to present it to her in front of the court. 'Strewth, how he feared her scorn.

With his cloak he concealed the unattached pile of sandstone holding his huge, square gift. When she had placed the cup beside the cask, he moved aside and gestured—not grandly, as he'd once planned, but with a flip of his arm. "It's your bride gift," he said in an undertone. "They all think I'm a fool to give a lady such a thing."

She stared, and doubt grew in his mind.

"It's the bear off my family crest," he explained. When she still said nothing, he cleared his throat. "Carved into a block of stone. To set on the top of the wall when it's finished. Like a gargoyle."

She lifted her gaze from the ugly creature of curved fangs and claws. Her eyes swam with tears, and she whispered, "A bear. You gave me a bear."

He didn't know if she cried from joy or distress until she flung her arms around his neck. "You are the most generous . . ."

The press of her body against his soothed him, aroused him. He wrapped her close, but she started, her hands loosened, and she tried to pull away. "I'm sorry," she apologized breathlessly. "Your neck—"

"It doesn't hurt."

"You don't like to be confined," she insisted.

"No, I don't." He shrugged in surprise. "I had forgotten."

But he released her, and she circled the bear. "Look at the great arms outstretched, the ferocious snarl, the wild hair." She touched the stone.

He didn't know what made him say it. " 'Tis I, set in stone and bound to protect you."

She leaped back as if his words made it so. Then, uncertain, she cocked her head and examined the bear once more. "It does have a resemblance, does it not?" She chuckled, a wavering laugh, but her smile faded, and she twisted her fingers until they were white. "I will join this stone one day, cold as the earth, staring out at the road, waiting for you to return to me."

Her agony sounded real, but he would do what was best for her, regardless of how she fought. " 'Tis better if I leave."

Whipping around, she pushed him with her hands on his chest. "Better for whom?"

He staggered backward and sat down with a plop in the mud. The courtiers cheered, but Raymond scarcely heard them.

"Better for you, perhaps. You'll be away from this provincial castle, away from the children, away from the responsibilities. You'll be at court, giving Henry his advice while I stumble along alone. Always alone. You'll be bringing your love skills to other women— prettier women, sweeter women, richer women, braver . . ." The words clogged in her throat.

A pain twisted in his chest, a pain greater than any he'd endured in all his loveless life. "Advising Henry holds no charm for me. As for other women"—he chuckled mirthlessly—"I'll never see another woman without seeing your face, nor hear a voice without recalling your song, nor—"

"Then why do you turn from me so coldly?" she cried. She pointed at the bear. "Here's the answer, is it not? You blame me for everything that happened at Moncestus Castle. 'Twas my failure to confront and curb Sir Joseph that caused it all."

He struggled to stand. "Confront Sir Joseph? You did. I saw you."

"I should have done it as soon as my father died."

Unable to pull himself out of the sticky embrace of the mud, alarmed at Juliana's despair, he put his hand down and pushed himself to his feet. "He would have killed you!"

"I doubt that." She took his filthy arm and wiped at it with her skirt. "I think it would have removed the sting from his tail most effectively. He wouldn't have influenced Denys, Margery would never have been taken, Bartonhale would not have been stripped, Felix's men wouldn't have been murdered, you would not have been chained—"

"Are you God to have so foreseen these events?" he asked angrily.

"Not God, but a coward." He shook his head, but she insisted, "I am. I avoid confrontations at every turn, and if Margery and you had not been in his hands, I would have turned tail and run. I have earned your scorn." She dropped her head. "I'm not like you, a warrior, never fearing. I'm only a snivelling milksop."

His hand, still rich with mud, cupped her chin. Lifting it, he looked into her eyes. "You labor under a misapprehension. When a knight prepares for battle, he's sick with fear. His hand slips on the hilt with sweat. His knees knock. His teeth chatter."

"Nay."

"Aye. 'Twas always so with me. 'Tis so of Lord Peter, and William, and Keir." She didn't believe him, he could see, and he told her, "Long ago, before my first battle, Lord Peter told me that courage isn't facing an enemy without fear. Courage is facing an enemy who terrifies you and doing your duty anyway. You're as valiant as any person I've ever met. Your life was smashed, destroyed by Sir Joseph and your father, the men you trusted. You rose from the ashes of fear and contempt to rebuild your life. I admire you, Juliana." His hand fell away, but her head remained high, and he realized he had dirtied her chin. Finding a clean edge on his cloak, he wiped at her skin. "I salute you for your courage."

Trusting as a child, she let him clean her while hungrily searching his face. "If you believe this . . . stay with me."

He realized he was caressing her neck, and jerked away. Glancing out at the court, he found them staring as if Juliana and Raymond were mummers providing entertainment. Lowering his voice, he said, "I will remain your husband."

"And stay with me?"

"Not far away."

"Nay. Stay with me."

"You tempt me even as Adam was tempted."

"Had Adam resisted, we'd not be here and I'd not have to beg you to stay with me." He snorted, but Juliana bent her mind to the puzzle that was Raymond. If he wasn't leaving because of her, then he must be leaving . . . because of him? Summoning the courage he praised, she said, "I do not fear you, nor the beast inside you. Do you believe?"

He nodded reluctantly.

"I do not despise you because a cruel and petty tyrant forced chains upon you. Do you believe?" He did not indicate he'd heard her, and she shook his arm. "Do you believe?"

She had to raise up to hear his thin reply. "Aye."

"I believe you are everything that is noble and knightly. Do you believe?"

"Aye."

"If you believe that I believe in you, then why do you wish to deprive me of my heart?"

"Because it's best."

She started shaking her head.

"Aye, it's best for you and the children. It will benefit the lands and . . ." His voice trailed off. He stared at her as if the sight of her daunted him. Taking flight, he marched to the wall with Juliana on his heels. He faced the cask, and with his face safely hidden, he confessed, "*I* don't believe in me. I can no longer live a lie, pretend I'm a knight when I know I have no right to that title."

They had reached the heart of the matter, and Juliana was determined not to falter now. "You fought eight men in one battle and beat them all."

He shrugged. "Of course."

"And your fury when you came upon Denys and Margery drove a whole troop of mercenaries to flight."

"Sir Joseph had his horse atop of the poor lad, trampling him to death." He pressed the inner corners of his eyes with his fingers.

Juliana wrapped her trembling hands around her waist to keep from reaching out to him. "Such mercy to Denys does you credit."

"He kidnapped Margery."

Remembering the penitence she'd been assigned by the priest, and the time she'd spent on her knees every morning for the sins on Denys's soul, she answered, "He paid for his foolishness."

"One can never pay for dishonor one brings on oneself." Fumbling, he pulled a tap from out of his purse and worked it into the face of the cask. Taking several deep breaths, he stated, "It stains one's soul forever."

A belief in the knight's code. A man who was only too human. It was a difficult dilemma, and with a craftiness she didn't know she possessed, Juliana asked, "Is Lord Peter a very wise man?"

Raymond smiled ruefully. "So he says."

"But you respect him?"

"More than any other."

Not wishing him to read the purpose in her face, she asked, "If a warrior cannot win a battle, what says Lord Peter?"

"If, after every attempt has been made to win, a warrior should do what he must to preserve his life, and live to fight another day."

"I know of a man, an honorable knight, who lost a battle and did what he had to to preserve his life." Raymond made a sound of disgust, but she ignored him. "And when he could fight again, this knight escaped, stole an infidel ship, saved the lives of all his followers, and won the respect of everyone. I have even heard a minstrel sing the song of this man."

He flipped open the tap, wine splashed at their feet, and he stared at it as if he didn't know what it was or where it had come from. "The Saracens broke me."

"It seems I have heard that before." Cup in hand, she filled it and shut the spigot. "I don't think you

broke. I think fragments of you broke. The cruelty
and indifference I see in knights every day are absent
in you, Raymond of Locheais and Avraché. But there
is one thing the Saracens never touched."

Grudgingly he inquired, "What?"

"Your pride." He jerked, and she drove eagerly
into the breech. "Your overweening, excessive pride,
that says Keir may bend to the Saracens, Valeska and
Dagna may bend to the Saracens, all those knights
you rescued may bend to the Saracens, but Raymond,
the almighty Raymond, may not."

"That's not true." But he looked as if he'd been
struck by the great sword of truth and suffered the
discomfort of facing his own conceit.

Taking swift advantage, she gripped the earlobe
pierced by his earring and pulled until he came down
to her level. "What's more, I find myself resenting it
when you reproach yourself for the very things which
I admire in you."

Still grappling with her first accusation, he glared
at her. "I don't think I'm better than Keir or Valeska
or Dagna or any of the other knights."

"Your compassion, the pleasure you take in the
children, in the everyday things of life, in me—that's
all because of your experiences in Tunisia. I'm sorry
about your back, about your neck, about the tortures
you endured, but you survived, and I'm not going to
let you throw away our lives for your pride." He was
listening now, and nose to nose, she said, "I will order
Layamon not to allow you to leave Lofts Castle."

He roared like a wounded bull elk. "I'll kill the
puny bugger!"

"Nay, you won't." Smugly, she mocked him.
"Your compassion won't allow you to kill a man for

performing his duties." She released his ear, but he still stood bent, with his mouth hanging open.

Then he shut it with a snap and looked around for something to vent his displeasure on.

Crossing the drawbridge was a scrimpy creature, covered from head to toe with mud, mumbling Gallic curse words.

Papiol had arrived at last.

The master castle-builder froze at the sight of the wall, a moue of distaste on his pudgy countenance. In high, amazed tones, he queried, "That is the wall we've come to christen? Nay." He stepped backward. "Nay, nay, nay."

He started toward the keep, and Raymond caught his arm. "What do you mean, 'nay'?"

Looking up at the warrior towering above him, Papiol's conviction warred with his fright. But his conviction won. With the lightning swift judgment of a skilled courtier, he both grovelled and replied. "You are a great lord. A greater lord than I will ever be castle builder. I do not dispute this. No one disputes this. But you are not a master castle-builder, and I will not be a party to this farce."

"What's wrong with my wall?" Raymond asked, a warning in his voice.

Papiol ignored the warning and told him the truth. "The stones are not set correctly. Inexperienced workmen." Touching the wall, he rubbed a bit of rubble between his fingers, and it fell to dust. "The mortar is crumbling. Cold weather. And you did not even use a batter."

Raymond's forehead crinkled. "A what?"

"A batter!" Papiol waved his arms. "A sloping base which strengthens the foundation and creates a surface on which to bounce stones. Nay, I will not remain while you christen this"—his lip curled—"this wall."

"Won't you?" Raymond picked up the ceremonial cup. "We'll see about that." He flung the contents at the stones, and the ruby wine splashed back at the force of his arm.

All parts of Papiol not already covered with mud were then covered with red, and he hissed in voluble exasperation. "Barbarian!" he accused. "English barbarian." He kicked at the stones. "That for your wall!"

"Be careful," Raymond warned.

Like a French peasant dancer, Papiol kicked, and kicked again. "That! And that for your wall." Then he danced away. "I would not stand there, my lord, for the wall will surely tumble from the impact of my little toe."

"Watch this!" With a grunt, Raymond picked up the bride gift.

Papiol sobered abruptly. "Nay, my lord, I beg you!"

Grinning like the bear on his shield, Raymond mashed the carved stone down on the waist-high part of the wall and ground it down until it sat securely, facing the world with a snarl.

"At least let us move Queen Eleanor," Papiol begged.

His distress seemed so genuine, Juliana looked up at the rock towering above her head. Every head followed hers, and the whole court, her whole household, held their collective breaths and waited.

Nothing happened.

More time. Nothing happened. Glances were exchanged, giggles stifled.

Raymond stood planted in front of the wall, hands on hips, and his gloating smile grew.

Papiol grew pale. "My lord, I tell you, your wall will fall ere much more time passes. The ground, she is saturated. The wall, she is on a hill. Only the best foundations—"

Juliana heard a pebble fall inside the wall.

"Only the best foundations—" Papiol repeated, but his fascinated gaze was now pinned to the wall.

The fall of one pebble was followed by a shower. Juliana stepped back. Nothing moved on the facade, but inside . . .

Eleanor called, "Raymond, perhaps you should move."

"I will not. This wall is as steady as—"

Papiol squealed, "My lord!" and threw himself at Raymond, knocking him aside as the bear and all the rock around it collapsed. The main portion of the wall remained, but it was no longer steady. As if a great snake lay beneath it, it trembled in ripples, then in waves. The stones groaned; the queen's attendants screamed.

Papiol no longer had to push Raymond; Raymond dragged Papiol, and when he reached her, Juliana, too, to safety. Unsupported by bedrock, loosened by the rains, the sandstone that formed the facade tottered. In a cacophony of noise, the line of boulders at the bottom of the wall slid away. Then the next line, then the next, skidded on the liquid mud—all the way down the hill. Madness ensued as the court, the servants, and Queen Eleanor herself scrambled to avoid the runaway rocks.

When the rumble subsided, the new wall lay flat as a Roman road, and a suspicious silence blanketed the crowd of people, broken only by Fayette's plaintive words. "Apple Tree Man mustn't have approved."

Raymond stared.

His wall. His beautiful wall. Flat. The rubble inside exposed and still escaping in little avalanches. All his work. All his construction. All his dreams of making Juliana's castle the most secure along the borderlands.

God's teeth. Juliana.

Escaping from the Saracens, fighting in bloody battles, participating in sieges, being beaten and chained, nothing had ever alarmed Raymond as much as facing Juliana.

Her jaw askew, she gazed incredulously on the ruin of her curtain wall. She gulped, and he thought she was going to cry. She gulped again and seemed to be struggling against some great emotion. Then, just like the wall, she collapsed—with laughter. Sitting down hard in the mud, she shrieked, she wiped tears from her eyes, looked again on the wall, and laughed. "Master castle-builder?" she sputtered. "*Master* castle-builder?"

Raymond went from being worried to being offended, from being offended to being . . . pleased. Dropping down on his knees in the mud beside her, he took her hands in his. "You really do love me, don't you?"

She sobered, although her eyes still gleamed. "I really do."

"You trust me to keep you safe?"

"I do."

"Enough to have an eight-foot-wide curtain wall?"

She tried to look severe. "No more than ten."

For her, he was as mushy-soft as the mud around them. "I love you, you know."

"I know." She took his earlobe again, but this time she struggled to release the golden ring that pierced it. Holding it in her palm, she showed it to him. "I don't think we need this symbol of your bondage anymore, do we?"

He touched it one last time. He'd sworn to wear it as long as he was enslaved by memories—memories now as broken as the curtain wall. "No. We don't need it anymore." Taking the earring, he threw it into the pile of gravel and masonry.

With tender fingers, she pinched his freed earlobe and brought it—and him—toward her.

When her lips touched his, he forgot. Forgot the mud and the wall, forgot the Saracens and his parents. She tasted like bread to a starving man. Her hands reached for his shoulders, crept around his back, clasped him as if she could never let him go. He pulled her toward him and they knelt, body to body, exchanging breath and life and promises without words, and she made his battered soul whole again.

A loud round of applause dragged Raymond and Juliana from their sensual mist, and like swimmers surfacing after a dive so deep they were giddy for lack of air, they looked out at their audience in astonishment.

Juliana collapsed back onto her heels and smiled at her husband, and he realized how much he'd missed her smile. "You won't leave me?" she asked.

"If I did, who would build your wall?"

Looking thoughtful, she said, "That's right. You're bound to me until I have a curtain wall." She glanced at the flattened wall and started laughing again. "A . . . a *standing* curtain wall."

He wrapped his arm around her neck. "I'll let the king's castle builder do it next time," he promised. "It'll take him two years to do it right. The little gazob." He turned her to look out over her lands. "But you don't really need a curtain wall. Here is your bulwark against fear. Acres of good English soil, dozens of good English people." Placing a smacking kiss against her neck, nuzzling her while she giggled, he added, "And me. I am your sword, your shield, and your right arm."

"And you," she agreed. "You are the love for my lifetime, and the foundation for my dynasty."

His grasp tightened, holding her as if she were a richness of spice, a cache of jewels. "You want me for my breeding purposes, only?"

"Nay, not only for that"—she leaned into the hand that caressed her waist, and pointed to the gravel still skidding down the ruins of the wall. "I want you to clean up this mess."

She leaped away, and he leaped after her, chasing her toward the keep.

Eleanor sank painstakingly onto a sandstone boulder and rocked to see if it was steady. "They'll secure the marriage bed against all comers, I trow, so bring the bread and cheese, and open the ale. If we can't celebrate the wall, then we'll celebrate their marriage."

As the courtiers and the servants gathered around, only Papiol remained apart. Hand tucked into his belt, he strolled to the bear that peeked out of the mud. "I told you it would not stand," he said, and kicked it.

The block of stone lurched. Papiol stared. The mud shifted. Papiol squeaked. With a noise that sounded obscurely like a growl, the bear skidded. Papiol scampered back, but the current of mud caught him and carried him, screaming and yelling, all the way to the bottom of the hill.

Reignite your passion for romance with these classic novels by

CHRISTINA DODD

Romance fans across the nation just can't get enough of Christina Dodd! This Golden Heart and RITA award-winning author has long been a bona fide favorite of readers, as she consistently spins exquisite and seductive tales of love and desire. You won't want to miss out on three of her beloved classics, now published with striking new covers...and available at unbelievably low prices!

"Treat yourself to a fabulous book—anything by Christina Dodd!" —JILL BARNETT

SPECIAL VALUE! $3.99

PRICELESS
ISBN 0-06-108563-4
$3.99/$4.99 (Can.)

TREASURE OF
THE SUN
ISBN 0-06-108564-2
$3.99/$4.99 (Can.)

CASTLES IN
THE AIR
ISBN 0-06-108565-0
$3.99/$4.99 (Can.)

HarperPaperbacks
www.harpercollins.com

Visit Christina Dodd's website at
www.christinadodd.com

CHRISTINA DODD

Winner of the Romance Writers of America Golden Heart and RITA Awards

ONCE A KNIGHT

Though slightly rusty, the once great knight Sir Radcliffe agrees to protect Lady Alisoun for a price. Now with his mercenary heart betrayed by passion, Sir David protests to his lady that he is still a master of love—and his sword is swift as ever.

"This love and laughter medieval romance is pure delight." —*Romantic Times*

MOVE HEAVEN AND EARTH

Fleeing the consequences of scandal, Sylvan Miles arrives at the Clairmont Court to nurse battle-worn Lord Rand Malkin back to health. But while this dashing rogue taunts her with stolen kisses, he never expects her love to heal his damaged soul as well.

"An unforgettable love story that will warm your heart."—Arnette Lamb

A KNIGHT TO REMEMBER

Passion becomes a battleground with no mercy given, as skilled herbalist Lady Edlyn is forced to secretly tend to the wounds of a man who is no stranger to her heart—Hugh de Florisoun, a knight renowned for his prowess in war as well as the bedchamber....

"Christina Dodd is a joy to read." —Laura Kinsale

MAIL TO: **HarperCollins Publishers**
            P.O. Box 588 Dunmore, PA 18512-0588

Yes, please send me the books I have checked:

❑ *Once A Knight* 108398-4 . . . .$5.99 U.S./ $7.99 Can.
❑ *Move Heaven and Earth* 108152-3 . . . .$5.50 U.S./ $6.50 Can.
❑ *A Knight To Remember* 108151-5 . . . .$5.99 U.S./ $7.99 Can.

SUBTOTAL . . . .$_____
POSTAGE & HANDLING . . . .$_____
SALES TAX (Add applicable sales tax) . . . .$_____
TOTAL . . . .$_____

Name _____
Address _____
City _____ State _____ Zip _____

Order 4 or more titles and postage & handling is **FREE!** For orders of fewer than 4 books, please include $2.00 postage & handling. Allow up to 6 weeks for delivery. Remit in U.S. funds. Do not send cash. Valid in U.S. & Canada. Prices subject to change.   http://www.harpercollins.com/paperbacks   M05011

Visa & MasterCard holders—call 1-800-331-3761